In Elizabeth Bowen's THE LITTLE GIRLS, a sudden flash of remembrance prompts Mrs. Dinah Delacroix to seek out two friends she has not seen in fifty years and relive a schoolgirl escapade interrupted by the tragic events of 1914. In that ill-fated summer, Dinah was Dicey, a beskirted hellion; Sheila was Sheikie, a precocious ballerina; and Clare was Mumbo, an irrepressible tomboy.

With delicate sensitivity, the years are peeled away as they unearth a long-buried time-capsule—a chest once possessed of shining remembrances, but now cruelly separating them. For the years have added something to the chest—a thing none of them can face.

THE LITTLE GIRLS

ELIZABETH BOWEN

AVON
PUBLISHERS OF BARD, CAMELOT AND DISCUS BOOKS

To Ursula Vernon

AVON BOOKS
A division of
The Hearst Corporation
959 Eighth Avenue
New York, New York 10019

Copyright © 1963 by Elizabeth Bowen
Published by arrangement with Alfred A. Knopf, Inc.
Library of Congress Catalog Card Number: 63-20834
ISBN: 0-380-39875-3

First Avon Printing, October, 1978

AVON TRADEMARK REG. U.S. PAT. OFF. AND IN
OTHER COUNTRIES, MARCA REGISTRADA, HECHO EN
U.S.A.

Printed in the U.S.A.

PART I

One

A man came down the steps cut in the rock. By nature agile, he made the descent with unusual caution, placing each foot first tentatively then extra firmly. He did well to—the steps, inexpertly hewn at some unknown time, were no two alike, and were this evening slippery after rain; moreover, he carried, balanced against his midriff, a lidless white cardboard box toppling with a miscellany of objects.

He arrived on to the floor of a sort of bear pit; that was, a sunken circular court resembling those in which, in old-fashioned zoos, bears keep house and are displayed. This was, if anything, on the large and deep side; it lacked a pole in the middle and had no railing, being overhung round the top by beards of creeper and scrambling and sagging roses. Dahlias bloomed at the head of the steps. Across the uneven rock floor, facing the steps, was either a shallow cave or a deep recess—or possibly, unadorned grotto?—now fronted by looped-back tarpaulin curtains. Within were trestles, across which boards had been placed; and a woman, intent on what she was doing to the point of trance, could be seen in backview, moving her hands about among the objects crowding the rough table. A jotting-pad, which she from time to time attacked with a stub of pencil, caught such daylight as entered the cave. She may not have heard the man, who was wearing espadrilles—she did not, at any rate, look around.

He said: "Here I am."

"There you are," she assented, taking his word for it.

"Getting on?"

This time, instead of answering she came out to meet

him, knocking hair back from her forehead with her wrist. Her sweater sleeves were rolled to above the elbows; out of a pocket of her slacks trailed a man's handkerchief with signs of being used as a duster. Shod as he was, she moved as soundlessly, lighting a cigarette as she came. To call her attention to his box, Frank Wilkins gave it a slight rattle. This acted: her fact lit up. "Oh, you *have*!" she cried.

"What did you think I was up to?"

"Let's see!" She made a grab at the box.

"Steady!" said he, protecting it. "Taken me most of the day, getting these together. Made me quite introspective."

"Took your mind off the telephone?"

"Mm—I suppose so."

"Good."

Amicably going together into the cave, they cleared space on the table and put his box down. He eyed the exhibits already there, if not critically, with no great enthusiasm. "Still all look to me very much the same."

"Same as last time, or the same as each other?"

"Same as each other, in pretty much the same way as they did last time. Not had anything new in since?"

"One lot, but I'm hardly surprised if you didn't notice. It is extraordinary, really, isn't it, Frank? I suppose the fact is, people *are* much the same, if one goes down deep. All the variety seems to be on the surface. When one comes to think, what's amazing is—" But she broke off, as she often did. She drew once more on her cigarette, let it drop, stamped on it. "Look, though," she cried with renewed fervour, "I've been cataloguing, before I forget what's whose. Once I *do*, there'll be little to tell me—or indeed anyone."

"How you expect posterity to make head or tail of it—!"

She smiled, otherwise took no notice. There are remarks which, having been once made, are repeated at intervals, on principle: Frank's was one of them. "Rightly or wrongly," she continued, "I never have done a catalogue before; yet this one's beginning to be so exactly like one— don't you think?" She held the pad with the jottings out at extreme arm's length, for admiration. He did not seem able to make sense of it. "Oh, bother you," she grumbled, "do put your *specs* on!" (That he was known to be slow to do, being loth to.) He objected: "We're right in our own light."

They were. Their two tall forms, backs to the entrance, not only overshadowed the table but further darkened the cave—blocking away from it outdoor daylight, which, down here, was subdued at the best of times. Only round noon did sun strike the circular pit's floor. It now was within an hour or so of sunset—unpent, brilliant after the rainstorm, long rays lay over the garden overhead, making wetness glitter, setting afire September dahlias and roses. Down here, however, it was some other hour—peculiar, perhaps no hour at all.

"Why not rig up some sort of lamp?" he wanted to know. "Don't you see, Dinah, the days will be drawing in."

"Dear, they've begun to!" She picked up a leather jerkin and, with his aid, slung it over her shoulders. Then Frank, whatever the visibility, could not resist giving a dig at his box—as nearly dispassionately as possible. A carved bone fan came slithering from the top. Dinah pounced on it, opened it, held it round to the light. "*This* won't do," she declared sadly, "it's an antique!"

"It was my grandmother's."

"But Frank, darling—no ancestors, we did say!"

"I should have thought, the fact that I'd kept it always—"

"Obsession about it, had you?" she asked, more hopefully.

"More, there's something of her in me, I've sometimes thought—that is, from what I've heard of her. In some way or another, a likeness. Though, mind you, I never set eyes on her: she died young."

"At least you haven't done that."

"Looks, more—possibly."

"Oh, then a beauty, was she?"

Frank, opening his mouth, glanced at Dinah sideways: she looked so bland, he decided she must be *méchante*. Straightaway, he was furious. "You're going to look on the whole of it as a laugh, this box? As a give-away—that's how you see it, isn't it?" he shouted, intercepting her hand on its way back to his box and holding it under arrest, by the wrist, in mid-air. She waited for him to quiet down, then, disengaging her wrist with a gentle tug, said. "No; simply as what we agreed—a clue for posterity. Or, poser?"

"That's what you *say*; but—"

"None of the others," she said plaintively, "made this fuss."

"I am not the others!"

"Oh, no. No, no."

"I am *not*?" he insisted.

"No, I tell you. They understood the idea."

"Ho, they did, did they?"

"Before it's quite dark, mayn't we unpack your box?"

So they set to work, racing against the fading of the light—till, in the silence, a cough was heard from above. It was a compact, contained cough: no other followed. Dinah said: "I'm sure that is Mrs. Coral." They left the cave, one after the other, both looking up.

Mrs. Coral, cased in a mackintosh amid drippy dahlias, stood looking down at them. Soul of integrity, she as ever held herself wooden-straight. Her wide-boned face with wide eyes and strong, blunted features was like a Saxon carving outside a church; the childlike hat she wore was turned up all round. Stalwart as a fourteen-year-old, Mrs. Coral appeared a typical forty, though past that. She lived, at the other side of the village, in a semi-detached stone villa, and took in students (generally, foreign) from a nearby agricultural institute. Carrying a plastic mesh bag with magazines in it, she took one more step, now, towards the brink of the pit. "Good evening, Mrs. Delacroix. Busy, are you?"

"Do come in, Mrs. Coral—I mean, come down!"

"I've come about the Mothers' Union."

"You know Major Wilkins?"

Mrs. Coral regarded Frank, then said: "Good evening." Considering how candid and expectant, as well as tolerant, her stare was (turned alike on man, woman, or child), she took in wonderfully little of what she saw. Never more than one thing at a time could be in her mind, and it was always important, at least to her. And it always came out at once: she was not inscrutable. "I've got your magazine," she said, temptingly raising the mesh bag. "And I'm sorry, but there's still the subscription."

"Naturally—how much?"

Mrs. Coral told her, explaining: "You're a trifle behind."

"I am *sorry*," moaned Dinah.

"Not feeling I ought to let it run on too far, and not

thinking you would care to have it run on too far, and not having noticed you at the last Meeting, I called in the other day, but you were in London."

"Oh, what a lot of trouble! And now I've left my money up at the house.—Unless *you*?" cried Dinah, turning to Frank in an at once inspired and pleading way. He tied knots with his eyebrows, but put his hand in his pocket. "Better than keeping Mrs. Coral waiting," she explained, picking the necessary silver from his palm. Mrs. Coral watched from above, neutrally, if anything favourably. It seemed natural that a gentleman should emit coins.

From up there, Mrs. Coral was seeing, somewhat foreshortened, a pair of ageless delinquents, whose random beauty was one of the most placid of their effronteries, or cheats: a cheating of Time. Nobody of their ages, it might be said, had any business to look as these two still did. It could be that looking as they did was the something in common which had brought them together. One hears of those who were behind the door when looks were being given out; but what about those who happen to be behind the door, or anyway elsewhere, when looks are being called in again? These two had, somehow, not handed back Nature's strictly temporary voucher. Possibly the collector had forgotten? They seem to have benefited by some oversight. Their teasing and needling of one another kept them in harmony, without rivalry, and was habitual. Tall and long-legged, they happened this evening to be, even, clad very much alike. His yellow springy hair and splendid moustache, lightened rather than grizzled by many summers, gave an additional glimmer to his countenance—in itself unusual, mobile, and sometimes wild. Her cut hair, slippery as a girl's, had darkened to the colour of vintage marmalade; her face was fair rather than pale. They were some time debating over the money: meanwhile, Mrs. Coral took them for granted.

Sum in hand, Dinah set off in a businesslike manner towards the steps.

"Now I must hand you your magazine," stated Mrs. Coral. "And I shall need to write you out your receipt. I should have a table, really. Is that one, down there?" Girding her mackintosh up, she eyed the descent. "Chickens were kept down here when I was a girl. Not a fox would

come down these steps—they're funny. Times change,"
she remarked, on her way down. "Starting cactuses, are
you?" She extracted the magazine as she neared the
bottom.

"Not cactuses; but we're starting something."

"I was told I was likely to find you down here, if anywhere."

Frank, as host, asked: "Know anything about the history
of this cave?"

"Only, Major Wilkins, that I always understood it was
prehistoric." Mrs. Coral looked into the cave, impassively.
"Now going to hold a jumble sale in it, are you?"

Throwing his head back, Frank gave a snorting laugh.

"Major Wilkins isn't laughing at you, he's laughing at
me," Dinah interposed, looking his way austerely. Mrs.
Coral took another look at the table. "I see: a small
museum. I beg your pardon. But you should take care,
working down here so late, particularly if you should
happen to be rheumatic. This type of rock perspires; it
always has done."

"That's what *I'm* always telling her!"

"All I hope is, you may not suffer from mildew on
your exhibits."

Dinah, at the very idea, half-sneezed, dived for the
trailing handkerchief, dabbed her nose. "It will soon be
airtight: we're going to seal it up."

"It won't, then, be a public museum, will it?"

"It's not a museum—or really anything like. If you'd
like to know, I'll try and explain. It's for someone or other
to come upon in the *far future*, when practically nothing
about any of us—you or me, for instance—would be otherwise known. We're putting these things in here to be de-
duced from. And by that time, hundreds or perhaps
thousands of years hence, think what a shattering dis-
covery! Imagine the theories it may revolutionize!"

"Why, yes," Mrs. Coral agreed, "I suppose it might do.
—Which theories are you referring to, Mrs. Delacroix?"

"Any, of any kind, about us. Look what a fuss is made
in newspapers, nowadays, about any odds and ends that
are come upon—one or two sad beads, or splinters of pottery! Enormously learned theories are based upon them.
Then of course there are arrowheads, daggers, and dinged-
in skulls; but they give such a fractious, bad-tempered pic-

ture of life, I feel they must make one unfair to the vanished races. So I'm looking ahead to when *we* are a vanished race."

"Well, I never!" said the awed Mrs. Coral.

"Oh, yes. But now we come to what is really the point! I don't know how you feel, Mrs. Coral, but I should imagine the same as I do—now would *you* wish, simply because you'd vanished, simply to be thought about as a *race*—all, I mean, stuck together in one lump? I do think we deserve to be thought of as personalities: you as you, Major Wilkins as Major Wilkins, me as me. So for that, you see, one's got to arrange. Those early races probably never thought; or what I suppose is still more likely, never really expected they would vanish. But we should be odd —don't you agree?—if the idea'd never occurred to *us*."

"Though, little is gained by brooding," said Mrs. Coral.

"How I agree! But the thing is, one should give posterity a break. One must leave posterity some clues!"

Mrs. Coral coughed. She then said: "Should there *be* any posterity."

"You won't get her to listen to a word of that!" remarked Frank, from a little distance away. Having moved off outdoors to light his pipe, he remained in the courtyard background, pacing and pausing, now and then looking up as rooks crossed the sky. For emphasis, he made a gesture at Mrs. Coral with his pipe. "She won't hear a word of it!" Mrs. Coral, looking from Frank to Dinah, for the first time in her visit appeared to dither—upon which Dinah, by dint of placing a hand on their visitor's mackintosh, at the elbow, confidently and swiftly reclaimed her audience. She went on:

"Clues to reconstruct *us* from. Expressive objects. What really expresses people? The things—I'm sure—that they have obsessions about: keep on wearing or using, or fuss when they lose, or can't go to sleep without. You know, a person's only a *person* when they have some really raging peculiarity—don't you notice that, Mrs. Coral, with all your friends?"

"Most of us have our little ways, I dare say."

"And the point is, all are completely different! . . . At least," said Dinah, looking with faint discouragement, or at least misgiving, at the clumps of objects, "so I've always believed. So you see now, don't you, what the idea's been?

I've been asking people for things (a dozen from each) which they couldn't have normally borne to part with. I started, of course, with friends; but I hope to be going much further afield."

"Found they could spare them, did you?"

"Oh yes," said Dinah, once more slightly depressed. "Some were glad, I expect, to get them out of their systems. One or two at first were a little bashful; some had difficulty in making the dozen up—expressive things do get lost these days, with all this moving about, like my silver pencil with the tooth-marks. I said it must *be* a dozen, as less than that could hardly give an all-round-enough idea. Personality's so extremely complex."

"Seem," remarked Mrs. Coral, tentatively, "to be quite a number of strings of pearls. None of them would be genuine, would they?"

"No, all fakes—but do look, though: one is a rosary. And you might say, numbers of pairs of nail scissors; but the same things mean something different to different people. Look, this pair has its tip broken: *that* means something. . . ." Exhausted, Dinah's voice ran down to a pause. Then, rallying, she declared in a firmer tone: "Will be a tremendous eye-opener, this cave—won't it?"

"*I* only," Frank informed Mrs. Coral, "brought in my stuff just now. Thought I'd think for a bit, look before I leaped. That's my stuff over there, if it interests you. On the whole, I've kept to the simple side. One oughtn't, in my view," he warned Dinah, "to be too upstage with posterity. Not too highbrow."

"I don't expect to deal with absolute fools."

"*You'll* be sitting up on a harp, playing a cloud—beg your pardon, I mean the other way round. . . . Well," asked Frank, shedding charm upon Mrs. Coral, "glad to have taken a look at our little circus?"

Mrs. Coral asked Dinah: "Who's going to seal it up?"

The effect of the question was out of all proportion with the question itself—and, as the minute lengthened, became still more so. Dinah first stared right through Mrs. Coral, then shut her eyes—which she opened only to stare in other directions, in none of which did the eyes light on anything they appeared to focus. Showing frantic estrangement from all surroundings, she beat one fist, irregularly and slowly, on the palm of the other hand. She seemed by turns to be seeking, listening, or dazedly simply waiting for some answer—that being far from any kind of answer she had been asked for. Among the cave's deepening shadows, her face looked white—not, by its expression, from distress: here, rather, was some consuming excitement. It hardly needs to be said that she said nothing.

"Well, that's not my business," said Mrs. Coral.

"I beg your pardon?"

"Merely wondered, who's going to seal it up?"

Back to herself (as quickly as she had gone), the organizer replied gladly and glibly: "Oh, whoever's the last!"

This was Frank's cue for another repeat-remark. "We may all go out with the same bang."

"Then the bang would certainly seal it up. You do make difficulties," she told him—setting to work to unloop the tarpaulin curtains. "The thing now is," she told Mrs. Coral, "to shut it up for the night—apart from anything else, it's extremely cold. Now we're all going to go in and have a drink. Drink in front of the fire, I do hope—if it's been lit. Did you say there was anyone in the house?"

"That young man who sometimes answers your bell did so."

"Good. Come on!"

"I'm afraid you'll have to excuse me."

"Oh no, you must, Mrs. Coral! Sherry."

Mrs. Coral, implacably raising the mesh bag, said: "There still are these other magazines."

Pulling, then tying the cave's curtains together was a ceremony amounting to locking up. That over, the owners left, to accompany Mrs. Coral across the garden. As they mounted the steps, the temperature rose. Above-ground, steamy flower-smells filled the air (more, still, that of a lingering August than of September) as the three followed a spongy serpentine grass path towards the house. On each side, the path was overflowed by a crowded border. Mauve, puce, and cream-pink stock, double, were the most fragrant and most crushingly heavy; more pungent was the blue-bronze straggling profusion of catmint. Magnificently, gladioli staggered this way and that—she was an exuberant, loving, confused and not tidy gardener; staking and tying were not her forte. Roses were on enough into their second blooming to be squandering petals over cushions of pansies. Flowers in woolwork or bright chalk, all shades of almost every colour, zinnias competed with one another. And everywhere along the serpentine walk where anything else grew not, dahlias grew: some dwarf, some giant, some corollas like blazons, some close-fluted, some velvet, some porcelain or satin, some darkening, some burning like flame or biting like acid into the faint dusk now being given off by the evening earth.

This had been an orchard. Twisted, old but only too fruitful still, such trees as had not been cleared away were to be seen in the near distance, their boughs weighted. Already an apple or two had begun to drop: it was felt that a week or two more of sun would be needed, however, before the picking. In an abundant year, indecision as to what to do with the apples became a burden. More interesting to greed were the vegetable plots, laid out in squares where trees were no longer. These looked almost professional—trenched where necessary, dotted with bell-glasses, frames, and, where frames gave out, sheets of cracked glass supported on bricks. Frank, at the price of a liberal rake-off from the produce, came over most days from his cottage and worked here: with his own garden he seemed to be less successful. Thanks to his and her industry, together with the prevailing mildness of the climate and excellence of the soil, her table and his were provided for most of the year round, nicely. They arrived, even, at raising Provençal and other exotic vegetables, the "musts" of the better cookery book. Little wonder that Frank, lagging behind Dinah and Mrs. Coral, now and then cast an eye gloomy with worry in the direction of what he was learning to call the *potager*. To pot it would all be going, before long, if Dinah's craze for the cave failed to abate.

Ahead, conversation came to its last lap. "And how are you?" asked Dinah, somewhat belatedly.

"I don't know whether you heard, but I lost my Indian."

"Oh, what a bother; how?"

"Took off on his bike one morning, not saying anything, then sent round for his things. Since then, not a word; just a postal order. Took offence, I can only imagine; but what at?"

"He must be dotty."

"He may not have hit it off with my Finn."

"What does your Finn think?"

"I didn't ask him. Or of course may have found something to suit him better."

"Has your Indian a girl, do you think?"

"I make a point of not hearing anything. Well, there it is: now I have a vacancy."

"Oh, but you'll only have to raise a finger to fill *that*!"

"So I'm generally told; in fact that I know. As to that I'm not worried; but I have been worried since it happened. It seems inhuman."

Dinah paused, plucked a Caroline Testout rose and silently gave it to Mrs. Coral—who, having looked at it for a moment in some dismay, stuck it into an upper buttonhole of her mackintosh. They walked on. "I have any number of vacancies," admitted Dinah, looking between the apple trees at her house. "But the inhuman thing is that I prefer them: when I can't have my grandchildren I'm happy knocking about with nothing but Francis."

Mrs. Coral was startled into glancing over her shoulder, with a query-mark. Dinah, putting the matter right, said: "No, Francis is my house-boy with the squint, who as you were saying sometimes opens the door. He's a Maltese orphan. Major Wilkins's name is nothing but Frank. He's got used to knocking about in a vacuum too, I think. He is so very lucky, there in that nice cottage."

"Something of a hermit?"

"Oh, yes. He's a little upset just now—becoming a grandfather at any minute."

"That should brighten him up?"

"Oh, yes." Dinah stopped in her tracks, in order to stand on one leg, draw up the other foot, and dismally study the soaking espadrille. "It never occurred to me it would rain. Also perhaps you're right about that cave; one does get forlorn down there, though without noticing. If Francis hasn't lit that fire, I *shall* die! Do you see any smoke?"

"Not from here, no. . . . A boy doesn't always think."

"That is a little beast I could sometimes kill; yet in his own way one is fond of him. He does *think*; he cerebrates like anything, one can see." They walked on again.

"I could get you a fire going, in half a minute."

"Not unless you're going to have a drink."

"No, you will have to excuse me, as I said."

The path brought them out on to a lawn, into uninterrupted view of Dinah's house—it was not easy to look at anything else. Applegate had been erected in 1912, by a retired haberdasher from Bristol. A substantial villa, it was built (like almost everything else round here, new or older) of stone, of a kind slow to weather or mellow. The house bespoke the sound workmanship which had gone into it; nothing had so far blunted the cut angles, gables, or mullions of the plate-glass windows (of which several projected into bays) or modified the new-quarried glare of the whole—which, by contrast, the lush green, wooded and pastoral, rolling Somerset landscape round it enhanced. Applegate promised to be much the same within as it was without, and was. Nothing rattled at night, even in a gale: the windows fitted, the doors shut properly. Neither the staircase nor any floor creaked. That may have been one of the reasons why she had bought it; another was the cave.

This was that only hour when land looks haunted. A farmhouse, to which the orchard belonged, had after many generations burned to the ground, just here, the year before Applegate was built, taking with it its hopeless, sonless master—thought to have upset a lamp when he came home drunk. Now the sun had diluted into a misty film, and this curious substitute for a sunset imparted a tinge of yellow to the successor's stone, or drew out an undertone that was there. Applegate stood up to the hour, as it had to others. Through a window, Francis could be seen moving about in his white coat, bringing in the drink tray. The lawn the women were crossing was scarred with outlines: crescent-and-diamond-shaped and circular ornamental flowerbeds, in other Septembers gorgeous with begonias, had been turfed in.

To reach the gate to the lane, it was necessary to skirt a side of the house. Out from this at a distance welled up a copper beech, under whose crimson-black canopy dangled a child's swing—unevenly, one rope being a trifle longer than the other. It caught Dinah's eye as though for the first time—turning her head as they walked, she continued to watch the swing in a peculiar, vacant yet intent way (the way in which she had looked at space, in the cave), which attracted notice. "Perfectly safe, is that?" asked Mrs. Coral.

"Oh, yes. Just, when it swings it twirls." Dinah answered —as though from another planet.

"So long as it's safe. . . . Oh!" Suddenly Mrs. Coral thwacked at the air with her mesh bag, magazines and all. Terrified, the rose leaped from her buttonhole. "*There* now!" Vexation, mortification reddened her face. "I went and never made you out your receipt!"

"Oh, have we to bother about that?"

"I believe in being particular, Mrs. Delacroix. But the truth is, you gave me such food for thought."

"I'm so glad. I mean, I am so sorry."

"I'll be dropping you your receipt in first thing tomorrow." They had come to the white gate, which stood hooked open. Regretfully, Dinah held out a goodbye hand, but her friend had not by any means done. "Or tonight my Finn might, if he's out on his bike. It would make an object for him. I expect he'd like to. The way *I* shall be situated is, I have jam to cover—and label, naturally. I should hardly like to tell you how many pounds! Plum. They are anxious to have it, so may be calling. Otherwise . . . Well, I am very much obliged to you, Mrs. Delacroix. I'll say good evening."

She put the resolution into effect. Dinah stood in the lane, unheedly waving, then came in—shutting the gate, with some idea of safeguard against the Finn. This gate was shut only very rarely, when there were cattle about. When Frank took off in his car, he would be dumbfounded. One cannot at once please everyone and be pleased oneself. This was a time when she could have done with a vacancy. Francis, when he had brought the drinks in, often either lay down or took a short walk, to refresh himself for the remainder of his evening duties. Or he might, with any luck, be shaving. If he were around, it would be necessary to make a scene about the fire—if she did not, Frank would on her behalf; if she restrained Frank, Francis, thwarted, would be well up to making the scene himself. She felt out of key with anybody likely to be tempestuous. *She* had food for thought.

Indoors, Frank had given himself his drink and was pottering round the room with it, watching Francis, who, crouched in front of the grate, was stimulating the new-lit fire by poking in small wads of newspaper soaked in paraffin. These he had carried in with him in a plated soup tureen, which, not yet emptied of them, sat on the hearthrug. "I shouldn't let Mrs. Delacroix catch you doing that," Frank was advising Francis, as Dinah entered: not only did there not seem to be bad blood, there was, if anything, an alignment. The situation between the three of them altered daily, one might say hourly—just now, if anybody was in anybody else's bad books, she was. Moreover, she saw in whose. "*That* seems to be going nicely," she tendered mildly; but Francis, reclaiming the soup tureen, rose to his feet theatrically and left the room, without so much as a glance her way.

Frank, seeing her, now observed: "There you are."

"Here I am."

"Mrs. Coral gone?"

"Mrs. Coral gone."

"Your feet look wet." (He had already changed into some slippers he kept here.)

"You're telling me," she said, kicking off the espadrilles. "And I could do with—"

"*I* needed *this*, I can tell you." He stared sombrely into what remained in his glass, then roamed away to the tray, to provide for hers. In the distance, he uttered a slight groan.

"Dear," she urged, "try and stop brooding about that baby. One must let Nature just take its course, like it or not. And a birth is one of the few things which *can* be normal. And Joan, I'm sure—"

"Oh, Joan is as tough as a rhinoceros: do her good! What's not normal is what it's doing to me."

"Oh, dear." She settled into her chair, looking across at him unresignedly.

"Oh, I'm a monomaniac, I know!"

"Don't begin to be furious, like Francis.—Oh good, thank you!" she said, taking her drink. But, holding the glass carelessly tilted, she forgot to drink—staring, instead, out of a window into the darkening orchard. " 'A thousand ages in Thy sight are like an evening gone,' " she meditated aloud.

"I've never somehow quite known what to make of that." Glass replenished, Frank headed for his accustomed chair.

"Frank, do you *know*," she suddenly cried out—drawing

her bare feet up under her, rearing up in her chair at him—
"I've been having the most extraordinary sensation! Yes,
and I still am, it's still going on! Because, to remember
something, all in a flash, so completely that it's not 'then'
but 'now,' surely *is* a sensation, isn't it? I do know it's far,
far more than a mere memory! One's right back again into
it, right in the middle. It's happening round one. Not only
that but it never has *not* been happening. It's—it's
absorbing!"

"Should be," said Frank, guardedly.

"They say—don't they?—one never is doing anything
for the first time. I'd say, there's been *a* first time—I'm
perfectly sure! Did you know I had a predisposition to
bury things?"

"Not me, I hope."

"No, no, no—I mean, for a purpose. One of the things
that's happened to me this evening is, I see what I've been
up to down in that cave."

"Ah!"

"That cave idea's been nice, and I'd never call it a fake,
but of course it's been really only a repetition.—No, perhaps not so much exactly that as a going back, again, to
something begun. Anyway, now I know."

"And for that you've taken everyone's favourite tooth-
brushes."

"Don't be stupid," she said, though without animosity.

"Fact is, Dinah, I don't quite follow you."

"Try to! . . . I called this 'a flash,' did I? More, it was
two flashes. First one, a question. Second one, the answer.
The first happened—would you remember?—down in the
cave, when Mrs. Coral asked, 'Who's going to seal it up?'
What made me then go so blah and go round in circles
was, knowing I *had* heard that: but how, why, *when*? . . .
Then the second flash was, when Mrs. Coral and I saw the
crooked swing."

"My dear girl, you see that swing every day."

"Yes, I know I do." Dinah paused, frowned, again
looked out of the window. She drank down most of her
drink as though in a hurry to get it out of the way.—
"Frank?"

"Well, go on."

"At the school I went to, there was a crooked swing."

He found nothing to say.

"And two other girls and I. There were three of us."

"A small school."

"Don't be stupid—of course there were dozens more! The girls I am telling you about are us. Three. What I now must know is, where are the other two? What do I do, do you think? How do I find them?"

"Need you find them?"

"I want them."

"There I can't help you." He wrinkled his forehead, however, with helpful intent. "You last saw them— when?"

"Then." She added: "*They* may not have seen each other since then, either."

"Heard—written?"

"Heavens, no!" she exclaimed. (The very idea!)

" 'Then,' " he asked, "being—when?"

"That summer," she said impatiently.

"Let's get this straight," he implored. "That summer when what?"

"When we were eleven."

"O-oh . . ." Frank said, at once enlightened and more nearly bored by several degrees. "Just little girls, then? I see. Little girls. Children."

"Little do you know."

"My dear Dinah, you'll never find *them* again."

"Why not? . . . Why shouldn't I?"

"You're thinking of two little girls."

"Three."

That was beyond him. "Can't you see, they are not there any more! I mean, *they* are no longer anywhere. By this time. Time goes by, you know. So those two you're thinking of—"

"Three."

"All you would rustle up, if you went ahead, would be two let us hope very charming but—er—decidedly well-grown ladies. Sorry to sound a brute, but that's how it is."

"Don't be too sure."

"Then find out for yourself."

"WE," she told him, with alarming composure, "are far from nowhere. Never have we been nowhere. Simply, the question is—"

"Dinah, don't be fey!"

She turned her head away haughtily.

Frank, one way and another, had had enough for the evening. He heaved about in the depths of the large chair, from which comfort had fled, moodlessly dandling an empty glass. From time to time he studied the ceiling. Later, he was moved to compare his wrist watch with her French clock—small on the high oak chimneypiece. One of the two was slow, and he knew which.—"Francis," he asked, "expecting me here for dinner?"

"I have no idea what he expects. You had better ask him."

Two

Francis's eye-defect was in fact not a squint but a cast—
one eye stayed riveted to his profile, leaving the other to
dart where it would. The arrangement seemed, if anything,
to suit him: he saw the more. Nor, and least of all here at
Applegate, where there was so much vanity in the climate,
did his vanity suffer: he met himself constantly in the mir-
rors and looking-glasses about the house not only without
turning a hair but with, by all signs, fortified self-esteem.
But if neither his vision (so far as one could make out) nor
his looks (at least in his own view) were impaired by his
peculiarity, he did yet feel that it narrowed his future. In
this day of the career open to the talents, the career for
which he deemed himself truly fitted, and to which he
fanatically aspired, was closed to him, talents and all, by
his mischance. What gnawed at Francis was, how far he
might have gone in the Secret Service. He had renounced
his intention of entering the Secret Service for this reason:
it would be impossible for him to assume disguises—that
was, effective ones. Agent X must not be an identifiable
man.

Origin need not have stood in his way; though Maltese
by descent on both sides of his family, he looked (as people who came to Applegate who had been to Malta at
once said) so Maltese that it was nobody's business. More
than one of his parents' relatives had perished in the bomb-
ing of their heroic island: these two gratuitously met their
end in a Bank Holiday seaside boating fatality. Luckily for
Francis, he had been left on shore in charge of unwilling

friends—so thoroughly had he blighted his parents' outing that they were sick of the sight of him: hence their sea-going. The tragedy attracted to the then infant an interest Francis never afterwards forfeited—since then, he had never not been taken an interest in, in one or another quarter if not several. He'd acquired a ring of adoptive uncles and aunts, together with sympathizers, legend-creators, sponsors, and would-be organizers—it had been from one of their number that Dinah'd heard of him. He was then seventeen. It had been considered he might do worse than be under her roof for a month or two, while he thought over his future and looked round. Country air, and fare, could be beneficial. Of course he must very shortly do far better. She had been awarded Francis on the understanding that this was to be temporary, only. "He won't mind doing a certain amount," she had been told, "so long as you take an interest." Resignedly, at the outset, she had done so. She now could not cease to. Francis was habit-forming.

He now was nineteen, and still at Applegate. Everybody told him, he told her, that he was throwing himself away. She assented fervently. However, no suggested alternative had, so far, been by half dazzling enough. No attempt to lure him out of the place, or to boot him out of it from within, had so far succeeded. Francis preferred, it seemed, to continue to entertain frustrated ambitions. And the longer he did so, the more swollen the ambitions became. He fed them by heady reading, lying on his bed, took them out for exercise with him on country walks, and altogether nursed, promoted, and petted them. Where they were not his masters, they were his *protégés*.

As an employee, Francis chose to vary. There were times when he staged a parody of his role here, travesty-ing the impeccable house-boy. There were times when he flattered and cheered Dinah by seeming to manifest a bit-ter devotion. There were times when he took little notice of anyone, still less of his duties, for days together. There were times when breathless attention, punctuated by cries of rapture or awe, had to be gummed by her to all things he did. Or he would devote days to some special skill, such as worrying at the inlay in her furniture with a toothbrush steeped in linseed oil. When he was into one of his talking

phases, that could seem ceaseless: he dogged his employer's
footsteps, stood over her, drilling in with his conversation,
wherever she was, whatever she did. He seemed to her
menacingly well educated. His vocabulary, in these two
years, had enlarged hers—by nature adventurous, she took
chances with hitherto alien words. He whisked newspapers
away as soon as they came (she had often to borrow
Frank's copy of the *Daily Express*) and evidently in-
gorged them: an inflammatory effect on his talk they did
often have. Frank opined that Francis was somewhat
politically confused.

"He needs chums of his age, I expect—don't you think?"
Dinah would ask.

"Bit of a lone wolf, possibly," Frank would comment,
when sympathetic—when not, it was, darkly: "I could tell
you what *he* needs."

She would then firmly say: "He needs more intellectual
life than he has in the country."

Francis never desisted entirely from work. It was clear
to him that if he ceased to do anything whatsoever he
might have to go, and that might not suit him. Meanwhile,
he compensated himself for being unable to be in the
Secret Service. In an unbreakable code he wrote in a fat
notebook, which he did not carry upon his person lest it
bulge, instead keeping it wedged among the bowels of
plumbing under the pantry sink. That came to be a hiding-
place known to all—for he returned his *cahier* to it
ostentatiously. Also, no letter entering Applegate was
unread by him, unless Dinah remembered to lock it up—a
precaution she rarely took; she had the impression that
Francis was probably able to pick locks. The stubs in her
cheque book, bills, Income Tax demands, and correspond-
ence with brokers were of interest also. No form of written communication was beneath his notice. Waste-paper
baskets never delayed him long: he was already con-
versant with what was in them. It was not surprising that
he by now knew how everything stood.

Dinah stowed all her papers inside her writing desk in
the drawing-room. This morning, Francis opened the desk's
flap with no keen or particular expectation—today's post,
arranged by him on her breakfast tray, had been unusually meagre, insipid-looking. Nor, even, would his in-

vestigation today have the charm of requiring stealth and
haste—she was off in her car round the village, which,
given her way of chattering in the shops and custom of
dropping in on the Major, meant (or did usually) out till
lunch-time. Francis therefore embarked on his routine
check somewhat listlessly, though in a practiced manner.
Then, though, all of a sudden he was rewarded. For here
(and certainly fresh since yesterday) was a wad of thin,
crumpled sheets in her handwriting—scarred with erasures,
corrections, inserts, loops, brackets, arrows, marginal
scrabblings. And all (that was, to judge by the first glance)
saying, or attempting to say, the same thing, here or there
with omissions or variations. He was sincerely puzzled—
what *was* she up to? Scooping the stuff from the desk, he
carried it to the neighborhood of a window, where he sat
down on a sofa to sort it out. Smoothing the sheets, he
compared them with one another. Drafting something—ha.
A document, was it?

It would have been this—whatever this was—that she
had been muddling away at late last night, till all hours,
after the Major left. Francis, weaving his way downstairs
to eat a banana at 1:30 a.m., had seen light still showing
under the drawing-room door. A new Will, eh, due to a
brainstorm? No: these repetitious jottings mentioned no
money. An advertisement: could she be advertising
Francis? At that thought, Francis wore a grimace which
Dinah (who'd come on it once or twice) likened to that of
an infuriated Chinese warrior's decapitated head, being
brandished about by a foe, in a gory drawing. . . . No,
however: calmer inspection showed him she had not had
the wits, yet, to think of that. He returned to work, which
was to say, analysis. Throwing out the more tangled convulsive sheets, early stages in her trial-and-error, he was
left with what finally she had let stand. Here, presumably,
were her "fair copies." They reduced down to five in
number, and ran as follows:

Will the former Clare Burkin-Jones and Sheila
Beaker at once get in touch with the former Diana
Piggott, with whom they buried a box. Imperative
Dicey confer with Mumbo and Sheikie. The past not
so buried as it appears. Write Box xxxx.

It is urgent that Sheila (Sheikie) Beaker and Clare (Mumbo) Burkin-Jones, once day-boarders at St. Agatha's school, Southstone, should, whether married or otherwise or living under real or assumed names, without delay get in touch with Diana (Dicey) *née* Piggott. They will know why. Crisis arisen. Write Box xxxx.

Sheikie and Mumbo, where are you? Your former confederate Dicey seeks you earnestly, in connection with matter known so far only to us. Whole affair now looks like coming to light. Essential we meet before too late. You or anyone knowing the present whereabouts of Sheila *née* Beaker and Clare *née* Burkin-Jones, who in 1914 were at St. Agatha's, Southstone, should at once write to Box xxxx.

Will Clare Burkin-Jones and Sheila Beaker, who took part in a secret rite with Diana Piggott, at once contact her. Unforeseen developments make a talk essential. Dicey will always stand by Mumbo and Sheikie. Write Box xxxx.

Where are Sheila Beaker and Clare Burkin-Jones, last heard of in Southstone? Anyone who can throw light on their disappearance is requested to contact their anxious friend, the former Diana Piggott. If alive but in hiding, the two should know they have nothing to fear from Dicey, who continues to guard their secret. Should they care to write, she will not reveal their whereabouts. Whatever the past, she would gladly see them. Write Box xxxx.

To the five drafted notices, Francis found, were appended various notes and queries:

Times, Telegraph.
? Would they read *Times*? Husbands anyway should, if any and living.
Southstone and area papers, how find out names of? ? Telephone Mayor's office?
Also cast net wider. Rest of England?—Scotland,

Wales, Ireland, also, oh my heavens! Do all places have papers? Telephone *all* mayors' offices?

Continent, Commonwealth, U.S.A.? What a bundle of hay. See what breaks *here*, first?

Which of my adverts to go into which papers?

Why not all 5 in rotation in *all* papers? YES. Place order on those lines—standing order? Cash advance necessary? Afterwards pay weekly?—monthly? Memo: remember *to* pay. See how Bank is, sell out something if need be. Why *not*? Get typewriter, get someone to type, get paper to type on, envelopes, paper clips, oceans of stamps. Get map of England.

What a labour of Hercules.

IDEA, though. Get hold of Packie. Knows all the ropes, always did—or *is* he still furious? No harm trying.

On NO account let—

At that point, the reader was interrupted. Francis's ever-acute hearing warned him of Mrs. Delacroix's car now in the lane—far off still, but tearing along. Vexed, he rose from the sofa. What a wrecker she was, what trouble she gave. Thoughtless. Of all scatter-brained homecomings, here was the most untimely. He set about restoring the many sheets to the disorder in which he'd found them, stowed them back where they came from, looked round the drawing-room. Why not partake of a little music? This, provided nobody was around, it was understood he should always be free to do. Showing of interest in his interest in music was a condition of having Francis assigned to one. Would there be a stereophonic gramophone for him? She had a record player. He strolled to it and switched on—letting the needle fall upon a record which dwelled almost permanently upon the player: "Rhapsody in Blue." Few were the days and still fewer the evenings on which either sustained bursts or torn-off snatches of this did not fill Applegate, Dinah having for years been as wedded to it as now was Francis, and Frank acclimatized to it, perhaps more.

Yet on this occasion it was with an air of mutiny that Dinah entered her sounding drawing-room. She was in a mood, but not one for this. She flapped for silence.

"I'm sorry, madam. I understood you were out."

"That doesn't alter the fact that I'm now in. Haven't you got anything to do?"

"There is no Silvo."

"Anyway, get out, will you? I want to telephone."

He at once shot at her, out of his mobile eye, a look of intelligence she could not fathom.

Three

The tea room at the top of a Knightsbridge department store was the place appointed; the time, 3:45 of an afternoon by now some way on into September. The *décor* nicely estimated the patrons' likings: tables low, chairs sympathetic, and carpet costly. Now and then a mannequin prowled through. There have been stranger places for a council of war.

A big woman wearing a tight black turban, and on the lapel of her dark suit a striking brooch, sat down, with all but no hesitation, opposite a woman already there at the table. The already seated woman seemed in two minds as to whether to rise or not. She advanced a hand uncertainly, took it back again, slightly opened her mouth but did not speak. Given her almost excessively *mondaine* air, her look of being slightly too smart for London, her inadequacy was in itself dramatic. Her hat was composed of pink roses.

First, each drew a breath, summoning her forces. Then, as though at a signal, they looked straight across at each other, then away again. Having got *that* over, they simultaneously uttered a sort of titter. Black Turban, settling into her chair, bumped a leg of the table with her knee, whereat Pink Roses tittered: "There you go, again!" She added: "Imagine seeing *you* again!"

"*I'd* been going to say, imagine seeing *you!*"

As airily as could be, Pink Roses hazarded: "You'd never have known me, I suppose?"

The other grinned, but didn't commit herself: "I don't say it wasn't a good idea to describe your hat."

"That was my husband's idea," said Pink Roses, in a

tone which made plain that it was her rule to do that individual justice whenever possible. "He said that as this
was bound to be embarrassing enough for both of us,
you and me I mean, it would be a mistake to start by going
around staring at the wrong women, inviting snubs. 'So let
her know what you'll wear,' he said, 'and be sure you
wear it.' He also hoped neither of us would be surprised if
we got a shock.—No, I don't suppose I'd ever have spotted
you if, in return, you hadn't described your brooch.—I
should like to ask you: is it Italian?"

"Not my type, in a general way," observed Black Turban, ducking a look at her lapel. "Too much of an eye-
catcher. Still, it's served its purpose."

Pink Roses narrowed her eyes, to continue to look at
the brooch, gluttonously. "Directly after I wrote you,"
she went on, "I thought, whatever made me say *this* hat?
Suppose it had rained? Coming up for the day, you never
know. And it's rather a summery hat for this time of
year." . . . Suddenly conscious of being studied, in a lei-
surely, neutral manner, across the table, she flamed up into
suspicion, became defiant. "Or perhaps *you* think—?"

"No," decided the other (still cocking an eye, though).
"I don't. No, you can still get away with it."

"Well, thanks.—China or Indian?" A waitress indeed
was waiting. The order given, the waitress watched out of
hearing, Pink Roses deliberately turned her head and
said: "Well, Clare . . ."

"Hello to you, Sheila."

They both leaned back as far as their chairs would go.

"You know, Clare, it's a curious thing—as I said, as you
now are I'd normally not have known you. That is, if not
for the brooch, and me looking out. And yet now, this
minute, with you sitting there opposite, I quite distinctly
see you the way you were. You so bring yourself back that
it's like a conjuring trick. I *had* all but forgotten you."

"And why shouldn't you?"

"Yes, why not, after all? If we had even known each
other as girls . . . But since we met's been the greater part
of a lifetime. We weren't girls then, even. What were we
both? Eleven. *Little* girls don't make sense."

Clare launched her bulk forward. "You, on the contrary, do the vanishing trick! To me what you've done's
the opposite way round. You still are (in some way?) like

enough what you were to make me actually 'see' you the way you *were* less clearly than I—for instance—did an hour ago, on the way here. Know what I mean?"

"No," said the other flatly, without regret.

"Aha, though, I'd know that 'no' of yours anywhere! It was always 'no'—when it wasn't 'oh.' "

"You must still be clever," said Shelia coolly. Not expecting an answer, she opened her crocodile bag, brought out a rolled-gold compact, tapped it open, and regarded herself in the lid mirror, without comment or, it seemed, curiosity. Not much of what now was her face was to be seen; for the roses, though receding above her forehead, showing a peak of blue-blonded hair, clung round her cheeks like a somewhat loose-fitting wreath. Her rouge blended in with them. Her long rather than large eyes, sea-grey, still tilted—as it could be remembered that they had. A long nose, tilted slightly up at the tip, had not lost its shapeliness with maturity: below it, a recalcitrant mouth, carefully outlined, wore the look of having resigned itself, not good-humouredly, to not saying much that it might have said, and also, probably, to having kissed for the last time. The flesh of her face had hardened, perhaps through the effort involved in resisting change. For the greater part of a lifetime she had been very pretty; she was still not bad.

Clare wore a look of sombre jollity. Her forehead, exposed by the turban, was for ever scored by the horizontal lines into which it rolled up when she raised, as she often did, her comedian's eyebrows. Bags underhung her eyes; deep creases, down from the broadened lobes of the nostrils, bracketed her mouth. Her pug nose and long upper lip (which she still drew down) *should* have been recognizable features, had the whole of her not so paralyzed Sheila's eye. Strictly, she was massive rather than fat: her tailor-made, tailored to contain her, did not minimize (as she sat in it at the table) shoulders, chest, bust, or rib-cage. Clare had arrived, you might feel, by elimination at the one style possible for herself, and thereafter stuck to it. It did not so much fit her as she it. If that had meant forgoings, they had been worth it. Contrary to what might have been once expected, she looked like something, and was unlikely to let herself feel like anything else.

"Yes," she announced.

"What?" asked Sheila, called away from her compact.

"You asked if I'm still clever."

"No, I didn't; I said I supposed you must be. Well, suppose you clever us out of *this*!"

Undeflected, the boaster went on: "I've managed to live!"

"You have had to, have you?" Languid, the daughter of Beaker and wife of Artworth, of Beaker & Artworth, Southstone, turned her head away to look for her waitress —nor had she far to seek. Their tray was wafted into the space between them, teapot towards the hostess—by whose order eatables were restricted to a smallish plate of minuscule cress sandwiches, strewn with more cress, at which Clare looked glumly. "Lemon?—or do you take milk?" asked Sheila, pouring. "I see," she went on, given countenance by her task, "you still sign yourself Burkin-Jones?"

"For the best of reasons."

"Then you never—?"

"*Oh* yes I did! Mr. Wrong came along, all right. That was a mess. So when I wrote that off, I took back my name."

"Oh."

"Or rather, my father's."

"Yes, you were Army, weren't you? You Army children were always moving along, and then on the top of that there was 1914. What a clean sweep that made at St. Agatha's, looking back! I suppose it must have felt curious, though I don't remember, when school began again after those summer holidays. You so suddenly gone, off into the blue . . . *and* her. After that, not a clue, not a word, from that day to this. Once war broke out, was your father ordered abroad?"

"Killed at Mons. August 23rd, 1914."

"Oh. Still, by now I suppose you must hardly miss him. Anyway, it seems late to say 'so sorry.' "

"Don't bother!"

"Don't bite my head off!" Sheila bit into a sandwich, then put it down. Nothing more was *she* going to ask; it was up to Clare—who, sure enough, banged back into the talk with: "So you married into the firm, like a good girl?"

"Mr. Artworth's second son; yes. The elder was killed."

"You might have travelled farther and fared worse."

"I did. I married Trevor eventually."

"You don't mean *Trevor*?"

"Why?" asked the wife, curiously raising her tilted eye-lids.

"I stuffed sand down his mouth and trod on his spectacles."

"So you did. He may not remember."

"I bet he does."

"He has never said so."

"You chased him up that sewer."

"No, that was Dicey.—Anyway," said the wife, "that was the past."

"They say, little girls and boys these days are little sweethearts.—Where've you been all this time, Sheikie, when not in Southstone?"

"Southstone. More goes on there than they suppose."

"Evidently."

"Just what do you mean by that, Clare?"

"What you mean, don't I?"

"I wondered.—*Don't* call me Sheikie!"

"Saw no harm."

"Sorry; but don't you see—it's this dreadful thing. Hanging over us. Really I dread to speak of it."

"But isn't that why we're here?"

"It could have been nice, meeting," said Sheila crossly.

"Come on, though," bullied Clare. "No more beating about the bush!"

"Then suppose you stop."

"Buck up. Come on. Cards on the table!"

Mrs. Artworth allowed herself one doomed shiver. Then, rallying, she unwedged from inside her handbag a manilla envelope: before handing this over she examined it, warily, on both sides (nothing was, in fact, written on either). "Here are mine—where are yours?" Miss Burkin-Jones extracted, from her more angular, larger black calf handbag, an envelope of considerably greater bulk. Sheila at once cried: "Where did you get all *those*?"

"Press-cutting service."

"Then they're all over England?"

"Not quite, yet. Give her time, though!"

Mrs. Artworth put her hands to her face, forcing them up her cheeks, pushing up the roses. So nearly hysterical seemed the gesture that one or two women glanced her way from other tables. She did, however, know when to stop—having withdrawn her fingertips from her make-up, one by one, she composedly glanced at each to see whether anything had come off on them. While thus engaged, she asked in a deadened tone: "Why is she doing this to us?"

"Oh, don't act up, Sheikie! The thing's a joke."

"For you, perhaps," the other said, with a bitterness which, if tinted by envy, was chiefly slighting. "You don't live anywhere."

Clare commented only with her eyebrows—given their expressiveness, was more needed? They shot up so high, and with such force, as to drive her turban further up her skull. She peeled open then shook her envelope, causing cuttings to shower, as from a cornucopia, on to and round her plate. "Well, here we are," she declared, in a lordly way. "Now let's match up with yours. Ten to one they're identical, but let's make certain."

"You are methodical," said the other languidly.

"That's gone far to making me what I am."

"By the way, what *are* you? I've no idea."

"Goodness, haven't you?" Clare asked, almost with awe.

"Don't be so pompous at me. You never said."

"Hardly thought that was necessary."

"Well, I'll tell you one thing you're not, Clare, from the way you go on, and that is, a prominent local family. Because clearly you seem to form no idea what these last weeks have been like for me in Southstone. And not me only; Trevor's been losing sleep. And how Daddy'd have felt, if he'd lived, I don't like to think. A thing like this *could* reflect on the firm. Beaker & Artworth, you may not realize, have not only been going more or less ever since the place was a place at all but have done as much as any firm in the place to make the place what it is today. Anybody in Southstone would tell you that."

"And be right, I'm sure."

"And never has one of us been remotely blown upon."

"And who is remotely blowing on you now?"

Mrs. Artworth opened her eyes. "You *are*," she said, "—aren't you?—really very extraordinary." Pointing a frosted-rose fingernail at Clare's dreadful plateful, she inquired: "You have *read* those, I suppose? I at least imagine yours are the same as mine. Yes, go on, do what you said: compare them—here are mine, right under your nose! Go on, shove them round as much as you like—only don't ask me to! A, I know them by heart; B, I could no longer touch them with the end of a barge-pole." Her voice thinned to a species of shrieking whisper or whispered shriek—"If you don't consider those damaging what is?"

Clare pulled yet another face, this time sideways. She conceded: "Make us look a bit silly. Could do, and since you feel they do, do do. But that's the worst."

"You think so?" asked Sheila, marvelling.

"That's my view," said Clare, with defiant firmness. But her pug nose seemed to tickle; she rubbed it suddenly.

"That hasn't been Trevor's view. Or anybody's who's in their right senses."

"Trevor's now out of his senses, from what you tell me," Clare remarked—though abstractedly: she was busied to and fro between the two hoards of cuttings. Unexpectedly quick of eye and nimble of finger, she picked, glanced, sorted. Finally she gave out: "Look here—these shockers of Dicey's reduce to five, or so I make out. You seem to have no variants, and I haven't, certainly. Five are enough, I grant. They've mounted into the number we have here thanks to her having seeded them far and wide, also to sheer non-stop pigheaded repetition. Won't take no answer for 'no,' or 'no' for an answer. Never did, did she? I'll tell you *one* thing—"

"I'll tell *you* one thing: if Trevor's not quite himself, there is every reason. Night and day our telephone keeps ringing. Everybody who's anybody in Southstone wanting to know what we intend to do, saying how they feel for us, asking, do we realize it's more than a laughing matter? Saying they've spotted another, have we seen that, or shall they bring it round or send it along? I am worn down."

"Wonderful friends, however."

"I am not so sure."

"Who got on to this first?"

"Trevor's office-boy. In the *Southstone Herald,* in the 'Miscellaneous,' among the rabbit advertisements. The chief clerk found him sniggering over something, so took it away and of course looked. He then of course thought it right to bring the matter to Trevor's notice. Needless to say we promptly rang up the editor, whom we have both of us known since the year one, who said he'd had no idea and would do his best. Next morning, however, three people sent us the one from *The Times.*"

"That was where I lit on it, first of all. Happening to

be on the hunt, as I now am, for a good-looking fur coat from a good home, I'd been running my eye down the 'Personal' most mornings."

"Another woman's? Oh, I don't think I *could*!"

"Then you couldn't."

"The nerve of her, Clare—an enormous paper like that!"

"The cash of her!—Now I'll tell you what *I* was about to tell *you*: wherever she may be and whatever up to, she's in the money."

"Why?" asked Shelia malignantly.

"Why, I'm unable to tell you. She clearly is, though. These," stated the self-made woman, indicating the bevy of cuttings, "cost. Run her into three figures, if she keeps going. Money, and more where it came from. To go bashing around like this, just for a whim—"

"They say sadists spend thousands, sometimes, torturing people."

"Those particular Piggotts, it's known, never had a bean."

Fortified by studying her own bracelets, Sheila asked: "Imagine she married a rich man?"

"Two, three, by now: who knows? She's had more than time to. And one leads to another, I've often noticed—*I* should argue, the last is dead and she's on her own."

"Don't try to make out to me that she's lonely!"

"Gay as a lark. But completely out of control."

Sheila remarked, pensively: "It's surprising, though."

"Nothing surprises *me*."

"Not when you come to think of her? Looking back, she was rather an awful child. Blinkety light-red eyelashes, and quite pudgy.—You were the skinny one." (Sheila's glance of renewed incredulity at Clare's torso was so artless as to be without offence.) "And scream and moan and create: I can hear her now! *And* bossy . . . wasn't she related to a baronet?"

"No idea."

"No, that used to be Olive Pocock. No, what *she* had in her family was a bishop: much good that did her character! You know, Clare, thinking her over as I've done lately—*did* she so suddenly leave because of the war, or under a cloud? What has dawned on me is, why should it have been the war when she had no father? Supposing,"

Sheila proceeded, with growing caution, "she never did have a father, at the best of times? There they used to be, simply she and her mother, stuck down in that cottagey house with no explanation. Things one may see as a child but not then think anything of seem peculiar later. That drawing-room of theirs smelled like a hothouse, always—who sent those expensive flowers? *They* never grew them; think of their garden! Then there were those pictures they had which made me giggle (I now see why) hanging right on the wall. Mother'd have had a fit. Her mother wore tea gowns. They had no gong. Those Saturdays you and I went to tea there—"

"Mrs. Piggott always laid on the most stunning cake. You got outside plenty of that, in your quiet way."

"I dare say; but did she seem like a widow?"

"Nothing fishy about the Piggotts. My mother knew them."

"Oh.—They were none of them mental, by any chance?"

"Not that I heard, ever. The bishop may have been."

"Not an Atheist, are you?—Anyway, in that case, *there* goes heredity!"

"Don't follow?"

"You tell me her mother was moral, and her family normal. Yet in spite of all her advantages, look at her now!"

"You know, I can hardly wait to!" burst out the incautious Clare.

Mrs. Artworth lightly frowned, as though vexed by deafness. "Sorry—say that again?"

"You heard me. Aren't *you* mad with curiosity?"

"You mean, see her?"

Clare puffed her cheeks out, then sucked them in. Pinned by Sheila's considering, mermaid gaze, she became delinquent: over-bold first, then shifty. She mumbled something.

"I beg your pardon?" asked Sheila.

"I said, 'Why not?' "

" 'Why not?' Because that is what she wants."

Clare looked at once hangdog and unresigned.

"You astound me rather, Clare, I can only tell you. You'd really dream of playing into her hands? There you go again, then—falling under her spell!"

"If anybody exerted a spell, *I* did."

Inclining her head in its pink bower, Sheila let herself smile. She said: "So you thought." Dibdabbing with her spoon at the disc of lemon afloat in her teacup, she smiled again. "She, though, *was* a born ringleader. She only did not succeed in ringleading us because, unfortunately for her, we were you and me. The two of us being *us* was just too much for her. So we know how that always ended: with her screaming—oh, I can hear her! But she never learned: it was try, try, and try again. Next time, she'd be back at her old game. And here she now is, trying it on once more.—Do as you wish, if you want. I simply instinctively warn you, if I were you I wouldn't go near her without me."

"Come along too, then?"

"Thank you, I'd rather die."

"If that's how you feel—"

"That is how I feel. Any objection?"

Tea-logged, the disc of lemon submerged—the point of the spoon, however, ran it to death at the bottom of the cup, goring away at it without mercy. Here and there a shred rose to the surface. "Well?" asked Mrs. Artworth, when that was over.

"Though," tendered Miss Burkin-Jones, a gleam in her eye, "it could be the one way of stopping this. However . . ."

"Since you can't wait to see her, Clare, which stands out a mile, exactly why *did* you wait, I should like to know? Her instructions were clear, surely? Why didn't you dash off a line to her straightaway? Why waste time, I mean, getting in touch with me?"

"Thought, no harm in you and me getting together first."

"Oh. Oh, then you did smell a rat?"

"Not exactly, but—"

"Did you, or didn't you? Yes or no?"

"Smart of me, didn't you think, the way I traced *you*? A typical brain-wave. Occurred to me, c/o Beaker & Artworth, Southstone, could hardly fail to catch up with you —if still living."

"I can't see why I should not be," said Sheila huffily. She reflected, however. "Now that I come to think, *she* could have done the same. First thing anybody might think of, one might have thought—sorry, Clare, but really it does seem obvious! With Beaker & Artworth boards, not to speak of notices, all over Southstone and through the area. There they have always been, and doubtless will be. There they used to be *then*, just as much as now. If she'd been bona fide, her way lay open. But not her, oh no! No, she had to rouse the world. No, apart from anything, that itself shows . . ."

"She took little notice of notice boards: too self-centred. And never had any memory."

"Exactly what," Sheila wanted to know, "is she having now, then?"

"Some sort of attack, with regard to us—call it a seizure."

Sheila brightened slightly. "Imagine she's breaking up? . . . It certainly was a relief when I heard from you, Clare. Where you'd disappeared to, of course I had not a clue."

" 'Alive but in hiding'—eh?"

"*Don't*!—Trevor pointed out, the best hope was your contacting us. He thought, in view of how rattled we knew you must be, it was probable that you would—and of course you did. Trevor was all in favour of sitting tight until you did show up. 'Give her time,' he advised me. He's attached great importance to our getting together. As he said, once I saw you—"

"Then, what?"

"Then we could talk this over."

"Exactly," Clare vaunted, "what we're doing!"

"Yes and no," Mrs. Artworth said, less contentedly. "We don't get far."

"How far were we meant to get?"

"*Somewhere*, surely?" The victim, side-glancing at her watch, complained: "It's already twenty to five. We can't sit here all night, you know: this place closes."

Clare did not seem sorry. "There's the bar at my club."

"I dare say there is; but there's my train. What Trevor hopes, and really I cannot blame him, is that you and I will decide on what we're to *do*. Once he's been told what that is, he can think it over. Oh yes, and he also asked me to tell you, he by now has of course already taken legal advice, though he's not as clear as he'd like to be what that came to. Our lawyer apparently hummed and hawed. Trevor expects you're in touch with your lawyer, too? The idea is, you and I should take action jointly."

"Oh, yes?"

"Well?" asked Sheila, extremely guardedly.

"Against whom, about what, and—quite frankly— why?"

Thus querying, Clare extracted a cigarette from a mono- grammed case (which Sheila weighed with her eye), lit it, after some to-do with her lighter, and went on to take two or three tense, inexpert puffs. Clearly (nor was this ig- nored by Sheila) she put herself through the bother of this performance only when it was needed to mark a crisis, build up a role, or convey an effect, as now. Heaving up her thorax, she supposed herself in the act of inhaling deeply: the brooch on her lapel knowingly winked and twinkled. Then—"Sorry!" she penitently exclaimed, jab- bing the case towards Sheila. "You?"

"Thanks, I seldom bother to.—Did I hear you ask 'why' take action, and 'what about'?"

"You did. Exactly what *is* complained of?"

"Innuendo," said Sheila promptly, colouring deeply. "In- sinuations—malicious, insidious, mischievous, damaging."

"Golly, you've got that pat!"

"She so words those things that anyone could think any- thing. And if *that* weren't enough, there may well be worse at the back—Trevor considers the tone is distinctly men- acing. Not blackmail yet, but that is what it could come to. Incidentally, how do we know that she's not a gang?"

"How, indeed?"

"Have *you* no character, Clare, that you don't want in- jured?—or professional capacity, or something? I repeat, I'm exceedingly sorry I've never heard of you. You do something, do you—what do you do, then? Or if you pre- fer it the other way, what *are* you?"

At once, Clare's expression became uplifted. She looked round her at the emptying tables like a big speaker depre- cating a small audience. The eyes she at length returned to her friend were dedicated and abstract—not, it seemed, to be focussed merely on one face. "I am MOPSIE PYE," she made known.

"Mopsie what?"

"You heard me," said the celebrity, severely.

Sheila could not forbear to giggle: her roses tottered. "Animal, vegetable, or mineral?"

"MOPSIE PYE chain of specialty gift shops operates

throughout the better-class London suburbs and outward into the Home Counties. When it extends to the coast, you will soon know. *I* started, have a controlling interest in, buy for, and operate MOPSIE PYE."

"Oh."

"Yes . . ."

"Did that brooch," Sheila asked swiftly, "come out of stock?"

Clare nodded. "Goes back tomorrow."

"I wouldn't mind taking it off you, for cash down. How much?"

"Nope, dear. Not out of hours. What a jackdaw you are, Sheikie, always were!"

"You do really run some quite nice lines, then, at Mopsie Pye," Mrs. Artworth conceded, though not in the best of humours, frustratedly closing the purse she had whipped out.

"Swedish, Spanish, Finnish, Italian, Provençal, Japanese, and Javanese novelties, and others. Driftwood, primitive art. Witch balls, wind harps. Neckwear, place mats, personalized dog dishes, book ends, saris, door knockers, goat rugs—"

"Yes, I expect so. But stop it: listen! How many people know you are Mopsie Pye?"

"Oh, I show up sooner or later at all my branches. Always have made a great point of that. Personality. Hare round and round in the Mini, six days a week. How am I to count my enormous public?"

"Most people," persisted Sheila, "do *know*, then, that 'Mopsie Pye' is Clare Burkin-Jones?"

"Everyone who is anyone. What about it?"

"That is what I've been wondering," said Mrs. Artworth, not only slowly but in her most ominous tone yet. "*What* about it? You don't think widely spread innuendo and menacing hints and allusions to secret rites, not to speak of threats to expose your past, will in any way blow upon Mopsie Pye? If you don't you're an optimist, let me tell you. Don't tell me scandal *is* good for business! And least of all in your line, I should have thought. No one can tell me anything about gift shops: we have seven in Southstone alone, to my certain knowledge. To me they are sissy, but they're respectable—and ever, *ever* so their clientele are! Dizzying round with joss sticks and Swedish pepper pots far, far from means their customers are abnormal: quite the reverse. It's respectable people who need to have fancy outlets. . . . No, do *look*, Clare! These days there are so constantly being such revelations, one can hardly wonder at everyone's being nervous. Spy rings, dope rings, art-thief rings, white-slave rings, Black Mass rallies (or whatever they call them), and of course always naturally Communists. A gift shop, so mixed up with foreign trade, could be cover for any of those, if you come to think—and a *chain* of gift shops, ever so much more so! You don't care if everyone's frightened off?—However, that's your worry: I'm merely telling you."

"Thank you."

"You hadn't thought?" asked Sheila, tilting a glance.

Clare's upper lip drew down to its glummest length. Her jaw sank into her chins. She returned no answer.

"Then really I think you should," said the other earnestly.

"You mean, I'm in more of a spot than you are?"

"Oh, I should hardly say *that*."

"One thing I won't do," Clare blustered. "Come hell and high water, won't do it. Won't get myself snarled up in a law-court case. Fine old figure of fun I'd be made to look —and you too, also, my Rosy-Posy! Even apart from the fact that in point of law I doubt whether we'd have a leg to stand on."

"How is *she* to know that? I didn't mean bring a case, stupid (and nor did Trevor, to do him justice). I meant, threaten one. We could give her a fearful fright."

"With a lawyer's letter? If she's still our Dicey, nothing short of a gun would.—Besides, damn it all, *I* still think she's just being friendly!"

"Oh, yes?" The pointed tip of a tongue licked its way slowly round Sheila's lips.

"Let me think!" Clare commanded.

"I'm not stopping you."

Before thought took place, it became devolvent on Clare again to go through the act with a cigarette. This time, it miscarried—she choked, spluttered, while water from her smarting eyes made gutters out of the pouches under them. A mannish, also monogrammed handkerchief set about (when it could at last be come at) to make good the damage. Mrs. Artworth meanwhile examined her faultless fingernails. Yet the would-be smoker did, in a way, profit by her mishap: it gained time for her, also the mopping handkerchief hid the spasm by which her face was apt to betray thought. Once back in order, and after one steady puff (to show that it *could* be done), she announced: "Leave this to me—I've had an idea."

"What ?"

"Leave that to me. Just wait."

"Oh . . ." said Sheila, moodily, indecisively. Swooning back in her chair, to denote exhaustion, she nonetheless keenly searched the other one's face. Though the prospect of handing over, of being quit of things, should have been grateful to Mrs. Artworth, it dissatisfied Sheila and thwarted Sheikie. "I can't see," she admitted, "why I should miss the fun, if there's to be any."

"Oh, there'll be heaps."

This was still ambiguous. "I hope it's a good idea?—a quite nasty one? When I think of that fat little bossy beast . . ."

"Those were the days."

"Well, *go* for her, Mumbo!"

The big woman, eyeing the pretty one with genuine fondness and affability, asked: "Ever had any?"

"Children? No, not—funnily enough," Sheila said with aggressive lightness, an air less of regret than revived surprise. She added: "However, Trevor, by means best known to himself, had already two."

"Wh-at?"

"What d' you mean, 'wha-at'?" asked the unblinking wife. "He'd been married before. Any objection? She was Phyllis Sissen—used to go to St. Monica's, not St. Agatha's. Fell off her bike if anyone yelled at her. I don't think you met her."

"When you found you required Trevor, you got her out?"

"She had died already. A chill, after German measles. Anyway, there you are.—What about you?"

"No issue. The fact was, Mr. Wrong gave me but scant chance to show my form." Clare's eyebrows went up jaunty, came down lugubrious. Then she pondered. "Wonder if Dicey's multiplied?"

Sheila shuddered.

She then asked: "What do I tell Trevor?"

"To hold his horses."

Bill on salver, the waitress stood like a conscience. They were quite the last. Everything had been spirited away. But that outgoing footprints bruised the bloom of the carpet, there might never have been a soul here—stretching into the distance, the sea of tables was disembellished neither by crumb nor speck. Agoraphobia threatened. All that there was not yet was silence: in the void, the clatter of tea tray stacking and china piling and tea spoon counting sounded ever more loudly. Not to be daunted, the Southstone lady slowly reread the bill. "I pay at the desk?"

"No, me, now, madam. The desk has closed."

"Oh? How peculiar.—What *is* the matter, Clare?"

"Dropped a glove," grunted Mumbo, dropping the other.

Four

꧁꧂

Ten days after Frank had become a grandfather, Dinah
pulled up her car at a lonely crossroads. She lit a cigarette,
then unfurled a map. This should be the place she had
said, but was it? Places on maps are unlike what they are
in reality. Space causes the same anxiety as time, when
one is at sea with regard to it. Here, though, all but on top
of her, was an excellent signpost—and better still, what she
learned from it was encouraging. It appeared that the roads
intersecting here *were* the roads she'd hoped. If this was
not the place, it ought to be. She could do no more.

She and the car were up on a hill, in miraculous early-
October air, which shone, making dazzling the emptiness of
the country. It was noon. Few were trees, far or near; of
those that there were each stood out in tinted and lonely
beauty, a smoky flame; while in distances a watery shimmer
was given off by roads whose surfaces caught the sun—
roads whose wide verges were bounded only by low stone
walls. Morning filled the Hillman, its windows open—she,
who thought she hated to wait, sat tranced, becalmed in
stillness as one only otherwise is in the midst of speed. She
had with her her transistor, a flask, *In Memoriam* bound
in once-violet suede, and *The Midwich Cuckoos*, but had
resort to none of them: while this lasted, everything was
enough. . . . But now traffic, having for some time been
sealed away out of sight and hearing behind the skylines,
began to come by in gushes—vans, lorries, a bubble car,
two or three great snooty ones, a tractor, motor bikes. She
began to wonder. Soon she was watching, searching the

road coming up on her left. Along that the taxi must come. Why did it not?

Sitting turned left, arm hanging over the seat-back, Dinah had in mind no other direction. It was, however, from straight ahead that a Mini-Minor came bounding towards the Hillman. Checking its eagerness as it neared the crossroads, it, once across them, slowed down to a crawl. In passing, sidling close to the Hillman, the driver took stock of Dinah's turned-away head. The Mini-Minor then came to a stop, correctly, on its side of the road, the requisite number of yards further along. Clare, encased in dogtooth tweed and wearing a claret variant of the turban, got out and walked back briskly towards the Hillman.

Distracted, at last, from her vigil by these manoeuvres and the plaguey sense of now having a neighbour, Dinah looked behind her to see what was going on. Seeing at once who it was, she flew into a rage. "What on earth—?" she stormed, leaning out of a window. "I told you to take a *taxi!*"

"I know, I know!" Buoyant, Clare came alongside.

"I *told* you the train!"

"Never take trains—what's the matter with this? I am on the dot."

"You have ruined everything."

"Boohoo!" said Clare, with veteran unconcern. Here they were back where they had left off—how long ago? Not a day might have passed! "Are you," she asked, putting a hogskin-gloved hand on the frame of the window, "getting out, or do I get in?"

"What are we to do with that car of yours?"

"Tail you home in it, I suppose, don't I?"

"But we shan't, like that," Dinah mourned, "be able to *talk*. Don't you see, that was the entire point—the whole point of this entire plan?"

"What I don't see is, why gallivant out here? Why not you simply have met the train?"

"Fat lot of good that would have been, when you weren't on it! But anyway, meet in a *station*?—No, really, Mumbo!"

"For your feelings, I was supposed to take an expensive taxi?"

"You old meanie, with that enormous shop of yours!"

Dinah's tone changed to one of dovelike complaint. "Yes, I know we do have the day, and there's my house—*there*, though, I'm so constantly overrun: wait till you see! So if you knew with what care I'd devised this plan—you and me, in my car, for the whole drive home. That's what I've looked forward to! As it is, we shall be a ghastly procession."

"Hum-ha, yes: could have been nice. Anyway, let's have a breather?"

"Budge, then—let me out. Let's sit in the sun."

Clare, watching Dinah's length snake out of the Hillman, remarked: "Fancy *you* growing into a daddy-longlegs!"

Dinah looked down at herself, brushed ash from her slacks. "Yes, haven't I!" In accord, facing towards the signposts, they walked a pace or two, mounted the grass verge, and sat themselves on a wall. From above, around, poured on to them the not wholly untender or hostile noon. The rumpus, during whose course they had truly met, left its benevolent influence behind. Dinah crossed her knees and, clasping the top one, rocked some way back and looked up at the sky; then, with much the same pensive idleness, round at Clare—who, bolt upright, unbuttoned her fitted coat. If Dinah's regard more rested upon than considered the newfound Clare, Clare's in return (out of habit?) was inventorial. "Yes, improved," she admitted, in an as-though-grudging tone.

"*Haven't* I! Apparently I was a most hideous child, so that's just as well. It's nice to look nice."

"Must be."

"But you look splendid, Mumbo!" Dinah cried, surprised that anything else could be thought for a moment. She rocked further back on the wall, then sat up with a beatific sigh. "You're glad, after all, we did gallivant out here?" she began to wheedle—but then broke off. "Look, oh do look, at those hundreds of birds! Off to Africa, can't make up their minds to start. All that organization, and all for nothing. What a dither they're in!—No, over there!"

In movement the birds were like shaken silk. At them, Clare did consent to stare: of the universe they transparently shadowed she would have nothing. Her known objection to scenery had been hardened by years which had shown her how sound it was. By now, she resisted many things; or, should she fail to, acted as though she did by affecting an extra nonchalance or jocosity. To be sardonic could be a refuge also. Count on Dicey, she thought, to lay on no scene without towering stage-effects. Meet in a railway station? Oh no, never. Or on a doorstep, or in a room, or even a bar. Nor might one merely meet, one had to converge—and in the middle of what? This great aching landscape. And what had she lifted this out of? Thomas Hardy . . . No, though: wait a minute—was not an older nigger in this woodpile? "This," Clare remarked, in what Mrs. Artworth would have called a distinctly peculiar tone, "could be quite a Macbeth meeting-place, could it not?"

"Bubble-bubble," Dinah said instantaneously. "Not quite a heath, this, or exactly the weather, but near enough. The *main* thing wrong is, being one short. First Witch, Hail. Second Witch, Hail. Third Witch . . . ? I can't understand her letting us down like this. When one thinks, I went to a lot of trouble!"

"And made it."

Dinah went on, unheeding: "No, it's been most mysterious about Sheikie: she never answered. You saw her—how did she seem?"

"Sore."

"Said so?"

"You've made her life hell."

"What absolute nonsense!"

"Come off it, Dicey! She has her life, and she has to live."

"Then why marry that house agent?"

"She more or less was one."

"Sheikie?—Dust to dust, I suppose, then, ashes to ashes: that's not my fault!—She didn't sound sore when she wrote, though. The way she wrote, butter wouldn't melt."

"*Wrote?*"

"What's up?—don't fall off the wall! Yes, she naturally wrote, why shouldn't she? You did. Hers came three–four days after yours. Rather slow off the mark, I thought, but then so had you been."

"Just this minute, you told me you'd never heard from her."

"Don't be dense: I told you she'd never answered. Never answered the one I wrote in answer to hers. As I say, the letter I had from her was quite merry. Said, to think of *me* being still around, what fun. Asked what my name is nowadays, and where I'm perching—meaning, living? Told me what hers now is, and where she perches—pretty permanently, I thought it sounded. Only two doors, apparently, from the old Beaker mansion in What-d'you-callums Gardens. Geographically she hasn't got far, has she! Something a bit wrong about that, surely? What became of her dancing, I do wonder. What she chiefly wanted to know was, whether I'd heard from you, whether you and I had made any plan and, if so, what, and for what day. I naturally told her."

"Damn Sheikie! Sly is her second name."

"Why?" queried Dinah. "Why shouldn't she? Three it was meant to be—*I* thought. Anyway, as I say, I jolly well told her. Told her the day (today), the train, and where to get off. Told her to keep an eye out for you on the train, as you'd have the further secret instructions—couldn't be fagged to go writing everything out all over again. You, I thought, could scoop her into the taxi. . . . I did, though, particularly ask her to let me know whether she would be coming along, or not. Not simply because of how many chops; more, because I *have* to picture a thing. I have to picture everything in advance. It's by picturing things that one lives, I completely think. Which," added Dinah—turning on Clare a not so much reproachful as exploratory glance (should reproach be risked, how far dare it go?) —"is, I expect, probably just as well. Because when, usually owing to someone else, something one's pictured does not, after all, work out, one has at least had one tremendous pleasure."

"True, I'm sure."

"Oh, but you sound so glum!—Anyway, as I began by telling you, not another squeak out of her, from that day to this. Gone to ground again, as though she had never been. That I do call mysterious: wouldn't you?"

"No. To me, her motives are clear as glass."

"Mumbo, *I* don't see why she wouldn't come. Or couldn't. Or why she shouldn't come, least of all."

Clare snorted. "Nor did I, at the start. (*Listen*, Dicey,

will you!) On the contrary, what could be jollier, thought
I. If you want to know, in the first place *I* put it up to her,
over that scrumptious tea she and I had. 'You come along
too,' I said, 'why not?' She was not on to."

"Not keen to?"

"Since you ask, she said she would rather die."

"Oh!" The wound made the crier-out not know where
to be. She blinked at and beyond Clare, then turned in the
other direction, to blink alone. "Then why did she ever
write to me?" she asked miserably. "What made her?"

"Second thoughts."

"I don't see—I don't understand!"

"Thought again. That should be clear, should it not?"

"No. What's she *up* to?"

"Sabotage. Who's being dense now?"

One way and another, this was not to be borne. Dinah's
scream rose. "Oh, bother, *bother* you two! *Cawing* away
at each other—you beastly bothers!"

"Boohoo, boohoo.—And if we're going to ask who's
been up to what," went on Clare, with cannibalistic glee,
"I've got various questions to ask *you*."

"I say, Mumbo, let's go home and have lunch!" In a
flash, Dinah was off the wall. Whistling, she walked ahead,
back to the cars, the prospect of a processional drive home
less distasteful to her, apparently, than it had been. Clare
was the one thwarted. And back Clare had to dart, to
recover a dropped good glove.

Waiting, Dinah held open the Mini's door. "Hop in. I'll
just go ahead and turn."

"At lunch, then?"

"Except for Francis."

"Francis?"

"You'll soon see.—One thing there won't be," Dinah
said, walking away again, "is Frank."

"*Who* won't be?" shouted Clare, through the Mini's
window.

"Not today: he's in London," called back Dinah, getting into the Hillman. She and it executed a lightning turn,
then slid past Clare (ready in gear) at gathering speed.
They were off. Clare drove with great intensity. Her
ferocious image was never for long gone from the Hillman's mirror, many as were the turns and twists of the
lovely roads. She seemed to be less tailing the car ahead

than hunting it. The run to Applegate, cross-country, was about fifteen miles.

Dinah, turning in at her gate, saw Francis framed in the porch, in his whitest coat. He stepped out to meet her—clearly, bearer of tidings. "Chops not come?" she asked, getting out of the car.

"The lady you are expecting is here, madam."

"I'm not expecting a lady; I have one with me." (Clare, entangled with cattle back in the lane, could be heard banging on her horn.) "So whoever this one is, she will have to go. Who did she say she was?"

"She appeared to know her own business, so I did not . . ."

"Never mind—where is she?"

"I put her into the drawing-room with the Major."

"Now you *are* seeing things, Francis: he's in London! Went by the early train."

"All I know is," Francis said in a hard-tried tone, "he walked in this morning, shortly after you'd left, saying he'd changed his mind. Said he considered today too fine for London. Not finding you anywhere, he asked where you'd gone. I could give him no information, beyond the fact that you were expecting a guest for luncheon. He appeared dissatisfied and put out, but took himself off for a prowl round the *potager*. He re-entered the house and rang for a drink shortly before the lady's taxi arrived. Having brought the tray in, I left it to the Major to do the honours."

"Everyone must be mad."

"We are also right at the end of the Noilly Prat."

The Mini came sailing in at the gate, to be brought to rest neatly behind the Hillman. Clare, saying something about the cattle, got out. She shook herself into order and looked round—taking in the lawns, the house, and the copper beech. "Nice," she remarked contentedly, "isn't this?"

"Sometimes. Today's an inferno. Mumbo, what *do* you think? Frank's not only ratted on London, Francis says, but now has a woman in the drawing-room!"

"Well, well.—Look, I should like a wash."

"Oh, come in, come in!" Dinah propelled her guest through the Gothic porch into the neo-Jacobean hall. "And welcome, of course, and everything, Mumbo darling!

I suppose this still is my house, though I sometimes wonder.—Straight up, first on your right. No, sorry, second!—
I'm all but out of my mind. The lengths I went to, ar-
ranging London: but oh, no—slippery as an eel! . . . I hope
you'll find everything," Dinah shouted, despondently, after
ascending Clare. "*I'll* just, I think, now go and see about
getting that harpie out."

She lost no time in tackling the drawing-room door.

The big-windowed drawing-room, at this hour, was more
dazzling than had been the open country. Sun, magnified
by the plate glass through which it poured (windows she
had left open were now shut), lavished itself on lavish
bowls and tureens of early chrysanthemums, late dahlias,
surviving roses, and with sunny malice lay on fine films of
dust over the satiny surfaces of the furniture. Armchairs
and sofas looked over-exposed and crushed. Blazing into
the fire, the sun all but brought off its trick of putting
the fire out; though wood ash, consuming itself at white heat,
made the air pungent and faintly blue: Frank's pipe, too,
had been going for some time. Nor in other ways was the
room as it last had been—a chic collapsible hat had become intimate with the faded needlework stool, opposite
Dinah's desk, on to which by the look it had been light-
heartedly flung, and a magazine glossier and more knowing than any accustomed to enter Applegate had glissaded
off something and lay sprawled on the floor. But at-
hominess centred around the hearthrug, on which stood
Frank entertaining Sheila, and Sheila svelte in a knitted
suit. He balanced a glass of lager, she held on to a gin and
tonic.

Into the room, not yet far from the door, Dinah came
to halt—diffidently, one might almost have thought. Be-
mused, she wore a look of regret, regret at being without
her sun-glasses. Slowly she drew one foot up, as though
uncertain how much of the floor was hers to stand on.
"So where have *you* been?" Frank asked, in a tone of
marked reprobation. Simultaneously Sheila, with aplomb,
nitched her glass on the chimneypiece, uttered a fearless
laugh, and swung right round, extending a hand. "Why,
Diana," she chanted, "isn't this fun!"

"It's not *you*, is it?"

"Oh dear, am I a shock? It's been such years, hasn't it?"

Frank, with an emphatic roll of the eyes, said: "Mrs. Artworth has had a rocky journey, you'll be sorry to hear."

"It's not that, so much," said the traveller pluckily. "But I *am* in a way knocked rather all in a heap—after all these years, Diana just walking in! And looking marvellous, Diana, all things considered. I honestly don't think I should have known you."

"I'm no longer 'Diana.' "

"Oh? Such a pretty name, I remember my mother thought."

"Mine didn't; she hated that bristly goddess. Cousin Roland bullied her into it."

"Not your father?"

"Oh, no."

"We are 'Dinah,' now," Frank told Sheila.

"You spoke of her as that, yes. I supposed it might just be a pet name.—Well, there you are: I *am* knocked all in a heap!"

"Weren't you," Dinah inquired, not only reasonably but with milky mildness, "expecting me here, though, surely, sooner or later?"

"You *were*," asked the other swiftly, "expecting *me*?"

"Well, no. I regretfully wrote you off. But life"—Dinah turned, now, upon Frank a gaze rendered ethereal by pure fury—"is full of surprises. Today especially. So you didn't feel up to London, Francis tells me?"

"Not when it came to the point, m'dear, no. No. Bit off colour this morning. In no right mood for viewing the kid."

"That poor, poor little unwanted baby!"

Sheila, during the combat, had snatched her glass back and polished off the contents. Now, picture of tact, she looked down her pretty nose, of which the tip was becoming pink. Tact went for nothing, unobserved: she abandoned it and let out a crowing titter. "Who's had a baby, I long to know?"

"Merely," said Dinah, seething, "his only daughter."

"Major Wilkins's? Oh."

"As you are here, Frank, do look at poor Sheikie's glass. Bone empty. And after driving such miles, *I* should rather like . . . Well, Sheikie, it's fun you're here, as you truly say, so let's let bygones be bygones. You were mysterious, rather, a bit, though, weren't you?"

"Fearful, have I been?" wondered Mrs. Artworth. "I truly did not know, up to the very last, whether I *could* pull out. One's so tied up, isn't one? One thing if not another. I actually was not sure till this very morning. I fully intended to phone or send you a telegram, but when it came to the point was in such a whirl, also knew you were bound to ·*be* here, on account of Mumbo.—And by the way, that is the first thing I meant to ask: where has *she*, now, vanished to? Not a sign of her anywhere on that train. Up and down, down and up I went, searching, searching. The ticket collector thought me rather peculiar. On top of which, I'd had to leave home at cockcrow. Southstone to right down here, in the same morning!"

"Very game of you," said Frank, bringing back her glass.

"Not *another*? I wonder whether I ought to." The doubt resolved itself. "Such luck," Mrs. Artworth continued, "that I happened to have your address with me! You see, you'd said Mumbo'd know about everything. Out I got, at the station—"

"Not a soul there," took up Frank, bringing Dinah a drink but nodding over his shoulder at the sufferer. "I could always have met her, as things turned out.—And meanwhile, where were *you* tearing off to? The wrong station?"

"A blasted heath."

"So I ended up in a taxi," said Sheila bravely. "I must say, you're miles from anywhere, aren't you? Chiefly, though, I was worried, and still am. What can have possibly happened to poor old Mumbo? Where she's got to, one simply hasn't a clue. I mean to say, where *is* our wandering girl?"

"Having a wash."

"Oh," said Sheila, by reflex. Slowly, though, the intelligence filtered through to her—she turned her face, which was colouring slowly, away from Dinah. "You can't mean, here?"

"Yes I do. Here. Why not?"

"How did she get here?"

"Motor car."

"When?"

"Just now. With me."

"You *said* she'd be on the train!"

"To which *you* said nothing."

"Oh, stop it, Dicey! Don't nag.—Does she know I'm here?"

"Know? No. We'd both sadly written you off."

"Oh," Sheila remarked, while her mermaid eyes became dreamy, then showed a decided glint. She smiled. "Then, in this case I'll really be quite a shock."

"Why? You're not half such a wreck as you seem to think. Anyway, she saw you the other day."

"Thanks. That was *not*, though, what I happened to mean—this time. What I meant is, she's about to look quite a fool. Caught out. I'm rather sorry to say, she's been underhand."

"Mumbo?"

"Oh yes, I know she's a soldier's daughter.—Still, enough of that for the moment," Sheila declared, lightly touching around her waves of blue-blonded hair with the hand not engaged in holding her glass. "The whole sad story would hardly be interesting to Major Wilkins.—We mustn't bore you, must we?" she asked him.

"On the contrary," Frank returned, though with not altogether his former vigour. Worn out by hoping the girls would at last sit down, that he at last might take his weight off his feet, he languished in the vicinity of a window. "Absolutely the contrary, couldn't be more so! It means something to me, I may say, to be told anything. As a rule I'm left in the dark as to what goes on; or so it seems to me—or is that my stupidity?" (Indignation recharged the batteries as he went along.) "In the dark absolutely as to plans for today—not aware, in fact, that anything *had* been planned. So far as I now understand, I have crashed a party, or—worse, no doubt?—a reunion. I can only say, no one gave me any idea. Efforts were made to get me out of the way, as I should have spotted. Been as blind as a bat. Should have been more popular—eh?— not here." He gnashed his teeth, beneath the splendid moustache, at Dinah—who, early on in the discourse, *had* settled into her large chair, legs tucked under her, thereby causing Sheila to seek round for somewhere to perch herself, which she had finally done, with West End grace, on an arm of the other large chair, properly Frank's. "London was indicated," he went on. "Up to the mark or not (and I'm not, this morning, can't tell you why), Lon-

don it was to be. Why I was not told why, I might well
wonder; but I'm damned if I'm going to—can't be
bothered. . . ." He let silence simmer, then turned again
to Sheila. "Sorry," he said, "too bad. But I'm not so
sorry, you know, as I know I ought to be. I've at least had
the pleasure of boring you for this last hour, and delightful
it's been! In case I don't see you again, very many thanks.
Now I must take myself home and look out some lunch."

"How sad."

"What there'll be in the house," ruminated Frank, "to
eat, that is to say, I have no idea. Something, let's hope."

"Let's," said Dinah serenely. "What *you're* to eat,
Sheikie, don't ask me. There are three chops."

"Then that should be just right, shouldn't it?"

"No. Two are for Mumbo."

"Yes, my heavens!" Frank, on his way out, loomed over
Dinah's chair. "Two for 'Mumbo,' by all means. 'Mumbo'
for ever! Who and what is 'Mumbo'—if I may ask one
question?"

"No, dear," she pleaded, looking up at him fondly. "Not
about anything more. Not now."

The hall through which Frank strode was, being prin-
cipally lit by the staircase window, darker in summer than
in winter: outside the window grew the copper beech, and
the tree when in foliage was a curtain. It still was in foliage,
black-crimson. But something further, foreign, not there
till now, intercepted the light dusked by the branches—
on the halfway landing, someone or something stood looking out. Like anything at a height it appeared to float,
though manifestly it was solid. The apparition (for such in
effect it was) not so much scared the man as angered his
nerves. If ever he saw a ghost, he had often said, he would
stand no nonsense. He was not required, however, to stand
anything: the impervious non-ghost affronted him by turning round. It remained in back-view, its thick, overpower-
ing stillness giving it an air not only of regardlessness of
all time but of being in possession of this place. Loose about
the house. . . . "Mumbo-jumbo!" he shouted to himself, in-
ternally, silently and violently. It had been his intention to
track down Francis and ask him for a couple of eggs, but
that he abandoned—he fled out through the porch out
into the sun. And once out there, in the clear, he gave a

shake of the shoulders and found himself all but mopping his brow.

The tree itself did not keep Clare at the window, beautiful though a copper beech is in its late tarnish. What she beheld, by looking down, was the swing—which she watched as she might have done if it were in motion, though it had no occupant. Under it, a small bald patch had been kicked in the grass. But no ground-kicking, from whatever angle, with whatever force, *can* steer an unevenly hung swing out of the twirl. Higher you go, the crookeder —leaning, lurching. Great it is to master a crooked swing: greater than straighter swinging. There were three masters. Sheikie a firework in daylight. Dicey upside down, hooked on by the knees, slapping instead of kicking at the earth as it flew under. Mumbo face down, stomach across the seat, flailing all four limbs. Pure from the pleasures of the air, any of them could have shot into Kingdom Come. But they had not.

Those were the days before love. These are the days after. Nothing has gone for nothing but the days between. . . . Clare now recollected having heard somebody, by the sound a man, leaving the house hurriedly— just now, was it? Or if not, when?

"*There* you are! Have you had a whole bath?" Dicey, at the bottom of the stairs, looked up as though from the bottom of a well. She beckoned Mumbo down, into closer hearing. "Now, I'll give you three guesses . . ."

"I shall only need one. It's Shiekie?"

"Yes, and indeed."

"Aha."

"I don't think," Dinah admitted, "*I* was really surprised, either. Anyway, come on. She's into the drink."

"How does that take her?"

"So far, butter wouldn't melt.—She's inclined, though, I think, to be sore with you."

An eight-egg omelette, *portugaise*, had been contrived in the kitchen, the idea being that it should stun appetite before the chops (which were cutlet-size) took the field. The idea had been Francis's, on the strength of which he personally handed the omelette round.

"Does your butler speak English?" Sheila wanted to know when Francis had reluctantly left them.

"Oh yes. He can do almost everything."

"Do you have other help?"

"Alternate widows. They clean. But the one here to-day, by fortunate chance, can cook—at least, *I* think so, don't you?" said Dinah, forking away at her share of omelette. "Otherwise, I do. But I can't cook and talk, so today I thought better not."

"The situation in Southstone is rather desperate. Fortunately, *we* have Trevor's devoted nurse."

"Who does she nurse?"

"She cooks, and muddles around. But one has got to face it, she'll soon be senile. And then, what?"

"Then you pension her off.—I say, Sheikie, how many children have you?"

"*I* had, actually, none."

"How d'you mean, 'actually'?" pursued Dinah.

"She has two 'steps,' " Clare said, sombre with boredom, raising her muzzle from her plate. She banged round her mouth with her napkin. "Better than nothing. Now ask her if they have children, and we'll be through."

"Oh no we won't!" said Dinah. "I have five grand-children."

"What did you start by having?"

"Oh, two sons."

"Oh, you clever girl, you," said Mrs. Artworth.

"I wish we could have some wine," said Dinah to Francis, who had re-entered. Butler-impersonation today had made him banish what was generally on the table, within agreeable reach, to a far-off sideboard. One was bereft of everything but the salt and pepper and a round of butter stamped with a lion's head. To wait at table, he had discovered, was one form of absolute domination: the waited-on ladies waited upon his will. Dared they rise and make raids while his eye was off them? He defied them to. Also, talk—keeping going, if not swimmingly—tethered them where they were. He had dug out, for the occasion, three large lace mats. He had the interest of noting that formal splendour, topped by his own perform-ance, cast gloom on one of the guests and needled the other—to the blonde it was obviously occurring that the splash being made was not for but at her, less to please than afflict her and get her down. Had that intention been Mrs. Delacroix's, he would have seen it as rightful and her as human. But the fact was that Mrs. Delacroix, tearing off in her car after doing the flowers, had omitted to tell him anything, other than there being about to be one lady for luncheon and three chops. He'd been left to use his discretion. Well was it that Francis had briefed himself, and thoroughly, as to the psychological background of this luncheon. The cut of the jib of Mrs. Artworth (whom, recall, he'd taken to be *the* lady) had caused him at once to whisk out the lace mats, then rehearse his "waiting" around the kitchen table, with, as thunderstruck stand-in, the day's widow. In him, discretion and malice were identical.

Kicking the door open, to bring a tray in, he had heard the ladies drop the subject of childbirth.

"That will be all, I think, for the time being," Dinah said—each chop having found a plate and the vegetable dishes completed their jiggling course. "Go and have a rest." Enraged, Francis left them. Sheila, doubting the door to be truly shut, said: "They say Orientals are all ears."

"*I* am, now, all ears." Clare took one slash at her chop, then, ominously, rested her knife and fork. She looked round the table. "All ears for whatever Dicey has got to say.—So are *you*, or aren't you?" she rapped at Sheila, who, though not yet fully adjusted, declared: "Of course!"

"Just what have you got to say for yourself, my girl?" the culprit was asked, in what was meant to be an objective manner. "You jolly nearly ran into serious trouble. *What* you thought you were doing, we'd like to know."

"Some explanation's due, I honestly think," supplemented Sheila, though declining to raise her eyes from the lace mat. "I mean, after what we've been put through."

"Well?" Clare boomed. "Come on, Dicey. We're waiting."

"*Mumbo*, don't be so pompous!" exclaimed their hostess. "And apart from that, what is all this about—so completely suddenly? I couldn't be more in the dark if I were Frank. What is this potion you two've been brewing up?—And I won't," she went on, wonderfully mildly still, "I won't have you make a scene while you eat my chops."

"I've not eaten your chop!"

"Then it will get cold." Dinah turned to her other friend. "You're eating up yours, I'm so glad to see, because

they are good, I think.—Sheikie, I wonder whether you
know you're said to have said I've made your life hell?"

Sheila, ceasing to masticate, turned an annoyed pink.
"I'm certain I *never*—" She looked daggers across at
Clare, who bellowed at Dinah: "That's what we're attempt-
ing to *talk* about!"

"Then let Sheikie talk."

"Sheikie come into the open?" Clare jibed. "Ever been
known to?"

"That," Sheila returned, "I must say, comes nicely from
you. Who did her best to give me the slip? Who said, 'Not
to worry,' then went one better—she thought? No, devious-
ness is a thing I can't understand! Nobody would object
to your being clever—"

"Good."

"Oh, have I sown dissension?" their prisoner asked.
"No, because look how it's always been! When you both
get into a state, you two have to fight. Look how this
always ends?" Yet she faltered, if for less than an instant;
or just barely—how barely?—overrode a misgiving. "Or
isn't this ending? Otherwise, I'll go on." Her demeanour
altered. Her beauty, having been up to now an indeter-
minate presence about the room, grew formidable and
stepped forward. From now on, she spoke to ignored
hearers, not only not looking at them but making it felt
that by not looking at them she spared them. "I begin to
see what you're both in a state about. Or could, if it wasn't
so inconceivable. You mean, the means I used to rustle
you up? Well? . . . What else was I to do?—No, more I
mean, in what other way should I do it? That was for US.
And you two minded—*you two*? Oh, then how pointless
to meet again—how you have gone down!"

"Maybe," Clare assented—collapsed, morose.

Sheila, in this instance the stronger spirit, said: "Yes, I
dare say. You don't happen to have to live prominently in
Southstone, or run a fairly well-known shop."

"Chain of 'em," Clare corrected, from depths of apathy.
She looked down at her heavy, projecting body. "As we
now are, my love, like us or not. As we now are, Sheikie
and I felt blown upon."

Dazed, Dinah marvelled: "Mumbo, what an expression."

Clare, having asked for that, hugged it with an awful
sort of contentment. Mrs. Artworth, however, stepped in

to reclaim her property. "Mine, in the first place, I think," she told Dinah briskly. "Any objection?"

"Not from you." Dinah shoved her plate off the lace mat, put her folded arms there, and leaned on them, studying them unseeingly. "*I'll Huff, and I'll Puff, and I'll Blow Your House Down*—Eh?—That I never thought of. I never thought."

She suddenly turned to Clare. Down her white face a tear made its bewildered way. One forgets that each tear is shed for the first time. "What do I do?"

"Try thinking. I warn you against the habit, but try it once." Clare was lightheaded. Within, she trembled and shook. An electrical happiness transformed her. Sighting her chop anew, she fell upon it—tenderly watched by Dinah. Sheila, whose mistrust of anyone's quoting anything was akin to Clare's objection to scenery, had since the offence brooded—in particular, for some cause she could not pin down, she misliked those lines Dinah had chosen. Now: "*Macbeth*, I suppose?" she warily asked. She remained unanswered. Tilting that look of hers to and fro, fro and to, she thought: "Who's now falling under whose spell?" She let a minute go by in regardful silence, before again, more loudly, raising her voice. "*Now*, then, we're to consider the matter closed?"

Base Clare, mouth full, said: "Sheikie, how sane you are!"

"It's as well to know. I was feeling a shade at sea. Because, am I wrong or wasn't it you, Clare, who insisted on bringing the whole thing up, *and* here at Dinah's own table, which from something she said I imagine she rather felt?—or didn't you, Dinah? Left to myself, I'd have willingly let the whole thing—"

"To hell with the whole thing, anyway!—which, if I may remind you, was my original standpoint, that day at tea. There's no such thing as 'a whole thing.' Anyhow, court adjourned."

"What do I tell Trevor?"

"I remember Trevor," mused Dinah. "Give him my love." As they should be glad to see, she was feeling better. "You'll be glad to hear, you obstinate mules," she said, "you cost me nearly a hundred pounds."

"Well, you beastly rich girl."

"You all but beat me. 'Not a penny over that hundred,'

I said to Packie. 'Squeak or not out of them by then, we then call it off—they win.' I'm not mad, after all."

"You *had* an accomplice?"

"You wondered? Yes. An old friend who's come back into my life, who knows all the ropes. Johnnie Packerton-Carthew. He's known to take on so much and be so dependable, most people call him Pack-Horse. I call him Packie."

Sheila, languidly leaning back, touching around her hair (with both hands, this time), said: "Meaning, he'd do anything for *you*?"

"No, I'm afraid he'd do anything within reason for almost anybody. So it's no compliment."

"He considered this was within reason, did he?"

"He entered into the spirit of the chase, like anything. And now, naturally, can't wait to meet you two. We must arrange. Meanwhile let's drink to Packie, out of full hearts!—Bother Francis, confiscating the wine again! And where's he gone to, wandering off like this? All this time, there should have been treacle tart. Here we sit and sit, when all we want is the cave."

"Cave?"

"*Cave*, did you say?"

"*The* cave," said the hostess, impatiently starting smoking. Both floored, her guests exchanged blank looks.

Clare said: "Dicey, we really don't think you've told us."

"But that's incredible! That was the start of this. No. I mean WE were the start of this, but the cave acted as a—as a precipitant. Though, on the same day, so of course did the swing."

"Someone precipitate off it?" Sheila tittered.

"No. No more than we did. You idiot, Sheikie."

Clare remarked: "I took a look at the swing."

Francis came in, accompanied by the treacle tart. Having slashed it up, he went on to hand it round—the blonde, a slimming demoniac if ever he saw one, would not so much as glance. Meanwhile, he listened to his employer launching off into her well-known preliminary to the Guided Tour —which did not, to his ear, go with quite its accustomed swing. Not having delivered it for some time, she always could, of course, be a trifle creaky. One had, too, to allow for the handicap she was under in having an audience who'd known her long and probably too well. This act of hers certainly *had* gone better. Her former delirium seemed lacking. Could it be that the cave neared the end of its reign? In that case, some hope for the poor Major's succeeding in winning her back again to the *potager*. Though she kept going, gamely, she seemed by no means sorry to interrupt herself by saying: "Francis, coffee in here—at once, please!"

"I'll bring it in here," was the most he could guarantee.

"So you see, now?" Dinah concluded, optimistically turning from Clare to Sheila. "You have, now, grasped the idea? You won't understand the cave if you've not grasped that; though I hope you'll grasp it still more when you see the cave." Her cigarette, sketching the final gesture, showered ash on to her helping of tart.

"I expect," Clare said, civilly, "we may."

"Full up, is your cave by now, did you say?" asked Sheila.

"Oh, brimming. One can hardly get in."

"Oh. . . . You have ever so many friends, then?"

"Hundreds, by now. Hasn't everyone—haven't you?"

Mrs. Artworth, for once, looked vague. She did not reply.

From along the serpentine walk, stocks which had breathed wet fragrance on Mrs. Coral were now gone. The turf of the walk was, today, dry and springy under the foot. Hedging the backs of the borders, Michaelmas daisies ran through all purples out into puce and ruby. Due now to be slain any night by frost, dahlias defiantly burned on from noon to noon—fewer, the fulsome staying-on roses looked less mortal. The latening sun lit not only those but the few twisted apple trees of the ancient orchard, some of whose fruit by lying bruised in the grass, not rotted yet, gave a cyder-like taste to the afternoon. The hour was now nearer to four than three.

Shepherded by Dinah towards the steps which were to take them down to the cave, the two strangers to Applegate found or made every reason to dawdle. They examined Dinah's gaudy autumnal flowers—uncommon, possibly, to them? They had, over the flowers and through the trees, glimpses of kind, unpoetic skylines. Sheila asked: "We're in Somerset, are we?"

"More or less."

"But that's the West, isn't it? I thought the West was mountains. . . . Well, it does all seem very far away."

"What does?"

"This does. Doesn't it to you, ever?" Turning to Clare, Sheila added: "Doesn't it to you?"

They approached the end of the walk: now, the cave drew near. "Turn left," their guide said. "Look, I'll go on ahead." She did.

But then Clare stopped dead. "Look, Dicey, don't think us perfectly beastly, but I *don't* want to go down that thing; nor, I'm sure, does Sheikie!"

"I'm not keen to," agreed the other.

"Oh?" said the guide, coming slowly round on a heel, hands in her pockets. She took a look at them. "*Oh* . . . But it's awfully interesting—awfully humanly interesting."

"Yes, but Sheikie and I don't know your interesting friends."

"Neither will archaeologists aeons hence," Dinah felt it devolvent upon her to point out. "If this interests them, why shouldn't it interest you?" She added, rather more sternly, "All things considered. . . ."

"What do you mean?"

"*You* know jolly well what I mean—you two."

You could have heard a petal drop, all but. Clare then said, with noisy bravado: "Ha, yes. *That*. Well—what *about* that?"

Sheila looked trapped.

"There's no 'what about?'" said Dinah. She walked right up to them. "Simply, when do we go there, when do we dig? How soon?"

"Dig . . . ?" asked Sheila.

"Un-bury."

"We put *that* there for posterity," Clare said doubtfully.

"*We* are posterity—now," the remorseless one said. "So, what night? Any night—how soon? There's no moon these nights, but there was no moon then. We shall again need torches. At St. Agatha's, hadn't we better meet? Agreed?"

Sheila said: "It's not there."

She was not at once understood.

"Didn't you know?" she said. "I suppose not."

A scarf formed part of her suit: she knotted it, first loosely, then drew it slowly tighter under her chin.

"Well, go on," they said.

"How do I begin? . . . As you may or may not know, we were shelled at Southstone." A snobbishness, far from unsympathetic, o'erspread her native countenance. (Anyone could be bombed.) "They lammed away at us, onward from 1940. I don't say every day; it was on and off. One of those fine days, St. Agatha's copped it."

"*Sheikie* . . . not all the girls?"

"Gracious, no. Girls?—they'd been long gone. That old place had not been a school for years. When it was hit it was empty and boarded up."

Clare said: " 'Into thin air.' "

PART II

One

❦

Thick cream glazed blinds were pulled most of the way down. Failing to keep out the marine sunshine, they flopped lazily over the open windows in the hot June breath rather than breeze haunting the garden. St. Agatha's had been a house, IV-A classroom probably the morning-room. The blinds were lace-bordered. There was a garlanded wallpaper—called to order by having on it a bald, pontifical clock, only a size or two smaller than a station one, a baize board clustered with lists and warnings, and sepia reproductions of inspiriting pictures, among them "Hope," framed in oak. Of oak were the desks, to which were clamped high-backed seats. An aroma of Plasticine came from the models along the chimneypiece, and from jars of botanical specimens near a window whiffs of water slimy with rotting greenery were fanned in—the girl in charge of the specimens being absent with one of her summer colds. Chalk in the neighbourhood of the blackboard and ink thickening in china wells in the desks were the only other educational smells.

A dozen or so girls, most of them aged eleven, some ten, some twelve, sat at the desks. All wore their summer tunics of butcher-blue. By turning their heads, left, they could have seen strips of garden, parching away, between restless lace and stolid white window sills. Politely, however, most of them faced their teacher; this they could do for Miss Kinmate, if little else. This was the first lesson after mid-morning break with its milk and biscuits—even the slight feast had thrown IV-A into a gorged condition. But this also was the Tuesday poetry hour, to which Miss

Kinmate attached hopes. Each girl (the idea was) chose for herself the short poem or portion of longer one which, got by heart, she was to recite.

One more of them had just taken the stand.

"There *was* a time when meadow, grove and stream,
The earth and—"

"Stop!" cried Miss Kinmate. "Before we begin, not *too* much expression. Wordsworth was not as regretful as all that."

"I thought he was. Like some old, fat person saying, 'There *was* a time when I could jump over a ten-foot wall.'"

"That would be silly."

"Well, this is silly, in a way."

"Your old, fat man would not be speaking the truth. Have you any idea how high a ten-foot wall is?"

"Yes."

"I wonder whether you have. Because, even a Greek athlete could probably not jump over that." (From a back desk, a hand shot up.) "*Yes*, Olive?"

"How high could a Greek athlete probably jump?"

"That would depend."

The child Clare, during this intermission, stood stonily contemplating her audience—hands behind her, back to the blackboard, feet planted apart, tongue exploring a cavity in a lower molar. At a moody sign from Miss Kinmate, she went on:

"—and every common sight,
To *me* did seem
Apparell'd in celestial *light*,
The glory and the freshness of a dream.
It is *not* now as it had been of yore;—
Turn whereso'er I may,
By night *or* day,
The things which—"

"Stop! Oh dear, what are we to do?"

"I thought—"

"Well, don't—*try*! Otherwise, go and sit down. Ruining that beautiful poem!"

"Yes, Miss Kinmate."

"And don't make eyes at the others. Next time, choose a poem you understand."

"I do know another. Shall I say that?"

Miss Kinmate looked at the clock. The whole class (but for Sheila Beaker, who couldn't be bothered, and Muriel Borthwick, who having picked at a good big scab on her arm now dabbed blotting-paper at the resultant blood) did likewise, in an awed, considering way. "Very well," Miss Kinmate conceded. "Go on, Clare—though remember, there are others to come."

The child, having drawn a breath twice her size, launched with passion into her second choice:

> "Last night among his fellow-roughs
> He jested, quaff'd and swore:
>
> A drunken private of the Buffs,
> Who never look'd before.
> Today, beneath the foeman's frown,
> He stands in Elgin's place,
> Ambassador from Britain's crown,
> And type of all her race.
>
> Poor, reckless, rude, low-born, untaught,
> Bewilder'd and alone,
> A heart, with English instinct fraught,
> He yet can call his own.
> *Ay! tear* his body limb from limb,
> Bring *cord*, or *axe*, or *flame*!—
> He only knows, that not through him
> Shall England come to shame.
>
> Fair Kentish hopfields round him seemed
> Like dreams to come and go;
> Bright leagues of cherry blossom—"

"Stop! Time's up, I'm afraid. A pity, because you were doing better." Miss Kinmate's eye roved round. "Diana, try and not sit with your mouth open—wake up! What is the name of the poem Clare's just recited?"

" 'The Drunken Private of the Buffs.' "

"Not exactly.—Well, who and whose poem next? Muriel: you!"

"I think I'm bleeding too much."

"What, cut yourself?"

"Not exactly."

"Better go and find Matron."

Gory Muriel left. Miss Kinmate had to cast round all over again. "*Sheila*, then. Sheila, we'll hear you now."

Southstone's wonder, the child exhibition dancer, rose, tossed back her silver-gold plaits, and habituatedly stepped forward into the limelight. An ornate volume, open at the required page and gildedly looking like a school prize (which it was, though not awarded to her), was bestowed by her upon Miss Kinmate, with what was less a bow than a flowerlike inclination of the head. She then half-turned, with a minor swirl of the tunic, and, facing the footlights, glided three steps sideways into the place of doom left vacant by Clare. Here reality struck the prodigy amidships. Bewitched, since she rose from her desk, by her own performance, she had lost sight for that minute or two of her entrance's true and hideous purpose. She was to be called upon not to spring about but to give tongue. A badgered hatred of literature filled her features. She did deliver her poem, though in the manner of one voicing, with wonderful moderation, a long-nursed and justifiable complaint:

> "Up the airy mountain,
> Down the rushing glen,
> We daren't *go* a-hunting
> For fear of little *men*;
> Wee folk, good folk,
> Trooping all together;
> Green jacket, red cap,
> *And* white owl's feather!
>
> Down on the rocky *shore*
> Some make their home;
> They *live* on crispy pancakes
> Of yellow tide-foam;
> *Some*, in the reeds
> Of the black mountain-lake,
> With frogs for *their* watchdogs,
> *All night awake*.
>
> High on the hill-top
> The old *King* sits.

He is now so old and grey
He's nigh lost . . . ?
. . . his bridge of white wits?
. . . his mist of white wits?
. . . *his* bridge?
. . . *his* wits . . . ?"

She ran down, ticked over uncertainly, gave right out, and turned on Miss Kinmate a look as much as to say: "Well, there you are. What else would you expect?"

"Never mind," Miss Kinmate hastened to say. "It went nicely so far. Though a little mournful—fairies are gay things, aren't they?"

Sheila had no idea.

"And one word wrong in your second line. It should be 'rushy,' not 'rushing.' How could a glen rush?"

"I thought it meant they were all rushing about," said Sheila Beaker, still more deeply aggrieved.

"Sheila chose a delightful poem, at any rate," Miss Kinmate informed the class—who knew to a girl whose the choice had been: Mrs. Beaker's.

Most of the St. Agatha's girls day-boarded. The school, scorning the plateau on which others were crowded, was out of town to the west, downhill. This suited children from the Camp and surrounding military villas; on the South-stone contingent (persistently sent there in spite of much education nearer to hand) it came harder. To cut out to-ing and fro-ing during the day, which was thought tiring, the Southstone children ate meals at school, and the rest had fallen in with this practice—which made, as Miss Arding-fay, foundress-head mistress, said, for girls getting to know each other really well. The school day, though necessarily long, was less arduous than might have been feared: organized games apart, there were times for loafing. The girls were back at their homes at varying times after six o'clock, carrying some prep. They supped, slept, bolted their break-fasts, and tore back to St. Agatha's. From noon on Satur-days till the St. Agatha's prayers-bell rounded them up again on Monday mornings, they were on the loose.

The school, though near enough to the sea for its lower garden to be fluffy with tamarisks, was not actually on it. From the far side of the tarred road passing the gates, there

was quite a high, steep drop down to the beach. Along that
side of the road ran a parapet, not supposed to be sat on.
St. Agatha's being some way above beach level made it less
likely, it was generally held, to be swept away during a
storm: certainly nothing had happened yet, pleasurable
though the excitement would have been.

The grounds, mostly, ran up the hill behind. The due-
south aspect was favourable to small, old greenhouses, some
now empty; and there were seats and arbours facing the
view, which was of the Channel. A croquet lawn, by now
rather bald, had at some time or another been terraced
forward. There were two overgrown thickets, which to the
outer eye looked more impenetrable than they were—between them, "walks" serpentined up; there were also
steeper, slippery dog-paths worn into being by impatient
girls. The higher you climbed, the more you beheld. At the
top of the grounds (which was not the top of the hill) was
another terrace: up here, from a stout frame, a swing hung
during the summer months. Miss Ardingfay had not had it
put up (it had been here) but equally had not had it taken
down. *Where* it was, it was possibly a slight worry: each
spring she had the gardener make sure that the ropes were
sound. As she had not a straight eye, and did not herself
swing, it remained unknown to Miss Ardingfay that the
swing did not hang as evenly as it should.

Today, in spite of (indeed, because of) the heat, Miss
Ardingfay strolled outdoors after lunch. She wished to be
sure that the girls now all in the garden were resting quietly,
not running about. Out here everything shimmered: a heat-
haze hung over the Channel. No France, today. The girls
were not running about. Everywhere was dotted with
butcher-blue, but it kept still. Having had it rubbed into
them about sunstroke, they kept in the shade, or what
shade there was—some lay flat, some were propped against
banks, trees, or each other, some leaned back on their
hands, some sat on their heels. A few read; the rest were
doing nothing particular. That they *had* been talking could
be gathered from the hushes that fell. She, in her large
rush hat and Florentine-belted green garb, was observed
by them. Shy in her own way, she passed on like the Im-
perial Votaress.

"For ever on the go," commented Sheila, on the whole

approvingly, to Diana, with whom she shared such inches of shade as were cast by a short escallonia hedge.

"Has to be, do you suppose?"

"Oh, she has to be. Makes her red in the face though."

Yet they envied Miss Ardingfay her free gait. What would kill them if it continued was inactivity. With sharp, clean thumbnails Sheila split blades of grass—she sat up. Diana lay on her back, now and then drumming with her heels. As Sheila bent frowning over her task, the immaculate shell-pink of her skull showed along the division of her hair. So dead straight was the parting—back from the centre-forehead, over the top and on down behind, where it served to allot each hair to one or another of the flawless pigtails—that her head looked as though *it* had been slightly split. Should it fall apart, it would do so in two perfectly even halves. . . . Cravingly, the addicted children thought about movement—when again could it start, how most could it be? Pure vision was Sheila's.—Flinging away the last bit of grass, she asked: "After tea, coming to the rink?"

(That was, the open-air roller-skating rink, at the more popular end of Southstone.)

"*Oo*, yes!"

"All very well saying 'Oo, yes,' but have you got any money? You know what happened."

"Oh, no; I haven't got any money."

"Well, there you are. Why d'you never have any? Or why don't *you* have a season ticket?"

"I don't know. Oh, I want to *go* to the rink!"

"Well, you can't, can you? Till you do go more, you'll never be any good."

"You show off at that rink."

"So you would, if you were any good.—Try and see if Mumbo's got any money."

"No."

"No harm seeing."

"It's too hot," said Diana, putting on airs.

"Oh, all right," Sheila said, unconcernedly (though not quite, since she was not supposed to go to the rink alone) tossing the plaits back. "You'll never be any good.—What shall you do, then? Just go home?"

"Unless," sighed Diana, unhopefully, "*you* had any?"

"I don't need any."

That was true, though not fair. Sheila was allowed a
bike, which she skimmed about everywhere on, like anything. And anything she had not got a season ticket for,
she could get tick to get into or on to, such as the pier.
She'd once got all three of them on to the pier free, to show
she could—alas, never again! The fact was the Beakers
were important: not only had they met the Member of
Parliament, they hob-nobbed with the Mayor. And on top
of that, their daughter was a celebrity. Dejected, Diana
rolled over on to her stomach, which gave a spiteful gurgle.
Sheila mimicked the sound lewdly but absently—she was
elsewhere. She announced: "I'm going to dance 'The Spirit
of Winter.' "

"Oh—why can't you dance 'The Spirit of Summer'?"

"Because I'm dancing 'The Spirit of Winter,' stupid. Any
lump could dance 'The Spirit of Summer.' I shall wear
frost."

"Where?"

"The Metropole ballroom."

"When?"

"The Gala, for prevention of cruelty, animals or children or something—I don't care; I don't know."

"But *when*? Soon, or after the holidays?"

"After the holidays. October."

Diana thought. She said: "October's not winter."

"I shall *make* it winter. And they're festooning the stage
with silver."

"Sheikie, do *you* ever think it's extraordinary to be you?"

"No," said the other, flatly and unregretfully. She transferred her gaze to the middle-distance. "Do look at Mumbo
scratching her head. Go over and ask if she's got nits."

Diana, too, took a look. She explained. "Thinking."

"I know she's thinking; and I jolly well know what she's
thinking *about*, and so you should. Go over and ask if
she's got—"

"What are nits?"

"Oo-*er*. What awful people have in their heads."

"Oh, bother. You go over and ask." Diana, pressed flat
to the breast of Earth, one cheek down on it, nonetheless
watched Sheila sideways, out of one eye. In return, that
prettiest, coolest little Sheila dealt out one of her most
supernatural stares. "I DARE you to."

Doomed Diana got up, behind first. She rambled across and off their section of lawn, crossed the path, and mounted to where, on the other side, Clare sat in an insolent solitude. Clare occupied, in the manner of Alexander Selkirk, a small, unaccountable grassy mound. She was—as Miss Ardingfay had noted but, not feeling up to a duel at that moment, had let pass, having reason to hope that the child might be pickled by foreign climes—full in the sun. Her back was turned to the path, which obliged Diana to ramble round: she ventured, even, a step or two up the slope. Clare was not sunk in thought but positively blown up with it, like a bullfrog. Her shortish, thick stiff hair sprang about, nohow. The glower she turned on Diana was not encouraging.

"I say, Mumbo, have you got—"

"No I haven't. So go away."

"What have I done?" asked Diana, taking offence. "And what were you making those awful faces at me at lunch for?"

" 'Faces'? I didn't know you were there."

"You did," contradicted Diana, emboldened by balancing on one leg, in spite of the slope. "If you didn't, you *have* got nits in your brain, crawling round and round." She added, in a more social tone: "After tea, Sheikie's going to the rink, she says. Are you?"

"Rink?" Clare examined the idiot from top to toe. "No."

"I would *like* to go. I don't get on very fast, when I never do."

"You like falling down, attracting attention."

"No, I don't. It hurts. And I don't knock other people down. You bang round knocking people down. They won't let you back on that rink, if you barge about."

"Who says?" Clare wanted to know, jibingly.

Diana hurriedly put on airs again. "Oo, it's hot. Is this the same as India?"

"Ho, *yes*, like anything!"

"Sheikie and I know what you're thinking about. Where we are, we see you scratching your head."

"Then go back to wherever you think you are.—I *would*," Clare said ominously, "if I were you."

That fascinated Diana. She could not but advance further up the mound. Re-establishing balance, she stood on the other leg. "Why, if you were me, would you go away?

If you were *me*, you'd know what you're thinking about—
is that why?"

"Oh—do—just go—AWAY."

"Oh—all—right—then—I—WILL. Anyway, you never
answer anything I ask, so I think I'd rather. You never
answer anything I say."

"You bleat. How can anyone answer? You just bleat."

"*I*," said the other, "don't go and ruin beautiful poems."

Clare banged shut her dark, rather prominent and now
furious eyes. "Baa-lamb!" she shouted.

"*Touché?*" At once, Diana broke out into a shrill, happy,
attacking chant. "*Ru*-ining that beautiful po-*em*. Ruin-*ing*
that beautiful *po*-em. Ruining *that beauti*-ful poem. Roo-
ining that—"

Clare snatched at the leg and expertly jerked it away
from under. Down came Diana, without even a shriek. Not
doubting she now was dead and in Heaven, she stayed as
and where she had fallen, placidly wide-eyed. Clare, for
her part, got up. She aimed a kick not at but over the
bright-blue upside-down tangle, tunic and bloomers, then
walked off. Diana arose, still looking surprised.

From the cool dark inside an open window, Mademoiselle, Miss Brace (the geography mistress), and Matron,
holding their coffee cups, looked on. They had seen much
the same thing happen before. The victim was plump, and
the lawn though hard-baked not as hard as the asphalt from
which the same child had rebounded the other day. Nevertheless they melted back from the window: Matron, whose
afternoon peace could be most imperilled, the first to do
so. Better have witnessed nothing.

Sheila, from under the escallonia, enjoyed the spectacle
and took note of its audience. Turning, she selected a leaf
from the hedge behind her, then set about splitting that.
But the glossed thick leaf with its saw-edges proved to be
more of a job than a blade of grass—green got into her
thumbnails, and pretty soon.

Two

❧✦❧

The Feverel Cottage drawing-room was—as Mrs. Piggott, asking for its exemption from any but guessing or the quieter card games, herself said—rather full of china. This was reputed to be or have been priceless. Precious it must be—why else should it have been mended with such care? Delicate metal stitchery underran dishes and saucers and held lids together; tiny alloy claws enabled handles to keep their grip on cups; cemented cracks formed networks cradling fine bowls, and where hatted and curled heads of shepherdesses or braceleted forearms of court ladies had been fitted back again on to throats or elbows, healed wounds were to be pointed out. And so on. . . . These ingenuities had for the children more merit than had the pieces themselves. Still "perfect" pieces seemed deficient—of those, however, the Piggott collection contained few.

Having no special cabinet, the china overflowed from the chimneypiece on to two and a half tables and a three-tiered whatnot, and, not content with those, rambled along the top of a low bookcase, whose doors dared not be opened lest the china be jarred. The piano only could count on being immune. The selfish china was borne with by the children, to whom its brighter-than-gold golds and unearthly colourings endeared it when in the mood. Also, some of the china had a secret lien with at least one of them: the scenery motifs spoke in particular to Clare. Their miniature vastness was of a size for her; their look of eternity could be taken in in less than a minute. She had lived within them. That she knew each landscape, to her a planet, to be linked in destructibility with the cup, bowl, or plate upon which it was, added peril to love. One saw, here, how china could break. One foresaw also how, one day or another, it must do so beyond repair.

Nor was china all. To the Army child, there was something mystic about this world of possessions. The Burkin-Joneses, in their austere, ordered movements from place to place, took with them little—brass bowls, framed photographs, trophies. Oriental rugs acquired along their course and, it might be, a scarf or two wherewith to deck yet another provided sofa or drape yet another hired piano. Round such existences, nothing but intangibles can accumulate: they do. Mrs. Piggott and Dicey had, by contrast, spun round themselves tangible webs, through whose transparency, layers deep, one glimpsed some fixed, perhaps haunted, other dimension. Feverel Cottage, from what one knew of their history, had not been their abode for long: yet who now could picture them anywhere but here? Their drawing-room bay window was tangled with muslin curtains—which, having come from some larger home, were too long and somewhat over-voluminous. Though bloused out liberally over tied-back sashes, the muslin found itself still with some yards to flow: it disposed of itself therefore in swirls and pools inside the bay and on the neighbouring floor. Muslin did not, however, entirely fill the bay, into which a delightful table had been inserted, with, at each end, space for one each of a pair of needlework stools. Further into the room, chairs dressed loosely in leafy stuff sat about in a state of sylvan indifference, sat upon or not. The walls wore a pearl-grey paper, faintly lustrous: through one of them, near a corner, had been cut what the Piggotts stigmatized as "a silly window": a casement sentimentally diamond-paned. Despised though it might be, it had its use. It supplied with daylight the head-end of the sofa on which novels were read.

Clare, this late afternoon, came in on her own. She wound her way silently into the muslin window-cave, slid open a drawer of the table and extracted a puzzle, and sat down with it. To disturb Mrs. Piggott once she was *in* a novel was known to be more or less impossible; nevertheless the child, for these first minutes, worked away at the clickety puzzle with some caution. It was her favourite of several: Chinese ivory. Only a roving bluebottle, which from time to time seemed to divide and become two, stirred in the air of the room. But for the periodic flicker as she turned a page, Mrs. Piggott, diagonal on the sofa, might have been a waxwork—Clare, at a halt with the puzzle, took a contemplative look at her through the curtains. The scarlet, brand-new novel, held up, masked its wholly-commanded reader's face. Though nominally she was "lying" on the sofa, the upper part of the body of Mrs. Piggott was all but vertical, thanks to cushions—her attitude being one of startled attention, sustained rapture, and, in a way, devotion to duty. The more flowing remainder of her *was* horizontal: feet, crossed at the ankles, pointing up at the end. She was as oblivious of all parts of her person as she was of herself. As for her surroundings, they were nowhere. Feverel Cottage, the sofa, the time of day not merely did not exist for Mrs. Piggott, they did *not* exist. This began to give Clare, as part of them, an annihilated feeling. She burned with envy of anything's having the power to make *this* happen. Oh, to be as destructive as a story! . . . She tossed the interlocked puzzle into the air, muffed the return catch, and heard it fall.

At that, a protesting stir took place deep in the being of Mrs. Piggott. She could be felt battling against reluctance. Alas, now she was in the throes of knowing there was something she ought to do or say. Not going so far as to lower the scarlet book or quite unglue her eyes from the cogent page, she resignedly said: "Oh, Dicey?"

"I'm Clare, Mrs. Piggott."

"Oh, Clare!—Good evening," said Dicey's mother, friendly as ever and made more so by what clearly was a reprieve. She went some way back to her reading, but was less happy. A minute later—holding the book away, this time, at arm's length, like a banished temptation—she resumed: "Do you know where Dicey is?"

"No, I don't."

"Then it can't be helped."

"Do you want her?" Clare asked, showing civil wonder that even a mother could.

"Sooner or later." Mrs. Piggott failed to repress a sigh which had, evidently, within her some complex origin. "Have you had a nice day?"

Clare scowled retrospectively. "It was Tuesday."

Mrs. Piggott, with that blend of boredom and commonsense which made affable her relations with children, did not point out that it was Tuesday still. She was occupied in coming to a decision. She must make a break with the novel—a ruthless, clean one: she did nothing by halves. Using an envelope as a marker, she shut the novel. She then reached round and put it right away, on the far side of a still water-tight *Famille Rose* bowl of wonderfully early and large sweet peas, on a small table. She went on to turn upon Clare the same, whole attention which had gone to her reading. "You don't think Dicey's gone to the Beakers', do you?"

"She didn't go off on Sheikie's bike. I don't see how else she'd get to the Beakers'."

"For a day or two, I think that is just as well. Don't you?"

Clare examined the puzzle—had the fall hurt it? She volunteered: "She didn't go to the rink."

"That I'm glad to hear! She comes back from there black and blue.—Clare, has your mother had a letter from Mrs. Beaker?"

"I don't know, Mrs. Piggott. She didn't say so."

"Oh, how I do hope not!—Or hadn't the post come when you left for school? It hadn't when Dicey left."

"I don't know. I never take any notice."

"I'm afraid she may; and surely you must know why.— Couldn't you come out of that lair of yours, don't you think? From here, I can hardly see you."

Clare, though perfectly able to see Mrs. Piggott from where *she* was, knew the sound of an order. She withdrew from the curtains and marched out into the open carpet. "Trouble again?" she asked, fair and square.

"Well . . . gelignite?"

"Everything happens on Tuesdays!"

"No, but it was last Saturday you seem to have done your best to blow up the Beakers."

"Just their bicycle shed. What I mean is, all *rows* happen on Tuesdays."

"My dear, dear child, it's just by the grace of heaven— isn't it?—that nothing's happened till now. As it was, they came on that box you left not till yesterday afternoon. Think what might have happened in the meanwhile!"

"Gelignite doesn't just *go* off; it needs a detonator, and a fuse."

"Then I hope you didn't have one of those, on Saturday?"

"Oh, yes. But that shed's miles down their garden."

"Do try not to be so calm! With any awful explosion, how can one know? There might have been poor Sheila, with no home."

"It was her idea.—Not," Clare added indignantly, "that I'd sneak."

"She is a curious child. . . . But for you and Dicey, *what* a way to go on—wasn't it? What a horribly heartless thing—surely?—even to think of doing. And so bad-mannered. And, I think, ungrateful; when the Beakers had so very kindly asked you to tea."

"I don't think they did. We stayed because we were there."

"Mrs. Beaker says, if this sort of thing goes on she'll have to stop Sheila playing with you and Dicey."

"She says that, Sheila says, almost every time."

"I don't think that's anything to—to guffaw at."

Sighing again, Mrs. Piggott dealt with a cushion which was escaping, somehow, from the small of her back. She also looked over her shoulder at the clock: her French one, busy in a small way on the chimneypiece among idling china. Clare stood around, meanwhile, making a face or two. "Well," confessed Dicey's mother, "it isn't for me to give *you* a wigging, is it, of course? I don't see why I should, and I hadn't meant to—as you know, I didn't even know you were here, did I? Dicey must have a wigging when she comes in, Sheila's idea or not. She must go to the Beakers' properly, wearing gloves, after a day or two, and tell them she is extremely sorry, as I know she will be, once she has thought things over.—Oh dear, what makes you three so rough?"

"We never really much thought it would go off."

"No, I don't for a moment suppose you did. But you none of you had any business to even try—had you?"

"We now are rather beginning," admitted Clare, in a gloomy, deflated voice "to wonder if it *was* gelignite, after all."

"It was written large on the box, Mrs. Beaker says."

"Oh, we wrote that!"

"Surely you might find other things to invent and do—I should have thought? You, after all—the clever one—could, I'm sure? Then if you did, the others would be delighted. It would be dreadful to think of you never doing

things, you three, but it depends what. Nobody'd ever expect you to be mice, and I'd hate you, I expect, if you
were muffs—but do, do try not to be inconsiderate!"

Clare, looking down earnestly at her black sandshoes,
vowed: "I honestly, honestly will try, Mrs. Piggott."

"Yes, but *all* try! You're only, ever, so tiresome when
you're all together. Then, what comes over you nobody
seems to know. It couldn't possibly be—could it?—that
you're bad for each other?"

"I don't know," said Clare, in her unconcerned way.

"I do so always hope not.—Dicey," said Mrs. Piggott,
with a tremble of love in her voice, "is silly. Sometimes
she's very silly.—Clare, she blinks so much more, sometimes, when she's been out with you other two. You won't
be bad for her—*you*, I mean, won't be bad for her ever,
if you can help it, will you?"

"No."

"But I wonder," cried Mrs. Piggott, "where she *is?*"

Restless, she made a motion of the arms, with a tumble-
down of summery sleeves, ending by pressing clasped hands
to the nape of her neck. Tired out? "I *would* go," Clare
began to explain, "but—" But Mrs. Piggott, by shutting
her eyes, signified that she wished for no word more. Clare
was glad, on the whole—she had food for thought.

What was clear, now, as to the gelignite situation was
that it was likely to go no further than Mrs. Piggott thought
well. Not herself adroit, the freak intellectual child saw
how everything had been handled, herself included. To no
lengths was Mrs. Piggott prepared to go—she might go to
some lengths to deter anyone else from going to any. Nor
had she any intention of knowing anything, other than how
the land lay: that she had wished to know, and very ably
indeed had she found out. Otherwise, how masterly had
been her nonputting of questions—for instance, how the
gelignite or supposed gelignite had been come by, she would
go to her grave rather than know. The poser remaining
ahead was the Burkin-Joneses. What their attitude would
be, had the matter reached them or should it fail to be
stopped from doing so, one could predict, alas, only too
well. Their unappeasable rectitude was well known. *Could*
the matter yet be kept from the Burkin-Joneses, and from
Mrs. Burkin-Jones in particular, Dicey's mother would by
any and all means do so—though not, it was to be realized,

for Clare's sake. . . . It was just possible that Mrs. Beaker's known regard for the military might restrain her (or have restrained her so far) from worrying Mrs. Burkin-Jones. The more ambiguous, solitary Mrs. Piggott might, at the start, be selected as sole target. Mrs. Piggott, once sufficiently worried, could be counted on—surely?—to speed to the Burkin-Joneses, as parents of her ewe lamb's companion in crime. The Burkin-Joneses would thus *be* worried (which, after all, was an aim) while Mrs. Beaker preserved, with regard to them, a front of forbearance and magnanimity. Might that be the Beaker policy? One dared hope so.

The Beakers seemed, as compared to the Burkin-Joneses, to present no problem to Mrs. Piggott, serene in her reliance on gloves and charm. She seldom spoke of the Beakers without remarking how kind they were. She seldom, however, spoke of them.

One could do nothing but admire.

Yet in spite of all that, now—look!

Clare refused to. She could not feel it was fair to. Instead, she trod with crushing deliberation from one to another and then the next of the carpet's barely distinguishable roses. The child had been (each time, through inability to get away in time) in the distasteful presence of grown-up persons who became "overcome"—whether by heat, sea-sickness, vertigo, stage-fright, or bad news. Of inferior calibre did she find them. With more like sympathy she had watched one soldier after another faint on parade. She had learned through reading that persons are apt to be overcome by joy, jealousy, anger, curiosity, greed, grief, or one or another powerful feeling, including the unspecified one known as "emotion," and lust, whatever that was. What overcame Mrs. Piggott?—for that, alas, *was* what was unmistakably going on. To be overcome is, to be got the better of.

What overcame Mrs. Piggott, getting the better of her, was anxiety. Anxiety tortures its prey through the sense of impotence: *that* was the matter with her, too. Many as were her gifts, she was, this minute, impaled on the lack of one—she was not clairvoyant. Had she possessed a crystal, it would have been useless—she would have "gazed" unavailingly, trying to ravish some, any, picture out of the lasting emptiness. One *should* be able to "see"

—how could one not? How could Mrs. Piggott not, in the
case of Dicey? It came hard on her. She had taken her
hands from behind her head; now they lay somewhere
about her dress, palms turned supplicatingly up. "You
don't know," she was driven to ask Clare, "if she possibly
went to the sugar mouse shop? No; I don't believe she had
any money?"

"They give us tick there."

"Oh, how greedy she is!—If she has no money, she
can't very well have got on a bus, can she?"

"They give us tick on the buses—anybody in a St. Agatha's hat."

"They ought," exclaimed Mrs. Piggott, with inordinate
anger, "to stop that, it's very snobbish."

"Then we might have to walk. Or some of us might."

"That's what she must be doing, mustn't she, for some
reason or other? Dawdling along . . . Clare, do one thing:
look at the clock for me, will you?"

"*Want* me to tell you the time?"

"Go on . . ."

"Five minutes to seven."

Mrs. Piggott heard: she said nothing.

"—Oh, Mrs. *Piggott*?"

No answer.

"Oh, Mrs. Piggott, now's just about the time Father
said he'd be here!"

Mrs. Piggott, in her now listless dress, moved on the
sofa. "I don't understand. What about your father?"

"He's going to come here."

"Oh."

"That's why *I'm* here. I mean, that's why I haven't gone.
He said, if you didn't mind he would pick me up here again,
like he did last time he was playing tennis at that house.
That house close to here, you know. So I'm waiting for
him.—Will that be all right?"

"Well, I suppose so," said Mrs. Piggott, in what was,
yet was not, her smiling and teasing voice.

"He said he'd only come *in* if you didn't mind." Clare
showed, for the first time, signs of misgiving: the announce-
ment properly should have been made before. She already
had had one try, but been cut short. "But if you're tired,"
she volunteered, "I can easily wait for him down in the

garden, or even outside the gate, then he could pick me up without coming in. Shall I?"

"That sounds a silly plan. No, he must come in. I shall be delighted to see him."

She was to be delighted almost at once. In what could be called the distance of the small garden, the gate—which was, strictly, an ironwork door in the wall—could be heard to open, then be closed with precision. . . . Suddenly Clare, turning not pale (she could not) but pale's equivalent, attacked herself wildly, all over, with both fists. "But he's *talk*ing to someone!"

Less concerned, Mrs. Piggott got off the sofa; chiefly to disinter a letter on which she'd till now sat. She put the letter away in her little desk. Any and all preparations were now over—apart from provision of cake for comers to tea, she put herself out in no way for any visitor. She and Feverel Cottage were to be taken as they were. Not so much as a glance in a looking-glass or cushion shaken or curtain straightened or fallen petal picked from the carpet. She did, however, do as she always did the minute before anyone from the outside came in—cast a meditative, half-solicitous look round at these multitudinous things of hers, not least china, wondering how the stranger might affect *them*. In this case, Clare's father would not be coming here for the first, second, or even third time. But a visitor alters, as each visit becomes one more.

Clare was blowed, as things were, if she would rush to the window—still less (as by nature one would) the door. She stayed studying extraordinary Mrs. Piggott, till asked: "Well—aren't you going to meet him?" She then did set out, though at slow march, for what at least was an observation post. Having re-tented herself in curtains, she stood stock-still, bristling, while you might count ten. She then let out a loud and most bitter snor. "I say, Mrs. Piggott, only do *look*—come here!"

Mrs. Piggott came forward, though not the whole way. Standing behind Clare, she looked through the muslin.

Major Burkin-Jones came up the garden, which was at a slight incline—white-clad, erect at his full height, bareheaded. Unheedingly carrying a racquet, he had with him a Panama hat. All the more in the early dusk of the garden stood out the sun-saturated and noble beauty of this man.

Everywhere was breathless, heavy syringa bushes increasing the look of hush. The look of evening, caused by the high walls over which rose many and close trees, was premature: the tops of the trees still netted the brightness of day. Along or above this coast, one could not both be sheltered and have a view—there now, though, was *a* view from Feverel Cottage: Major Burkin-Jones. The neglected grass of the lawn, already growing up into seed, created a sort of pallor round his feet: nothing splashed anywhere with colour, except where a meagre delphinium leaned through ferns or ungirt cabbage roses burned purple-pink. This came to be a garden like none other—or was it always, perhaps? The moment could, at least, never be again. Or, could it—who knew? Happy this garden would be to have such a revenant, were he ever dead. Though who would be there to see, were they all gone? . . . Nearing the house, Major Burkin-Jones gave it a smile, also raising and moving a hand in vague salute—vague because, so far, he could see no one.

As the sounds had proclaimed, he was not alone. At his heels capered Dicey, as pleased as Punch.

Three

❧❦❧

Wednesdays went better than Tuesdays, always—if they had a fault, it was a tendency to be uneventful. Today, the heat was a little less, which insofar as it was to blame for the disturbances of yesterday was as well. The weather continued to be set fair: Tuesday's nervy little hot breeze or breath having died at sunset, Wednesday's blue warmth was extremely still. And yesterday's sun had, in spite of all, ended by going down on nobody's wrath—the Burkin-Joneses had heard nothing from the Beakers about the gelignite; Mrs. Piggott (inferring this to be so from Major Burkin-Jones's uncloudedness) had not given Dicey really much of a wigging; and the two girls, having buried the hatchet while waiting about in the Feverel Cottage garden for Clare's father to say goodbye to Diana's mother and take Clare home, had parted, before the end of the evening, on the good terms on which they quite often were. Sheikie had been deflected from the rink, and possible trouble, by happening as she was biking thither to sight the Sissens (non-St. Agatha's friends) accompanied by the elder Artworth boy, so going bathing with them instead.

She, as she mentioned to all and sundry, still felt, in spite of a bath between, encrusted with yesterday evening's brine when she re-entered the sea on Wednesday morning.

She did so with the school bathing party, which comprised all St. Agatha's girls other than those afflicted by summer colds and, more strangely, some of the bigger ones, who were for some mystic reason debarred. The dedicated smugness with which they bore their exclusion made such girls as ludicrous to their juniors as did, already, their bulging forms. The rest oozed through the gap in the parapet, and poured, zigzag, down the cement steps to the orange beach and glassily waiting sea. That the beach was private made the sea seem so. Over bathing suits, wriggled into up at the school, flapped wraps to be worn for crossing the road. Rub-down towels awaited them in the school cloakroom. They wore, to the sea's brink, sandshoes, against the hurtful pebbles. Some wore frilly bathing caps, others not. Those first in shrieked and beat at the sea, bobbing. Watchful, Miss Brace and Miss Kinmate paced to and fro, the steep shelving drops of the shingle, under the surface, being one of the few perils of this beach—of treacherous off-shore currents there were none. A non-swimming girl, taking one step too many, could find herself, in an instant, out of her depth. Both Miss Brace and Miss Kinmate were, therefore, armed with deterrent whistles. Miss Brace dreaded the role of life-saver, and Miss Kinmate, herself *unwell* today, had not the slightest intention of going in.

Dicey was, rather surprisingly, not a bobber. Swim well was one of the few things she could do—Cousin Roland, who was almost a merman, having taught her to when she was five or six. She could swim faster than Sheikie, farther than Mumbo. Her disappearances in the direction of France had caused flattering outbursts of whistle-blowing. This minute, though, she was liking simply to float—some way out, seaweed-like hair awash.

"Muriel's stung by a jellyfish," she sang out, though dreamily, to Olive, who, working away at a breast-stroke, came thrashing by.

"Kick up a fuss?—*Ouch!*" said Olive, swallowing sea water.

"*Jellyfish!*" bawled Clare from some way off.

"I *know*."

St. Agatha's stared denudedly out to sea: alien became its dead-still tamarisks, cream-cheese gables, and garden patterning up behind. Sheikie, nosing that way in a long, swift, sleek streak like a surfaced shark, with scorn sighted two of the left-behinds teenily framed in a french window. *She* wore a scarlet bathing cap. She made a turn, submerged, came up again not far from Dicey. "Race you, lazy?" Thus showing how good was her mood, since she lost always. For a minute more Dicey let herself lie, the not even plaything of the indifferent, not even swelling sea, aimless as she, whose strength could only be felt in that it would not let her sink. Then they did race. There being no goal—no buoy, raft, boat, rock, nothing in sight —it was racing for speed's sake.

Voices across the water.

" '*The further out from Eng-e-land the nearer is to France—then turn not pale, beloved snail . . .*' " chanted one of the bobbers, watching another swim four strokes after making a depth-test with her toe. Miss Kinmate half-blew her whistle, looked at her watch again, saw she *was* wrong, there were still five minutes to go, let the whistle swing away on its cord. And, "It *is* a cornelian!" shouted a girl ashore, holding a pebble up to the eye. "I see red light through it—I do!" Those coming out picked their way up the beach to look for their sandshoes, amid brittle-dried starfish, pod seaweed, razor shells. The coarse, clean smell of the beach met those coming out of the scentless sea. Shoes being higher up than they'd been left was the one sign that there was a tide at all—it was going out.

When some half of the girls were already on to or up the cement steps, wraps plastering on to their sea-wetness, Miss Kinmate really did blow her whistle. Miss Brace, not to be outdone, blew hers.

The sole school incident, that Wednesday, was a visit from an aunt. Thanks to being a day school (though one day-boarded there) St. Agatha's was not much plagued by relatives—the girls, should that be wished, were on view at home. But this, it seemed, was an aunt "down for the day," who had sworn an oath not to return to London without a glimpse of her niece. She had also said she'd like a glimpse of the school. Miss Ardingfay had been warned by telephone on no account to let Elfreda escape —which, this being a games afternoon, she might have done. The displeased Elfreda (fond of rounders, and good at them) was kept hanging about.

When the aunt came, the more athletic girls were indeed gone. Three afternoons a week, St. Agatha's used the playing-field of its one neighbour, St. Swithin's, a preparatory school abounding in horrible little boys—no little boys, happily, were at those times anywhere to be found. The field was large enough for cricket and rounders to be, in summer, played on it simultaneously, provided each game kept out of the other's way. There were also available two tennis courts. Even so, that left girls unaccounted for, there being sixty-eight at St. Agatha's in all. Miss Ardingfay strongly held that everyone should play something, or at least try to—therefore efforts were made to see that the same girls were not left out of games afternoons too often. Those most rarely left out were the keener ones (those, that was to say, who were any good).

Those left behind, within St. Agatha's grounds, met their fate with a varying resignation. They played pat-ball on the old croquet lawn, or poked about looking for lost balls, which were many, the lawn having no net round it, and hard to locate, age having turned them a dark green. Dead-seeming when hit, the balls could nevertheless bound away downhill with great velocity; some, it was thought, had ended up in the sea. Or, struck upward with anything like force, some plopped, for ever, into the dense thickets. A girl purporting to look for a lost ball could fade from view for the rest of the afternoon. When all balls were lost and most of the girls, the pat-ball came to an end.

More green balls being supplied, unfailingly, each games afternoon, had made it come to be held that Miss Ardingfay bought them in by the ton, third-hand.

Dicey, suffering from pique, sat on the garden roller kept up here that it might from time to time fruitlessly roll the croquet lawn. She was still wondering whether to look for tennis balls when Elfreda placed her aunt on a close-by seat, muttered something, and hurriedly went away. Dicey perceived why. To the aunt's look of avidity and intentness was added the aimful glitter of pince-nez. Worse, the woman, though clad as far as the neck in a way which seemed neither here nor there, had topped herself off with a largish black straw hat which, by the sticky look and still more smell of it, had been lately touched up with hat-dye, known to be poison, and had upon it what could only be magpie's wings. The effect was not of poverty or bravura but, far more, that of both hat's and wearer's having been chemically reconstituted, and of that's having so acted on *her* as to send her out robbing a charnel hedge. For the wings were not sporty hat-ornament but sheer dead bird— of which the child on the roller was subject to an overmastering horror. And living, even, one magpie is of ill omen.

Having been rushed uphill, the aunt could have been hoped to be out of breath. She was not. Lean, she was active-looking. She cast around, then marked down her prey. "And what's *your* name?" she keenly asked.

"Diana. But I'm afraid I have to look for tennis balls."

"Oh, no, nonsense—there are plenty of others!" (Balls, or girls?) "Why not come over and talk to *me*?" The hat-woman patted the seat beside her. To the outer (only the outer) eye, Dicey came across like a bidden dog. "This game," the captor went on, slighting the pat-ball, "I expect is rather for duffers only?" Evidently she saw through Elfreda's plan, which had been to deposit her—for how long?—somewhere where there would be something to watch. The child batted her lashes and said nothing. "However, you're all very happy, Elfreda tells me, here at this school of yours, in your various ways? Plenty of freedom?"

"Where has Elfreda gone?"

"Oh, *Elfreda*'ll be back to her old aunt! Meanwhile, there's plenty more you can tell me.—For instance, isn't this near where the Romans landed?"

"I don't know. I think somebody said so."

"Now that is *very* exciting, isn't it!"

Dicey, though shrinking back from the hat, reflectively peered at the speaker under it. Anybody more truly sharp than the aunt could have noted her to be hoarding something away. At the moment, however, she said nothing. The aunt, nonplussed, altered her tactics. "Are you, I wonder, the little girl who dances?"

"No," said Dicey regretfully. "She's my friend, though."

"And will she be a famous dancer when she grows up?"

"I don't know. She's very famous now."

"And what do *you* mean to be when you grow up?"

"I don't know."

Weighed on by witless negatives, the poor aunt attempted to inspirit by an upward toss of the head. She succeeded only in making the magpie quiver. Dicey, shutting her eyes, quite ill, backed further away. The jerk to the hat also had stirred up poison-fumes—it was out of a nimbus of those that the aunt declared: "Well, now, we shall have to think about *that*, shan't we? So let's see . . . What are you interested in?"

"Interested *in*?"

"Interested in, dear. Yes."

"I was in tadpoles, but something happened to mine. I've got kittens now."

"Ah! You like looking after them, I expect?"

"No, our cook does."

"So what *do* you like to do?"

"I like to play tennis, but everyone bags the courts—I mean, proper ones." Dicey sadly stared at the croquet lawn. "I like looking for things," she added, "or hiding things, wondering who'll find them. Or doing anything I can do, like getting on people's nerves or swimming."

"Ah . . . ?" said the aunt. She made back on to firmer ground. "*Elfreda's* going to be a doctor.

Dicey conveyed, by silence, that she did not believe that for a single moment, and anyway could not have thought it a good plan. "Did you ask her," she questioned, "or did she say?"

"Old aunt asked, and, wondrous to say, was told! Her father's my brother, and *he's* a doctor, as I expect you know. Careers do frequently run in families.—What's your father?"

"He's dead."

The aunt was nonplussed, again.

The child stole a very cautious look at the hat, out of the corner of her eye—the magpie at any rate had subsided. Steeling herself, she again searched under the brim; this time, more outright calculating than formerly. "Did Romans leave anything about—did they leave anything behind? Would that be there, if anyone hunted?"

"There are interesting, fine Roman things in museums. There should be many in the museum here.—It a little surprises me," said the aunt, glittering a disparaging glance downhill at the comatose back-view of St. Agatha's, "that all you girls shouldn't have been shown them!"

"Oh, we've been shown them; but all those things *have* been found. Would there still be anything there, anywhere?"

"You could always go with your little spade and see!"

The child, at the sound of the laugh, frowned, haughtily turning her head away.

"You never know, you know—one can never tell!" the woman continued.

"Did Romans live underground?"

"No, dear—my goodness, what *do* they teach you here? But the Romans, I'm sorry to say, have been long gone, and as time goes on things bury themselves."

"Oh. Doesn't anyone bury them?"

The aunt wore, pinned to her chest, a watch beneath an enamel bow—now she dipped her beak to take a peck at the time. "I don't know," she was forced to confess, with chagrin, "what can have become of that girl Elfreda! I think, Diana, perhaps I'll just potter down.—Are *those* all the girls, I see, coming in from games?"

She did see the girls coming in from games. In a drawn-out straggle, in flopping white linen hats, they proceeded along the winding coast road from St. Swithin's and turned in at the gates of St. Agatha's. Tea-time. Dicey gummed herself to the aunt as the aunt rose. "Have *you* found anything, ever?" she by now deeply wanted to know. But the fell aunt did all she could to cast Dicey off. "Your history mistress will tell you about the Romans." She readjusted her hat, with a fearful whiff. Lolloping down the slope after the aunt, she child mourned: "*She* tells us about the Greeks."

"Well, that's nice."—The aunt waved in a gratified, slavish way down at Elfreda, who glared up at them from the foot of the path.

"No. The Greeks never came here."

"There you are," Elfreda severely said. "I've arranged about tea for you, in Miss Ardingfay's drawing-room—that will be all right, because she's out." The ignored Dicey slid past the family group, to fling herself in at a back door, happily open. Before, or almost before, she had drawn breath, she was at the tea table—one of those long, long trestles—safe in between one tomato-hot and one cucumber-cool friend. She panted: "I've had Elfreda's aunt."

"What, the Suffragette?"

"*Oo?*"

"That's," Clare said, "what Elfreda says."

Sheikie blew lightly over the tea in her cup. Then: "Oh yes," she said. "She's been chained to railings."

Four

✦✦✦✦✦✦

The box possibility—though it had taken form at St.
Agatha's and would involve use of the school terrain—was
discussed, in the interests of greater secrecy, elsewhere, in
a series of meetings outside school hours. One, at an early
stage, was held or meant to be held at Feverel Cottage.

It was Saturday. Mrs. Piggott sat playing Debussy in
the drawing-room; other parts of the house were disturbed
by being made ready for Cousin Roland. Two of the three
girls sat, not patiently, on the lower stairs, waiting for
Dicey to come down to them. When she did, it was with
an armful of squirming kittens. That the kittens were or-
phans, much to be felt for, did not make them less of a
complication—hastily they'd been garnered up by her from
the spare-room bed, on which, in ignorance or defiance
of peacock counterpane over snowiest blankets and freshest
linen, ready for Cousin Roland, they had all been sleeping, some of them making messes. Clambering over her
friends in a worried way, she went on downward to the
door of the dining-room, which in spite of kittens she
managed to fling open. She then pelted the kittens, one by
one, at the old cook and very odd other maid, who were
in there polishing brass and silver. (Why in there, why
at this hour?)

The stir preceding a visit from Cousin Roland had origin
chiefly in the cook, who saw it as owed not to him only
but to herself. Mrs. Piggott suffered it, on condition that
it cease—and *have* ceased, leaving no ripple—before he
possibly could arrive. Cousin Roland was known to like

calmness only. Distaste for fuss, of any kind and at any
time, was one of his silent characteristics. He did not so
much "arrive" at Feverel Cottage as return thither: each
time, he resumed a life, plummeting back again into depths
which he thereby deepened.

Dicey had to break to her friends that, as things were,
the one place likely to be inviolate seemed the bathroom.
The garden, they could see for themselves, was being
raked over fervently by the jobbing gardener, egged on by
the cook. Dicey's room opened off her mother's; and who
knowing Mrs. Piggott could be certain when she might not
close the piano and sweep upstairs, to go over her winter
furs, or some-such, or settle down on her end-of-the-bed
sofa, to go on with a book she had left there? Safer the
bathroom. Having locked themselves in, they seated themselves in a row along the edge of the bath, formally. Fresh
from bossing kittens, Dicey showed her true colours. "Not
chickens' bones," she laid down.

"Who said chickens'?"

"You said if we took humans' we'd go to prison,
Mumbo."

"I know," put forward the local girl, "where there's a
wood with a dead sheep in it. Some boys showed me."

"You never said."

"Well, I've been saving it up. But that sheep won't be a
skull for a bit yet; we should have to wait."

"No, we can't. Oh!—Our Unknown Language?"

"Either of *you* started inventing that?"

"You said you'd know how to. You did, Mumbo!"

"I *could*, like billy-o. Only I can't if you two insist on
sticking your noses in—last time, both of you said you
meant to."

"Let her, Dicey! Who cares?"

"One head's better than three, any day," said the head's
owner.

"All right, Mumbo—go on. Don't invent it so's it's unknown to *us*, though: you swear and promise? We must
know what what we have said is."

"Writing *that* out's going to take so long, we might as
well wait for the sheep, I should have thought.—What
about the rich jewels?"

"And the pistol: how are we getting those? Hasn't your
mother, or someone, got any, Sheikie?"

"Not a *pistol*, she hasn't," the daughter said, thoughtfully.

"We can't burgle," laid down the Burkin-Jones child, adding: "You mean revolver."

"*I* mean pistol. And I didn't," asserted the leading spirit, "*mean* burgle! I mean, why can't we get hold of things?— Let's, though, not have the rich jewels and not bother. About having any rich jewels, we only said. A pistol, I know we can."

"Seen one, somewhere? Or was," inquired the expert, nastily, "what you really saw a revolver?"

"Well, I—*Sheikie*, where are you going?"

"I'm going away." The lovely dancer, off the bath, already was at the door, unlocking it. "I," she declared, with a backward toss of the plaits, "call this silly! I don't want to go on playing this: it's babyish. Babyish, with your old chickens' bones *and* no jewels. You two 'say,' then you're frightened! I'm going home." She reflected. "I'm not going *home* either; I'm going Somewhere Else." Thumb on the key, she paused, for an instant, to let the instant sink in—whereupon, something beyond the door caught, and held, her scornful attention. She turned to the two on the bath, with utter finality! "Well, there you are.—And there *you* are, anyway, Dicey: here comes your mother!"

Yes, it was Mrs. Piggott, calling "Dicey?" as though some pleasing idea had struck her, from halfway upstairs. A scuffle resulted: Dicey, having got control of the door, answered: "Yes, Mother?" opening it an inch. However, once she let go the handle the door, in a manner known to Feverel Cottage, swung open, behind her, as wide as a door can. "You poor creatures in there!" exclaimed Mrs. Piggott contritely. "Nowhere else for you? (Good afternoon, Clare; good afternoon, Sheila!) Listen," she went on, "don't think it's not delightful having you here, but I wondered how it would be if you all went out?—How would you like to? How would it be to go into Southstone and all have tea—with ices too, I should think?—at the Geisha Café?"

They looked at each other.

"If I gave you five shillings . . . ?"

At that answer to prayer they again looked at each other, sharply and sternly.

"Or are you tired of the Geisha?"

"We go to the Blue Bird, now. We like that better."

"That sounds lovely. Because," went on Mrs. Piggott, taking them into her confidence, as her way was, "I think possibly Cousin Roland after his journey might like a quiet tea. So now, I expect you will want to go? Wait a minute, then." She disappeared, to devote the next five minutes to hunting for five shillings, upstairs and down.

Money to lay out altered the picture. It re-engaged Sheikie. The three being again in concert, decisions went on to make themselves, as ever. Tea to be gone without, light refreshments possible. Shelving the jewellery question, go straight for fetters. . . . Not wearing St. Agatha's hats cut both ways: they had to pay on the bus, but could be licentious once into town. Dropping off the bus into crowded Southstone, they shoved their way through to the Old High Street. Halfway down that was Fagg's goldfish shop: this not only dealt in but provided for dogs and all but all kinds of pets. More than sunless, Fagg's inside was dark as a cellar: clicks, fumblings, and rustlings, from cages stacked to the grubby ceiling and barricading the small-paned window, animated the awesomely smelly gloom, in which how many hundreds of pairs of captive eyes watched? The only form of life missing, when the girls walked in, was Mr. Fagg: in a minute, however, he put that right, coming through the arch from the rabbit vaults to behind his counter like an old he-owl. "Well, ladies, what can I do for you?"

"A chain for a large bloodhound," panted Dicey, again well to the fore. Mr. Fagg looked sceptical. "Or Great Dane —any kind of mastiff," Mumbo put in, in her at once more slighting yet man-to-mannish way. Sheikie confined herself to pointing out: "Any ordinary chain would be no good."

"Haven't got your dog yet, then?" asked Mr. Fagg. "I wouldn't touch a dog that size if I was any of you. Not at your ages. You wouldn't have the muscle to pull against it. What any of you want is a nice terrier. Now I have a litter of *nice* terriers, it so happens."

"We don't want a dog; we want a chain."

"Life's nothing without a dog."

"A large chain. We can see some, there, hanging up."

Mr. Fagg, shown his way round his own shop, merely plucked at a wart, turning over resentful thoughts. Well was it that he did nothing more—for Mumbo, now, whistled a piercing warning. Not merely was somebody coming in, but the somebody was a St. Agatha's bigger girl, Hermione Bollet. Fifteen if a day, Hermione picked her way to the counter—her escort, a very much smaller brother, made for a corner where he tormented mice. By the look of her, Hermione had been making Saturday afternoon experiments with her person: she had tied back her hair in a wide black bow which something or other had since knocked sideways, and reefed in her anatomy, halfway down, by tightening the belt of her nice pink dress. She carried (probably because it would not go on without further damaging the bow?) a straw hat wreathed with maidenly rosebuds. Every inch a lady—and as at present so many inches went to the making of this girl, she was lady to a tremendous extent.

St. Agatha's out-of-school etiquette ordained that not more than the briefest glare be exchanged between encountering parties. The juniors slithered away along the counter into a bunch at its far end, to watch and listen. "Don't mind about *us*!" Dicey, at her most gracious, told Mr. Fagg—who was not intending to. "And what can I do for *you*, miss?" he asked Hermione, though in a by now not optimistic tone.

"I wanted some ants' eggs. But, Mr. Fagg—" "Then what's your trouble? I have them." "One of my goldfish died." "Well, we're all but mortal." "But another's begun to come out in blotches: are you *sure* your ants' eggs are quite all right?" "Those fish of yours, were they ever healthy?" "Beautifully healthy, always. They came," said Hermione, colouring with social consciousness, "from Harrods." "Thought *I* never supplied them! Well, if they continue to play you up, miss, I should tip the whole lot out and begin anew." "But I'm very, very *fond* of them, Mr. Fagg," expostulated the almost mother.

"Take it from me," he said, "all fish are the same." He got out ants' eggs, two packets, and planked them down. "Here's what you asked for. Want them? That's your decision—I can help you no further. Now dogs do show difference in character. It so happens, I have a nice litter . . ."

"No, we have dogs, thank you." Hermione bit her lip, then finally drew off a white cotton glove, the better to poke about in her purse. Mr. Fagg slid the packets, grudgingly, into a paper bag. She was nearly safely out of the den when Clare bawled: "Hi, you've forgotten your brother!" Disengaging the child from the mice took time.

"She makes me sick," Mr. Fagg said, flicking her money off the counter into the drawer-till. "Sobbing like that."

"Are fish the same?" little Dicey asked.

"They could be, for all she would ever know. To me, no. No, there are no identical fish—how should there be? What did you say you were after?" he asked, more favourably than he had yet spoken. "A large dog chain?" He unslung the fetters from their hook.

Their cost was shocking. "*And* that one's rusty!" pointed out Sheikie swiftly. It was not; it was the one they wanted. "You're a sharp little thing, though," recognized Mr. Fagg, in tribute to which he knocked off threepence. "This isn't going to travel far in a paper bag, you understand?" He demonstrated, dropping the chain in, then giving a good hard shake to the bag, which at once burst, dripping chain through. "There, now . . ."

"You haven't some *strong* string, and some *strong* paper?"

"No, I haven't."

"We can't, we can't, we *can't* carry fetters," stormed Dicey, "in broad daylight!"

"Well, you are going to look funny without a dog, aren't you?" said Mr. Fagg, unconcernedly going back to his wart.

Crisis. They tugged each other away into the mouse corner for consultation. Sheikie, unusually excited, declared: "I've got it—one of us has to wear it!" "Round their neck?" "Stupid, in broad daylight? Round their middle, under what they've got on. Me, it will have to be—Dicey's too fat, and *you* come apart in the middle." (Clare was never a frock-wearer, and her scanty blouses were known for coming untucked from her skimpy skirts.) "All I ask," requested the dedicated one, "is, dust it properly, first!" . . . The chain was wound around Sheikie, rather a business, in the cramped half-dark of the Fagg earth closet, out at the bottom of the yard beyond the rabbits. He'd been anything but keen on their going there. "What you'll find won't be much to *your* fancy, probably. However, if whichever it is of you can't wait, go on." The chain went easily more than once, not completely twice, round the dancer's

average-slender middle: they reefed it out with blue baby
ribbon unthreaded from Sheikie's Saturday frilly knickers.
When she had shaken down again into place her nicely
starched frock and embroidered petticoat, true enough
nothing was to be seen. In the front shop, happily, Mr.
Fagg now *was* interesting somebody in his litter. Putting
down two shillings, they told him the rest would have to
be tick, and, saying "Thank you so very much, Mr. Fagg,"
left. By the time he roared they were out of hearing, all
but.

While still in funds, now for the coffer. . . . The more
battered the better. From a wreck, or a crack in a rock?
Try at the rag-and-bone shop, down near the harbour.
Ahead they would have been forging, but for Dicey. "Now
what's up?" she had to be asked.

"I am not too fat. That *would* have gone round me."

To brighten her up, they had to buy six ounces (two
each) of lemon sherbet powder: this not only fizzed de-
liciously on the tongue but enabled one to froth at the
mouth ad lib, bright yellow. Sheikie, seized by doubt as to
whether, as Miss Beaker, she ought to froth at the mouth
in the open street, remained on to do so inside the sweet-
shop: the unrestricted others went on ahead, frothing away
in particular at an unknown clergyman whom they hoped
might think them possessed by devils. In a rush, before
Sheikie could catch up, they made for the picture-shop
window—a short way further down, on the Fagg side.
This was an Old High Street window not to be missed: it
guaranteed a sensation like no other—that of looking at
pictures of where one was. The back of the window built
itself up with masterpieces, among them "Hope," still
clutching her harp, but the front showed water colours
and etchings of the Old High Street—far more queer, as
a street, than one had thought. Top parts of buildings
stuck out, hatted by too large gables, black beams squeezed
doors, windows, and archways out of shape. Nothing high
but the crooked chimneys. Toy shopfronts were frowned
over by dimmed sign-boards, from under which they looked
ready to fall forward. . . . All this was to be wondered at
through two layers of glass—the picture shop's window's
and the glass in the gilt or ebony frames. But the greater
wonder was that, outside the pictures, there the Old High
Street actually *was*. You could verify simply by turning

round: there, it indeed remained—a magnified picture. So seeing it, one saw it for the first time. . . . Moreover, a portion of the Old High Street (that exactly across the way from the picture shop) reflected itself not only in the shop window but in the glass of these numerous pictures of itself. The reflection itself looked like a large painting. The gables, etc., were there twice over.

"All right, then, I *am* picturesque!" the street must have said. And soon, sorry it must have been. It came to be overrun by pokers-about, strikers of attitudes, and gazers. Much in the way they were—and would have been more so, but for the hope that their days were numbered: they could be run over, deafened, or given fever. Though the Old High Street, steep and extremely cobbled, was shunned by the traffic of most of Southstone, it had traffic of its own, which did as it liked. The din between the low gables was very lordly. On top of that, bicycles whizzing downhill so bounced and rebounded upon the cobbles that the bells on their handle-bars rang whether rung or not. And the street had deep-seated smells of its own, which, as none could be certified as downright insanitary, the denizens saw no reason to put a stop to. These mingled with smells always travelling up from the Old Harbour's fish market, oily old engines, and scummy puddles. Southstone's most (and, to be honest, only) picturesque quarter was seldom visited twice by the same visitor. "It certainly is a place to be seen *once!*" was said of it, with wary enthusiasm. Trophies from it, including water colours and etchings, were usually borne home. Superior paintings of it, by local art groups, hung in most of the drawing-rooms on the plateau.

Clare, sucking the last of the sherbet powder out of the cavity in the lower molar, studied these representations of where she stood, one by one—as she always did—in absolute silence. Dicey again wondered, again aloud, what it would feel like being an artist. Warned by a third reflection, they jumped round from the window in time to stop Sheikie from lobster-nipping them—a form of friendly surprise she favoured. "*I* knew where I should find you!" she said scornfully. She thought nothing of pictures, perhaps rightly. Off again they started, downhill, top speed.

"Look where you're going, can't you!" yelled someone, leaping out of their path.

"We are!" They were. Racing drivers of themselves,

they matched speed to space. Darting birds in the air could not have been surer. Last-moment swerving, at high velocity, was their forte—to bump into anyone meant enormous loss of prestige for the bumper-in. So, no one had anything to complain of. (Shove they did, but that was another matter.)

A clock at the top of the street, then one at the bottom, struck one—two—three—four—five. "*There* you are, you see: it's practic'ly night!"

"You took ages frothing."

"I saw jewellery. Pretence, but it flashes—sixpence for ruby rings!"

"Ho, in the *toy* shop?"

"We SAID, next was to be the coffer!"

"You won't buy a coffer in a jiffy, so you needn't think! Why can't a box do?—What *is* a coffer?"

"Oh, tell her, Mumbo!"

"I've *told* her—and shut up, shouting! Is this secret, or isn't it? Go on, do—let the whole *High* Street know, you two silly antelopes!"

Right she was—spies everywhere! They looked fiercely uphill, behind them, downhill, ahead.

"There goes Hermione again, down there!"

"Hoo, look at her! Wobbledy-wobbledy-wobble: she does look silly! She can't walk straight.—What's she done with her brother?"

"Sold him as a slave."

"She's got three paper bags, now."

"Gone off her head and think's she's in Harrods!"

Pink-linen, Hermione vanished into a doorway, which proved (when they'd hastened down to it) to be that of "Curios." "Curios" chiefly ran to the second-hand. What was chiefly curious about things in "Curios" was that anyone could ever have wanted them or be hoped to do so ever again. "From auctions," discerned the Beaker & Artworth child. To make sure what Hermione *was* doing, they took turns at squinting in at the window—under shelves on which fish knives and forks, half dozens of napkin rings, pepper-and-salt sets and so on tarnished away embedded in faded velvet; over trays where assortments of fancy tea spoons, tied up into bunches with rotting ribbons, lay among tangled corals, dishonoured medals and lacquer and other blemished visiting-card cases; and in between verticals such as statuary, domed or naked clocks, decanters with dust in their cut glass, grand jettisoned oil lamps, cruets for ogres. "Choosing a cheap birthday present to give her mother, I expect, or aunt, or something," opined Dicey. "Now," she further reported, "she's starting sobbing—I expect everything's too expensive?"

Mumbo came elbowing back for a second peer: longer, this time, and closer. Her spine stiffened, her knuckles whacked at her skirt. She used a shout-sized breath for a held-in whisper: "*They've got a* COFFER *in there.*"

Three noses flattened against the glass. Sheikie, though, stepped back after a minute. "If that's all a coffer is, we've got two at home!"

"You never said!"

"Well, you never asked. Well, there they *are*—doing no good, either. Nobody uses them ever, or ever wants them. Nobody knows about them, so far as I know. . . ." Sheikie came, at this point, to a meaning pause. "Nobody'd *miss* one." She lightly tilted her eyes at Dicey, then turned coolly away.

"But, *Sheikie* . . ."

But the dancer was elsewhere. This instant, a bronze, a nymph, in "Curios' " window had seized her fancy. Fancy, merely?—something more was at work. Inspiration set in. Knowingly, calmly, from every angle, Sheikie studied the pose of the statuette. Poised on a toe on a green alabaster base, the nymph spiralled up to the topmost fingertip of an arm flung upward over her head. Selecting a spot on the pavement outside the shop, Sheikie herself went into the pose. She held it.

Oblivious, Mumbo gnawed at a thumbnail. "*I* don't know," she admitted, scowling with indecision. "No harm to at any rate *ask* in there?—if that fat ostrich would buck up and get out."

"She's looking at tea spoons now, for her poor mother," Dicey thought likely, having in view the window from which Mr. Curio's hand had removed a bunch. "That coffer they've got's exactly just what we SAID."

"If it had anything wrong with it, like no bottom, we ought to be able to make them knock something off?"

"It wouldn't be very much good to us with *no* bottom."

"*I* vote we go on to the rag-and-bone shop!"

"This coffer in *here's* exactly just what we—"

"Yes!—But they don't try anything on at the rag-and-bone shop."

"If we went there, could we probably get some bones?" Sheikie changed toes, to try the pose in reverse (other arm up). This went, if anything, still better. She now spoke, also—though lacking a marble base, she managed to give her tone a remote altitude. "Do as you like" said she.

"We're going to. Only we don't know what, yet."

"If you like throwing good money after bad, oh do! At home we have two coffers, I merely told you."

Clare glared no higher up than the lower air. "Ho, yes! *Yours*, are they, by any chance?"

"My own family's," mentioned the voice from above. "And Daddy'd give one to *me*, I know."

"And would he want to know why?—*oh*, no! Or your mother would come along, and she'd start asking."

"Do as you like," said Nonchalance, "oh, do!"

Deadlock, unbearable. Dicey screamed: "Bother, oh *botheration*! Oh bother, *be* bothered—oh, *bother* you!"

"That's right," Clare told her, "go on, collect a crowd!"

Sheikie already was doing so—in a small way and, be it said, undesignedly. She suffered the increase of starers round her with the indifference of the artist—till one or two of them started chucking pennies. News of a pretty little living waxwork's being on exhibition somewhere at the bottom of the High Street was, from all signs, spreading like wildfire. Outside where "Curios" was, the Old High Street started not only to flatten down but to widen, being about to debouch on the Old Harbour. This was where good-humoured Saturday people, doing nothing particular, made it their custom to stand and be. By now the sun was off them, but had not left them—from where it was, in hiding behind the High Street's roofy hill, the sun went on heating the toast-brown shadow, in which the colours, darker than earlier, seemed brighter, brightest being the pink peppermint rock being licked by infants.

No, till the coppers started pelting the pavement round here, she hadn't turned a hair. She might have been alone in a nymphly glade. "Keep it up, miss!" was shouted: there was otherwise, for that minute or two (nothing lasted more than a minute or two), a hush. Forth into the midst stepped Hermione, out of "Curios." She had put her hat on. Biting her lip, she looked neither to left nor right. The natives parted before Hermione, who become lost to view till next Monday morning.

Sheikie out of the pose, the three sped on. A minute had to be sacrificed to restraining Dicey from doubling back to pick up the pennies. She mourned: "There were four of them. I counted them. Four of them would have bought—"

"They're Sheikie's; she didn't want them."

"I would have liked them."

"Looking for bones now, are we?" asked Sheikie, in a tolerant tone. The High Street bent to the right, before dying out: ahead was a V of sea. An artist was to be seen in the act of sketching. "Mostly, that place has old leaky kettles—" She broke off. "Hullo, *Trevor*—where's Aubrey?"

Trevor, not there a minute ago, came into being walking beside them. "Playing cricket," he answered.

"So I'd have *thought*!" flashed Miss Beaker, with a toss of the head.

The shrimp of a boy in the round school cap looked sideways, meditatively, out of the corners of his spectacles at the three girls. "What are you doing?" he then asked them.

"What are *you* doing?"

"I've been down at the harbour. Watching," he added—seeing he ought in some way to fill in the picture—"boats."

They asked, with foreboding: "Where are you going now?"

"Back to the harbour."

"Why on earth didn't you *stay* there, then?" (It took, alas, but one half-minute of Trevor to drive one wild.)

The boy was surprised that this need be asked. "It was tea-time. I wanted some tea."

"You don't mean you've been the *whole* way *home*?" cried Sheikie, with rapidly mounting frenzy.

"That would have been too far," he explained to her, "as I was coming back again. So I thought I would go to the Blue Bird."

"Oh, you did, did you!—You *went* to the Blue Bird?"

Trevor showed signs of patience (visible patience lent force to his bearing at times like these). Had he not made his movements perfectly clear? "It was nice, there," he thought it enough to say, looking replete.

At that, Dicey paused in her tracks and began to sway. "*Trevor*, don't be so cruel! How *can* you? Telling us, when we're weak and fainting and hollow! When all this whole afternoon we've had nothing to eat *or* drink *or*—"

"Stop it!" she was advised. Too late. Her hullabaloo had brought the group to a further and frantic halt, in which Trevor was felt to begin to ponder. Never averting his spectacles from Dicey, he backed as from a swaying cobra, but gave attention to her complaint. As a thinker-out, Trevor was slow but sure. Two and two were about to be put together. "You didn't any of you have any tea, then," he concluded. "Why?"

Clare stony, Dicey artless as ever. Sheila, in the clear bell note she kept for taunting, sang out at him: "*Wouldn't* you like to know!"

That, the boy considered. "No," he finally told her, "I only wondered." He then directed a look of liking, longing, and devoted intelligence away from them, at the harbour and its activities. Those you could not have enough of. Yet when the three pushed on again, he fell back into step with them: they were his fate, apparently, for what remained of Saturday afternoon. "Where are we going to go?" he asked open-mindedly. "Anywhere particular, were you going to? I don't mind, so long as I'm home by seven."

Ruin. . . . They dared not look at each other. Demoralized, skidding, stumbling, they repeatedly bumped one another—and indeed others. It ended by Trevor's steering them to the parapet: on to its top they—at his considerate invitation—hoisted themselves, to sit in a speechless row. It was highish. "You see well from here," he informed them, "or at any rate, fairly." *He* sat facing outward over the harbour, feet contentedly dangling over the nauseous water on which bobbed craft: his companions sat with condemning backs to it. Trevor now tugged from a pocket a small pair of opera glasses (mother-of-pearl: how come by?) which he proceeded to focus on a distant trawler. It was Mumbo who broke the thunderous silence. "I say, Trevor, that gelignite of your friend's was beastly. It never went off."

Trevor, having adjusted the glasses slightly, continued to use them. "I heard it hadn't."

"*Who* informed you, pray?" burst from Sheikie.

"What I mean is," the boy said, "I'd have heard if it

had. You did something not right to it, I should think.—
If you got it back from your mother," he said to Sheikie,
"I'd take a look."

"You can if you like. We're tired of that."

Silence fell again. Now, Trevor focussed his glasses on
the horizon—along which (fortunately) a pair of funnels
trailing some limp smoke could be seen to move: a tramp
steamer making along the Channel, westward, pretty far
out. This riveted Trevor. His captives seized the occasion
to shuffle along the parapet on their bottoms, to a distance
where they could begin to mutter. It was decided to make
for the Beaker home, least distant residence on their route.
A cache could be made at the Beakers', Sheikie now being
anxious to get the chain off—not only had it begun to
gall her but she had reason to fancy it might be slipping.
While there, no harm in taking a look at the Beaker coffers. . . . And mortified Dicey confessed to a baser crisis:
a great flea had caught her—in Fagg's, probably? As fleas
do, it had taken a short rest after its change to its new
surroundings, but it now was active in many parts of her.
"Everything," they told her, "bites you, Dicey."

"Mother says I must be succulent," said the poor child
miserably. Barely could she wait to get to the Beakers' to
tear all her clothes off, truly to search. "I'm not going
home with this flea on me," she droned on. "Supposing it
hopped on to Cousin Roland?"

"We don't want your flea staying with us."

"If we all could find it, we could kill it with soap.—You
killed a flea with soap once, Mumbo, you told me."

Sheila was asked sternly: "Where is your mother?"

"Out."

"Are your sure? Where has she gone?"

"Spending the day at Irene's, at Herne Bay." (Having
been "an afterthought"—an inspired one—on the part of
Mr. and Mrs. Beaker, Sheila had among other distinctions
two married sisters, one of whom was prominent at Herne
Bay.) "Not back," the daughter could guarantee, "till the
nine train."

How to get to the Beakers'? Sheikie's bike; which could
stretch to two passengers (handle-bar, back mudguard),
had been unforeseeingly left at Feverel Cottage. Bus, yes—
but everything cost, cost, cost! Heads turning as one, they
eyed Trevor's profile. Economics were simple: money of

Trevor's would be tick: inroads on *their* fund, what could ever repair?

"We're going home now, Trevor!" Sheikie announced.

So incredulous was he, he not only turned but lowered the glasses. She, pushing off from the parapet, executed a beautiful outward leap on to *terra firma*. The arc of her movement, still more her in-balance landing, were accompanied by a distinct sound—the girls heard it, merely; Trevor harkened more closely, "Sheikie," he said, "you're clanking. Why are you clanking?"

Poised, she on the instant showed vast confusion—on his behalf. Vexed, but far, far more scandalized, she looked away from him, down that nose of hers. In a hushed tone, which followed a pained hush, she said: "Trevor, I don't think *you* ought to ask."

He turned pink.

"Oo, *Trevor* . . ." breathed horrified Dicey, promptly.

He turned bright scarlet.

Clare, in her simplifying way, offered him a chance to buy back his character. "Trevor, *you've* got some money."

"Some," he admitted. "Why?"

"We ought," she said, taking him a little aside, "to get Sheikie home."

A short line of carriages, open, some having awnings, waited all day down here by the Old Harbour, hoping for the best. Extruded from the plateau by the vogue for taxis, the horse carriages—in their heyday known as "victorias" —not seldom succeeded in scooping up footsore seekers after the picturesque, inducing them further to take the air along the bowery, sea-girt Lower Road, under the steeps crowned by the Promenade. Such carriages mounted to Upper Southstone by gradients known to themselves only. . . . Trevor, stuffing the opera glasses back into his pocket, walked off stiffly, on hire bent. He was to be watched accosting the driver at the head of the line. A bargain was on the eve of being concluded when Sheikie shrieked weakly: "One *with* an awning!" The third carriage, therefore, was set in motion: horse still dreaming, it crawled to meet them.

On the wide seat, under the languid awning, they disposed themselves in a noble row. Dicey, keeping a clutch on the place where the flea was, overflowed graciousness down on to the boy: "Oh, poor Trevor, aren't *you* coming?" In return, he regarded her with demented blankness. Here was his half-crown, sweating on the palm of his hand . . . there was the harbour. . . . The carriage began to move, so he leaped in, seating himself back to the horse. The driver whipped up. The horse not only woke but began to trot. The victoria's splendid springs cradling them gaily over the cobbles, away they bowled, admired by all—Dicey, letting go of the flea, waved.

Five

❧❧❧

The front door of 9 Ravenswood Gardens remained on the latch all day. One turn of the knob, one push, and one was within. Only strangers rang. This might have seemed out of character with the Beakers, but was not, since it served to direct attention to the law-and-order imposed by Beaker rule. Loitering on the part of suspicious persons did not occur in Ravenswood Gardens. Burglary was as unthinkable as a sack by Goths. "No Hawkers" notices were unnecessary, nor did street musicians venture into the place—which consisted of fifteen houses facing a railed-in glade. This not being a wood, there were no ravens. There was an orderly twitter of smaller birds, some of which when maddened by spring sang—an expiring trill or two was still to be heard in the otherwise June-ish hush of Ravenswood Gardens, as the carriage drew up.

Sheikie considered it better to stop the carriage—imperceptibly lightened by the descent of Trevor near *his* family mansion, two corners back—opposite No. 11 rather than No. 9. Her father always might be at home. He was, as cigar smell filling the hall from out the ajar dining-room door proclaimed. The Beakers lived chiefly in their rich dining-room, their drawing-room being for entertaining. Clustered on the thick mat, the girls eyed the stairs: could a rush be made? No. An enormous gerrumph sound, belly-deep, issued from what could only be Mr. Beaker. Though passive, it had an expectant note in it. The little light-of-his-eyes knew what was owing. She sketched a "Won't take a minute!" gesture at her friends, then swung round the dining-room door at him. "Hullo, Daddy!"

"Hello, my duckie!"

The others looked through the hinge crack. There Mr. Beaker sat, looking pachydermatous. The armchair from which he protruded was of leather. The cigar from here being out of view, he appeared himself to be fuming, like a slow incense-cone, though of different odour. Comatose, reconciled to the absence of his spouse, he sickened with love at the sight of his little daughter duly: he would as soon not have. Dote, however, he always had, so he did. "Thought I heard you come in," he said. "Been out?"

"Yes. We're going upstairs."

"Go where you like, m'duckie; go where you—I *say*, though!" Unmanned by a memory, Mr. Beaker crouched his head in his collar: gripping the arms of his chair, he hauled his bulk round, hauntedly, to the windows. "Minute ago, thought I heard a carriage. *Wasn't* a carriage, was there?"

"There was *a* carriage. It drove away, though."

"Drove away, did it?" He gerrumphed again. He subsided—as though under the touch of a childish hand coolingly-knowingly placed upon his forehead. Out came the root of the trouble. "Thought it was callers."

"Dad-*dy!*"

"Y'never know, y'know!" He *had*, after all, been through deep waters.

"But Dad-*dy*, anybody *we'd* know would have come in a motor car—now, wouldn't they?"

"You're quite right." He stared at her, dwellingly. She would go far.

"Now, we're going upstairs!"

"Go where you like, my duckie.—Give me a kiss?"

She did.

Mr. Beaker had taken a minute, if hardly more.

One of the Beaker coffers was wedged in under the hall hat-stand, tented by dejectedly hanging overcoats and having as neighbour the vast brass evenly dinted gong. It contained two discolouring billiard balls and a whistle. The other was on a landing, under a table with an ample chenille cloth over it and Oriental fern pots. This one was empty. Both coffers were only too near the desideratum: the moralists spied on them noncommittally. Everyone pounded on up, up the flights of stairs.

Sheikie's room was surely the prettiest in Southstone?—

probably England, possibly the world? Round the frieze
darted swallows, sprays of pink blossom in their beaks: the
little dressing-table, on which the little mirror supported a
trophy boxing glove, was draped in lovingly laundered
flounces. Enamelled furniture shed an ivory gleam. From
within the cupboard, tissue-wrapped dancing dresses (ac-
cordion pleated), block-toed dancing sandals (satin of
every colour), and rainbow dancing scarves made their
existences felt. Vestments. That these should cohabit with
her St. Agatha's winter reefer, serge kilts, games boots,
hockey pads—such as any girl has—made the room not
less of a little temple; though, it might be, a more curious
one. Her castanets, on a ribbon, hung over a knob of the
little bed: on the pillow, the teddy bear wore a bow to
match. Her tambourine had the rather more restless air of
an object constantly shifted from place to place. On the
chimneypiece was a signed—how obtained?—photo of
Pauline Chase flying in at the window as Peter Pan, and
an unsigned more frantic photo of child tennis prodigy
Suzanne Lenglen. There were three of Sheikie—one with
wings, one as a bacchante, one in a mantilla.

She also was a collector of Free Samples, sending for
any the makers offered. Lynx-eyed was her look-out for
them. Patent foods packeted in miniature, tiny but strong-
scented cakes of soap, creams in jars the circumference of
a shilling, unguents or dentifrices or anything else squeez-
able out of baby tubes, condiments or lotions in bottles
small enough to be swallowed. . . . The collection lived
on display on the top and flap of the little desk at which
she wrote nothing. Mutilated, the magazines from which
she had chopped the coupons stayed piled on the window
seat, which had frilly cushions.

Now she *had* got the girls here, her manner towards
them became critical. "Why can't you tuck your blouse
in?" she asked Mumbo; who, having made for the magazines, was banging pages over with a stare or a whistle;
and who, at this, stuffed some part of the garment in off-
handedly, absently, not caring either way. She proceeded
to frown up, and round her, at Sheikie's swallows. "Flying
lower, today. Looks like a storm."

"Thank you."

Clare transferred her frown from the swallows to

Sheikie's middle: here *was* reason to ponder. "Where do we put it, next—once it's off you?"

"*Get* it off me first, then!—I'm sore, I tell you!"

Investigation. Scissors would be required. "In my *work*-basket!" fumed Andromeda, chafing. "*You* haven't got a workbasket!" "Yes, I *have*!" And so she had—sticky wicker, plump inside, satin-padded with scarlet. Loops for thimble, and so on. Thimble, and so on, right-and-tight in their loops. Goodness . . . "You never said," Dicey, viewing the basket. Having ascertained that the flea was no longer with her—it had got off, somewhere—she was back again into the picture; indeed its forefront. The flea was probably driving, now, back again across Southstone in the victoria. She bore it wonderfully little malice, in view of the gluttonous bites it left behind. Abstractedly scratching at them, she directed: "Into that nice coffer."

"Which?"

"The one on the landing. It had more nails, I thought."

The scissors sawed at the obdurate ribbon knot. The chain fell from Sheikie, noisily, on to the carpet. It—they (fetters)—was taken down the flight and a half of stairs and consigned to what by this very act came to be recognized as *the* coffer. Clare, even, said nothing. The house, with the dead man down at the bottom, was conspiratorially silent. "I expect," said Dicey, as they returned upstairs, "your father *would* give it to you, without asking?"

"I told you."

"Yes. You could give him another kiss."

That hour at Ravenswood Gardens was to prove fateful. Things having gone Sheikie's way through the first decision, she forced a second way. By the time her friends left, to walk to the bus (no way out of this), an addition to the first project had been accepted. Each girl was to place in the coffer, before its burial, one undeclared object, of which the nature was to remain known to herself only.

"What's she got in her head, that she's keen to put in, would you say?" Dicey asked, as they waited about at the bus corner.

Clare wore her thought-inflated look: she refused to answer.

"If one of my kittens died, I could put that in—I suppose? But I hope it won't, though."

"Well, don't *talk*! Don't *tell* me!"

"You think this extra-secret is good, then, Mumbo?"

"It's an idea. . . ."

"*I* think it's a good idea. We shall see, though."

"No, we shan't." Clare, turning her back, made a show of scanning in the distance for a bus. None came.

Where they waited, a hedge protected a corner garden. The privet, just into bloom, had been clipped today—perhaps rather cruelly? It gave off a knife-freshened but injured smell. Here, too, was a scarlet pillar box. Dicey leaned up against it, to ask: "Why shan't we?"

"Because that is the idea. We shall never know."

In the next days, not much was outwardly done. Dicey devoted her evenings to Cousin Roland; Mumbo, at work on the Unknown Language, was seeing no one; Sheikie simply went off to the rink and tore round and round. Anyone might have thought they had broken up. Summer-evening concerts began in the Pier Pavilion, which like a lit-up musical box admired itself in the glass of the darkening mauve sea—above, the chains of lamps along the Promenade etherealized strollers in evening dress, from the big hotels, bright-ghostly baskets of pink geraniums, and the fretwork balconies they were slung from. . . . What *was* important was that St. Agatha's, at its foot of the hill, was at such an hour extinct completely. To Dicey it fell to make sure of that—she accompanied her mother and their cousin on one of their after-dark turns in the open air, on his last evening. A taxi, part of the celebration, wafted the Feverel Cottage party to the fashionable scene —"Like a ship's deck," Cousin Roland said, looking up and down. His friend had gone down on the *Titanic*. They went across to the rail, to look out at what the Promenade lamps had now transformed into utter darkness: nothing was left but the pier below. The throb coming up—was that the concert? Wanting company, Dicey nested a hand in a pocket of her mother's tussore dust-coat. They joined the procession, taking no part in its night-hushed laughter: with it, they attained to the far end of the Promenade, turned, and came back. They ascended some marble steps into the Grand's palm lounge, where they sat down. Over them was a great chandelier. "You look lovely, but shabby," said Cousin Roland, turning his uncle's eye upon

Mrs. Piggot, who answered: "Yes, I am." He and she each
drank a glass of hock, the rest of which misted from view
in the slender bottle—iced lemonade with two long straws
was brought for Dicey. Talk turned, desultorily, to plans
for the later summer. The child, when she had syphoned
her glass empty, left them: she went down the marble
steps, outdoors. This very grand, high-up Grand was at
the St. Agatha's end of the Promenade—mounting one
rung of the horizontal railing, she crooked her stomach
forward over the top, searching round and into the gulf
where the school must be. There was nothing *but* gulf. . . .

Reported, next morning.

Clare merely said: "All went to a ball."

"Miss Brace—and Miss Kinmate, and Mademoiselle,
and Matron, and Miss Coots-Wray, and the cook, and—?"

The joke's maker cut that short. "What I mean *is*, last
night was a fluke, who knows?"

"That was what I saw."

"Miss Ardingfay," Sheikie gave out, "has a secret husband. She loves him." She went off into giggles.

"*You* see for yourself then, one night, Mumbo."

"Me go and spy about on that old Promenade? And,
when? My mother doesn't go and sit in the Grand. No,
there'll never be any night when we *can* be certain. We'll
have to chance it."

By Friday, an otherwise empty greenhouse, halfway up
the St. Agatha's garden, contained the coffer. Swaddled in
magazine pages, corded up with a skipping rope, it had
been transported thither at dead of tea-time by a hanger-on
of Aubrey Artworth's, Cuth Barnes, who believed it to be
a ferret cage—true, a heavy one. Secret ferret-keeping
and still more girls' schools were ideas which excited Cuth
Barnes deeply and strangely: he was a well-found agent.
Not otherwise highly thought of, he owned a motor bike.
Though to be a chartered accountant, he looked by nature
much like what he'd been told to look like—someone
delivering something at the back door. Anonymous, un-
complaining, and, best of all, challenged by nobody, he
heaved his burden uphill behind St. Agatha's and kicked
it into its designated place. The greenhouse, it being one
of several, wore on its doorknob Sheikie's pink-dotted
hankie, with a pink "S" swanning across one corner. Cuth
Barnes pocketed the hankie—whether from knightly love,

out of fetishism, or with some idea of blackmail, who was to say? Not he. He further, before leaving the premises, treated himself to a sideways squinnie in at the dining-room window. Munching in long rows, or talking at one another menacingly with their mouths full, the girls of St. Agatha's at this hour failed to stir up erotic thoughts. He banged his bike back into action and chuffed away. "That, let us *hope*, was the plumber," said Miss Kinmate. There'd been a vexing stoppage in the staff bathroom.

Clare had been kept in the dark as to this transaction. She could know later: that had been thought better. Any-way, she was incommunicado. By as soon as was humanly possible after six o'clock she was back home—glued to work on the syntax, under a monkey puzzle near the end of the garden of the house at present tenanted by her family. Rather deep in a valley running inland, overhung by the hill topped by the Camp, Virginia Lodge looked old enough to be almost permanent. The creeper which named it draped the verandah, on to which gave french windows —this evening open. Above, lightly streaked by the creeper, were gables, each with a dark-green spike. Since the Camp had come into being, this residence had had but one func-tion—that of being let furnished to married officers. Nice for children, convenient for entertaining, it engraved it-self pleasantly if dimly on the memories of successive regiments. It was a trifle large for the Burkin-Joneses, ex-cept when their son returned for the school holidays, bring-ing with him usually a friend or two—boys, as a rule, whose families were on service abroad. He had been their elder, now was their only boy. The blow was, poor fellow, he had bad eyesight: not a hope for the Army. The other, of bright and unblemished promise, had died of meningitis in England while they were in India.

Flat as a carpet along the floor of the valley, the unen-chanted garden was set out (as were the rooms indoors) rightly, if with no great inspiration. Ornamental trees, various shrubs, and some clumps of pampas dotted the lawn. When Clare with her two exercise books (red for grammar, yellow for glossary) first settled down on the ground, in what felt like hiding, nobody had shown signs of being about. But Mrs. Burkin-Jones, having in her the makings of a gardener, had this year planted annuals in

the flowerbeds; and this was to be one of her evenings for
tending them. In black sand-shoes similar to her daughter's,
the necessary number of sizes larger, she was now stepping
about purposefully with a watering can. The evening,
though warm and tranquil, was overcast, which gave a
peculiar glare to her very clean though last summer's white
piqué skirt, as it dipped in and out of the margin of Clare's
vision. Not till she reached the flowerbed opposite the
monkey puzzle did the mother realize the child was near
her. Just possibly, could she have wished things otherwise?
Solitude gave her an opportunity to muse. However . . .
"Prep?" she cheerily called across. "What a lot they give
you!"

Clare chawed on her pencil. Honour was in the air.
"Gnagna," she restricted herself to saying.

"Look up, when you answer," advised her mother.

The child looked up, looking terrible.

"These nasturtiums are not doing very well." The can,
having been giving warning by growing lighter, of a sudden declared itself all but empty. Tilted at whatever angle,
it barely dribbled. Mrs. Burkin-Jones shook the final
drops, fair-mindedly, over the defaulters—more than they
deserved! She then put the can down, looked back at the
house, and waited: by clockwork, out came the soldier
servant bearing a can of the same size, filled to a nicety.
Exchange was effected. "Too much in the shade, here?" she
went on to speculate. "I wonder. They ought to be doing
better."

"I hate nasturtiums."

"You can't 'hate' a flower. No one 'hates' any flower."
Yet, before moving on with the can, Mrs. Burkin-Jones
took thought. Could Clare be, possibly, doing too much
brainwork? She took a look. "Try not poke over what
you're writing. Mightn't you be better at a table?—*Your*
eyes," she asked, with unavoidable coldness, "aren't beginning to worry you, Clare, are they?"

"No."

" 'No' what?"

"No, Mother.—Thank you."

"Which reminds me, you have to go to the dentist."
Mrs. Burkin-Jones, further along the flowerbed, was
cheered by a thriving patch of love-in-a-mist. Freely she

showered that: the prettiest blue! Everything early this summer, except nasturtiums. . . . "Would you like to ask the others to tea tomorrow?"

"Why?"

"Tomorrow's Saturday." Certainties, of this calibre, had supported Clare's mother through changing scenes. As she spoke, she detected a shoot of groundsel amidst the fuzz of love-in-a-mist—shelving the can, catching her skirt up with her left hand, planting her right foot forward into the flowerbed, she stooped to pluck the intruder out. That done, straightening her back again, she went on: "Surely, by now, it must be your turn to invite them here?"

"We don't take turns." Clare spoke more than half absently. Her eyes flickered sideways, covertly, up the garden, dodging pampas and shrubs. They rested, less than an instant, on the verandah. They flickered back again. "Ever," she added, "Mother."

"I think you ought to. *I* should like you to ask them— this or next Saturday. It's not fair to be always round there at Feverel Cottage. Or, for that matter, at Mr. and Mrs. Beaker's, wherever they live."

"I don't want them. I'm busy."

Nobody seemed to hear.

"Besides, I'm tired of them."

Mrs. Burkin-Jones, not particularly tall, had stature. In a way, she was "character" embodied. Her grey-blue eyes were honesty's very colour. They gained extra lightness, bottomless clearness also from the ruddy weathering, round them, of her face. Her forehead was fearless. Plus all this, she turned to regard Clare. She had paused, before turning. She paused again. She then said: "What a way to talk about friends. . . ."

Clare was stunned.

"They may not be very clever little girls, though Diana has very good manners (it would be better, sometimes, if yours were better) like all the Piggots; and Sheila seems very energetic. But that's not the point; that's not what we're talking about. They are your friends. You never must say anything like that again, you know. Do you understand?"

Clare was intent on trying to drive her pencil, point down, into the ground beside her.

"What are you doing to your pencil?"

"Nothing," said Clare, stopping.

"No wonder you never have anything to write with," Mrs. Burkin-Jones remarked—but remarked only. She had done. It was over. No passion having, ever, been in her voice, nothing was left to die down when the voice ceased. It knew when to—not by persistence was it that she successfully cauterized her loved ones. She swished the can about again, evenly, at arm's length. "Really rather annoying," she told her daughter, in a woman-to-woman tone, "earwigs have begun again in the creeper. And on the deck chairs, some are walking about. Many people don't like them."

"Oh," said the dulled girl.

"Your father back yet, I wonder?"

"I suppose so. I saw him."

"Just now? Where?"

"Drawing-room window."

"Coming out, going in?"

"Standing."

Major Burkin-Jones's tendency to do simply that mystified his wife often, his daughter never. It arose not from infirmity of purpose but out of his happening, from time to time, to find himself where he was. Clare collected her books, untwisted her legs. Her mother asked: "Going in?"

The child walked away, then ran. She entered Virginia Lodge not directly, by the verandah, but roundabout by the porch of the kitchen wing. The long service passage, tiled, scrubbed, already heated by cooking, had at its distant end a baize swing door.

She catapulted herself round the swing door, all but into her father—again standing, this time in the hall. (Beyond, through a doorway, appeared the dining-room table, set with trails of smilax for a party of eight.) "Good evening," he said. "Busy?"

"Yes!" she said wildly.

"You're a better man than I am, Gunga Din.—How are the girls?"

"All right."

Glossy-covered, the red and the yellow books slithered against each other under her elbow: she gave them a hitch up. He gave them a glance. "Prep?"

"No." Taking his measure, not anew only, as though for the first time, she said: "An Unknown Language."

"Write me a letter in it?"

"You wouldn't understand."

"You never know."

Clare locked herself up again, more violently, into the Unknown Language, in a wedge-shaped box-room inside one of the gables, under a spike. The place was lit by panes of glass in the roof: when nothing but night came through those, she had to stop. Downstairs, she could have found a bit of candle. But downstairs was all party voices and, worse, laughter.

Six

"What have you written it in?"

"Blood."

"Good."

"It should have been all our blood. That is more usual."

"You were not there."

The assembly was in the dark of the hollow middle of the thicker of the St. Agatha's thickets. Electric torches were held downward, nozzles against the ground—now and then a beetle of light escaped. All was ready: out of the dug pit breathed raw, chalky earth—blisters were on the hands gripping the torches. At the pit's edge, the agape coffer was known to be. They saw it no more than they saw each other. Words had a night sound.

"Read it, then!"

The outside world, when they left it, had been extinct rather than, yet, dark. On the ledged hill, as for the last time they looked down, a rain of ashes might have descended. The steel sea was not yet one with the sky. Glimmer still haunted the panes of the empty greenhouse when, having shut its door for the last time, they looked back once. Even to the last of their laden journeys, it had been possible to see. They had closed the secret entry into the thicket behind them by lacing together branches. *In* here, they were into blackness itself.

"Go on."

The scroll could be heard being unrolled.

"Go *on*."

"Torches!" came the command.

Two torches rose, to bend on the writing.

In Southstone, a celebrity was playing the cello. Everybody was now in that place, listening. St. Agatha's *was* deserted, not merely looked it. And Feverel Cottage, Virginia Lodge, and 9 Ravenswood Gardens, too, had been emptied of authority. Departing, the concert-goers had asked no question, other than: "You will be good?" Nor stayed for an answer. No lie had to be told.

"Ready?"

The reader's mask was reflected, monkish, over the lit scroll. The lips parted. One by one, intoned, came forth Unknown syllables. No echoes had they: leaden they sounded. Someone shivered against a small tree: a tennis ball fell. The reader ceased. The ball, startled, fled down the sloping ground. Nobody stirred, neither did the torches. Below, the tennis ball landed on to the croquet lawn with a dead plop.

The reader asked: "Am I to go on?"

"Are you making this up?"

"I *made* it up."

"But can you read your own blood?"

The shiverer, controlling the shiver, asked: "How are we to know this is what we said?"

"Do you want this Unknown, or do you not?"

"Not."

"All right. Put out the torches."

They did. Having vanished, she spoke:

. . "*We are dead, and all our fathers and mothers. You who find this, Take Care. These are our valuable treasures, and our fetters. They did not kill us, but could kill You. Here are Bones, too. You need not imagine that they are ours, but Watch Out. No wonder you are so puzzled. Truly Yours, the Buriers of This Box.*' "

Silence, followed by a voice, marvelling: "That is what we said?"

"Yes."

" 'Truly Yours.' Are we truly theirs?"

"That's a mocking laugh."

The tree which again recorded a shiver can have harboured no other tennis ball, for none fell. Instead: "That would still more puzzle them," was said, "if it wasn't all in Unknown: they won't understand it."

"I dare say. But we said."

"Yes . . . And it may all be the same, by then? They may have no language."

"When are we going to put things into the box?"

"Now. Come on."

"When is each of us to put in her secret thing?"

"First."

"Now? Then we *must stay* in the dark. No one must listen, even. Stop your ears!"

When ears were unstopped for the third, last time, there was heard a jagged, over-strained sigh. Emanating from each, it was of all of them. A complaint, almost. Eyes, needlessly tight-shut against the dark during the dark of the three deeds, sprang again open. Blazing back into life, three torches focussed upon the coffer—taking in, on the margin, bits of flint from the pit, glinting fetter-links, sparkle from an acting-box tiara, one of the soil-clotted trowels, a scatter of the vertebrae of some larger mammal. . . . One torch broke away and played into and round the pit. "Hadn't we," asked the bearer, "better put that coffer into this hole now? When we have made it full, it will be heavy."

"No. Once it's in there, we can't get at it."

"All we have to do is to drop things in."

"All . . . ?"

"Oo-oo?"

"We are going to seal it up."

"Going to seal it up?"

"We said."

"Oh?" inquired the coolest voice, with no great concern. "Are we? Who's going to seal it up?—What with?"

"Wax.—Red."

"And a seal?"

"*Seal*? We are going to use our thumbs."

"Why our thumbs?"

"To leave prints."

"Hurts," said a voice literally from the pit (she had climbed down into it: it was by three inches deeper than the coffer). "That hurts."

"Not if you lick your thumb."

"I am not going to use *my* thumb."

"Think it will incriminate you, do you, Dicey?"

"I am not *going* to use my thumb."

Seven

The day after St. Agatha's broke up for the summer holidays came the Pococks' picnic, for Olive's birthday. The place was Wanchurch, known for immense sands which stretch out to and along the sea from under the grass-topped sea wall defending the Marsh. The Pococks were thought highly of for this choice by all children asked. By now, halfway through the long summer, everybody was sated with pebbly beaches. Out there at Wanchurch, with its ghostly name, grew sea pinks and even yellow sea poppies. And the place was your own. Its great distance away to the west of Southstone, twelve miles, made to be going there a great outing. The thoughtful Pococks had overcome what could have been a problem for some guests by chartering a small motor charabanc—open, but having a canvas hood able to be erected in case of rain. The July weather had been causing some though no great anxiety. To be on the safe side, children were asked to bring mackintoshes, on the understanding that their having done so would make it still more improbable that they would need them. Also, own rugs for sitting on. Of all things else, the Pococks took charge.

"The Pococks' picnic." "The Pococks' picnic." The sound had the spell of alliteration. Or incantation, chanted round and around IV-A classroom while school days ran out and the weather played cat-and-mouse. Every girl in IV-A had been asked, of course.

Not all the party came in the charabanc. Two or three families from the Marsh, known to the Pococks, who had a wide acquaintanceship, came over on bicycles or in pony traps. The Pococks, with the exception of Olive (who made a queenly journey amid her schoolfellows), came in their large motor car, bringing hampers, napkin-covered baskets, cake-boxes, string bags stretched to bursting-point, and so on. Aubrey Artworth borrowed Cuth's motor bike and deposited Sheikie—only, then, to tear away somewhere else. Mrs. Piggott, one of the few mothers to be invited, was gladly an occupant of the charabanc. To keep the picnic within manageable size, it had been decided to cut down on parents as far as possible. Mothers here today were old Pocock family friends—not so Mrs. Piggott, who had been asked because Mrs. Pocock often thought she looked sad. "I often wish," Mrs. Pocock had often said, "one could know her better." Here was an opportunity.

There were three or four popular fathers, and one uncle, vouched for by his owner as being funny. All were civilians. Clare Burkin-Jones's father's joining the party was, alas, known to be unlikely. "Not much hope, I don't honestly think, Mrs. Pocock," his sombre child said. As for little boys, they were not in the majority. Most of them were girls' brothers. There was a small, not highly esteemed representation from St. Swithin's. Trevor Artworth, met by Olive with Sheila, had chivalrously been invited by Olive—brushed off the Cuth motor bike by his elder brother, who'd asked him if he imagined this was a bus, he had to make a rush for the charabanc, into which he'd succeeded in squeezing himself at the last moment.

Motor conveyances drew up, there to wait for the rest of the afternoon, on the landward side of the sea wall. When the charabanc came to port, the Pococks, like noble humanized ants, still were staggering to and fro with hampers. The children out of the charabanc cataracted down off the wall at another point, shouting—at the foot, however, they fell silent, looking around them, calculatingly, at the large spaces. Mrs. Piggott, wearing the tussore dust-coat and with her hat bound on with a chiffon motor veil, scrambled up the land side of the sea wall among the children, on the heels of her daughter. When she reached the top, wind caught the transparent mauve ends of the veil, sending them flying against the sky—which was so lightly grey as to itself seem a veil over wide light. There she stood a minute, looking down at the sands, smiling at the beginnings of so much pleasure: a weather-signal. She was the first indication that there *was* a wind, playful so far.

French cricket got going, thanks to the uncle's being an eager player. Though loose, jumbled, and powdery and swept up into ridges under the wall, sand elsewhere was sleek as a seal, firm underfoot. Younger ones, who'd cluttered the journey with spades and buckets, started digging with senseless enthusiasm. Barefooted escapers, among them Dicey, went wading forward into the sea, girls stuffing their starched frocks into their bloomers of stuff to match—wade as you might, however, mile after mile, the sea was not yet up to your knees. Thinly running over the flats of sand, the water here was as warm as June, warmer than today.

Would the kettles boil, though? Up there in the encampment among the sand ridges, over which rugs were already spread and on which dozens of cups balanced, sounded grown-up laughter bright with anxiety. Little stoves' methylated blue flames danced sideways, all but flattening out: the enthroned kettles were seeming barely to notice the flames were there—driftwood fires *might* after all have done better? Fathers knelt down like camels, interposing their forms with coats held open, manfully between the flames and the blowy draught. Mothers unpacked scones and potted-meat sandwiches or cut up gingerbread tensely but steadily, as though nothing were happening—or rather, not happening. Mrs. Pocock, imploringly watched by Olive, landed the birthday cake on to its silver platter. "Sand won't blow on to it, will it?" asked unheard Olive. Holding back her long glossy dark hair, worn flowing today, Olive leaned over the cake, to read her name.

In the valley of the kettles began a humming. Heads turned that way, glances were exchanged—not yet did anyone dare speak. Like a medium giving off ectoplasm, the leading kettle gave off a wandering thread of steam.

Instinct now drew the children towards the camp. The game broke off; waders turned in the water and came back; young diggers stepped out over the battlements they had patted into existence round their castles. Mannerly, not sandily trampling over the rugs, all the assembling children moved one way: they surrounded the cake in a dense circle—those first there giving place that others might see. All in silence looked down upon the inscription, written in curling pink sugar handwriting on the white iced top. Some had to decypher it upside down.

A sort of victory wreath surrounded the words—*glacés* cherries, crystallized green angelica set like jewels into the icing. Twelve candles rose from the sugar in a coloured grove.

"Olive," said the first to speak, "this is your cake?"

"Yes."

"When are you going to light the candles?"

"Soon," Olive said, looking apprehensive.

"Twelve . . ." said another, who, having re-counted the candles, looked at Olive across them not yet with hostility but across a gulf.

"Yes," Olive said. "Isn't it extraordinary?" She licked a finger and held it up to the wind.

Turning away, in response to a call to sit down to tea, the children made determinedly for places on the more

eligible rugs. The grown-up servitors threw themselves into
action. Successful search having been made for tea cloths
wherewith to grip the now white-hot handles of metal tea-
pots, a brimming cup, or for juniors a mug of milk, soon
found its way into every hand. One of the licences of this
feast was that it was to be possible to *begin* with jam: Mrs.
Piggott, entrusted by Mrs. Pocock with the jam jar, dealt
out dollops on to split buttered scones extended towards
her by many applicants, doing so equitably and beautifully.
The uncle conjured into existence a mandoline and went on
to strum on it, though for some time given no great encouragement. He began to hum, in a manner which made
it clear he would later sing—under cover of the uncertain
music an almost complete marquee of held-up coats came
into existence round Olive and the cake. Ceremonially
handed a box of matches, she stretched forth a royal, un-
trembling hand: she succeeded not only in lighting all
twelve candles but in blowing them out again before the
wind could. One whiff came from the charred wicks.

Something about the destruction (for so it seemed) of
the moment of the candles let loose not exactly disorder
but an element of scrimmage about the party. Outcasts
upon an outlying rug, the St. Swithin's boys started punch-
ing each other cautiously but repeatedly. A Marsh girl by
sticking a foot out suddenly kicked in the kidneys Muriel,
seated in front of her. Diana Piggott, singled out by a
sand flea, bumped down her cup and began to scratch—
the cup heeled over, partially scalding Trevor, who made
away on all fours to a safer rug. The uncle incurred the
scorn of Clare Burkin-Jones—in vain he trailed cheery
choruses: not a voice took up. "Fool," snorted the child.

"If you call anybody a fool, you go to Hell, I may as
well tell you," said Sheila Beaker crisply, over her
shoulder.

"Where did you pick up *that* information?"

"Sunday school."

"*You* never went to—"

"*Oh* yes I did. Till I took up toe-dancing."

The birthday cake made its rounds as something to
eat. Shattered pink writing clung to the icing tops of the
slices. This was a cherry cake, very rich in fruit.—"Olive,"
quoth one of the fathers, helping himself, "this is a day we
shall long remember."

"It's very kind of you to say so," Olive returned, with her usual composure. Stillness fell, for an instant, on the grown-ups (who resting from their duties sat in a group), transforming them into figures in a *tableau*—once animated again, they were never more so. Mrs. Piggott was busy rescuing the spoon from the deep jam jar into which it had sunk. The spoon came out sticky all the way up: with a candid stealth like her daughter's she licked her fingers, then wiping them on her handkerchief. "We shall most of us be going away," she remarked, "now." This was true of many. August stood for dispersal. The Pococks were known to be going to Switzerland, D.V.; Mrs. Piggott and Dicey were off (as soon as tomorrow) to Cumberland, where a delightful old rectory had been taken by Cousin Roland for these holidays, for them and himself. Sheikie was off, shortly, to grace Herne Bay for as long as Daddy would spare her to Irene. The West Highlands were the bourne of one family, the Lorna Doone Devon moors of another. Muriel owned a grandmother on the Isle of Wight. And so on. The Burkin-Joneses only spoke of no plans.

Mr. Pocock took out his half-hunter watch. "Three-legged races, next?" he said to his wife.

"Oh, Mortimer, do you think so?—Just after tea?"

"Those make them fight, you know," said a mother. "They fight one another if they don't win. Freddie came back from some sports with his ear bitten. Not badly, of course."

"Who by?" asked Mrs. Piggott, gazing out of the triangle formed by the brim of her hat and her mauve veil.

"As I was saying, his partner—some little girl. 'Don't be a baby, another time,' I said to him, so I don't think he will."

"Even at egg-and-spoon races," said another mother, "they knock each other down."

"I don't believe we have brought eggs," said Mrs. Pocock. "Or did we, Mortimer?"

"We decided not to."

"Prisoner's base? French and English? Follow my leader?"

"Most of them are too big, I'm afraid."

"What we have brought," said resolute Mr. Pocock, "is an excellent rope for a tug-of-war." He walked away to the hampers, to look about for it.

Too late. The children were singing. It was a terrible wolf-like ululation, with a spectre of tune in it. Some, heads back, simply droned aloud to the sky. Any true voice, so far as it ever led, was once more drowned. Singers astray in a verse for a line or two boomed back again into the chorus with the greater vigour. Liked, the song seemed on whole known. Overwrought by what he had brought about, the uncle cantered behind them with the accompaniment: some few notes twanged, lunatic, on the air.

"*Wa-ay* down upon the Swan-eeee River,
Fa-ar, far away,
The-ere's where my heart is turning ever,
The-ere's where the old folks stay.
All up and down the *who-ole* creation
Sa-adly I roam,
Still longing for the o-old plantation,
A-and for the old *fo-olks* at home.

"A-ALL the world is SA-AD and drear-*eeeee*,
EV'RY-where I roam,
O darkies, how my HEART grows WE-E-EARY
FA-A-AR from the old folks at home!

"*A-all ro-ound* the little farm I wander'd
Wh-en I was *young*;
Then any happy *da-a-ays* I squander'd,
Ma-any the songs I sung.
When I was playing *wi-ith m-y* brother,
Ha-a-appy was I.
O-o-oh, take me to my kind O-O-OLD moth-er,
The-ere let me live a-a-and die!

"A-all the WO-O-ORLD is sad A-AND drear-ee,
Ev'ry-WHERE I roam,
O darkies, HOW my heart GRO-OWS wear-ee,
Fa-a-ar from the old FO-O-OLKS at home!

"O-one little hut *amo-o-ong* the bushes,
O-o-one that I love,
Sti-ill sadly to my *mem'ry* rushes,
No-o-o matter where I rove.
When sha-all I see the *bees* a-humming
All *ro-o-ound* the comb?

When *sha-all* I hear the *ban*-JO strumming
Do-own in my *go-o-ood* old home?

"A-ALL the WO-O-ORLD is sad and DREAR-ee,
EV'RY-where I . . ."

"How they enjoy it," said Mrs. Piggott, to nobody in
particular. The grown-up group was smaller by two fathers,
who had paced away from it frowningly locked in talk,
smoking cigarettes. The mother of Freddie scooped up a
palmful of loose sand and absorbedly watched it run
from between her fingers in slow skeins, as sand runs
through an hour-glass. Two others murmured to one another
with tense rapidity—caught at it, they moved apart. A remaining father reclined with hat tipped forward: his moustache beneath it was inexpressive. "Not a cheerful song,"
Mrs. Pocock laughed, "for a birthday, is it!"

"But there is not going to be a war, is there?" asked Mrs.
Piggott.

Mrs. Pocock stood up. Signalling to her husband, who
was making his way back with the coil of rope, she cried:
"Races *would* be better—you were quite right! They had
better run."

Everyone started moving outward from the encampment
on to the firmer sands, which were growing larger. The few
breakwaters, sticking out far apart like teeth left in an
otherwise broken comb, ended, high and dry, so far short
of the sea that seaweed here and there clinging to them like
dead ivy was the one sign that they had ever been anything
but alone. Also, considerably to the west of the encampment (for no one cared to picnic in its vicinity) a vast
iron drainpipe, flaking with rust, issued out of the base of
the sea wall. Though not carrying, probably, anything more
noxious than overflow from the dykes draining the Marsh,
the thing had the look of being a sewer: its mouth was
slimed on the lower lip by a constant trickle which, on its
way seaward, grooved for itself a miniature river valley
before exhaustedly losing itself in the sand. This had to be
crossed, for the sports ground, demarcated by the fathers
and uncle, lay beyond.

Everything from now onward was a matter of distance
—distance from what? The organized running or staggering or hopping or crawling of the children (for the races

now being put afoot without intermission and like clockwork were of all kinds, relay, three-legged, one-legged,
wheelbarrow) dazzled away out of the view of watchers
in the sharp light coming, level, between the accentuated
clouds. Nor were sands and sky resounding with shouts
and laughter: over the contests reigned a demonic silence,
punctuated only by whistle-blowing or words of command.
No part of the picture was for an instant still—each athletic
event took place in a nimbus of scuffle in which few on-
lookers failed to be taking part. Exactly what *was* going
on was hard to discern.

The mothers, having been piling cups together in the
encampment, were the last to leave it. Soon after they'd
crossed the trickle, on their way to the sports ground,
Trevor came tearing zigzig towards and past them, in the
direction of the drain-pipe. In pursuit was Dicey, abetted
by Muriel. Sand not only caked his knees but was round
his mouth. His spectacles were, it was to be seen, gone: he
ran all but blindedly. His pursuer incarnated most of the
cast of *Struwwelpeter*, most strikingly Cruel Frederick,
"the great, long, red-legg'd scissor man," and Harriet-and-
the-Matches—she brandished a matchbox (Olive's?) from
which flew many of the contents.

"Dicey!" expostulated her mother.

"A little over-excited," said their hostess.

Both looked back. Trevor ducked, doubled, and disappeared up the drain-pipe, Dicey after him like a terrier.
Muriel stuck her head in, but thought better of it: "Stinks,"
she said, making a *moue* at the grown-ups. Dicey came
shunting out of the drain-pipe, behind first. Her mother,
retracing a step to be better heard, asked: "What *are* you
doing?"

"Playing," explained the child, knocking back her hair.

"Suppose he gets typhoid in there, poor little boy?"

"*Whoosh!*" cried Dicey, flailing her arms at Muriel—
who in turn fled. She was given chase to. Mrs. Pocock,
having taken this opportunity to appraise her friend's little
girl, said, with a spontaneity the greater for having surprise
in it: "She's going to be pretty, you know, when she grows
up!"

"Oh, I do hope so," breathed Mrs. Piggott.

"She moves well."

Mrs. Piggott went to the mouth of the drain-pipe and, bending down, said pleasantly: "Trevor?"

His voice, coming whonging along from some way up, answered—with a frigidity one could understand: "Yes, Mrs. Piggott?"

"Won't you come out?"

"I like it in here, thank you."

So they walked on. Mr. Pocock, coming to meet them, said: "I thought we might soon finish up with the tug-of-war. Where did I put the rope?"

"It is near the rugs." Mrs. Pocock went back with her husband to the encampment, to begin to make ready the lemonade for the athletes and further sandwiches, ham this time, with which the picnic was to conclude. Mrs. Piggott, left to herself, decided that Dicey had better not take part in the tug-of-war—it would be better for her to calm down. She then went away into other thoughts as (other mothers being some way ahead) she advanced solitary towards the *mêlée*, searching for her child.

Children had collected along a breakwater—some leaning, some climbing about on the iron stanchions, some sitting along the blunted top. Among them was Clare. She had taken off one sandshoe, in order to pick from the thin black sole glass particles of Trevor's trodden-on spectacles. She was working away at this with listless intentness: her wiry hair fell forward, darkness encompassed her—she neither looked up nor spoke. Dicey came flumping against the breakwater, close by. "*That*," mused Dicey, contentedly sticking her nose over Clare's task, "will teach him not to be so superior another time.—*And*, look!" she commanded, thrusting her rust-reddened hands into Clare's view. Little notice was taken. "Oh, stop picking away at that old shoe!"

"I don't want glass to work through and cut my foot."

Dicey took back her hands, to admire them herself. "This is out of the inside of that pipe. What do you think I did? I struck matches at him."

"Couldn't have, in this wind."

"Oo, but he doesn't like the *noise*, even! So he rushes away from that, even. . . . So what *I* did's going to teach him not to be so superior another time, too, isn't it?"

Not another particle glittered on the black rubber. Clare

tugged the shoe on again, pulled the lace tight, knotted it with a jerk. "I don't care who is superior another time."

"I don't know what you want. You won two races."

"Three.—Well?"

Dicey resignedly heaved round and hung herself on her stomach over the breakwater, head down. She plucked about in some ancient seaweed. "There are some shells," she reported, "caught in this, but they're no good.—I say, Mumbo?"

"Well?"

"Who did kill that Australian duke?"

Confounded the minute she had spoken, the fool child hung for a minute longer upside down, as she was, in shame. Then she righted herself and got off the breakwater. Had the skies fallen? Every one of the children was staring her way.—No, though, not at her but beyond Mumbo at Sheikie, who was executing a tightrope two-step. This was going on further up the breakwater, where the structure heightened as it approached the wall. To and fro, backward then forward along the wood-bone, bone-dry, dry-slippery edge of the top-most board jaunted the airily balanced dancer—going away, returning, turning each turn into a nonchalant pirouette. She danced her music.

Her hair, in honour of Olive, wore four bows: one behind each ear, one at the end of each plait. *She* wore an American new-style little girl's dress: chequered gingham. Her sandshoes, from whose points she never descended, were not only sandless but snow white. The clean fine pink line dividing her skull in two was to be seen when she turned her back, as was the line of big black American buttons. She was distinct as a paper doll.

Wind came in a gust at her, bending her over. She wobbled once—once was enough! Off she sprang from the breakwater, of her own volition. Away she strolled.

Clare had turned her head away, heavily, towards the dance. Why not? It remained away, though the dance was over. "What are you *still* looking at?" Dicey wanted to know, uneasy. "Or what?"

Better have let Clare be: she came back doomfully into profile. "Austrian," she enunciated, "Archduke. Get that into your head."

"Oh, all right, Mumbo," said the willing learner.

"*It's not all right!*"

Mrs. Piggott's little girl recoiled, as though hit at. "It's not my fault. . . ."

Clare said: "Nobody said it was."

"Oh, look—there's Mother!"

Mrs. Piggott and Dicey, all by themselves, walked calmingly along the edge of the sea. But it receded, slithering back, stealing away. So they came to a stop, side by side, to watch. A chill had begun. Mrs. Piggott was carrying Dicey's jersey, so she pulled it on over the child's head; then, when the arms had angled their way into the sleeves, on down. She then buttoned her own dust-coat, which for this evening as it had turned out to be was a little light. The masterful wind again and again tugged untied the bow of her veil, so she gave up and with her right hand held the chiffon gathered together under her chin. The child's hair blew into briny rat's-tails.

They watched. The withdrawing sea washed over less of the sand each time. Its retreat made land seem itself to be an advancing tide, hard sleek wet sand-ripples dulled only by clottings of dead form. From across the shrinking watery miles came an expiring sigh—not like the sound of wind, a sigh in itself.

Or, desultorily, the mother and daughters stepped here or there picking up shells, which by being wet seemed more rare than they were. Dicey from time to time took a look back, up the long stretch, at the far-away picnic—which though in view, in miniature, was in hearing only in gusts and starts.

"They're at the lemonade, now. *And* eating something."

"I'm sure there'll be some lemonade left, darling."

"I don't care. I would like a sandwich, though—if they're ham? I mean, sometime."

"There are hundreds of sandwiches: I saw them."

Next time the child happened to look, there was being a disturbance—*not*, anybody could see, of a catastrophic kind, nothing like a wasp. No, what was occurring was a surprise, by the look of it a complete one, delightful in particular to the grown-ups, though no children showed signs of objecting to it. Yes, there was being an arrival—*had* been one (for there was an extra figure) but was in a way still being one, insofar as nothing had yet subsided. The extra figure stood out not only for the reason that it was standing (as for that matter were several others) but because it was, from here even, unmistakable. Fair, tall, and with that carriage of the head, this could be no one but Major Burkin-Jones—into mufti and with his usual air of unconcern.

The child said nothing, merely went back diligently to amassing shells. Mrs. Piggott roused herself from her thoughts to ask: "They're not packing up yet, are they?"

"No. I think somebody else has come."

"Poor Clare, I wish it was her father."

"I *think* it is."

Mrs. Piggott, indicating a fresh wet patch of uncovered sand, said: "There are more there." (The two of them were about to start on making a shell box: this would be something to do if it rained in Cumberland.)

Sand deadens steps till they are near. Not till Mrs. Piggott saw Dicey waving did she also, not startled, see Major Burkin-Jones. She let her veil go that they might shake hands. He said: "You're off tomorrow, Clare tells me?"

"Yes. We—"

The child hastened up, to tell the beautiful man: "This is our last day!"

"Rather windy," smiled Mrs. Piggott, in extenuation of the behaviour of her veil, whose flyings and flutterings round her he watched intently. "But it has been, is being, a lovely picnic!"

"*Mumbo* said you couldn't possibly come!"

"Nothing like being unexpected, is there?—No," he told them, in justice to his daughter, "at one time this morning it didn't look like it. Then I found I could, for a few minutes. That seemed better than nothing. So—"

The child asked, somewhat austerely: "You wanted very *much* to come to this picnic?"

"Didn't you?" he parried.

"Oh, yes. But I'm not sure whether I have enjoyed it. It's been too long."

"Pity we can't change places—times, I mean. Mine's too short."

"Why did you waste time changing your clothes?"

"I don't know. Habit, I suppose?"

"You could have come in your medals."

"I don't think I have any."

"I suppose you will."

"I thought," he said, deserting the daughter for the mother, "I'd like to wish Olive luck, see how you were all getting on, pick up Clare while I was about it, and so on.— Cumberland's where you're off to, tomorrow?"

"We're going to be there till the end of August."

"End of August. Some wonderful country up there, I've always heard."

"Yes, I believe there's the most beautiful scenery."

"You'll like that, I know," he told her, looking at the eyes which would see the scenery. "So you'll be happy there. So it will be something to know you're there. To think of you there. *You*—" He stopped.

"Mother, will there be caves?"

"I don't know, darling." She turned to him as though to ask: now they were looking each other in the face. "I don't know," she repeated. "I don't know. Do you?"

"No. It's beyond me. Altogether beyond me. And always will be, as long as I live."

Folding her arms she pressed them against herself, over the light coat.

"You're cold!" he cried out.

The child looked up.

"No," said Mrs. Piggott, "but I think Dicey and I ought to walk about again. And you go back to the others, to the picnic. There can't be many more of your minutes left, are there?"

"No."

"Well, then." She held out her hand. "Goodbye."

"Goodbye." Her hand had been ice-cold.

"Good*bye*, Major Burkin-Jones!"

"Goodbye, Dicey."

But the child held him in that lost-looking stare which may mean nothing. "Be good," he said, for something to say—and this time did smile.

Mrs. Piggott looked away to the west, along the ink-clear line of the wide bay, from one to another of the martello towers, some whole, some broken. Her daughter came and hooked herself to her elbow, while the long, few steps they had heard coming towards them were to be heard going away. They ceased to be heard—the child twisted her head over her shoulder, to see. She jerked the elbow. "Mother, he's not gone, yet!"

Still not far away from them he had stopped, turned and

was standing. They saw him. He saw them, calmly and with great clarity.—Was there more he wanted, could there be anything else? Mrs. Piggott, though moving no more than he did, may have sent some wordless inquiry. He said: "Just goodbye." His eyes rested on their alike faces. "God bless you," he said to them—turned, and this time was gone.

"Mother?"

"Yes?"

"Why did he say that? He said—"

"I know, darling."

"What made him? He—"

"I don't know, darling."

"He never—"

"Oh, Dicey—*Dicey!*"

So the child fell silent, sometimes rubbing her cheek slowly against the tussore of the coat sleeve, sometimes rolling her face round against it and breathing into it, with a low loving continuous snuffling sound. Where the warmth of the breath made its way through the stuff moisture remained. Mrs. Piggott asked: "Have you said goodbye to Clare?"

"Say goodbye to *Mumbo?*"

"Haven't you?—Aren't you going to? Wish her happy holidays."

"She's not going away."

"But you won't be seeing her, don't you see, for some time: it will seem quite a long time."

"She'll be gone now, won't she?"

"Go and see. Go and try—run, darling!"

Off went Dicey. Alone, her mother began to walk again. A pile of shells earlier built up no longer was where she last saw it. Even since he had gone there was more land.

Clare would have been gone (her father, expecting to have been gone, waited for her at the car) had she not been called back. The reckoning following on a picnic had laid bare not only her mackintosh, name-taped as St. Agatha's demanded, but what by elimination only could be the Burkin-Jones rug: all others had been by now claimed. Now on the trudge to the car for the second time, she dragged the belongings behind her like a fallen tent. Her blouse, all of it untucked from her skirt, ballooned in the wind, making her skinnier by contrast. Her shock of hair waged its individual battle with the wind. She was plodding her way over and through the loose sand under the sea wall to the first place where the wall could be climbed up.

Could the runner's course, diagonally up from the sea, intersect that other? Dicey had started late.

The sobbing runner, desperate, could not shout. Too great the wind, too little her breath. Wasting seconds by halting, she tangled her arms up into signals and pointings —might not somebody see her from the encampment? Might not somebody see her and shout to Mumbo? Somebody saw, did shout—but did Mumbo hear? Not she. Nor was she seeing anything: on, on pigheadedly she was pegging. Now she was nearing the place where you climbed up.

"*Mu-u-u-umb-O!*"

Now she was at it. Now she *was* climbing up, scornfully hauling the tent-things after her. Now, on to her feet, she dragged the unfortunates across the grass of the wall's top, to hurt them (as though to perdition) ahead of her. And now?

Alone in the middle of the empty sands wailed Dicey.

"Mum-BO-O-O!"

The rough child, up there against the unkind sky, on the rough grass, glanced at and over the sands once. She threw a hand up into a rough, general wave. Then she leaped down on the land side of the sea wall. She had disappeared.

PART III

One

❧❦❧

"Is Miss Burkin-Jones here?" asked Dinah, walking into the Mopsie Pye shop.

She addressed herself to the younger of two women who, alike in aubergine jerseys, each lightly exhibiting some sports jewellery, stood about to meet customers' any needs. The shop held nothing so formal as a counter: more inspired use had been made of space—wide shelves, with receding others above them, ran along both side walls; narrow tables only, not many, were in the middle. The length no less than the glitter of the prospective made the shop surprising to enter, after the smallness (stylish though that had been rendered) of the street-frontage. Probably, a back yard had been taken in: whether or not, the extension was for the greater part roofed by glass— through which, this morning, misty October sunshine came wandering in, to be met by lit though seductively shaded lamps throwing glow on the wares on shelves and tables. The newcomer blinked, as anyone might. The wares were some grouped, some spread, in measured profusion. Some dangled, even a little above the eye—and were a-twirl, at the moment, in the current of air from the door. Nor was any of this in vain. When Dinah entered, five or six gazing persons were moving about in a tranced state which looked like culminating in buying.

The shop's far end was cut off by a partition, in which was an archway partly masked by a curtain. "Or is she busy?" added the tall visitor, subdued.

"Well, she's checking in stock. But she's expecting you, isn't she? Mrs. Delacroix?"

"Mrs. Delacroix. Yes."

Clare appeared in the archway, shoving aside the curtain. She filled the archway. Over her top part she wore a light cotton jacket (half-length overall) unbuttoned. Beneath it she was encased, decisively as ever, in something dark. The amount there had come to be of her, not in bulk only, had to be reckoned with.—The other day, had the dazzle up on the uplands dissolved her somewhat? Here, on her own ground, the owner was out of proportion to her shop. In it, she threw everything out of scale. "Hullo," she said. "You're early."

"Am I?"

"Never mind. Come in."

She stepped back, to let Dinah through.

Shelves, at this other side of the archway, multiplied. The glass roof continued. This back room was partly store, partly office. Much *was* being unpacked, and all space seemed taken. On a stout table stood a crate-sized carton, top flaps open: yet to be tackled, another waited below. Progress so far made could be estimated by the number of the empties stacked in a corner. From under a bottom shelf protruded a major packing-case, metal-cornered, formidably intact. These shelves were more, and more inchoately, crowded than had been those on the showroom side of the arch: floods of checked-in stock, requiring dusting, had as islands among them a saturnine-looking telephone and a box lid serving as tray for carpenter's tools. Deep litter hid most of the floor from view.

"Well, you found your way here."

"Yes," agreed Dinah. "Nice to see me, is it?" she tendered hopefully—then, not waiting, knocked back her hair and rather wildly burst out: "Oh my heavens, though!"

"I don't wonder. Whatever time did you start?"

"I don't know. It was still rather dark."

"And drove like blazes. Any breakfast, had you?"

"Oh, yes. Francis was wide awake."

"Stop for coffee anywhere on the way?"

"I hate stopping."

"You hate coffee?"

"I said, I hate stopping!"

"*That* one can see. Eyes starting out of your head."

Dinah instantly, in a quoting voice, said: " 'Oh, dear, am I a shock? It's been such years, hasn't it!' (No, you

missed that one: try another.) 'Any objection?'—Not a
squeak out of *her*, by the way, since. Or have you had?
Nn-nn?"

Clare said merely: "Better have coffee now, then." She
turned her head to the arch and bawled: "Phyllida!" The
younger aubergine, eager, came into view. "When there's
a minute, be a very kind girl, will you, and nip along to La
Poupée? Coffee for two."

"Surely!"

"Need money, or we do we have tick there?"

"Tick there, Miss Burkin-Jones."

"Good.—Oh, and Phyllida, buns!"

"Mumbo, I don't *want* buns!"

"Well, I do, or shall." The sprite having vanished, Clare
rolled round her heavy eyes in their heavy pouches. "What
are you," she demanded to know, "in a state about?"

"I'm not in a state—state yourself! I just don't want
buns: surely that's not abnormal?"

To show, Dinah lighted a cigarette and drew on it at
some length, abnormally calmly. She then looked back
through the arch—from where she stood, she saw the shop
in reverse. In reverse, it confounded her still more. As
minutely as could be possible from a distance, she examined all things (twice over, those which hung in the air)
with a blend of ignorant wonder, deference, some suspicion,
though not mockery. Clare seized the occasion to finish
unpacking the opened carton: anything in it, now, being
near the bottom, her arms plunged in up to the shoulders.
Shavings gave out a deprived rustle as, one by one, wrapped
objects were mined from their bedded depths, to wait on
the table—from which, all being done, Clare deposed the
carton. "Well?" she then asked, brushing her hands together.

"We-ell . . . My Weird Sister, you *have* got a kitchen
here! I mean honestly, haven't you? Trade terms for your
weirder sister, I do hope? Anything in my line, have you
this morning? Any wombats' wombs or anything—pow-
dered, naturally?"

"*Tcha!*"

The frivolous one, making use of some shelves by standing leaning against them, was in good spirits. Whether or
not she had been funny, she thought she had; in any event,
she had quite revived. Contentedly simmering with mirth,

there she was. Clare's reaction was to remark, grumblingly: "First time I've seen you properly dressed." This referred to the suit worn today, to the burnish given to the hatless head, and to well-behaved though supple long narrow shoes: Italian, extremely probably. On them, Clare concentrated for so long that the wearer ended by drawing one foot up, to take a look herself—meanwhile seeing no harm in pointing out, mildly, though in her tone of withheld reproach: "This is only the second time you have seen me—since the gap." She went on in her mother's voice: "I'm sorry, though, if I was untidy the other day. I was in a hurry to get to the blasted heath. And I'd no idea we were going to be so grand: you, Sheikie, Francis. Frank in a tie, even, as though for London.—You never saw him."

"No, never saw him."

"He half-saw you."

"Better than nothing," said Clare affably—her attention, however, was on the move away. She directed a calculating scowl at her last (it might have been lifelong) enemy, the impregnable-looking packing-case. She side-longed a glance at her armoury, chisels, hammer, etc., as though fingers itched in her mind. She confined herself (for the time being) to moving in on the packing-case, laying hands on it, and giving it a tug, haul, or attempted heave. *How* heavy? Ton weight: budge it did not. "What about him?" she asked.

"Frank? He's a neighbour."

"I see. Nice neighbours on the whole, have you, down there?"

"Oh, *yes!*" said Dinah, with vague fervour. She asked: "How have you been?"

"Since when?"

"Last week, was all I was meaning."

"Much the same. And you?"

"Oh, Mumbo—anything *but!*"

In came Phyllida, with the La Poupée coffee tray. Sanely, with her ministrant smile, she brushed *débris* from their end of the table. "You'll need *chairs*," she went on to say, discerningly: two were found, cleared, given a flick with a duster, placed face-to-face.

"Thank you so much!"

"Not at all, Mrs. Delacroix. (Rock cakes looked nice this morning, Miss Burkin-Jones!)"

Round these cups, indeed around all this china, dolls danced ring-a-ring. All were brightly got up—amongst them danced teddy bears. "I thought *those* were over?" blinked Dinah, suddenly, closely gazing. No bear wore a bow. She shaded her eyes from the top glare.

"Traditional, by now, aren't they?" Clare poured coffee. "Don't your grandchildren have any?"

"I don't know," admitted the other, looking distracted.

"Too much light?"

"We-ell . . ."

The proprietor rose, rather harshly pushed back her chair, and unwound a cord: down from its roller rolled a taut dark overhead green blind. Their end of the table entered a thought-dark arbour. Clare remarked: "You didn't mind all that sky."

"Where—when?"

"Up on that hill of yours."

"No.—Oh, you were too bad, you *did* run out!"

"When are we talking about?"

"Last time. The *end* of the other day! All of a sudden, gone. Off, in a flash. No warning, barely goodbye. Running jump into that car of yours, door banged, whizz, pouf—out of Applegate gate!" The complainer paused, took a gulp of coffee. She then stared at Clare, straight across the table. "Could *you* not bear it a minute longer?"

Clare put her nose in the air. She went into profile. Mopsie Pye stated: "Had to be off. Was already late on the road. Am pretty busy, you know. Time's money."

"Oh, yes . . . But there she and I were left, you see. Two strange women. Totally disconnected, from that moment. And on top of that, poor Sheikie could hardly stand; she drooped like—"

"Nonsense. Strong as a horse."

"Anyway, her nose began to go blue. She had had rather a day, if one comes to think. Bleary was not the word, though I couldn't blame her. So what did we then do? Oh yes, I gave her tea."

"That cannot have cost you much: one lemon?"

"On the contrary, she got outside lashions of buttered toast, I was glad to see. She may simply not like eating when you're about, like some animals won't eat in front of their captors."

Clare all but blew up. "*That* come's nicely from you!—as she'd say herself."

"Not at all. I just gave a whiff of the bait, you rounded her up. Yes you did, too, Mumbo! Unilaterally whatnot-ing in that Harrods teashop."

"Not Harrods. However. Go on."

"You're staring at me, aren't you?" asked Dinah, stopping.

"You're coming on, you know."

"Mentally? That you could have noticed the other day, I should have thought."

"Was in a riot of impressions," said Clare rudely.

"Well, when the toast was gone I had an idea. I put her into the car and we went to Frank's. 'We'll have drinks with him,' I said to her, very slowly and clear, on the way over. 'Then, what he'll love—though sad that you have to go—will be, to take you in his car to your train.' "

"That brighten her up?"

"She faintly opened one eye. Anyway, there I left her.—What I never shall know is, how I got the car home. Even that short way, Mumbo, that short way. (No, not drink: anyone knows about that.) When I had, I looked at my bed and thought, 'Soon, sleep'—lay down, to see how sleep was going to feel, and never got up. I slept, slept, slept, slept. I was pole-axed."

Clare let slip: "So was I."

"*You* slept, slept, slept?—Even," Dinah was not to be kept from saying, "though time's money?"

"Even though."

"Where were we both, I wonder?"

Clare said: "More coffee?"

The visitor, receiving her cup back, ground out one cigarette in its saucer, then lit another. "Mind where you chuck that match away!" Clare said sharply. The smoker looked appreciatively at the floor—which, still more since the emission from the late carton, was awash with shavings, flammable-looking wadding, thin twists and untwists of flame-hungry paper. "Yes, we *could* blaze up, couldn't we! All the same, what do you take me for?" She got up, crossed to one of the shelves, and extinguished the match into a dish. Not content with that, she immolated her cigarette, grinding it out into the dish also. She then went back and looked into the dish again. "Who's 'Paul'?"

Clare, who'd been gazing up at the dark-green blind, asked: "Who?"

"Written at the bottom of a dish."

"Oh, a dog, then. Yes, we do line in those."

Dinah, pacing, clicking a thumb and finger, called: "Paul! Paul! Paul!—Sounds out all right," she had to admit, "but could a dog not be a prig, with a name like that?"

"I saw no dog in your country home?"

"Francis could never feel for one, he says. So what would become of the dog when I went away?"

"You go away often?"

"Now and then. Here or there. Frank has a Labrador, but it bites, so it mostly stays at his cottage. . . . *Mumbo*! Not a squeak out of Sheikie one can just bear; but . . . ?"

"Sorry, sorry. Busy."

"Oh, yes. You said."

"Rude? Should have written a bread-and-butter?"

"Even that," said the sad one, "would have been better than nothing. I wondered whether you'd telephone."

"Well, I didn't."

"No.—Last night, when *I* rang up, you sounded so cross."

"You made me jump, suddenly coming through like that."

"That's the worst of telephones. What were you doing?"

"Well, I was in my flat."

"Of course you were, else you couldn't have answered. What were you doing?"

"Thinking about you," said Clare crossly.

"And why not?—What's your flat like?"

"Well, it's a flat."

"Can't I come and see it?"

"If you like. If I'm there."

"Oh, you're so genial!"

Clare looked into the coffee pot: not a drop more coffee. Dinah's forgotten cupful the more annoyed her. Reclaiming the cup, she stacked it with other La Poupée items on the gay tray, then walked off and poked the tray through the arch. "Phyllida! Can we get this out of the way?"

"Miss Burkin-*Jones, nobody's* touched the rock cakes!"

"Oh? Take 'em back, eat 'em. Do as you think."

"Are you terribly tired this morning, Miss Burkin-Jones?"

"No."

"Shall I *shut* the curtain?"

"Do as you like."

During the colloquy, Dinah'd remained in mid-air, mouth open. Coming back, Clare sighted a look of perplexity, dereliction, in the beautiful face. "Sorry," she said —going nevertheless to the other, working end of the table, where she set about unwrapping the things from the carton: veined milk glass cereal bowls or saucers, greenish, heavy enough in cut to seem alabaster, all alike, one by one came to light. Dinah came nearer, saying: "Couldn't I help? Couldn't I put those somewhere?"

"Nn-nn, thank you. I know where they go."

"You could tell me. They're pretty, aren't they—rather? What are they for, though?"

"What they are for!"

"You never answer. I sometimes don't think you hear me."

"Oh, I hear you all right, when I like. I heard you just now. Now look *here*, Dinah—"

"Don't call *me* 'Dinah'!"

"You are Dinah. One becomes—you've become. So look here, *Dinah*, try and have sense! Sad though it was that we lost touch, you and I have got on perfectly well without one another for going on fifty years—"

"Oh, no!"

"I said, 'going on.' "

"I didn't mean that. I meant, have we?"

"Well, look at you. Look at me."

"Look at Sheikie."

Clare raised her voice. " 'For the greater part of a lifetime,' as Sheikie put it."

"Oh yes, at Harrods. What does one mean by the 'greater' part?"

"Don't argue: listen! To have met again has been very nice. But we cannot keep in-ing and out-ing every two days. We have lives to live."

"That sounds like Sheikie, too.—This has been a week."

"And so?" asked Clare, forbiddingly staring.

"If you meant to go again, why did you come back?"

"My heavens, *you* ask that! Practically blackmailed?"

"I'd thought it was more Sheikie who'd felt that."

"You're right: I take that back. *I* was glad enough."

Idly drawing a finger round the rim of a mock-alabaster bowl, Dinah said: "Oh, I've had a nice time—I agree completely. In most of my life, I mean. I mean, as things go. But one can miss without knowing what one misses. Miss —can't one?—without even knowing one *is* missing?"

"I have no idea."

"I don't want to make you angry. I didn't see I was going to be a bother. You mean, you haven't got time for me— now? Or," she added, looking round the restricted, encumbered space, "*room* for me, really? Phyllida thinks," she went on in a lowered voice, with a glance at the area, "I can see, that I'm wasting your time. Mumbo, is she right?"

"No."

"What must I not do, then?"

"Rock the boat. Unsettle me." Clare piled bowls on each other and, without warning, thrust them at Dinah. "Here," she said, "put these up on the shelf (one from the end, two from the top) where the others are, will you?"

"Oh yes. I saw the others—they're yellow, though?"

"Yellow, yes. Then come back for the rest. When they're all up there, count them."

Dinah was good at that. She then roved the shelves. "If I could dust some of this . . ." she said cravingly. "No good, though, till the floor's swept. I *couldn't*—?"

"No. There is still the packing-case."

"I see a broom—not a small patch? We should be less inflammable."

"Keep your talents for home."

"You didn't see much of it the other day. Applegate. Only the bath and that dull dining-room. Then, till you left, no-cave, so nothing but pottering."

"I walked back into the house, you know, on my own."

"I know when: I was showing Sheikie the *potager*." Dinah beamed round on Clare. "Oh, I'm glad!—Drawing-room, did you go into?"

"Where your mother's clock is? Yes." Clare paused. "China's all gone, I suppose?"

"No. Up in my room."

"Where's that other needlework stool?"

"Up by my bed: I keep books on it."

"She's dead, Dicey?"

"Yes.—You know, we never went back to Feverel Cottage."

"How should I know? We were gone.—Then where did you go?"

"We stayed on up there. I mean, Cumberland—Cousin Roland made us. He got in a state about leaving us, when the war'd begun, when it didn't seem going well. Didn't want us anywhere nearer Germans. 'What good would it do,' he said, 'hearing those guns?' No, better in Cumberland, he said.—At least I *suppose* he did, I suppose it *was* that? Anyway, there we stayed. So a house was found.—Where did you go?"

"Mother and I? To my grandmother's."

"Oh, Mumbo."

"Yes, well.—Then all your things went to Cumberland?"

"No. That was a furnished house. They went into store."

"I cannot imagine her without them."

"You only have to try for a few years."

"Then, after Cumberland?"

"There was no after Cumberland. There still was me, of course. There was Cousin Roland."

"*Oh,*" said heavy Clare.

"Don't be sad," said Dinah, turning back to the shelves. She went on: "What I don't understand is, where all this new stuff's going to go? The shop as it now is seems just enough—won't all this overcrowd it?"

"Quite half that stuff that's now out there's going out."

"Heavens—to where?"

"Why, another branch. That's the entire principle: keep things stirring."

"How do you know all this—how did you find it out? How do you do it?" Dinah, sobered, said: "Clare, how able you are! Aren't you?—Things, you did always like, but you either would never touch them or always dropped them. Now they're your living?"

"Now they're my living. Yes, you are perfectly right: I have great ability. Could have done almost anything. Yes, I mean that—for once, for a wonder." Clare, giving Dinah her most stoical stare, told her: "I'm not joking."

"But you were intellectual. Shouldn't you have been educated, or something?"

"By now, what matter? Who cares!"

"I care."

"Now don't start any of that."

"I'm not starting anything.—And I tell you who is mysterious, and that's Sheikie. In ways, she's more fascinating than you are."

"Oh, yes?"

"Yes. More barnacled over. Far, far more barnacled over than you or I are. Wouldn't you say? She's certainly thickly covered with *some* deposit. Thanks to which, she is tremendously 'the thing'—almost never not, doesn't one notice? Partly, that chic Southstone set she seems to be in? And Time, of course, also has done its work—it's so far failed to give coating to you or me. One could say, she's simply become *more so* (as no doubt you have, and I suppose I have) yet I ask myself whether it's that only? You wouldn't say she put up a bit of a front? Well, she always did—but now more than she did, and for more reason? Because, what I'm now coming to is why she's fascinating: under all that, Sheikie's *capable de tout.*"

"So are we all," Clare said somewhat vaguely, "aren't we?"

"No, I don't think so. Not *capable de tout* anything like Sheikie. She always was, you would say? And you could be right—all I'd like to point out is, one thing Times does is, make anyone *capable* capable of still more. To my mind, there are various mysteries about Sheikie. What *about* that dancing, what became of her dancing? And that no-children: does she, or not, care? And I tell you another thing she's done: she's invented Trevor—doubtless for some good reason. We all knew Trevor. That 'Trevor this,' 'Trevor that' she is always quoting is not Trevor."

"You were not nice about Trevor the other morning," Clare pointed out, "sitting on that wall. 'Why marry that house agent?' you shrieked."

"Were wildest horses to tell me that *was* Trevor? Her letter had only said she was now an Artworth."

"Why not? He was in the succession."

"Was he?—Well, to go on: Sheikie's certainly dauntless. I bet you she defended Southstone like simply anything, that famous time around 1940—I see her seated up on a cliff, don't you, lobbing anything-everything back at those poor Germans. No wonder they were too terrified to land. Oh, brave as a lion—but then, so are we all: what's also outstanding in Sheikie is calm efficiency. Would make an excellent nurse or excellent murderess. You'd agree?"

"Well, that's quite a thing to be asked."

"Well, I'm only asking.—Why did she marry so late, too? What happened first? She *could*, I suppose, have not been anything more than 'a fair but frozen maid,' but I deeply doubt it. And what made her cut up like that about my advertisements? Went on like a maniac, you told me."

"I did not."

"Well, that's the impression you gave me."

Clare, having during the discourse unzipped a stylish brief-case and brought out papers (invoices, checked lists, and bills of lading already were tucked under much of the checked stock), now looked at her watch—ostentatiously, in the manner of one who has done so, in vain, before. She put on spectacles. "Sorry, but I've now got to—"

"Have a conference?"

"You're surprisingly right."

"Well, that's what you look like.—Who with? Oh, *not* for five minutes more?"

"You've talked enough."

"I only talk when I have something to say," said Dinah contentedly, lighting a cigarette.

"An excellent rule.—Sorry, but there are matters to be gone into."

"That means Phyllida in again?"

"No. T'other, this time. T'other's boss here, if any. Got more sense."

"Oh, has she?—What's *her* name?"

"Mrs. Stokes."

"Why Mrs. Stokes, when the other's Phyllida?"

"She's a widow."

"Well, I am a widow, but you show me no special consideration. Can't you wait till I'm gone?"

"When are you going?"

"Not for a few minutes, I hadn't thought?" Dinah started fishing about in her deep handbag—which since it was last resorted to had hung open on its strap from her arm. "Here it is—thought I had it! Engraved on her Azure Bond." Her next move was made with decision, though no haste.

"*Dicey*—what are you doing to my telephone?"

The other began arrangements for what should be a protracted session—hooked a chair from where it was to where it should be, sat on it, saw to it that the "Paul" dish was in position, then, reaching round, removed the telephone bodily from its shelf on to her knee, where it took on the air of a favoured nurseling. So placed, she orientated towards Clare—and facing Clare, it was clear, she planned to remain. Her determination to do so was engaging. "One squeak," she said, "just one squeak out of Sheikie, wouldn't it be a triumph to obtain? A Message from Mars? Come on, come on, come on—leave Sheikie out of this?"

"We have sung her praises."

"Oh, but I don't feel that's quite the same!—How do I get Long Distance on *this* telephone?"

Not told, she found out. Southstone then came through, supernaturally soon.

"Oh, hul-lo! Who's that?—Well it doesn't matter, but do you think I could speak to Mrs. Artworth? . . . That would be very kind. Tell her it's urgent. (D'you know who I bet that was? Trevor's devoted nurse. Bright as a button. She says she *thinks* Sheikie's there," said Dinah, wearing a look of awe. "As simple as this, after all these years.) . . . Oh, *Sheikie*, hullo! . . . Why yes, of course I am me! (She knew my voice.) . . . I was just telling Mumbo, you knew my voice. . . .Yes, of course she is here. Or rather, I am with her. . . . In a Mopsie Pye shop. . . . A garden of all delights. (She wants to know what your shop's like.) . . . I was telling Mumbo, you want to know what her shop's like. . . . She's very well. (You are, aren't you?) . . . I am *very* well. But the real point is, how are *you?* We wondered. Are you *very* well? . . . Yes, I see. (She's run off her feet.) . . . But otherwise well? . . . That is an undertaking, isn't it? (She's taken on running the White Elephant stall at some vast bazaar.) . . . Oh, were you? Well, all the more lucky to have caught you, but we mustn't keep you. (She was just on the point of dashing out of the house, to get to the White Elephant, when the nurse caught her.) . . . I was just putting Mumbo in the picture about the White Elephant. Oh, *did you get back all right the other night?* . . . Good. We wondered. . . . Oh, dear. (She did, but she was all in.) Well it's nice to know you are there. We wish you were here. . . . Well, yes, you easily may be, now I come to think of it. (Will she be seeing us, she wants to know.) . . . Almost any time. Any evening Mumbo can get away. We are at least going to *try.* . . . I can't believe there's no St. Agatha's *garden.* . . . Yes, but they may not have dug

the whole *place* over. . . . Well, then don't, Sheikie. . . . I
know, but we think it's worth trying a slight probe. . . .
I know, but this isn't a dog. (Let sleeping dogs lie, she says.
Rather late in the day, I should have thought?) . . . I do
see. How can you, when you're so prominent? . . . Well,
if we run into trouble, we run into trouble. . . . Yes, but
who is to know you know us? *We* would never let on.
Only if all went well, we would then come round. . . . Well,
that's very nice of you, Sheikie. (Drinks, she says.) . . .
Good: then we'll let you know.—Oh, one last thing: have
you ever killed anyone? . . . What? . . . I see . . . I only
wondered. . . . No, Mumbo thought not. (You did on the
whole, didn't you?) . . . Ha-ha, yes, like anything. You bet.
Well you should have been here. . . . Yes you *must*, or your
White Elephant will go rogue. See you soon, then. . . .
(Mumbo, Sheikie says to wish you all of the best.) . . .
Sheikie, Mumbo says to wish *you* all the best, too. . . . So
long!"

Dinah put down the receiver slowly, giving it an affec-
tionate look. She remarked to Clare: "The one thing
Mother stopped me doing that Sheikie did—and I think
your mother was the same?—was saying 'So long!' You
know, in spite of that old bat Mrs. Beaker, Sheikie always
was *avant-garde*." The telephone, after its brief good time,
had to go back on to the shelf. "I'm glad we did that. She
was pleased, I think. It was nice.—Her life *is* human, you
know."

Clare chose to be stuffy. "What a thing to ask her over
the telephone!"

"Why? Her line's not tapped, is it?—Or is yours? Well,
look, since you have that conference on your mind, you
had better get started, and I'd better get going. Fair enough;
I only asked for five minutes. How far's London?"

"What *did* she say?"

"You don't have to know, if you don't approve. She
said, 'Not exactly'—having thought for a minute. She took
it very calmly, in good part. On the whole, she seemed
pleased at being asked, I thought. People like to be taken
an interest in. Set or no set, I don't think Sheikie has many
friends."

"And one other thing, Dinah. *What* is this project?"

"Why, what we were in the middle of planning the other
afternoon! You know: in the orchard at Applegate, when

Sheikie suddenly dealt us that frightful blow. Oh, it was *a* blow (so much so that I've been fighting to put it out of my mind). But not, you know, thinking the matter over, necessarily a blow to our plan. As Sheikie remarked just now—and as I think one would have imagined even if she hadn't—everywhere there's been built over with new houses. But new houses, in places with nice views, often have pretty little gardens, don't they? And to make pretty little gardens, one quite often uses fragments of gardens which have been there. I've known of that being done, at least. Haven't you?"

"I'm damned if we're going there," said Clare.

"And I shall be not damned but very much surprised, indeed, if we don't." Dinah now looked at her watch. She reiterated: "How far *is* London?"

"What part?"

"Where one has lunch. Oh, and I must tell you who I am having lunch with: Packie! We must, must arrange— that, really he is entitled to! The *least* he is entitled to," said Dinah firmly. "Then, as I made rather an early start, I think I may go round to William's and sleep. If I go there, I'll probably stay the night."

"William is?"

"My son." A second search was being made in the bag —car keys?

"I thought you had two?"

"Well, of course I have! Roland lives near Canterbury. William and Annie, though, are in Rutland Gate.—Mumbo, no, don't come out with me: you're busy. Oh, *don't* all of a sudden be so very polite—*aren't* you? I shall have miles to walk, too: nowhere, nowhere was there to leave my car. Where *was* the Mini, where had you put the Mini? I looked for it everywhere in vain. This is a very, a very animated town. Are all these places like this, where you have your shops? How do you remember where you are?—I mean, which you're in? Are you going to another place today?"

"Yes, this afternoon."

"At the first glance, I thought I'd been here before, but I think I can't have. And the thing is, I'll never be here again. Next time I see you, it will be some other place? I—"

In the archway, though tentatively, stood Mrs. Stokes. The senior aubergine carried a loose-leaf jotting-pad and a gold-banded pen (present from her late husband?). "Sorry," she said.

"No, come in."

"I could come back, Miss Burkin-Jones."

"No. Mrs. Delacroix's just going."

Two

꿎꿎꿎

Dear Mumbo,

This morning when I was in your shop, I saw something I did very much want. A butter knife, suitable for a breakfast tray. Blade quite short, 2 to 2½ inches, I should say, but handle huge (quite out of proportion), gnarled and dark and with a knuckle bend in the middle. The more I think about it, the more I want it.

Unfortunately this butter knife was in the wrong part of the shop (yours, I mean). Otherwise nothing could have been simpler. Sheikie told me she took a beating trying to buy a brooch you had on your chest at that secret tea. If I may not buy it, will you give it to me? I know that giving anybody a knife is supposed to cut a friendship, but that is made all right if you give the giver 6d or even a penny in return. You need not worry that you would be giving me a dangerous thing: that knife (I tried it) would cut nothing *but* butter, and very rightly. And you need not worry if it is a symbol, as practically everything is, as we now know. Certainly everything is in your witch's kitchen, as your customers know?

Could you (or would that be a great bother?) telephone to Mrs. Stokes or Phyllida, probably the former? What I am so hoping you won't reply is, that that butter knife belongs in part to your Board of Directors. I know how complicated business can be. But I do want it. Only when I am able to look at it every morning, first thing, shall I be able to tell you why. And with a handle that size, it can never get lost.

The Grand (Southstone) would be the best place for us to meet, as with where we are going to so changed we might miss each other. We had better be there while there is still some daylight, to get our bearings, but then wait in the car till it gets dark. So be at the Grand at 5, or as soon as you can. I will bring everything necessary in my car. The *end* of next week would be best, as I am rather busy before then and expect you are. So, that Thursday. Unless I hear from you that you prefer Friday, I shall be waiting for you in the Grand on Thursday. *I* shall be in the Grand, come what may.

I did not after all sleep this afternoon, as I took the children out in a boat while Annie was at the osteopath's, so am looking forward to doing so tonight, in fact now. I wonder how you got on with that packing-case. I could have opened it for you in half a jiffy.

Yours affectionately,

D.

Three

"Still very grand," maintained the Grand's former *habituée*. She and her friend, making their way out of the carpeted catacomb, passed entrances to two or three bars and a cocktail lounge, alike in being dark and unechoing: nothing open yet. "Not its finest hour," Clare had cause to remark. But the other was making a heel ring on each white step of the shallow flight they were going down, exclaiming: "Marble!" She added: "There's a flask in my car."

Few people were about on the Promenade. The early marine evening was clear and sunless, the sea autumnal. "Places evaporate, don't they?" Dinah said, looking about her emptily. "The poor harmless things."

"*This* never said much to me, at the best of times," Clare said, looking at the Promenade with the more curiosity. They went round the Grand to its car park, which was not crowded. "Now," Dinah asked, "what about your Mini? Come by here and pick it up afterwards, on the way to Sheikie's?"

Both got into the Hillman, which trickled clear of the plateau then swooped downhill. The passenger, looking orthodox, pulled on one then the other of her good hogskin gloves. "Let's be clear," she began, "as to why *I'm* here—"

"Oh no, don't let's analyze anything!"

"Last hope of keeping you out of jug."

The car took a sharpish bend of the hill; a slithering clank was heard from the boot. "There go the spades, again," said the driver. "They've been keeping that up, on and off, all the way from Applegate. Francis can't have stowed them in very firmly.—Quick, *which* turn left? Look how many there are!"

There is seldom anything convulsive about change. What is there is there; there comes to be something fictitious about what is not. At a first glance, what had been the site of St. Agatha's, grounds and building, looked like being impossible to determine—the coast road had somewhat altered in course: the coast had somewhat altered in shape. The drop from the road to the beach had become less, though a balustrade guarded it. A white concrete-and-glass pavilion, deserted, half-closed for winter, interrupted the balustrade for some way along. And for some way along, opposite, the base of the hill had been embanked, strongly, with rusticated stone. There was no way up till the embankment had cornered itself off: then, a steep road did begin its ascent. Well kept, the road was no longer new-looking: the impression it gave of reserve and privacy was confirmed by a notice at its foot, saying: "No Through Way."

To see up the hill, it was necessary to get out of the car. The revenants stood back, backs to the balustrade—above them, ten or a dozen nice-looking houses, spaced out over the hill's face, harmlessly contemplated the Channel: garages, their doors painted pastel colours, sat on ledges surrounded by landscape gardening. More land than St. Agatha's could account for had evidently been taken in. (*Where*, indeed, now that one came to think of it, was St. Swithin's?) In general the gardens were veiled in the thinly dusky yellows and coppers and bronzy purples of midautumn: however (to the left of the roadway), darker and more opaque patches of growth were to be discerned. Husky vestigial remnants of former planting *had* been incorporated into the more diaphanous later scheme. Once located, the two ex-thickets were unmistakable. One above the other, modified out of being groves into being strips, they stood out like two conspiratorial dark moustaches.

Dinah said instantly: "The lower one."

"Yes, I believe you're right."

"I know I am. There was nothing below it but the croquet lawn; then below that those banks with those seats and things.—Now we must dash up there, while the light lasts, and make out *which* of those houses' gardens it's got itself into."

"That's going to be all?"

"Wait a minute." The owner locked the Hillman. "We don't want anybody getting at our drinks—when we've come down again, we can have those while we wait for it to get dark. And I've brought sandwiches."

Trimmed escallonia hedges topped boundary walls on either side of the private road. Gates, opening on drives of varying lengths, each announced the name given to the home within and had by it a post with a lantern lamp, not of course yet lit. Trees which doubtless flowered in spring here or there overhung the hedges—and at a point there projected also a Beaker & Artworth "For Sale" board. "Trevor won't have *that* on his hands for long. A very desirable property, I should say?" The escallonia being too high to see over and dense to see through, the prospectors had the bother of turning in at one after another of the left-hand gates. "*There* it is—see?—down there! Dinah cried at last. On their way out, she memorized the gate. "It says, 'Blue Grotto' ... Blue Grotto."

"They honeymooned there?"

"They couldn't have *in* there. That was Tiberius."

"Don't know whether you noticed," remarked Clare, as they neared the bottom of the road, "but the greater part of Blue Grotto consists of glass."

"Then they can't throw stones. Who do they think they are, anyway?"

"Who do we think we are?"

"Don't caw." Dinah, opening the car, asked: "*You* don't know whether we put a curse? I'm not certain."

"I bled like a pig writing that out."

"I expect you did—but really this is important! *We* could be receiving the full blast."

"I shouldn't let that worry you."

"Well, it does rather."

"Then lay off—couldn't you? You've had a nice look round; now leave it at that. Don't *tamper*, as everybody has told you! Sheikie's got twice your sense."

"Oh, yes." They settled into the Hillman, to be stationary during the watch ahead. "And four times yours."

Dark took long to come. Dinah heaved the provisions out of the back seat into the front. "You spoke of a flask; I'd call this a bar," Clare said.

"I'd call it a choice," said the host. "One thing I don't yet know is, what you really like."

They drank with coat collars up, one window down on the sea side. Colourless glass dusk was like a glass dome over a stopped clock. The sea was out of action. Here on the coast road unlit cars slid by with cargoes of ghosts—observant ghosts, however, who turned their heads. "They wonder what we are up to."

"What are we up to?" wondered Clare, refilling her Perspex glass. Behind the Hillman, a door banging (caretaker coming out?) must have started echoes in the empty pavilion. "Did you say there were sandwiches?"

"Oh, here! . . . Any news of the butter knife?"

"I am negotiating."

"Mumbo, what became of the Unknown Language?"

"Gone."

"Back into your head?"

"An attic, if so. And the key's lost."

"It sounded awful," Dinah said, still with awe. "Nobody ever heard it again?"

"No. I wrote a letter in it."

"I don't understand—someone else understood? Was there an answer?"

"It got there too late.—Aren't *you* eating anything?"

"In a minute." Dinah looked out of each of the car windows, hoping that at least one might bring better news —but no. Not so much as a shred of darkness! "I don't see why a watched pot should *never* boil," she complained. "What's the matter with it? We haven't come here at sunrise by mistake, have we?"

"Getting darker in here," Clare said. "I can hardly see you."

"I can hardly see you; but what's the good of that? Outside, no. No, not nearly enough. Waiting's like a curse in itself, isn't it? At the bottom of one road one can't see up, on another horrible road one can't bear to see. This is a dream doom."

"Then drive on."

"Where to?"

"Then walk about."

"*Here?*"

"Then don't get so tensed *up!*"

"Knocking me about, like you always did."

"Can you wonder?"

"No. But you did knock me about."

"What we need," said Clare, "is a pack of cards. Or a band.—What are you flinging yourself about for, now?"

"Oh, I am only hunting for my transistor. . . . Here we are. What's on on the Light?"

She obtained a concert. Throughout it and some part of its successor, which was Variety, the listeners, arms folded, sat with their eyes shut. When at length they opened them, darkness had truly fallen—with, indeed, the thoroughness of a collapsed wall. Dinah jumped and put on her parking lights. She then turned to Clare. "Now's the hour—come on, Posterity!" She took two torches out of the glove compartment, got out, went round to the back of the car, and unstowed the other necessities from the boot. "I brought this pick-axe—save blisters, this time. Carry it, will you?" Clare, like an automaton, took the pick-axe. Nothing did she say, so they set off.

Up the hill, shallows of electric lantern-light alternated with gulfs where the black road surface blotted into blackness of shadowed walls. Seen or unseen, the close escallonia sent out its humid, varnishy smell. Between the lamps, trees had beneath them caverns—out of one of which stepped a figure still webbed like a black cobweb to the shades out of which it had taken form. It waited, waiting to be neared—then said: "Well, you two?"

"*Sheikie!*"

"Don't scream the place down. Lost yourselves, did you? —Hullo, Mumbo."

"Aha."

"How did you get here, Sheikie, though? Did you pass the car?"

"I came down from the top."

"It says, 'No Through Way.' "

"No through way my eye," said the local girl. As Mrs. Artworth, she had made herself both striking and, in intention at least, invisible. She wore a black mackintosh, had swathed head and throat tightly in black chiffon, wore black gloves—but should have been masked, for her make-up was phosphorescent.

Clare said: "This is very sporting of you, Mrs. Dracula."

"I intend to be there if that box *is*. What did you suppose? Leave you two to root about in the bottom?"

"The secrets of the tomb . . ."

"That was what it was intended to be, Clare."

"We are in the wrong," said Clare, turning to Dinah.

"This is not what we said," Sheikie drove in. "It is *not* what we said."

"Not that it will be there."

"How do you know?"

"How can it be there?"

It was there.

It was empty.

It had been found.

The moment when the pick, through the loosened earth, struck upon the sounding lid of the coffer happened to be rendered apocalyptic: it was the moment when the lounge of Blue Grotto chose to blaze into light. An unbroken succession of door-windows floodlit the terrace they gave on. Non-indigenous maples flamed from the top down. Brittle Japanese foliage and laden berberis were stereoscopically in Technicolor down to the last vein of a leaf and hue of a berry. As the garden descended, a statuette of Pan or some unknown faun, a white scrolled Regency garden seat, and a shell-shaped bird bath floated one after another on the illuminated darkness. Though that became less bright as it sifted down, the thicket was entered. One could see down into the bottom of the empty coffer.

Clare, kneeling, fingered round the edge of the raised lid till she detached a fragment of macerated red sealing wax. Dinah, putting down the pick, knocked against a tree which with a creak gave out an ancient shiver. But Sheila stared up the slope like a night animal hypnotized by oncoming headlights. "This is about to be the least of our troubles, let me tell you."

True enough, in part of the window stood a man. Face to the sheet of glass, *he* was also staring. What he would chiefly be seeing would be the reflection of his lounge and himself. "He looks like a Yugoslav," said Dinah. No longer content, apparently, with reflections, he slid aside his part of the window and came out. He crossed his terrace, came down his steps—on which he made one thick-set but rather histrionic pause, looking about—then came on steadily down his garden.

Clare pushed herself heavily up from her kneeling posture, saying: "Well . . ." Mrs. Artworth, in the almost contented tone of satisfied terror, said: "O My God in Heaven."

"Make yourself into a yashmak, you silly fish!"

Sheikie, with her wonderful reflexes, had chiffon above the bridge of her nose and had tightened it in a single flash. Her eyes, dark for the first time, looked out over the yashmak glazed by an Oriental passivity while Dinah walked out of the thicket to meet the man, saying: "Good evening."

"Well, I don't know so much about that," he said.

"I'm afraid you will think us rather unconventional. We were looking for something we hid as children. We had no idea this was *your* garden."

"That's what it is," he said, turning and taking a look up at it, giving himself top marks.

"How did you know we were down here?"

"Well," he said.

"Our torches, I suppose?"

"You never know."

"You didn't know what you might have been walking into. There *are* only three of us." She invited his attention into the thicket, in which her friends rather oddly stood like a non-matching pair of caryatids in transit. "That," she said, indicating Sheila, "is a friend of mine from Somerset —I live in Somerset. Unfortunately she has toothache this evening. And that is Miss Jones, who works in London; she and I were at school together, down there—" She indicated the sea. "I really don't think we have injured anything."

"I see," he said.

"Did you build that house?"

"Yes and no," he said, extra cagily.

"It would be nice to signal from, if one wanted to."

"I don't know," he said.

"We wondered who chose the name?"

"That was my wife. My former wife, I should say."

"You don't think your *wife* can have found our box?"

"Not that I know," he said, with the greatest indifference.

"You don't find the gales are bad for your rare plants?"

"Not that I've noticed."

"Well," she said, "we must be going, I'm afraid." She went back into the thicket, picked up the pick, and handed it to Clare. He watched. "The ground here's rather hard, don't you find?" "No," he said. She collected the spades, fork, trowels, then looked into the pit, saying to Sheila: "We might as well leave the coffer where it is, I think, don't you?—Or would your father have objected?" Sheila chawed once or twice on the chiffon, but then thought it better to confine herself to an inclination of the head. Dinah told the man: "This is a coffer of the kind many people like to have in their hall. You might like to?"

"Not that I know," he said.

"Come on,' she said to the other two. In single file, as they had come down, they went level by level up the garden: he followed, keeping them under observation as far as the gate. They left. Sheikie, whose car was up at the top, said she thought she'd go on and get out the ice. "Number 11, remember, not Number 9!" were her parting words. Posted under the lantern at his gate, the man looked dully after the friend from Somerset.

"Careful!" Dinah said, stepping clear not for the first time of Clare, who was swinging the pick with too great emphasis, as they went downhill. Later: "There's the car, still," she said, in a tone of surprise. As they got into it, she remarked: "No wonder she left him."

"I should have thought you'd have thought he had done her in."

"Oh, no; too busy spying."

Later: "You're not driving very well, if I may say so," Clare ventured, after minutes of it.

"I'm dying laughing."

"I don't hear you."

"Oh, then perhaps I'm not.—Look, here's the Grand coming: we'll have to think. Do we—or don't we, I hope not?—*not* know the way to Ravenswood Gardens? . . . You had better do the hitting-and-missing, if you don't mind," Dinah added, as she stopped in the car park and Clare got out, "and I'll follow."

The Mini turned in at Ravenswood Gardens, with the Hillman already some way behind. Ahead, opposite No. 11, a cream Triumph coupé had come to rest at the kerb. Clare pulled in behind that, looked back over her shoulder, switched off her engine—a minute later, some way back down the Gardens, the Hillman's engine likewise ceased to be heard. There followed a dead, untwittering silence:

birds were in bed. Sheila appeared in the door of No. 11, saying: "Well, come in," less disparagingly than usual. Not unwilling, Clare bundled out of the Mini.

"But where's Dinah?"

"Somewhere there in the distance. . . . Wake up!" Clare shouted back at the Hillman. "We've got here. What are you doing?"

"What *is* she doing?" Sheila complained, from the top of the steps.

Clare shrugged. She briskly came up, explaining: "She'll come when she fancies."

"Oh. *I* want to shut the door."

"Leave it on the latch?"

"What are you talking about?—*These* days?"

"Risk it."

"I'm alone in the house."

"Oho. No Trevor?"

"Over at Herne Bay."

"Why, yes. How is, is, is—?"

"Irene? She's no more. That's why he's over at Herne Bay: he's her executor."

"That's too bad, Sheikie. Awfully sorry!"

"We all come to it sooner or later, don't we? Not that I shan't miss her—that I cannot pretend." In the Nile-green hall the guest got out of her overcoat, which was spirited on to a hanger in a built-in closet. The other of the Beaker coffers had been polished up and was prominent. "On up," directed the hostess, with a nod at the stairs.

No sooner was Clare into the large lounge than she hurled herself on to a striped settee placed diagonally to the electric log fire. She puffed and blew, as one is entitled to do after a strain—then turned to eye a nearby table on which magazines were set out in overlapping rows. Seizing upon a top one, she set about staring her way through it. Sheila asked: "Think she's come over funny?"

First, the magazine-addict no more than grunted. Then: "Why?" she finally said, without looking up.

"Search me! Because, *what* a laugh, after all!"

"Mmmm . . ."

"Well, what about it?"

"A drink? I should not object."

Down there, the door-on-the-latch clicked shut. A step

began to explore the carpeted stairs. Clare changed magazines, remarking: "Well, there she *is*." Sheila turned, to issue directions. "On up!" she called.

The room, in shades of beige with touches of colour, was brilliantly though indirectly lit. The late-comer, having entered, headed with the aloofness of a somnambulist for a space in the middle: there, she stood gazing round. The sight of one object appeared to wake her. "Sheikie," she cried, "what a beautiful scarlet telephone! That's the one we had such a happy time on?"

Sheila, staring, said: "You're as white as a sheet."

"Well, the game's up."

"Look, I should perch myself somewhere, if I were you. . . . We didn't do too badly, all things considered. *You* lied like a trooper: I give you that!"

"I don't mean—"

"Oh. Then what *do* you mean?"

Dinah blinked. She looked round the lounge again, for about a minute. Then: "What a nice big water colour *that* is of the Old High Street!"

"What, that? Yes, it was a wedding present."

"From the Mayor?"

"No, he did us somewhat better. Still, that picture's come to be of historic interest, as Trevor frequently says."

"Why?"

"Why would you suppose? You can't make an omelette without breaking eggs, can you?"

"I suppose not," said Dinah, hand to her face.

"What remained was found to be unsafe. The street they've put there instead is quite picturesque-looking, however. Quite a hang-out for gift shops.—How's business, Mumbo?"

"*Comme ci, comme ça*," said the occupant of the settee.

The settee's owner said, drily: "Comfortable, I hope?"

"Couldn't be more so, thanks. This is very snug."

The third of them, wheeling round, cried: "You are there, Mumbo?"

"So far as I know. Why?"

"So long as I know . . ."

"We all shall feel better shortly," guaranteed the hostess, making for the cabinet in which bottles were kept. The cabinet, extending out into flaps at the front and sides, already was hospitably open. "Scotch, for all?—or anyone not?"

No sooner had Dinah clutched at her filled glass than she said: "When I've drunk this, alas, I shall have to go."

Sheila, pausing before the next stage of her ministrations, smoothed her *taupe* crêpe dress over her hips. It fitted: she need have had no anxiety—and indeed probably had not. (*Had* this dress been present, under the mack, all the time during the exhumation?) The skirt gave a swirl as she half-turned, in order to say to Dinah, lightly: "What can you be talking about?" To which Clare, giving a plunge round on the highly sprung settee, added: "You may not know, but you've only just come."

"Yes, but I have to get back."

"Your home," pointed out Sheila, "won't run away."

Dinah examined the speaker, before saying: "That's what it *has* done, Sheikie." She took a shaky gulp at her drink. She added: "Everything has. *Now* it has, you see. Nothing's real any more."

Clare reached over the back of the settee, to receive her glass. She drank angrily and at a great rate, then said: "Nothing?"

"Nothing's left, out of going on fifty years."

"Nonsense!"

"*This* has done it," said Dinah. "Can't you see what's happened? This us three. This going back, I mean. This began as a game, *began* as a game. Now—you see?—it's got me!"

"A game's a game," Sheila averred, glancing down her nose.

"And now," the unhearing Dinah went on, "the game's collapsed. We saw there was nothing *there.* So, where am I now?"

"At Sheikie's, one would have thought."

"But *you're* real, Mumbo."

"Oh, good."

"You were there before."

"I still less see, Dinah," admitted Sheila, "why you're in such a fuss about getting home."

"No, I have to get back! I have to get home—there are people there. I, I have a great many irons in the fire. A *great* many irons in the fire. Oh yes. And I'm looking after Frank's dog.—Sheikie, I hope it didn't bite you?"

"It had a good try.—Frank away for long?"

"I don't know. And Francis is no help; he won't go near it.—Mumbo, do please remember: you *are* reality. Now I'll start, I think."

"Hi, wait a minute!" commanded Clare, withdrawing her muzzle from her glass. "You don't mean, Young Lochinvar, you're making a dash back into the West *tonight*?" Sheila, prising open a drum of cocktail biscuits, stated: "*I* don't think that she should."

"I want to go home."

"Yes, yes, you shall," promised Clare. "But do it by stages, why not? Why not Canterbury, or as you say, 'near Canterbury' (you are quite near Canterbury now) and Roland?"

"My goodness, Dinah," cried Sheila, "is that old cousin of yours still going?"

"No, he isn't. He's my son—I mean, Roland is. Apart from anything else, Mumbo, he's in Leeds, and so is Teresa."

"Then what's wrong with London: William and Annie?"

"At this hour? Anyway, they're in Port au Prince.—No, I'd like to sleep in my own bed."

"You'll sleep in your own grave if you don't look out."

"So why not," Sheila wanted to know, "calm down?"

The culprit at any rate sat down. She fell silent, from time to time looking from one to another of the three windows, which were heavily curtained in light beige. Clare asked Sheila: "Who is in Number 9?"

"It's a nursing home. For elderly people."

"Quiet neighbours, then?"

"Very. Many of them are failing, some rather rapidly."

"Who's failing in your room?"

"I haven't a clue. They've installed a lift."

"Number 10—no longer those Pomeranians?"

"Yappy little beasts. No. He's said to be a psychologist, or a psycho-something."

"Convenient neighbour?"

"He doesn't analyze anyone, just researches. He's let off his top to friends from London. Trevor handled that; it was rather a tricky lease. One's a Hindu, I hear."

"Tut!"

"Well, I don't know. Sometimes *I* think one might do

worse. Living in the whole of an empty house takes it out of one. Of course, there'd be much to be taken into consideration—for instance, our stair carpet shows every mark. And on top of that we now have another facer. Mother had made her home with Irene."

"Ah. How is your mother?"

"Mother's wonderfully lively."

"And so now?"

"That remains to be seen. Any day, of course, she could begin to fail."

"*You* could install a lift?"

"It may come to that.—Yes, Dinah, what do you want?"

"May I look out of one of your windows?"

"Oh, do."—But at that the barbarian set about manhandling the nearest curtains, fighting her way through. Sheila, with a patience learned from her husband, said: "There's a cord you pull."

The curtains handsomely sailed apart. The maker-free then threw open the window, pushing up the sash as far as it would go. The night, so content to be dark, so moveless and mild, was spilled out upon by *this* overlit room. Unlike the Blue Grotto man in that she cared what she was doing, Dinah knew herself wickeder than he—it would be pitiable, at this minute, to be a bird in this part of the glade. All the same, the night could not have been done without for a minute more: here it was, understanding something of the good it did, inexhaustible. Changeless and unhauntable. The little low railings along the glade were now painted white, and probably not the same. Ravenswood Gardens was what it always was: a place to be left to go back to one's own home.

"*Dinah*, another?"

"What?"

"Drink. Where on earth have you put your glass? And, sorry, but shall you have finished with that window? It's giving me gooseflesh.—No, *I'll* shut it (one doesn't want it to bang)."

Sheila found the glass and purposefully carried it to the cabinet.—"No, please not, Sheikie! I've got to drive."

"Famous last words."

Clare, from the other end of the room—she had risen from the settee and was standing not actually with her back to the electric log fire (that, its ferocity made impossible) but a little to the left of it—shouted: "I'm not so sure, Sheikie, that she *hasn't* had enough!"

Dinah was annoyed, and showed it.

Clare said: "Then don't be a fey bore. Pull yourself together!"

"You're so military."

"Such a way to go on!"

"*I* haven't just been sitting there wolfing magazines *and* biscuits and taking no interest in my surroundings! All this because I looked out of a window. The thing about you is, Mumbo, you can't bear to have anybody's attention off you for a single instant."

"Speak for yourself.—Have had a shock, have you? So have we all had a shock."

"Yes, and who kept *me* out of jug, ha-ha?"

Sheila, giving a light tweak to the top of her dress, said: "Girls, girls . . ."

"It's as well for Trevor," said Dinah, "that he's at Herne Bay. Which is his chair, though?—Where does he usually sit? What do you and he, Sheikie, generally do up here in the evenings?—He *doesn't* bear us any malice, does he?"

"You know," said Sheila, "you're still a peculiar colour."

"He hasn't gone to Herne Bay because of us?"

"Frankly, he has no idea you are here, either of you."

"Oh."

"All very well to say 'Oh.' You know as well as anyone else how Trevor puts two and two together. Well, then? You'd expect him to think you'd come nipping over from Somerset and Mumbo'd left Mopsie Pye to go to the dogs simply to drop in here and have a drink, no more? Well, *then*? Wanted to have him flapping about after us, arguing, while we were digging around for those old bones? Or alternatively, keeping on and on and on, afterwards, till he'd found out all? *Well*—then?"

"I do see. You were right."

"Well, then."

"I think I would like that drink."

Glass in hand, Dinah addressed herself to the picture. "So this will be the Old High Street for evermore—this lie!"

"It isn't as bad as that, is it?" asked the owner.

"If it's any consolation, Sheikie, if it were slightly better it would be very likely to be a still worse lie."

"To me," said Clare, coming up also carrying her glass, "it appears correct in every detail."

"Oh, it is—look, you can read the right names over the right shops. And *that's* not a bit what I quarrel with: don't think so! It's just that something has given the man the slip, so in place of what's given him the slip he's put something else in."

Sheila, examining the work of art for the first time, said: "It looks to me like a picture; and I should have thought that was the idea? Pictures are what people go for: who wants a street? Streets are six a penny. Quaint as that old street was, we went there to shop.—Also let me remind you," she added, with revived animosity, "you two were for ever goggling in at that window at pictures no better than this (*and* not half so big) of the same thing."

"But then we were *in* the street."

"Oh," said the sceptical Mrs. Artworth.

"You say," asked Clare, rolling her eyes in what tonight were their heaviest pouches round at Dinah, with a blend of combativeness and curiosity, "that this would be a worse lie if it were a better picture?"

"Oh, yes," said the positive one. "Because this poor chap has at least only been trying to portray what he thought he saw—and as we see, beyond getting the details correct he didn't see much, and what he did see he didn't see right. But if he'd been a bit better, then he'd have waded in and started portraying or trying to portray what he thought he felt; and as we know, what anyone thinks they feel is sheer fabrication.—Not that it doesn't have quite a powerful effect, though: in *or* out of pictures."

"What effect?"

"Well, I'm thinking more of what it has an effect *on.*"

"What?"

"Oh, Mumbo—people! People are glad to feel anything that's already been fabricated for them *to* feel, haven't you noticed? And those things have been fabricated for them by people who in the first place fabricated for themselves. There's a tremendous market for prefabricated feelings; customers simply can't snap them up fast enough—they feel they carry some guarantee. Nothing's so fishy to most people as any kind of a feeling they've never heard of."

"What would you say, Sheikie?"

"I've no idea what she's talking about, I'm sorry to say."

"I don't think Sheikie does have prefabricated feelings. She simply behaves in a prefabricated way—and indeed why shouldn't she, if she wishes to?"

"Well, thank you."

"What bone's sticking in *your* throat, Mumbo?"

Clare conveyed by a formidable silence that any bone in or not in her throat was her own affair. Shouldering past Dinah, closer to the picture, she read the names over the High Street shops. By no means discouraged, Dinah went on: "And I'll tell you one great centre of the prefabricated-feeling racket, and that is anything to do with anything between two people: love, or even sex. Except that one knows it's not, one could at times be tempted to suspect that the entire thing was a put-up job. Look at the complications which go on: they're totally out of relation with Nature's purposes. The fact is, many people prefer to be distraught. Even if they don't enjoy it (and you bet they do, mostly) they feel they ought to be. Nothing more convinces them than a tremendous to-do. If one for an instant says, 'But couldn't this be simpler?' they become furious.— So much is so simple."

"For you," said Clare, though not bothering to turn round, "probably."

"It seems so particularly ridiculous," said Dinah, "nowadays, with so many new horizons. So much more to get on with. So much more than there used to be to get one's hands on to. Outer space—"

"Leave *that* alone, there's a good girl!"

"I've no intention of tampering with that; I was merely giving you an illustration. No, all I'm trying to say is this, Mumbo: so many of these fanciful devices by which people have got into the way of keeping themselves going are, now, not only unnecessary but obsolete."

"Still, you can't go round pointing that out."

"I don't see why not."

Clare thought. "Disaffecting, for one thing."

"You're being military again."

"Right—then I'll speak as a shopkeeper. Bad for business. You'd put more than half the world out of business, including novelists. And not to speak of Trevor, insofar as home-seeking is a matter of whimsy.—And then what would become of *you*, Sheikie?"

"If you'll excuse me," said Sheila, who for some time had

been holding the vacuum ice-container to the breast of her dress, "I'd like to go down for more ice; we are running low."

"Sheikie, I'm going to stop!"

"I'll believe that, Dinah," said the hostess candidly, "when I hear you."

"She only talks," explained Clare, turning her back on the Old High Street in order to look paternally at the ceasing speaker, "when she has something to say."

"All I want to add is this, we did *know* those things were in that box. That's, perhaps, why this evening has been a shock?" About to depart, the guest looked, for the last time, at the water colour. "Also, I owe an apology to this picture. It is not such a lie, really, as lies go. I was too ready to think it must be a lie because of its even attempting to be a picture. Also because it's here, and the street's gone—you tell me? It might be better to have no pictures of places which are gone. Let them go completely."

Four

The Hillman's tail lights steadied out of a wobble and disappeared out the end of Ravenswood Gardens towards the West—watched from the steps of No. 11. "There *she* goes," Sheila remarked. She added: "I wouldn't worry, Mumbo, if I were you. As I see it, her bark is worse than her bite. With no one to argue with she'll get bored with driving after an hour or so and wander into a Trust House."

"You could be right," said the other, willing to think so.

"And now," said Sheila, turning upon the remaining guest with her coldest nonchalance, "*you* will want to be off. So do make a start as soon as you like. I am not keeping you."

"You're not throwing me out?"

"Why, no," was admitted, with elaborate detachment. "Do as you like."

"Trevor not back tonight?"

"No. He has a valuation appointment at Herne Bay first thing tomorrow."

"I'm in no great hurry, then, Sheikie."

"Aren't you? Well, as I say, do as you like. But you don't *have* to stay, let me make that clear."

"Your point has been taken."

"Care to come for a turn, then? In Trevor's absence I have to take out the dog."

"*You* haven't got a dog?"

"Not actually, no. It belongs, or did, to a patient in Number 9. Trevor and it for some reason best known to themselves took up with each other; and now this has come to be where it lives. It was that, the nursing home said, or putting it down."

"And the patient said?"

"Oh, that patient is failing rapidly.—Why don't we get our coats, and I'll root it out. I must warn you, it's no prize-winner." At the back of the hall, a push-back given by Sheila to a swing door revealed a flash of pastel kitchen, one tubular light on over the frigidaire. "Come on," said Sheila neutrally, "buck up." The dog came out. It was an Airedale model with something wrong with it, bleached to the colour of a soiled sheep and resigned, evidently, to its own lack of temperament. Sheila, having slid into a mohair coat (no call for the black mack on *this* expedition) swiftly selected a walking-stick from the closet. "You don't," Clare asked, "flog the thing along with that?"

"No. Just attract its attention—it's somewhat wanting. It would take Trevor to land us up, at the end, with a dog like this."

"You never embarked on a dog you could fancy more?"

"They get run over."

Number 11 had, since Dinah's departure, relapsed into a tomb-like silence. Clare, struck by a thought, asked: "Where's the old woman?"

"What, Trevor's nurse? Out bowling."

"Wha-at?"

"Well, watching her great-niece. That girl's building up into a champion, by all accounts. I'd like," Sheila admitted, "to see her."

They set out. Clare, in passing, looked into the cream coupé. "Yours?" "Yes. Trevor's is on the firm." Leaving Ravenswood Gardens, they entered another area of the plateau. Once into here, the atmosphere altered. Roads were wide, gloomily tree-infested, empty, and much alike. Massive houses, built rather far apart, loomed up into the night out of evergreens—their forms being, where visible, of that hue in which dark red brick invests itself after dark. Within one dim-lit porch could be numbered many electric bells. Tops of boundary parapets were pitted where fanciful ironwork must have been snatched out during the frenzy following 1940. Gateposts were gateless or else had flaccid gates propped back with a look of desuetude. Leaves deadened the pavements; here or there a late-fallen chestnut fled from under the foot. The dog probed ahead through a slight groundmist.

Clare asked: "*Have* we been here before?"

"I don't know—weren't we?" It's been here since the Flood."

"You know every stick and stone?"

Sheila hit hard with her stick at a stone parapet, to recall the dog and remind it what it was out for. She said: "It's always pretty in spring."

"Chestnuts flowering, may, lilac, and so on?"

"And so on. All the works—every spring. *I* should know."

The dog came back into view, selected a lamppost, slowly went through its performance, looked round to make certain this had been noted. "That's *that*, anyway," Sheila said. The dog, with an air of heightened prestige, resumed the lead, conducting the women out of the road they'd been in into another exactly the same. Clare said: "What I don't see is, why you never got out."

"*You* mean, don't you, what became of my dancing?"

Clare, starting as though Dinah were at her elbow, said: "Right—what did?"

"That's the world's shortest story. It came to nothing."

"But you were good?"

"Never saw me, did you?"

"Only on that breakwater."

"What breakwater?—You heard I was good. I was better than they said. I could have been twenty times better than they said."

"I knew you were good."

"I could have been better than you knew. I had it in me. That is, I *had* it in me."

"Well? And so then?"

Sheila, slowing down only very slightly as she lightly stepped beside Clare, who pounded along, started tapping ahead of her with her stick, as though doing a heartless parody of a blind man. "Daddy and *Mother*, of course, wouldn't have heard of my doing it for money; professionally, that was. It would have shocked them out of their skins—in those days. But I wouldn't have hesitated, Clare, to have done that to them, or indeed worse, when it came to the point. *Had* it come to the point—which it did not.

Till I could see my chance, I wasted no words; keeping on meanwhile dancing away at charity performance after charity performance. Oh, such showers of bouquets! All that time, though, I was casting round, keeping an eye out: finally, I *did* find where I should go. *The* place, in London it was, that was tops then. The place there could be nothing possibly better than, for anybody going truly to be a dancer. The real works. By then I was eighteen. So I took myself up there. 'Dance,' they said. Dance I did. They watched me. Then, 'Stop,' they said, after a short time— and didn't they say it kindly. For a bit after that they said nothing. They then said, 'No, it's a pity.' I said, 'What's a pity about my dancing?' They said, 'You've got into certain ways.' Vulgar they meant I was, Clare; I mean, my dancing. Vulgar was what they meant.—They said, 'You'd have too much to unlearn.' 'Why too much?' I asked. They said, 'More than you could by now.'—I can't say they sent me away; I took myself off."

"May they for ever rot."

"They were right, Clare."

"I expect they were. May they for ever rot."

Sheila said, almost with triumph: "So back I came."

"With flying colours. Yes.—But you stayed *on*?"

Sheila, turning her face scornfully, primitively, and blankly towards Clare, asked: "Why would you suppose?"

Clare hazarded: "A man. Man here?"

"Where else would you suppose?"

"I see. Well, there's always something," said Clare, "thank God."

"I'm not so sure that I do. I was eighteen. And *you* ask *me* what happened to all those years!"

"Not Aubrey, then, or any of those?"

"Aubrey'd been killed.—And I said a man, didn't I? I didn't say a boy."

"Didn't marry him?"

"*Marry* him!" Sheila gave an unheard laugh, of the kind probably best unheard. Then she reflected. "Yet what else had I but that, with my dancing gone?"

"What else had you but him?"

"Getting deaf, Mumbo? I said, what else had I but that?"

"That being so," said Clare, looking away, "what ended it?"

Sheila whistled twice—once to herself, softly, once aloud to the dog. "His death."

"I see. Shouldn't you—couldn't you, though—have got out *then*?"

"Where to—*by* then? And Trevor had come along. One prefers to marry."

Clare said dubiously: "Well . . ."

"Come," cried Sheila, impatiently, not unkindly, "you had a try yourself!—Well, so here I am. Surrounded"—she looked round her, whether inimically or mockingly, at trees, houses made phantasmagoric by the hour—"by tender memories. There are two things, curiously enough, which I can't stand: one's spring, and the other's this time of night."

"Well, I'm glad I'm here."

Sheila extra slightingly said: "Well, drop back in spring! —Now the dog's done, what about homeward bound?"

"And I *shall* now, Sheikie, have to be getting on the road."

"Then one for the road first!" Mrs. Artworth said. Suspecting herself, rightly, to be unlistened to, she got a hold on Clare's elbow and wheeled her round. "Home!" she loudly said (as though to the dog) to her big, slow-motion, unheeding friend. No response came. The dog, demonstrating its better sense, had dodged round and was heading the movement back. Sheikie gave a lobster-nip to the elbow. "Say what you like, *you're* worrying!"

"Where Young Lochinvar *has* got to, it would be nice to know," Clare admitted.—"This," she burst out, suddenly loud with anger, "is how I saw her send her mother nearly off her head!"

"Well, you're not her mother. Far from it, I should have thought."

Clare made no answer.

Sheila remarked: "She has everything, hasn't she?"

"Don't know what you mean by 'everything,' " said the other, defensively.

"I do. Notice how she gets everything she goes out for? ("You're as wax in her hands, as I told you you would be.") Still, let *that* go—one could call it a gift. What makes me so mad is the way things are showered on to her that she hasn't the sense to value or understand. Showered. That man Frank, now, to give you an example—I wouldn't want him because I don't, now, want anyone; but he's a man anybody would look at twice. (You didn't see him?) He's a selfish man, and he acts up more than a bit, but in his own way he is nuts about her. Being nuts sometimes does more to a selfish man, when it's once got him. And she?— Oh, she likes to have him around. At times. When not, does she ask what he does with himself? *I* could tell you. Loafs about on his own in that stuffy cottage with that vile-tempered dog—my goodness, I'd rather have this poor chump! No, she's never yet outgrown being a selfish child."

"Look, Sheikie, give her a chance!"

"You give her too many.—Frank's, however, the least of it. If it were that only—"

"What more?" asked Clare, weariedly.

Sheila paused, to adjust her voice to a not unfair mimicry of Dinah's. " 'Oh, two sons!' " she announced, with an audible smirk—then returned to her own furious tone. "Want them?—She hadn't had time to want them. Oh, no. Along they came, like everything else. There they were, and so that was very nice. Very nice and such fun, like everything else is. What did *she* want two boys for—to play house with?"

Clare made no answer.

"Eh?" Sheila demanded.

"Look, we're none of us perfect."

"We are *some* of us human!—Apart from that, she's perpetually flinging them in one's teeth. 'My son this,' 'My son that.' You may notice, not one opportunity does she miss."

"No now, Sheikie, really, that is unfair! Those two sons don't crop up for hours together."

"Expect *me* to be fair?" Sheila was thunderstruck by Clare's stupidity. She waited till she could speak more calmly before saying: "I could have done with them."

Clare, heavily startled, rolled her eyes round. "I didn't know."

"What do people expect to have when they marry? I wasn't old; I was thirty-two. And Trevor, as had been demonstrated, could have children. What else do you think I thought there would be, when I went into that?"

"I hadn't any idea . . ." declared Clare, sorrowfully and humbly.

"That's good news, in its way," said the other, crisply. "You were not intended to. Nobody was intended to."

"Thirty-two," pondered Clare. "Then you've been married to Trevor a long time?"

"Why not?"

"Never looked sideways?"

"No, thanks—never," said Sheila lifelessly. She added, as though in extenuation: "You have to watch your step in a place like this."

"Did you formerly watch your step?"

"Not so successfully as I'd thought, as it turned out."

"Still," said Clare, "with time, and so on, one lives things down?"

"With time *and* patience, yes. If one gives one's mind to it. And that Trevor did me a good turn, coming along when he did, I cannot deny. I've returned, I think I may claim, Clare, to being as Daddy would have liked to see me."

"I congratulate you, Sheikie."

"Well, thanks. That is the one thing that I *have* done."

"You hit it off all right with Trevor's children?"

"Phyllis's children? Yes, they were nice kids. They were all right."

"Where are they now?"

"Married.—However, there are times," said Sheila, returning to Dinah, now more genially, "when one has to laugh. For instance, this evening. No sooner was she into the house than like a wild animal in captivity she went on, didn't she? You saw the way she went for my curtains? One might have thought she'd know: she must have spent quite a bit on those Applegate curtains, to do her justice—surely they would have cords?"

"There was a time when curtains were drawn by hand. This evening she may have become confused."

"If she didn't know what century she was in, she could have asked. Couldn't she, instead of savaging all before her? Yes, and then did she keep on, talking, once she *had* wound herself up! Yes, and where did she get all that from? As a child, as you often so truly used to say, she mentally used to be something of a baa-lamb. Now, to hear her talk one would think she had invented the world."

"She thinks, therefore it is?"

"I shouldn't have thought *thought* was her strong point.

Yet in her own way she's quite sharp. You heard that question she asked me over the telephone?"

"Well, yes."

Sheila merely repeated: "She's quite sharp." Going in, as she spoke, at a gateless gateway, she threshed about in evergreens with her stick. "Come out, you fool!—It goes into there every time. What gets into animals?—Knows I can't stand that house?"

"You don't think, a bitch?"

"It's got no sex.—Well, I should *think* so," Sheila said as the dog came out. The dog and its two women shortly afterwards crossed the dividing line (a substantial avenue) between the Poor White swamps and Ravenswood Gardens. Seldom had the latter appeared more spruce: in the comparatively copious lamplight brass door knockers and knobs shone, steps were solid white, and the doors themselves, enamelled, as dark as gems. There appeared to be, however, one disadvantage. Sheila Artworth stopped dead, shut her eyes, and said: "*Look!*"

"What?"

"Well, *look!* That is Trevor's car. Trevor's home."

"Aha."

"I don't know what to say, Clare. I do feel bad! But all things considered—?"

"I'd better be off?"

"I do feel bad."

"High time I *was* on the road.—*Pssst!* You and the dog go in."

Mrs. Artworth drew a hand over her brow. "*What* we've all been through . . ."

Clare got herself into the Mini, slid back the window. The dog, followed by Sheila, went up the steps. The about-to-depart one put her head out and said in a hoarse whisper: "Good night, Sheikie!"

The woman on the steps turned. "Good night, Mumbo. Good journey. And, oh—thanks!"

The Mini left Ravenswood Gardens, in the direction of London.

Five

❧❧❧

"What's this?" asked Frank, picking up the butter knife.

"I couldn't tell you," said Francis.

"What's it doing here?"

"Looks mummified to me, doesn't it to you?"

"How did it get into the house?"

"It's for butter, according to Mrs. Delacroix."

"But how did it get into the house?" Frank liked the knife less the longer he looked at it. "Looks like something intended for the cave."

"Far from it. *It's* in high favour—it's to go on her tray."

"Where did it come from?" asked Frank, altering his tactics.

They were in the pantry, Francis's headquarters. The butter knife, till Frank interfered with it, had been seated on a satirically bright, clean fragment of green baize, dug out by Francis from somewhere. No wonder it had not failed to catch Frank's eye.

Francis launched into an account of his relations with the postman. "I cured him of battering and ringing when it was a parcel. What's a porch for? I pointed out to him. 'You leave whatever it is there—what do you think it's going to do, blow away? You ought to have more sense, at this hour of the morning.' That, as you'll understand, Major Wilkins, was at the beginning of the summer, when Mrs. Delacroix's personal circle were so lavishly responding to her appeals to stock up the cave. There were mornings when I thought the postman would tear the house down—sleep as she may at the other side of the house, Mrs. Delacroix was showing signs of alarm. Therefore I finally spoke to him about it. I can't say he took it with good grace. If you ask me, that battering and kicking and ringing was his revenge for having to carry the parcels—many of which, I must fairly say, were of a size to rightly have come by rail. However, if post offices *had* accepted them, that was his trouble. Since then, he appeared to have subsided: as it turns out, he was merely biding his time. A registered packet, requiring not only to be taken in personally *but* signed for, gave him exactly the opportunity he'd been waiting for. Such a renewed outbreak as we had this morning! Worse than any poltergeist, I can only tell you.—And now, this voodoo."

"What voodoo?" Frank asked—tossing the butter knife, negligently, back on to the piece of baize.

"Looking for a sixpence. It's now hoped, Major Wilkins, *you* will be able to provide one. Mrs. Delacroix's discovered she once again has no money of any kind in the house, and I have no silver smaller than half-a-crown.—You're with us early, this morning," remarked Francis, glancing at the pantry's electric clock.

"Touch of frost's what we've been wanting for the celery."

"Quite a tingle in the air, isn't there? Rather a sharp frost, I should say, to have come so suddenly.—Which reminds me," Francis went on, at this point turning his eye on Frank at once impressively and cautiously, "with winter descending upon us at such a rate, what's going to be done about the cave?"

Frank, shrugging his shoulders, extracted two boxes of matches then a third for luck from the supply drawer (quest for these having been in the first place what had brought him padding into the pantry). He grunted: "Better ask Mrs. Delacroix."

Francis accentuated the look he had given Frank, then diplomatically withdrew it. Galvanized by the briskness of the morning he was about to make a tour of Applegate, indoors and out, oiling all the locks, so was busy getting his kit together. Meanwhile, from the end of the kitchen passage could be heard the opening-then-shutting of a glass door. This would have signalized nothing more than the arrival of today's widow from the village, to be about her duties—but no. It was Mrs. Delacroix, in again from the garden. Francis whisked the butter knife out of view: baize and all, it vanished into the cutlery drawer. Any further to-do about this newcomer he was not, for some time to come, prepared to abide.

The chatelaine, framed in the pantry doorway, wore two jerseys: heavy, high-necked, pulled on one on top of the other. Gardening gloves crammed bulkily into a pocket distended one hip of her narrow slacks. Raked into tails by the battle into the jerseys, her hair hung round a particularly shining morning face, etherealized rather than clouded by a look of grief. "Well, it's come," she told Frank. "The frost's got the dahlias!"

"My dear, I'm sorry."

"Now I must spend this morning cutting them down."

"But look here, I'd rather thought—" he objected.

"It's cruel to leave them looking as they are this morning. You should see them—no rather you shouldn't: nobody should. It would be kindest to burn them at once, I think."

"Autumn's autumn." Rubbing the palm of a hand against the back of his handsome head, Frank contemplated her. "Not the end of the world."

"Madam was away when this happened last year," remarked Francis.

"Otherwise," cried Dinah, either revivified or bent on seeming so, "it's a heavenly morning!" She looked from one to the other. "Now, what's going on?"

"Francis," said Frank disloyally, "is wondering what's going to be done about the cave."

"Oh, *Francis*, do mind your own business!"

"I should be glad to," said Francis, "but that the matter forced itself on my attention, as sooner rather than later it will be doing, I should imagine, on that of others. Happening to be strolling in that direction, the other evening, I was met by a really nasty and musty smell, coming out from behind those mackintosh curtains."

" 'Strolling'?" jibed his employer. "Poking about!"

"Like it or not, you know, Dinah," moralized Frank, "you can't leave all that junk you've collected in there to rot. It was sent to you for a specific purpose. And—judging at least by my own experience—quite a bit of trouble was gone to hunting it out."

"Everyone concerned thoroughly enjoyed themselves, rooting about in their personalities," declared the cave's organizer, mutinously. "You included. If what you're in a fuss about is your grandmother's fan, go and take it out."

"If the collection *is* to be considered to be complete," interposed Francis, meanwhile testing the quill he was proposing to stick into the locks, "why not regard the matter as closed, twice over? Wasn't somebody then going to seal it up?"

"Get a mason in," the rash Frank said, going one better. "There's that chap in the village I can get hold of. And the sooner the better: the masons are pretty busy."

"*Mason?*"

"Well, it's no good counting on a bomb, as I always said."

"*Wall* up my cave? Then where would my cave be?—gone."

"Pity you didn't think of that in the first place."

"I didn't expect to survive it, I suppose," admitted the miserable one.

Francis, kit now got together, was ready to leave the pantry for his round of the house. He lingered, however, to offer further advice. "Why not make something of a ceremony of it? Invite the donors. And there would be no harm in having a representation from the village. And without attempting anything too formal, a few words probably should be said? With any further arrangements, I'd gladly charge myself. It's coming to be a considerable time, madam, now that one comes to think of it, since we had a party. It's a pity to drop into being too much of a recluse."

"You know, he's got something there—or wouldn't you say?" Frank wanted to know, though guardedly. He rather liked society.

"Nobody," said Dinah, "yet seems to have said anything about a band. Where are we going to get the band from?"

"Now, now!" warned Frank—for him, rather sharply.

"What *you* secretly want," cried Dinah, turning on Francis, "is to be a barman. Oh, very well then. I know three or certainly two people who are looking for a barman. Sorry as we shall be to say goodbye to you—"

Francis, disdaining to reply, quitted the pantry. "And don't go dripping that oil all over the carpets!" she hurled after him. "Oh," she said in a general way, "how he can annoy one!—Well," she told Frank, "I must be going out again. Coming? What I can't remember is, why I came in."

"I'd thought," he said, "I'd take a look at the celery." But he spoke, if not gloomily, uncertainly.

"What's up, Frank?" she instantly asked.

"You're very jumpy, you know. Nothing's happened, has it?"

"Only the dahlias. Did I cut up? I'm sorry."

"You've seemed to me jumpy ever since I got back. Nothing frightened you or gave you a shock of any kind while I was away?"

"Perhaps I missed you?" she asked.

"I should like to think so."

"It's lovely that you are back.—Come out. What are we doing standing about in here?"

"Wait a minute," he commanded, sliding a hand down into his money pocket. "You want a sixpence?"

"Indeed I do.—Oh, *good*! Thank you, darling Frank. You see, I must immediately send it off: Mumbo's sent me a butter knife from her symbol shop. Oh, where is it?—Oh, where *has* Francis hidden it? I want to show you."

"I took a look at it," he said, "I may as well tell you." Together they went down the passage towards the glass door dazzlingly at its end, out into the yard, out through the yard door into the garden, into the vindictive and sparkling beauty of the first frosty morning.

Six

Applegate.

"A pilot's thumb, wreck'd as homeward he did come."
That's what it is. I saw what it was the instant it came,
this morning. And why I wanted it. The most over-
looked line in that whole play. DON'T miss the 6d,
will you? It's in this envelope, but might wedge itself
down into a corner and get thrown away. Thank you
very much; I can hardly wait for tomorrow and my
tray. Will not write more now, as we have got an
enormous bonfire going in the garden. A woman near
here makes extraordinary masks, at a great rate. Why
not for Mopsie Pye? They would catch on. It would
be the greatest help to this poor woman, who has to
support not only a mother but an abnormal brother.
Any Sunday, we could take a look at them. Which
Sunday?

Yours affectionately,
D.

Sunday church-bells started their work on the tawny
evening while goodbyes were being said to the mask-maker
at her gate. She conveyed by a gesture at once resigned
and fanatical that everything else must be now suspended.
She cast a look upward, as well she might.

Her village (no great distance frome Dinah's) was famed
in this part of Somerset, and indeed beyond it, for its
ringers. Rooks, evidently familiar with the bells, streamed
through the sky filled by the pandemonium, and villagers,
facelessly there in their darkening doorways or stuck in

groups outside the blinded shops, seemed as inured. For non-natives, the disturbance was elemental. The village was hard to get out of—the frantic Hillman darted hither and thither, a thing trapped. One had been caught in a raid.

This seemed no fair way to announce Evensong—and continue doing so, as the ringers in their frenzy of virtuosity were intending, for the next half-hour. It was a half-diabolical way to announce Evensong. Holy-unholy changes, slicing and climbing on one another, no one wholly to be driven out of the air, followed the fleeing car into open country, loudening over fields made hollow by dusk and coppices made hollow by autumn. Nothing was left to slumber: from tracks and field-paths and wells and the scars of quarries rose everything latent and unremembered, till the centuries were as opened wounds. This beset tract was landlocked, no aid from the sea. The hour was one which should have drowned soundlessly when the sun set. The sun had set—though by glimmering as they ran past the car windows stone walls and gateposts still were memorials to the space of light which had been today.

The bells were long in letting their prey go.

"Phew!" said Dinah, shaking the last off by giving a violent shake to her head.

"Well . . ."

"Always running you into *something*, aren't I!"

"Chance, no doubt?"

"It's handsome of you to say so, Mumbo."

"I didn't say so."

"Still, you did like the masks?"

"Yes. But this is the finish, you know, Dicey."

"To what?"

"To dashing about like this."

"Oh, no—you don't mean that? 'The Last Ride Together'? No, you mustn't say that. I'm, I'm not feeling well."

"You're looking perfectly well."

"Frank, though, says I have had a shock."

"Surely *you* should know?"

"Yes, but he sees me every day. And those are the people who know, aren't they?"

"I've no idea. Nobody sees me every day."

"Then I don't know, Mumbo, how you can have any idea what you are like."

"Your mother had some idea what I am like."

"Why?—I mean, how did you know?"

"Your mother told me not to be bad for you."

"*Did* she?—Mustn't she, more, have been thinking of us all three?—Nothing's ever really got going when there wasn't Sheikie too. Look at the other night."

"That is true," Clare said. "And that she knew. But I was the one she gave the wigging to.—Dicey, what happened to her in Cumberland?"

"She didn't go vapouring over a crag while gazing at the moon."

"Not she!"

"Some thought her dreamy. No, she went down in that plague at the end of the war. That Spanish Flu, that was like a war more. Why had people to live through that, then die then? Anyway, they had to. That, like war was, was the common lot. And the common lot's good enough for anybody who's any good, isn't it? Good enough for her. It was very bad up there where we were, in those isolated places. Everywhere such awful dismay. There she was with nobody but me, doing what she could—so often, in vain. You can nurse sickness, but what can you do against dismay? She never turned a hair—he would have been proud of her."

"Who?"

"Your father."

Clare said first nothing, then only: "You didn't get it?"

"Some children didn't—did you? . . . Mumbo, it all was rather confused, confusing, the other evening? I mean, at Southstone."

"I should stop thinking about that."

"All right.—What *did* you think of the masks?"

The car smelled of masks inside. Clare sat with three on her knee, samples—only lightly wrapped, in view of their fragility, in thin paper. Another, bought by Dinah outright, grimaced all by itself on the back seat. Taking her three out, Clare re-examined them, more by touch than sight. "They're good," she said. "You were right."

"I'm glad. Glad not to have brought you down here for nothing; also for her—you *are* taking them?"

"She'll have to keep at it. No good me creating a demand if she can't supply: bad for the shop."

"She looked puzzled but pleased, I thought."

Clare, absently, held up one of the masks to her own face. The driver waited till she had negotiated the Hillman past a party of bicycles—the road was seeming to narrow; their reflectors, caught in the Hillman's side lights, strung out into a series of scarlet warnings—to more than half turn round, crying: "Don't do that!"

"What are masks for, then?"

"To hang on walls."

"Dicey . . . I am not now hearing *more* bells, am I?"

"Only my church's; they wouldn't hurt a fly.—We're back, all but. I thought we'd go round by Frank's."

Clare re-swathed the three in their tissue paper. "Oh? Just as you like."

"He'll *be* at Applegate, probably."

"What's the point, then?" (Frank, who had made an exception of this Sunday by going over to lunch at the other side of the county, had yet to be met. Clare, Sabbath or not, had polished off one or two pieces of Mopsie Pye business along her road from London, so had not got to Applegate till about two o'clock; not too late, however, for an excellent pheasant. Francis had been active during the meal.) "See the cottage?" she said, more pleasantly.

"What I want to do there is, tack up this mask."

"Ah. A surprise?"

They came to a stop at Frank's neat gate. Clare took a look up the short path. In this late light, the face of the cottage was dark-engraved against trees behind it—seen by a newcomer, and through no veil other than that of evening, it had the somehow sinister sentimentality of an illustration to one of those books of tales over which bygone children wore out their eyes. Two top windows were squeezed under heavy eaves; two below looked out over clumps of box. Care and time, by all signs, had gone to the upkeep—not a weed sprouted between the cobbles of the path; the porch, the door, and the water butt at the side had lately been painted a scarab-blue which kept sheen even in deep dusk. Yet the cottage, like others on promotion, had about it a look of askew destiny. A television aerial, over the dipping roof-line, showed that the owner had at least one resource. Only the aerial seemed of normal size.

"Should fit the man like a glove, I should imagine?" Clare said.

"There was keen competition for it, I can only tell you."

"Ever get any sun?"

"Oh, dazzlingly in the early mornings! It faces east."

"Where is a car put?"

"Yes, that *is* a bore for him. Somebody else's barn."

"Looks locked up?" said Clare, sounding optimistic.

"*Oh*, no." Dinah, advancing upon the drop door-handle (which was an example of village ironwork), gave it a practiced wrench. As the door yielded, horrible growls and snarls were heard from within—entrance being directly into the living-room, the Labrador came at them round an oaken settle, teeth bared. Dinah pushed past the dog. "And don't try anything on with your Aunt Mumbo!"

"It had better not!"

The black beast, having run out of snarls, went off and became *couchant* under a side table: it continued to watch them disagreeably. "One oughtn't to talk about it," Dinah said, "because it listens. But I sometimes think that by having such a horrible character it draws off any bad out of Frank. He has a very nice character, as you'll see." She held her hand, experimentally, near to the white ashes powdering the hearth. "Dead cold. Out since last night, I should think. So he probably only looked in just now, just for a minute, to leave the dog back, so didn't bother." She looked round for somewhere to hang the mask.

"It *has* been out, then, the poor brute?"

"Oh yes, he took it to Shepton Mallett. Most people will stand for anything once. Better have the top light on for this job, I think?" Click went the switch. With no less certainty, Dinah unearthed a hammer and a tobacco tin of assorted nails.

Top-lit, the room made a clean breast of it. Little to declare, nothing to conceal—exactly what *was* the nature of the reading-matter stuffed back into a recess deep enough to be still shadowy was the only mystery to remain. The walls' plaster bulged over ancient stonework; the low ceiling was kept where it was by two hoary cross-beams. The settle, out at a right angle from the hearth, was the only quite unamenable piece of furniture—a rather concave large chesterfield in a garment of Jacobean linen looked comfortable, as did the saddlebag chairs upholstered either in hide or a good substitute. Apart from the pearwood table having under it at the minute the Labrador, there were other, smaller ones, on which were many ash trays, each looking as though it might have a history. There were two shaded table lamps, though it might be suspected that Frank when left to himself lived with the top light on, as it now was. Any disorder was on the floor: Sunday papers, dishevelled, lay where they had been impatiently dropped, and more than one of the rugs had been kicked up at the corners or rucked across by some frenetic movement— surely only the dog's?

Dinah, though already holding the point of a nail in position against a place on the wall, turned when she felt Clare to be examining the room. Her eyes, slow and soon left behind, followed Clare's earnestly on their tour. "Nice?" she wanted to know.

"*You* choose that?" asked Clare, reverting to the Jacobean linen.

"Oh, no. Why should I? But I like it."

Yet another recess was crammed with dinted black japanned tin boxes. "I don't think he's ever unpacked, properly," said Dinah, seing them being studied. "How he came by those lawyer's boxes, I've often wondered."

"Never asked?"

"I don't think so."

"What would be in them?"

"That I have no idea."

Clare bit a yawn off. She sat herself on the uncushioned settle.

Dinah seemed disappointed by the choice. "I don't care much, ever, for that settle. But his wife liked it, as far as I can make out. She apparently believed it came out of a Welsh farmhouse—and it does keep draughts out; that I must say it does. Unfortunately, you see, this room has that other door at the other end, straight into the yard. It used to be two rooms. However, one learns to put cushions against that."

"Where is Mrs. Wilkins?"

"Oh, she's been for years in Heaven!—at least I should think so; I hope so. Frank's a widower."

"How does he like that?"

"How could anybody possibly? It's a hardship. Still, it's another thing he and I have in common.—You're not sneezing? *Not* in a draught, are you?"

"No harm in a little through ventilation, as my mother would have said."

"May I tell you one thing I have often wondered?"

"Well, what?"

"Why did he marry her?"

Clare's back stiffened against the settle's. She out-stared Dinah, but nonetheless consented to take thought, ending by coming out with: "I asked her that once, one day. She thought honestly, then gave a tremendous laugh, saying, 'D'you know, I don't think he's ever told me!'—As a marriage, you know, Dinah, that was all right. She was born Army. We make dynastic marriages."

"You didn't."

"No, but then I'm a muddle. No."

"Did you ever wish she was not there?"

"Well—"

"Did you ever hate her?"

"My mother? No, never," Clare said. That was that.

"*I* liked her," said Dinah. "She was nice to me, and friendly to Mother."

Clare said vaguely: "Went out of her way to be."

"Does it ever seem to you that the non-sins of our fathers—and mothers—have been visited upon us?"

Clare said: "I thought you were going to hang that mask?"

"Indeed I am!"

Easier said than done. A well-worn cottage comedy ran its course—outbursts of hammering, each in a fresh place, each ending with the rebounding nail falling to the floor. "Bother! . . . *oh*, bother! . . . bother all ancient walls! As you can see, poor Frank only could hang his pictures where he could." Now she said so, that was to be seen. But as they were all bird pictures (Peter Scott) and birds are often at different altitudes, it might not matter.—"Don't breathe; I *think* this one's staying in!" Dinah hastily hung the mask on it, stood back. The mask looked well.

"So now, I suppose—"

The mask fell to the floor.

"Perhaps," said Dinah, picking it up, "it was not MEANT to hang here?" She moved a pottery jug with some twigs in it on to the table with the Labrador under it and propped the mask against the jug. "*Here*, it hardly can fail to catch his eye?"

"Hardly, I should imagine."

"I wish," said Dinah, looking about her once more when they were leaving, "we *had* lit the fire in here, even for a short time. And in a way I wish I hadn't brought in that mask—however, there it is. You see, I love this cottage. I wish it was mine. Directly I am in here I feel safe again—it's a long, long time since anywhere else has given me the same feeling. Feverel Cottage was only called a cottage; I suppose it was not one really—but there were many times when it felt like one. *This* cottage has got some syringa bushes in the back garden, and the smell is the same. And also here there is a pane of glass in the roof, upstairs, which one can hear the rain pattering on. I am sure the people who lived here before Frank must have kept kittens, because there occasionally still is a smell of them.—I, I don't suppose you see what I mean, Mumbo?"

Clare did her best—she shut her eyes. But club chairs and ash trays remained imprinted.

"You don't?" said Dinah.

"Dicey, this is not *like* Feverel Cottage!"

"Oh, no. No. No, of course it isn't.—Come on!"

"Now, where?"

"Back."

The way was short. Two minutes after leaving the cottage, the car turned into the home lane; four more minutes, then there would be the white gate. Never much used after dark, the lane was empty—never had it led, beyond Applegate, to anywhere but another farm. And last week's frost had terminated the season for outdoor lovers, though to-night again was no more than chilly. Some few trees, so far as it could be seen, posted the way.

A cat came out of the ditch, conspiratorially turning the lamps of its eyes to meet the car's—it shrank back, just not too late. Dinah said hurriedly: "May I ask one more thing?"

"That depends."

"Now that it's all over—"

"What's all over?" (Clare steadied the masks, which had given a wobble on her knee.)

"*What* did you put into the bottom of the coffer?"

Clare seemed to be bargaining in her mind. "You won't get anything out of Sheikie," she pointed out.

"No—but what did you put in?"

"Oh, all right. Shelley."

"You don't mean *Shelley*?"

"What's the good of asking if you don't believe me? I'd given him up."

"You must have been mad?"

"I thought he was WRONG."

"You must have been mad! I put in a gun."

"Nonsense."

"What's the good of asking if you don't believe *me*?"

"I didn't ask.—What on earth do you mean, though?"

"What's now called a gun. A pistol—or could it have been revolver? Somebody's shooting somebody else with it now, probably. I told you two I knew there was one, but you took no notice."

"Expected us to believe you?"

"That's a mistake you may make once too often, Mumbo. Still, that's that—here's my nice white gate!"

There it was: bland if phantom. For ever open. As large as life. "*No*," Clare cried, again restraining the masks, "you crook, you don't get away with that! Wait a minute, can't you?—Pull *up*!"

"No," said the driver, driving on in. "Frank will have heard the car."

He had not; he was playing a loud record. It rather than he came out to meet them. In the hall, Dinah flung her overcoat at a bishop's chair, then waited to do the same with Clare's. They harkened.

> The runaway train came down the track,
> She blew, she blew,
> The runaway train came down the track
> And she blew, she blew,
> The runaway train came down the track,
> Her whistle wide and her throttle back,
> And she blew, blew, blew, blew—

Dinah, going ahead of Clare round the drawing-room door (which had been ajar), said, "Oh, really, Frank!" though in a pacific tone.

"Makes a change," he said, stopping it not without regret—he was on his feet anyway, near the player. "Well,

here you *are*. I was beginning to think you'd gone to
church." He then looked civilly, if not exactly expectantly,
towards Clare. Dinah introduced them: making their way
towards each other, they shook hands. "Missed meeting you
the other day," he told her, "by a few minutes." She said,
yes, she had heard that that had been so.

"If we didn't go to church, it wasn't for lack of asking,
was it, Mumbo?" recollected Dinah, shuddering. "Oh my
heavens!—Frank, what did you have for lunch?"

"Pheasant, chiefly."

"Oh, then you didn't miss much. Who was there?—No,
that can keep," she told him, on second thoughts. "You can
imagine what Mumbo and I need, first of all.—I say," she
asked, looking about, "where's *your* drink?"

"I was waiting for you," he said with unusual formality.
"What may I get you?" he asked Clare.

She told him; then, looking at Mrs. Piggott's clock, remarked: "We are quite late, I see."

"All the nicer to be home!" sang out the homecomer,
contentedly coiling into her chair. "*Perch* yourself somewhere, wouldn't you, Mumbo; or not yet? As you know,
everything here's yours." She went on: "This *is* a fire!"
gazing at it with love and awe.

"Not bad, is it?" asked Frank, turning his head—he was
at the tray at the other end of the room. "You told Francis
to go to some French film?"

"I did, but I hardly believed he would—has he? On his
own, or who with?"

"Mrs. Coral's Finn."

"Oh, good."

"This as it should be?" Frank asked Clare, entrusting
to her the well-filled glass.

"By the look of it, exactly, thank you." She tried it, it
was. She said: "I met your dog."

He said: "I don't understand. Where?"

"Yes, Frank," cried his neighbour cheerfully, "we went
round by the cottage—into it, for a minute."

"I'm afraid you didn't see it at its best, then," he told
Clare—speaking from a distance: he was back at the tray.
Standing there frowning at a decanter, he said, as much to
it as to Dinah: "If I'd known, I could just as well have been
there as here."

"Naturally," she said, a little irritated by having to say

anything so simple—dodging her head to see him between or over the various objects interposing between them, cushions along the top of the back of the sofa, lamps, a high bowl of spindle and other berries, and so on—"it would have looked nicer with you in it."

That's being true did not reflect particularly upon the cottage—almost any surroundings would gain by surrounding Frank: this room was doing so at this minute. Still wearing and strikingly well become by the suit in which he had been over to Shepton Mallett or its neighbourhood, he looked like Sunday, a Sunday of an enjoyable, by which need not be said wholly secular, kind. Any slight touch of fantasy about his appearance he could carry off. This fortunate man not only liked his clothes but was liked by them—not always is the liking reciprocated. Whether or not (Dinah said, not) in his life Frank had had the recognition he deserved, he looked fortunate, and how far better that is than to look deserving.

"I dare say it might have," he said, "that is, I hope so. But that's not the point. I left the place in a mess, and as cold as the tomb."

When all three of them were provided for, and Clare had decided upon a place on the sofa, he settled, finally, into his usual chair—from which he returned his attention to the visitor. "I hope," he said, "this afternoon went to plan? As I understand, you were to pay your respects to our local witch. Find her congenial?"

"Largely, it was a business trip," said Clare. Facing the fire, she unbuttoned her coat—the tweed of her suit, this time, was more sombre and less aggressive in pattern than the tweed last time: with the same sardonic discretion she wore a dark silk shirt, high at the neck. Her being without the turban made no great change, since her hair had been moulded by successions of turbans into their shape. What more seemed unusual was her wearing earrings: square, big, good-looking pearl stud ones. She looked handsome— there was a slight touch of fantasy about *her* appearance. She added: "Nothing like talking shop."

"I agree with you. And you had a march past of the masks? My idea is, she gets many of her ideas from living under that belfry. Result is, *I* shouldn't care to live with one of those things. Come home late, open the door, and find one of those grinning at me?—no, thank you."

"Oh, Frank—now you *have* put your foot in it!"

"What on earth do you mean, Dinah?"

"Wait till you see. Oh, dear!"

"Short of talking shop," he went on, to Clare, "provided
there's anybody to do it with, there's nothing like talking
over old times, is there? Those, one never gets to the end
of, still less the bottom of. Seen Mrs. Artworth lately?"

"You unfortunately *haven't*, have you, Mumbo?" interposed Dinah hastily.

"Too bad, her living so far away." He brought out his
pipe, considered it, put it back again.

Clare, changing her attitude on the sofa, knocked a
cushion overboard with her elbow. Dinah, in an outburst
of loving showmanship, pointed out: "Mumbo always does
that.—Frank, having by now met us all three, wouldn't
you say St. Agatha's was to be congratulated on the way
we've turned out? We may not be much, but we could
have been far worse. Looking back, I think Miss Ardingfay
had ideals."

Frank, having waited to see whether more was going to
come, and if so what, said: "Good." Clare recovered the
cushion and put it back again. Dinah, evidently disappointed with both of them, turned away and looked into
the fire: she continued to do so. Frank fixed his eyes on
her: "Tired?" he said accusingly—for one or another
reason she failed to hear.

"*What* do you think can have tired her?" Clare asked—
with, for the first time, a mocking deference.

"Overdoes things," he said—for the first time, curtly.
"She overdoes everything."

"What I was thinking," said their friend, coming to the
surface, "was, wouldn't it be better, later, to have an
omelette? There's that other pheasant, cold, but that might
be stupid. But soup could be nice, from the bones of the
first? If so, the bones ought to start now."

"Now?—nothing easier," Frank exclaimed. With alac-
rity, taking his glass with him, he rose and left them.

"Can cook?" asked Clare, looking after him.

"Everyone can now, can't they?"

"I couldn't tell you: I eat out.—*Now*, what about that
gun?"

"It was at the bottom of Mother's glove drawer."

"In Feverel Cottage? I don't believe you."

"There you go, again! Yes—I was looking for some place to stow sugar mice: wherever I had them in *my* room that odd maid we had detected them out and ate them, and it was no good tale-telling to Mother because she said they gave me spots. But I happened to know there was that drawer full of I don't know how many pair of long, long gloves, folded up and beautifully put away. As at Feverel Cottage she no longer wore them, why should she go to that drawer? So then I lifted the gloves up, to stow my sugar mice underneath, and there was the pistol or revolver. That was how, as I told you, I knew there *was* one."

"Taking it was another thing," said Clare.

"I don't see why, when she never used it."

"Nevertheless, you robbed her."

"Everything that was hers was mine, she told me."

"What about everything you had?"

"I was hers."

Clare sat scowling, thumping a knee with a fist thoughtfully. "What can have been its history—*why* was it there?"

"Cousin Roland thought of it as a thing no widow should be without? No, he couldn't have been so silly. Not only was she not nervous but there was nothing—*then*, if you remember?—to be nervous about. More likely, it was one of the things she'd inherited that she didn't exactly know what to do with. Not that it looked antique; it was fairly new-looking."

"Loaded?"

"I thought it was safer not to look."

"My heavens, and you dragged it round in that thicket!"

"Well, it didn't go off. . . . It may, of course, have been Father's; but if it was he can't have been keen on it. I mean, if he'd been keen on it he'd have used it, wouldn't he, instead of going under that train?"

Clare's "*What?*" froze on her lips.

"I'm sorry—I'm terribly sorry, Mumbo!" cried Dinah, shaken. "I thought you knew; I imagined everyone knew."

"You were how old?"

"Shortly to be born."

"*What* a thing to do to her, to do to *her!*"

"There was some reason, something he couldn't bear. Something gave way underneath him, all of a sudden. *And* I expect some worry, partly money? Nothing to do with her. They'd been so happy."

"Too happy, possibly?"

"How could it ever be possible to be that?—Anyway, that was how Cousin Roland came to take us on."

"Who was that man?"

"Cousin Roland? Mother's first cousin. He thought of everything. He paid my school bills, I *think*; but also, which was still nobler, all those years he kept Mother in flowers and new novels. From which I suppose there may have been those who manfully tried to argue he kept Mother: if he had, she could hardly have cost him more—those were the only two things she wanted; but those she could do with any amount of, and did. Otherwise, she was very independent."

"All she wanted?"

"Poetry, but those books she already had: they were up in her room."

"She should have married again?"

"*Again?*—Even I have never wanted to do that. Oh, no. No. There are shocks you don't take the risk of twice."

"You didn't, though, have her kind of shock?"

"No, but it was *a* shock. . . . Bill died. That happened while the boys, still, were little. Widows," said Dinah, "run in families." She rose from her chair and went to the door, calling: "Is that you, Frank?"

"Coming," came his voice from the hall. "Are we in the kitchen?"

"We like eating in the kitchen, Mumbo—if you don't mind?—when Francis is out of the way: he so rarely is."

The Applegate kitchen had a substantiality given it by its 1912 builder and not made less by any few changes, such as the substitution of a white Aga cooker for a probably larger iron-and-steel range, and of chromium taps over the sink for brass ones. Round the walls ran racks, brackets, and shelves; there were ample cupboards and, in the middle of the red tiled floor, an abiding-looking, heavy, clean-scrubbed deal table—with, now placed ready upon it, a basket of eggs, a mixing bowl, pots of pepper and salt, and a large pat of butter stamped with a lion's head, on a willow-pattern plate. Other preparations were on the dresser. A steam of pheasant came from the simmering bones.

"All very snug," said Clare, at a halt as much in the

middle of everything as the table permitted. Frank clattered two omelette pans out of hiding, to compare them for size; while Dinah, dark-purple sleeves pushed up, set about compounding a dressing for the salad. The guest added: "Nothing *I* can do, I expect?"

"No. But why don't you come and live here too, Mumbo?"

"Thanks very much."

"It would," said Dinah, methodically busy with the wooden spoon, "be very nice." Frank left the kitchen for the pantry, where, not too far away down the passage, he could be heard getting silver, glasses, and so on together on a tray. Dinah continued: "If you retired?"

"Couldn't afford to, thank you."

Dinah added a pinch of something to the dressing. "It *would*," she repeated, "be very nice."

"Why?"

"We should have more time, then. Plenty of time."

" 'Make *me* a willow cabin at your gate?' "

The spoon stopped. Dinah went white.—"How *dare* you? As a matter of history, Frank bought that cottage before he met me—before he had any notion that I existed, and why should he? Why do you try and ruin *everything*—why?"

"Only for myself."

"Trouble-making, wherever you go!"

"Sorry."

"And *you* had the nerve to criticize Shelley!"

Timely return of Frank, carrying the tray. . . . Supper, when ready (which it was not immediately), went surprisingly well. Dinah added a tinful of ready-made pheasant soup, and later sherry, to the liquid from the bones. The omelette, as sometimes does happen with those made under unfavourable conditions, turned out to be one of her best. Claret was enjoyed. "You're not," Frank asked Clare, as the meal drew to a close, with mellow and genuine if not deep concern, "really taking the road again tonight, are you?"

"Yes, she is—she says. She likes dashing about."

"Got to get back, unfortunately," said Clare. She looked stoically at her watch.

"That, I am greatly against," said Frank.

"*What* are you greatly against, Frank?"

"Dashing about." He dealt Dinah a look, and more than a look, from under his eyebrows. "Life's too short.—You got that sixpence all right?" he asked Clare.

"Yes. You put it up?"

"I was glad to.—I'd better make up that fire, in there, again," he told Dinah, "before *I* go." He left them. She lit the burner under the coffee. "Everybody's going away now, I suppose," she said, though as though to herself.

Somewhat faintly, music came from the drawing-room:

> The runaway train went over the hill,
> And she blew—she blew.
> The runaway train went over the hill,
> And she blew—she blew.
> The runaway train went over the hill,
> And the last we heard she was going still,
> And she blew, blew, blew, blew, blew—

They harkened. Dinah, waiting for the coffee, stacked some plates up and landed them in the sink, saying: "Doesn't waste a minute, does he?"

"*This* is a blazing fire to be left alone with," she said, coming back from having seen off Frank. "Or, to be going to be left alone with." Clare, standing about, was studying some curled-up family snapshots, found in a bowl. Many of them featured the same five children, some of them small; others, the same two girls (or quite young women). "Which is Annie," she asked, "and which is Teresa?"

"Teresa's the one with the hangdog smile: she *is* the more fascinating, I suppose. But Annie goes to one's heart for some different reason. She has always been plump—see? —plump as a robin. And her back's all right now."

"No longer goes to the osteopath?"

"Thanks to the osteopath, no.—You would love them, both of them," said Dinah timidly. "Anybody would love them. I do wish that we—I do wish that you—?"

Clare, as though not hearing, re-examined the children, one by one. "None of them are like you, either now or— or, then." She dropped the snapshots back into the bowl. "Well, you need never lack for company!"

"No, oh, no. No, I never need lack for company."

One log's giving way under the weight of the other logs,

consumed, causing the fire suddenly to blaze higher. "How good he is," mused Dinah, reminded, isn't he . . ." Then she struck her cheek with her hand, crying out: "*Oh*, and I never warned him about that mask! How could I not have? What had I better do—telephone?"

"Too late, I should have thought."

"I could say I'm sorry."

"If that's how the man feels, why put it there?"

"Mumbo, he'd never *said* so, until tonight! How was I to know?—at the worst they bored him, I thought. What an idiot act of mine, all the same! I wanted a reason to go into that cottage."

"You need a reason?"

"I thought you might laugh at me.—But *now*, what a thing to have done to him, when he's worried anyway! He's less happy, and I'm making him less happy. Everything I've done's been stupid and wrong: I should never, for instance, have lent him *The Midwich Cuckoos*.— You've read *The Midwich Cuckoos*?"

"No, I haven't."

"Well, that's the *last* straw!—How am I to explain? Frank's terrified of children. Otherwise, he's the bravest, most fearless man; but he has, perhaps, got a conspiracy complex slightly. He's terrified that some terrible Hostile Race, which will go on to drive everyone else out, is at any moment going to begin to be born. He was highly suspicious of his own grandchild, even: convinced that *that* poor little thing would have Yellow Eyes—which was why he wouldn't go next or near it (last week, he finally did, I'm glad to tell you). When I went and lent him that book, the damage was done.—Yet, was it only *The Midwich Cuckoos*?"

"You welter in superstition down here in Somerset?"

"Oh, no.—Though it *was* no book for a pending grand-father, I admit. When I tried to argue him out of it, things went worse. 'If one's a Hostile,' I said, 'one is that at any age.' He gave me a long, rather searching look, saying, 'Well, perhaps you're right.' What *am* I doing, when he's so dear and good to me, as you see? And apart from that, also, I often bore him—nor, I may say, is he the first I've bored. But then, boredom is part of love."

"That I deny!"

"Well, of affection."

"*That* I doubt."

"Then you've no affections.—Mumbo, are you a Lesbian?"

"Anything else, would you like to know?"

"I only wondered."

"You 'only wondered' whether Sheikie had killed anyone."

"She said, 'not exactly.' "

"Shall we leave this at that?"

"Are you annoyed?"

"Why?" asked Clare imperturbably. "As you remarked at that same time, 'People like to be taken an interest in.' That is true of all of us." She paused. "All the same, you know, one can injure feeling. You are worse in saying that I have no affections."

"*I* don't care what you are!"

"That is the worst thing you have said yet."

"But I care *for* you!" cried the bewildered one. "And you care for me—or so I had thought? I wanted you. I wanted you to be there—*here*, I mean. Whatever you think of yourself, you are very strong; and also, I thought you would understand. Who else am I to talk to, without frightening them? Stay with me for a little, can't you?"

"Look, Dicey, what *are* you frightened of?"

"I hoped—" said the other, but broke off, hopelessly.

"All your life, I should think, you have run for cover. 'There's Mother!' 'Here's my nice white gate!' Some of us have no cover, nothing to run to. Some of us more than *think* we feel."

"That's not kind, is it?" asked Dinah, puzzled.

"What makes you expect me to be kind? *Was* I ever, particularly?"

"Your father was."

"Whatever you have become," said Clare, angered, "and what you have become is in many ways very wonderful, as you do know, you are what you were always, and that's a cheat. A player-about. Never once have you played fair, all along the line. Simply, you play your particular kind of game better than you did; so well, by now, that you probably hardly know that you *are* playing it when you are. Nor have you learned, it seems, after all these years, that it's a game you can play too often. Well, now I am telling you: you can. *This* is once too often. Frightened? I don't believe you—you enchantress's child!"

Dinah was at the far end of the room. Target, she stood like a target, flattened against a wall with, behind her head, one of the pictures Sheikie had giggled at. She found nothing to say but: "But you loved her?"

"Yes. But once is enough."

"I am also—"

"Well, what?"

"I am also my father's child."

Nothing from Clare.

"Like a drink?"

"I've done well, thank you."

" 'Famous last words'?"

"Well, *I* can't stay here," Clare said, slapping a pocket of her coat. "It's late, and I have to go."

"It *is* late to start. If you slept here, you could start tomorrow at cockcrow—cockcrow?"

"I have nothing with me," said Clare, buttoning her coat.

"If I gave you a toothbrush, a new toothbrush?"

"*No*—Circe."

"Very well," said Dinah gently, turning away.

Seven

The room was over the drawing-room, and of the same size—it appeared longer. There being no end window, that wall was occupied by a canopy into whose curtained distance the bed ran back, drawing the room with it. From the foot of the bed, a carpet with roses stretched to the door at the other end of the room: yet, coming in, one was struck by the austerity of the perspective. Why?—for the bed was as wide as it was long, which is voluptuous. But it was the marriage bed of an early widow, having about it, whether or not since visited, a look of unbanishable half-emptiness. And, these last days, a growing remoteness from all things else had caused it to take on the look of a death bed—or more, perhaps, one for lying in state? The woman on it lay unlivingly still, straight, her narrow form outlined by the covering which it hardly lifted. She lay along the edge, close to which was pulled up a needlework stool—on her other flank extended the desert. Her eyes (so far as could be known in that tent of shadows) remained closed. The one sign she gave of sickness was this indifference, but it was an indifference so great as to be a sickness in itself.

The windows there were looked out, as did those below them, across the lawn into the orchard. One, a wide bay, held the dressing-table; the other, nearer to the bed, was open at the top. The early-November day, having been since morning resigned and sunless, was now drawing to a close: what was left of it came through the big panes. The room was warmed by a fire kept burning in the grate, at the door end: the door stood half-open, a darkening oblong.

In a chintz armchair by the fire sat Sheila Artworth, knitting. Now, after a second cautious glance at the patient, she risked switching on the table lamp at her elbow—perhaps for company?—so tipping the shade down as to protect the bed. *She* was framed, thus, inside a circle of light: now and then flashes came from her crystal needles or violet sparkles from her three-strand necklace. In the warmth she had taken her jacket off; she was sleeveless in a pleated orchid blouse. Her head of blue-blonded hair stood out clearly—above it, and above the circle of light, the china-crowded chimneypiece was spectral.

"*You* can't knit?" came a voice from the distance, faintly.

"Oh, hullo, Dinah."

"Hullo."

"Lamp worry you?"

"How long have you been here?"

"Since this morning."

"How long have I been here?"

"I wouldn't worry. What about a cup of tea, now you *are* awake?"

"Am I?"

Just as nothing but silence came upstairs out of the house and in at this door, there had not, either, come through the open window anything but the witless or disenchanted note of a bird. But now, somewhere in the hinterland of the orchard children began inquiringly shouting to one another. Sheila Artworth gave ear. She said: "There they are."

"What, Sheikie?"

"I said, 'There they are.'"

"Yes." A hand of Dinah's came out and explored the empty top of the needlework stool. "Where are my books? —Why are they gone?"

"You don't want them, do you?"

"I want them by me."

"Well, they're only over there," said the accommodating nurse, nodding towards the top of a chest and beginning to get up (even *this* sign of will in the patient was encouraging). "All I thought was, they rather crowded you up. And with them off it, that makes somewhere to sit for anybody coming to see you."

"Is anybody coming to see me?"

Down in the drawing-room sat the sons—Roland in one, William in the other of the armchairs facing each other across the fire. Having come far to see what ought to be done, they could so far find nothing to do but this. The tea tray decreed by Francis (they had got here about an hour ago) and shortly afterwards placed between them, was in more than one sense filling a gap. Apart from a certain clear fairness of skin, neither of them had inherited his mother's looks—which was, as she had pointed out, as they were sons probably just as well. Their marked and pleasing likeness to one another suggested that they had inherited their father's. They had in common a look of steadiness (though this was by no means a look of heaviness) and of knowing where one was. There may have been truth in her story that each of them, one two years after the other, had, when ceremonially first placed in her arms after his birth, taken in the situation at a glance—not at least without some optimism, and certainly kindly. Had they guided her, rather than she them, throughout the problems of their fatherless childhood and then youth? If she had made a good mother (to the surprise of many) it was owing to them—or so she held. Gratitude mingled with the love she bore them. Their marriages had not only rejoiced her but seemed to allay some fear—had she perhaps feared to outstay her welcome?

William, the one facing the window, saw out into the orchard; for Roland, there was its tarnished reflection (should he wish) in the mirror some way back over his brother's head. Somewhere out there, long ago lost to view amongst twisted apple trees, each had a daughter. On arrival, the children had instantly taken to the woods—that is, if an orchard can so be called.

Had bringing the children been a good idea? It had had the hallmark of having emanated from Mrs. Coral. "Don't be too alarmed," Mrs. Coral had written, "by anything you may happen to hear. But should you think of coming, which might be well, those two would serve to brighten her up, which is at the root of most troubles, is it not? I shall be glad to have them to sleep with me, that house as one might expect being upset. They would be nice for Coralie, my second daughter's little girl, that is, who is here with me from Nuneaton after her adenoids and rather a lonely little elf."

Nothing made sense. Vaguely wild, the early reports from Applegate had been, as Mrs. Coral foresaw, alarming. Later, censorship seemed to have clamped down. What did the doctor say? There had been no doctor; she wouldn't see one. She was being looked after by people from the village. Somebody, clearly, would have to move in here and take charge. Annie, for instance, or Teresa? Both girls had confessed, so far, to a sort of diffidence. Constantly on the telephone to each other, the two had frantically consulted. Teresa, quite off her own bat, had got through to that curious old card Frank Wilkins: she had nothing against him. It had not been satisfactory, she had had to admit to the tense Annie. "Do you think," asked Annie, "they had a fight?" "At their ages—what would they fight about?" "How did he sound, all the same, Teresa?" "Lost." "*What* d'you say, I can't hear you?" "Lost."

Meanwhile, talking of taking charge, a Mrs. Artworth had arrived this morning, with, according to Francis, apparently every intention of doing that. She had arrived, as she had done the time before, in a taxi; this time with a so-called overnight bag which had seemed to him to be of ominous size.

" 'Artworth'?" repeated the sons, when greeted by the news.

"Curious name, isn't it?" asked Francis, swivelling his eye from one of them to the other.

"Anyway," Roland said, ignoring the eye, "this is exceedingly kind of Mrs. Artworth." (The sons' adoption of a would-be repressive policy towards Francis was a sign not of overbearingness in their natures but rather of the optimism of which their mother had spoken.) "She'll ask you for anything she wants, I hope?"

"She's been doing so."

"Knows the house, then. Often been here before?"

"Once."

"Well, thank you, Francis. That will be all."

Francis dealt the speaker a look of sheer incredulity, and rightly. There'd be far, far more of *him* before they were through.

"At any rate," they said to him, "for now."

He inclined his head, professionally, and left them. Tea done, the sons lit cigarettes and looked round the drawing-room. No comment—other than the light patter whenever a desiccated berry fell, from the high bowl of spindle and other berries, on to the satinwood table behind the sofa. Roland got up out of his chair and walked round to examine the small-size record left behind on the player to gather dust. A Children's Favourite. This waking the father in him, he said: "They won't have had any tea?"

"Well, they bolted off. Mrs. Coral will give them a feed; won't hurt them to wait. . . . What about Mrs. Artworth?"

"A word with her?"

"No harm?"

The moment was psychological. As the two at the bottom looked up the stairs, a lady from the top began to come down. Round the turn of the banisters, she came down towards them smoothly as though descending a waterfall, nonchalantly balancing a tray. The copper beech being now denuded, but for some tatters, evening came freely if faintly in at the staircase window: it silhouetted her—silverly outlining the hair, the strong though light figure, the bare arms.

She was at an advantage. What gleams there were fell, from behind her, down full on their upturned, youthful-looking, Huguenot-descended faces. They knew themselves bare to a cryptic gaze they could not see.

She came to a stop a step or two above them, saying: "You're the sons, I suppose?"

"Mrs. Artworth?"

"Yes. Look, I wouldn't go up there just now, if you don't mind."

"We wondered if we could have a word with you?"

"Oh, I see. I'd been going to say, she's a little confused, just now."

Roland said: "But she does know we're here?"

"Well, she's been told."

William said: "so long as she knows we're here?"

"She forgets, you see."

He looked at her with a dismay verging on horror.

Roland said: "And knows the children are here?"

"Well, sitting up there with her, *I* heard them."

"Mrs. Artworth, have you any idea . . . ?"

"Sorry," she said, with, in her mermaid glance, a blend

of teasing regret and hospital sternness, "but I can't stop now—something's rather urgent. Later, if I can? Had a talk with Francis?"

"But you are the one who now—"

"Yes. But he was the one who found her."

"If you ask me," said Francis, "that other one put this Mrs. Artworth up to it."

He had not been asked. That did not alter the fact that he felt it now to be time for an interrogatory. He was as capable of conducting *that*, as a one-man show, as he was (as his employer had long known) of making a scene without outside aid should he consider one to be due. Now, again, he had got the sons pinned into the drawing-room: he had removed the tea tray, brought in the drink tray. ("Upset"?—the house, on the contrary, ran like clockwork. Any trail of disorder left by its owner had been obliterated —true, there lay corpses of berries on that table: at them, while he spoke, Francis levelled a frown which was partly abstracted and partly not.) Wearing an all but dazzlingly white coat, he had taken up his position near the door—*he* could make an exit at any moment, which was more than they could. Morally, his position was as propitious: he was forcing a duty upon the sons. If they shrank from hearing what had happened, why had they come?

He was moving in on the subject from its periphery; beginning with those birds of ill omen, "those two ladies." Occasion had been given for his opening remark by Roland's having told him to take a drink up to Mrs. Artworth. Join them in the drawing-room, it was to be feared that she would not—she was unwilling to leave her patient for so long.

"This one's object being," continued Francis, "to succeed in keeping everyone else out. That you will soon see. Gin and tonic is what she drinks, if you want to know: that is to say, so far. I would not put it past her to switch to Scotch as the night goes on. . . . However, the other is at the bottom of it, if you ask me. Battering and ringing? —she beat the postman; but that her instrument was the telephone. *She* was the one who'd been here with us the Sunday it happened, as you no doubt know? Nor when gone was she gone—anything but! Oh, no. Opened up on the telephone early in the small hours of Monday morning, while the Major and I were getting Mrs. Delacroix into bed. (I'd telephoned to the Major once I took in the extent of the disaster, so round he'd dashed.) Ring-ring-ring-ring that instrument started going, right by the bed. *That* I soon put a stop to; I switched off that extension and off it's stayed, but ring-ring-ring-ring kept on down here. Came to stop for a bit, then struck up once more. 'Go,' said the Major, 'and tell 'em to go to hell.' I did better; I told her, 'You've got the wrong number.' She knowing my voice as I knew hers. Then onward from 8 a.m. there were further outbursts—sleepless night had been had, from the sound. From then on, I adopted a regular procedure. 'Mrs. Delacroix is unable to speak to you,' I informed her, each time, previous to hanging up. One time, she succeeded in jumping back on me—'*Unable?*' Well, she had asked for it, so she got it. 'Mrs. Delacroix has nothing to say to you, at the present time,' I said.

"It was the Major, I'm sorry to tell you, who sold the fort. Yesterday. Roving around this place in the unoccupied way he's taken to doing, *he* went and answered the telephone—that one, there. *I* arrived on the scene a minute too late. 'Packed up,' I heard him telling her. 'That's all I can tell you, she's packed up. . . . No,' he said, 'no one. Who should there be? . . . Yes,' he said. 'Sunday night.'

"Whereupon *she*, if you ask me, went straight off after this other one like a pack of bats. '*You* go,' she'd have said to her, 'my name's mud there. You've still got a toe in the door; *you* get yourself there, p.d.q., and spy out the land.' Nothing like planting an agent of hers in this house, was there?"

William distastefully asked: "Are you off your head?"

"Six of one of them, half-a-dozen of the other, however, no doubt. What a pair," Francis said piously, "my goodness! Little did *she* know what she was doing, when she stirred them up."

"I should shut up, Francis, if I were you."

"She advertised for them!"

"That's enough!" Roland said, sharply and with authority. "You've got no business to talk like that. What's come over you? Those are my mother's guests. Either less of that, or you'd better go."

Uncertain what might or might not be the connotation

of the word "go," Francis looked thoughtfully, twice, at the senior Delacroix.

"Nor should either of them be 'she' to you," William pointed out. "They've both got names, haven't they?— What's the other lady's?"

"Burkin-Jones—Miss. Name mean anything to you? . . . No, I thought not."

"And not only don't do that but do what you're told, will you?" Roland requested. Hastily going to the tray, he caused gin to flow freely into a glass, wrenched the cap off a bottle of tonic. Francis, watching, said: "Rather more ice than that; we like plenty of it. *Two* slices of lemon. I shall need a tray to take that on; we are very particular."

"Go and get one, then."

"First, you will want to hear about Sunday. I rarely go out, but it happened that that evening I attended a French film with a Finnish friend. Not in this village, I need hardly tell you; no, it was at the Agricultural Institute. They have cultural activities there on Sunday nights, therefore this was a psychological French film, *avant-garde*. When I returned here all the lights were burning, which surprised me in view of the fact that the house was silent as though empty. I concluded that Mrs. Delacroix must have forgotten and gone to bed—she could not be out, as her car was before the door. *I* had better turn out the lights, I supposed. Only when I came in *here* did I find her.

"She was not in her chair but in the middle of the sofa —there, where I'm pointing to. She was leaning back. The back of her hand was against the middle of her forehead— where that great bruise, they tell me, has since appeared. She did not see me."

"How do you know she did not see you?"

"She did *not* see me. I said, 'Is anything the matter, madam?' She did not hear me."

"How do you know?"

"She did *not* hear me."

"What made you think she was not asleep?"

"Her eyes were open, under her hand."

"What did you think?—you thought she was dead?"

"I thought I was still looking at that film."

"Anything else strike you?"

"How cold the room was. They'd had a big fire going

in here, by the look of the ashes, but it had burned out.
She was alone."

"So you've already said, in so many words."

Francis, for the first time, curtained himself in a look of
stupidity. He said: "Everybody had gone."

"What *induced* you and Major Wilkins not to get a
doctor?"

"We did what we could; we got her to bed. She then
said: 'If you bring anybody in here, I'll go through that
window. I don't mind glass,' she said, 'I'll go through the
glass.' "

"That doesn't sound like her."

"She was not like herself. So the Major said: 'Let her be.'
He stayed up there with her through that night, in that
chair Mrs. Artworth's sitting in now. Major Wilkins was
satisfied that it was not a stroke; he's seen many strokes.
And Mrs. Artworth is satisfied that it is not a stroke, and
she's had experience of nursing."

"It could have been severe concussion."

"Mrs. Artworth is satisfied that it's not concussion."

"Mrs. Artworth came on the scene late. You two took
the most frightful responsibility."

"That," said Francis, fixing one then the other of them
with a Roman eye, "I have never shrunk from. Nor, I
should imagine, has the Major."

"I see. Thank you," said Roland. He turned to his
brother. "The thing is, to see her."

"If you can," said Francis. He picked up the glass of
gin and bottle of tonic, to go away with him to be put on
a tray. "Thank *you*, Mr. Delacroix," he said, dividing the
appellation between the two.

While trays went to and fro, up and down (Mrs. Artworth, having taken her tea tray down with her to the
kitchen, where she had a word with the widow about *bouillon*, was while down there run to ground by Francis, who
handed over the tray with the gin and tonic, which *she* had
to take up), one of the Delacroix children effected entrance
by means of the front door, and by means of the stairs
ascended to her grandmother's room.

She first stared in, in a general way, from the threshold.
She then came in far enough to assure herself there *was* no
one in the fireside chair. No, no one: nothing left of the

keeper but a cocoon of knitting skewered by glass needles. The field was her own—she advanced, humming like a bee. From the foot of the bed, she gazed along the perspective which was her grandmother with some interest. "Hullo?" she inquired (no harm trying).

"Hullo, Emma." (This was the child's name, after the book. She was eight.)

"When are you going to get up?"

"When I have a bath."

"Can you have a bath when you've got a cold?"

"Where have you been?"

"We can't go into the cave, it's tied up with string. And the *swing's* gone."

"No, the swing's there."

"No, it isn't; the swing's *gone*—you go and look out of the stairs window!"

The grandmother stirred in the bed—an event, had the child known. Moving herself up, so far as one could, on the flat pillow, she looked about over the expanse of the bed for her yellow dressing-gown: she was allowed to keep it there. She saw it, but it was out of reach. "Now," she said, "go and turn the taps on. I want my bath."

"Have you still got that duck I gave you?"

"Yes."

"Does it still swim when you have your bath?"

"Yes.—Give me that yellow thing, Emma."

"Shall I put the duck in when I turn the taps on? Or won't the lady want you to have a bath? She isn't the big lady who was in the garden, is she? *She* tried, but *she* couldn't undo the knots of the cave; that string has all got itself swollen up. She said, if we want to go into the cave we must have a knife; she says you have a knife made like a thumb—*is* it?"

"I've lost my slippers."

Emma looked under the bed. "They're there," she reported. "Why are there so many people? Why does there have to be Coralie? She was hiding here when we came; she keeps rushing after us. She keeps telling us things. We don't like her—yet."

"She belongs to Mrs. Coral."

"Why are we sleeping at Mrs. Coral's?"

"*Are* you sleeping at Mrs. Coral's?"

Emma sneezed. "I think *I'm* getting a cold," she said

competitively. "Down there at the bottom where the cave is, it *was* cold. Coralie says no fox will go down those steps."

The grandmother threw back her coverings, pushed the needlework stool out of the way, and sat on the edge of the bed pulling on the slippers. When Emma'd provided her with the yellow thing, she stood up, garbing herself in that. Now that she was out of the dark tent (in which it had no more than looked like a dark stain) the bruise she wore stood out in full magnificence—a marble boss in the middle of her forehead. The child ran to righten the tilted lampshade, the better to admire the bruise's colours—she returned, devotedly staring, saying: "May I touch it?" (Seeing was not enough.)

"Not hard, Emma."

"What *did* you do?"

The grandmother blinked.

"Hit against something, or something hit against you?"

The owner lightly explored the bruise with her own finger—evidently, however, its history was either a puzzle or a secret, for all she would say was: "Now, my bath . . ."

Emma bustled ahead. She turned on both taps, full blast, then launched the duck on to the churning waters.

Not best pleased at finding the bird flown, Sheila Artworth straightened the empty bed, then returned to her knitting. (She *had* extracted an explanation through the bathroom door. "All right, Sheikie, I'm not opening a vein." "I dare say, but are you all right in there?" "I can swim, you know.") She tipped the lampshade the way it had been before—who'd fiddled with it? Resorting from time to time to her gin and tonic, she thought about sons —or, glancing from the breast of her orchid blouse to a flowery arm of the chintz chair, thought how well the two colourings blended.

The patient, back from her bath, trailed past as though her nurse were part of the chair. She got back into bed again and lay flat as ever, saying, in the voice of one aloud continuing a train of thought: "You huffed and you puffed and you blew my house down."

"*Macbeth?*"

"What?"

"*Macbeth*, I suppose."

" 'Was my father a traitor, mother?'—that's *Macbeth*."

"Isn't it about witches?"

"Not altogether. . . . 'All is the fear and nothing is the love'—that's *Macbeth*. And, 'What are these faces?' I don't think most tragedies are sad, they are only tragic; but *Macbeth* is. It's full of particles of sadness which are seldom noticed—deluded expectations, harmless things coming to a dreadful end. King Duncan arriving to stay with the Macbeths in such good spirits.—'This castle hath a pleasant seat.' I know the feeling, driving up to a friend's house in the evening, enjoying the smell of the air as one gets out of the car, looking forward to everything—but *one* isn't murdered. And Banquo going out riding with his son, coming back in the nice dark fit as a fiddle, looking forward to dinner. And Banquo talking about the nesting swallows. 'This guest of summer, the temple-haunting martlet.' "

"That bath has brightened you up, I must say."

"Say, 'This guest of summer, the temple-haunting martlet.' "

"You've just said it."

"I want to hear it."

" 'This guest of summer, the temple-haunting martlet,' " said Sheila, with justifiable coldness.

The patient listened. 'It didn't make me weep this time —but never mind. . . . Yet Macbeth is the one I'm sorriest for."

"Ought you to be, from anything I've heard?"

"He'd done an irrevocable thing."

"I wouldn't worry, if I were you."

"He did at least, though, know what it was. Could one fear that one *had* done an irrevocable thing, without knowing exactly what it was?"

"That's beyond me, frankly. Better ask Mumbo."

"She's gone."

"Look, Dinah, you'll have to sit up: there's some *bouillon* coming."

"Oh, dear. I—"

"If you can march about, you can sit up."

"Yes; but I'd rather have curried eggs."

Alerted by sounds outside, the justly incensed nurse flounced to the door, saying not without satisfaction: "Here *comes* your *bouillon*!"

But it was Mrs. Coral. "Thought I'd just look in—I've come for the children." She looked consideringly at the bed. "Better, are you, this evening? I expect you are." She held up a small pot of special jelly. "I've brought you a little something to make a change and cheer you up and so on." The patient lifted her head to gaze at the nostrum: the jelly gave forth a cornelian glow. "*And* it's nice for you having your friend here now." Mrs. Coral turned her candid, wide, carven face to the chintz chair. "Mrs. Arkword, isn't it?"

"Artworth," said Sheila crisply.

"Sheikie," said their hostess-in-absence, "this is Mrs. Coral."

"Oh, you *are* brighter!" rejoiced the visitor. "(She really is brighter this evening, isn't she!) And wasn't it a surprise about your sons! Either of them had a peep at you, so far?'"

"Have either of them had a peep at me, Sheikie?"

"They'll be coming up later, for a little," said Mrs. Artworth.

"They wouldn't of course want to over-tire her," Mrs. Coral agreed, hastily if a shade perplexedly. She sighed. "I'm afraid what *they're* going to want to know"—instinctively, she continued to address herself to the authority now in the chintz chair—"is, why a doctor hasn't seen her."

"And well might they," said Mrs. Artworth, looking down that nose of hers at her knitting—swifter and brighter flashes flew from the needles. "*I* only took over this morning, as you may know, and I *do* wonder. Oh, they'll wonder, all right!"

"No, they won't," said the patient.

Mrs. Coral, still holding the pot of jelly, betrayed an unusual indecision by not seeming to know where to put it down. Might it feel more at home amongst pots and bottles? —She went over and lodged it among cosmetics. "Why, it *is* dark!" she remarked, standing at the dressing-table, looking outdoors through the bay window. "We shouldn't," she asked of the chintz chair, "soon be beginning to think of drawing the curtains?"

"No," said the patient.

"All your books gone, I see?" remarked the visitor, eyeing the bare stool.

"She can have them back," said the nurse. "She has only to ask."

"No, don't bother, Sheikie."

"Still, that leaves some place for anybody to sit, doesn't it?"

"Won't you come and sit on it, Mrs. Coral?"

"No, you'll have to excuse me—*I* have to go. Mrs. Delacroix, you wouldn't want to worry your boys, would you?"

"Would *they* want me taken away in a sealed van?"

"Now, that's *no* way to talk—it's silly; it's really wicked!"

"Stop it, Dicey!" commanded Sheikie.

"Or perhaps, Sheikie," went on the unsubdued one, "you could get me a room at Number 9? Since you say I'm not dotty, then I'm just failing."

"That's not funny," said Sheila, in a voice like a whip.

"And Major Wilkins worries," said Mrs. Coral.

The patient not only lay flat, she appeared to have pasted herself to her lower sheet. No squeak more from her, for some little time.

"You're accustomed to nursing, I expect?" said Mrs. Coral, turning to Mrs. Artworth.

"I could have made a nurse," agreed the other, reaching into a synthetic leopard-skin knitting bag for another ball of wool, "I expect, yes. But for one and another reason, I never trained."

"Experience is what counts, in the long run," meditated Mrs. Coral, "if one has had it, that is—I should probably say."

"I nursed a friend to the day of his death."

"*Well*," said Mrs. Coral. . . . "Well," she repeated, "as I say, I just looked in for a minute. Already, quite enough excitement for *you*," she informed the pillow. "Tomorrow, you'll feel up to seeing the children, who knows? Now I must go and find them."

"Mrs. *Coral*—?"

"Yes?"

"Couldn't they, though, stay here?"

"Well you see, I am ready for them, now."

"But their rooms are here, that they always sleep in. Their rooms are here . . ."

"I've got that nice top room, till I replace my Indian."

"How are you going to get them over?" asked Mrs. Artworth—having by now sized up (as it proved, correctly) the probable income-level of Mrs. Coral.—"Or *have* you got a car?"

"No; and I haven't got a bike, either, you may be surprised to hear. I prefer my feet," said Mrs. Coral, throwing a nod down at the trusty pair. "But now, as you say, there'll arise the problem of getting their luggage and bits and pieces and so-ons to my home. It's wonderful, the amount and the sort of things children want with them, at the last moment. You should see what Coralie brought; you would almost laugh. And *these* two have quite a pile, as I just now saw. Piled up down there, just inside the door, ready to go out again. Therefore what I wondered was, whether either of their fathers could kindly run them, myself, and their bits and pieces over to Rosebank—which is the name of my house—in their car? Wouldn't take long. Major Wilkins would have, I'm sure, but I see no signs of him."

"I can't see why that shouldn't be arranged," said Mrs. Artworth. "I'll go and see." She rose. "The next thing that will be coming, Dinah, will be your *bouillon*."

"Will it? I've lost count."

The active women, now about to get going, glanced before doing so at the canopy. Dinah had raised herself on an elbow. Down her white face, under the ignominious bruise, a tear made its bewildered way.

"Now, cheer up!" enjoined Mrs. Coral. "You'll see them tomorrow."

"Yes."

The children, anything but anxious to leave Applegate, had, after all, a reprieve: the fathers, though prepared to transport them to Mrs. Coral's, set their faces against doing so immediately. "Sorry, Mrs. Coral, but we're now going up to look in on Mother."

"Won't that be nice! But wasn't that to be later?"

"We'll be going up later too, I should think."

"That may depend, rather," said Mrs. Artworth.

"I'm afraid you may find her a little doleful, just at this minute," said Mrs. Coral. "Five minutes before, she seemed quite bright. She varies."

"Most of us do," said Roland.

"Sorry if this throws you out in any way, Mrs. Coral," said William, though with no less firmness than that shown by his brother.

"Never you mind!" cried the good woman. "With everything at sixes and sevens, who can wonder? But *I'll* just be off, I think, to adjust the oven: everything's *timed* for six. I've got a light little tea for them, their first evening, cheese-and-egg flan and baked chocolate pudding; but all the more I shouldn't care for anything to be spoiled."

"No, indeed."

"I could take Coralie with me," said Mrs. Coral—struck by that good idea, looking about. But the elf was nowhere.

The sons, a phalanx of two, wheeled in the direction of the staircase. Mrs. Artworth already was at its foot, saying: "I think I should go on ahead and tell her you're coming."

"Really, you need not trouble. She's quite used to us."

Turning her speculative look from one to the other, meanwhile touching around the hair on her pretty head, she thought that over. "Why, yes; I suppose she is. . . . You'd like her to yourselves?" she asked.

They were stunned by the question. "Well . . ." said one, "don't you think?"

"Really, I couldn't say—who am I to know? Well, if that's the case, I'll go out for a bit. I could do with some fresh air." She drew a breath deep into her bored lungs, at the very thought. "Yes, go for a stretch," she said, stretching her arms.

"You realize it's rather dark?"

"Oh, I shan't go far," she said, looking as though amused by them, in a small way. "Not outside your gate. I'll keep near the house. Quite frankly, the country gives me the creeps.—How's Frank Wilkins standing up to this, by the way? Seen him?"

One of the sons, after an instant, said: "Well, we half-saw him."

"Oh. He might be able to put you in the picture, I should have thought?"

"Saw him," said the other son, "for a minute, more or less in the distance. He seemed to be making off somewhere. He made off."

"Oh," she said, with her curious inflection. "He can't have seen you two, then?"

"You'll ask Francis," said Roland, "for anything more you want?"

"If it's there," she said, "couldn't I help myself?—Anyway, what I want is a breather, first."

They said: "See you at dinner, then?"

"I suppose so," she said tolerantly. "Yes."

Handing over the stairs to them (as it were), she went away to seek for her mohair coat. She undug it from under their overcoats on the bishop's chair. Having selected a walking-stick—to remind her of the dog?—she let herself out of the inner glass door of the porch, into the dark.

Yes, there had been something crepuscular, uncomfortable, about the half-seeing of Frank—which, but for Mrs. Artworth and her lightning question, would have been consigned by the two sons to the silence of their in-common memory. It had happened between an hour and half-an-hour before she jumped them into admitting that it had. The drawing-room had been still in that lampless state known as blind-man's holiday; outdoors, it was drawing towards the end of that hour in which land seems haunted.

Francis got rid of, they had been talking—William still in his mother's chair facing the bay window; Roland, on the move, from time to time taking a desultory look out of any of the three. Anything but desultory was their talk: a break-through would have to be made and they were planning it. So far, the situation at Applegate made rather than more sense with every minute—thanks to the bafflingness of Mrs. Artworth, the spider's-web ambiguities of Francis. The idea (later acted upon) of announcing they were going to see their mother, then walking upstairs, began to commend itself more and more. Having agreed upon it, they drank to it.

A figure came into view through the end window (the window which had no fellow in the room above, that wall being occupied by a canopy). From the figure's manner of crossing the frame of the window, it might have been that of a vagrant—a vagrant apathetically expecting at any moment to be asked what he was doing or what he wanted. Barely, in the now less than half-light, would the man have been distinguishable from the grass and trees, but that he moved—and there being about his movement some trace of what had been there formerly, he was recognizable.

"There," remarked Roland, "goes poor old Frank."

William, having dodged his head in order to see between or over the various objects interposing between him and the end window, came to the same conclusion. "Yes," he said.

"What's he up to?"

"Doesn't look as though he knew?—Anything one ought to do, do you think?"

"Bring him in?"

"He'd bring himself in if he wanted, wouldn't he? . . . He's probably the one, you know, that one really should be having a word with: he was on the spot. And seeing her as often as he did, he should be able to throw some light— as to whether, for instance, this thing really only did start last Sunday, or whether there'd been any trouble before."

"Yes."

Frank, meanwhile, had temporarily disappeared from view. The sons felt a temporary relief—they turned, however, to watch through the windows overlooking the lawn for him to come into view again on that. "Cheer him up in any way, could one?" asked William, while they waited.

"Well, I wondered. Take him out for a drink?"

In reply William, shrugging his shoulders, looked expressively at the crowded drink tray. "Out?"

"I know," said Roland, acknowledging the tray. "But what I had thought was, change of scene?"

Frank, as foreseen, was in sight again—diagonally, now, making across the lawn towards the orchard. William, having taken another look, said: "I doubt if he'd thank us."

"What *is* on his mind?" asked Roland, more uneasy than he had probably ever been. "Something that he knows and we don't?"

"He always has acted up, to give him his due."

"Yes. But—?"

"And I tell you another thing," said William, "He easily could be the type who can't stand illness: resents it, goes to pieces at the idea of it, is panicked by it. That isn't always necessarily selfishness, it's a phobia. And that kind of phobia gets worse with age, so would have with him. Naturally, I suppose—when the time's come when you yourself never know at what moment *you* may not be going to crack?"

"Well, *I* don't know," said Roland. "I don't know."

While they debated, it became too late. Frank gave a look, so swift as to seem perfunctory, up at the windows above those through which he was being watched, then went off into the ancient darkness between the boughs. "He may, you know," Roland said retrospectively, "have come over to see whether there was anything he could do, then thought twice about coming in. In that case, I should feel badly."

"Or, simply have come over to say hullo?"

"Then why didn't he? . . . One thing we must on no account fail to do, though, sooner or later, is have a word with him."

"I agree. It could be a great mistake not to have a word with him."

"Yes."

"Look, why *didn't* he send for a doctor?"

On learning that an extension had been granted, the Delacroix children tried to get hold of Francis, that last August's gin-rummy sessions around the pantry table might be at once resumed. (Coralie would have to try.) But Francis proved to be in no mood. "Your grandmother will not be the only one," he prophesied, "to be having a breakdown, if this goes on." He and Mrs. Throes (the widow) were getting dinner.

"But Fran-*cis*, not until eight?"

"I shall have to shave."

They watched him bringing rarities out of the glass cupboard. "What are those for?"

"*For*? They're finger bowls."

"They're very dusty, Francis."

"Well, I should *think* so. Now run along—do you want to get on my nerves?"

So they thought of something to do instead. Taking possession of the empty drawing-room, they extracted the cutting-out scissors of last August from the string drawer in their grandmother's desk (that was, the children of the house did: Coralie watched), hauled the hoard of slithery magazines out of the hollow inside the spinet, settled themselves down in a row on the sofa, and got down to it —that was, the children of the house did: Coralie, though a pair of scissors had been issued to her, waited. "What are we doing this for?" she wanted to know.

"Because we are," explained Pamela—scissors already flying around a dinosaur. (Pamela, not called after the book, was five and a half months older than her first cousin.) Emma hummed, busy with an Aztec altar.

"This is a nature magazine you've given *me*, isn't it?" asked Coralie, her suspicions deepening.

"There are coloured birds in it—or there were." (Truth to tell, that particular magazine had been heavily mutilated last August.) "Don't you like birds? Or here's a motoring one. Motor cars are easier to cut out."

Emma hummed. Coralie, leafing her listless way through a Motor Show now long ago glossily over, seemed to be missing something—her adenoids? Jabbing her scissors into a Jaguar, she said in a lugubrious tone: "Isn't it awful about your grandmother?"

"What's awful?"

"I said, isn't it awful about your grandmother? Disfigured for life *and* her mind gone."

"Yoo-hoo, Coralie!"

"It's all round the village."

"If *you* go all round the village you'll get smallpox."

"*That's* a lie!" cried Coralie, tossing back the blonde elf-locks which were her sole claim to be an elf.

"One and one make two, then."

That was too much. Re-attacking the Jaguar, Coralie recklessly made known: "Everybody's sorry for the family."

"What family?" asked Pamela absently, fine-pointing the dinosaur's tail with an expert snip.

"All of you."

"We are sorry for *your* family, Coralie."

"She had a bath," said Emma. "I turned the taps on."

The conversation lapsed. Pamela, having completely detached the dinosaur from its former surroundings, placed it beside her on the end of the sofa, anew to behold it. Emma, possibly delayed by her own humming, only now reached the base of the Aztec altar. Coralie wrote off the Jaguar as a total loss and turned her attention to a harmless Austin. Beneath them the sofa and at their feet the hearthrug came to be littered with coils and snippets. Coralie gave, in a general way, an omniscient sniff.

"*She* didn't take the swing down," Emma told Pamela. "Someone did."

"As soon as her back was turned."

"That lady was disappointed, too."

"She couldn't have swung on it, though; she is too heavy."

"If you mean that person," said the now helpful Coralie, "what do you think she did? She walked up your lane. She had her car, but she left her car in the village. *She's* funny, isn't she?—What's she doing out there? Coming up and trying to speak to us. 'If anybody comes trying to speak to you,' Mum says, 'you take no notice.' You went and gave her encouragement. 'See the cave?' she said, 'I've never seen the cave. Let's try!' Had she any business to? She looked funny."

"Mrs. Frog," said Emma, who liked frogs.

Pamela had picked up a bygone *Vogue*. She pored over corset advertisements, tore a page out, and set her scissors to work round a heart-shaped lady. "Wanted to know how Grandmother was, I expect," she said.

"Then why didn't she go to the door and ring and ask? That's what Gran does when anybody's ill—goes to the door and rings and asks."

"She asked me," said Emma, in a satisfied tone. "I said: 'She's in bed.'"

Coralie acted nervous. "Where's that person gone off to *now*, do you think?"

"Grandmother's friend?" said Pamela. "I suppose she's somewhere."

Clare had been grateful to the children. She'd been sorry to hear they were to be exiled from Applegate that night—her fault. But again, if it hadn't been for her they wouldn't be here now, in the middle of term. "Where," it had come into her head suddenly to ask Pamela, while the two of them were breaking their nails over the same knot, "did your grandmother afterwards go to school?" She had struck lucky—the history-loving child beamed. "After St. Agatha's? No school: she did lessons with some children in Cumberland. Then, after that war was over, Cousin Roland said she must go to France."

"*You* ever set eyes on Cousin Roland?" Clare asked.

"No, I suppose not."

"He was dead," said Pamela petulantly, as though mentioning some rather tricky peculiarity of her relative's. "So my father's called after him. Why—did you?"

"Once or twice, in the distance." Clare added: "That, he preferred."

"His brother was Cousin Claud. Cousin Claud was a bishop."

"My goodness, yes—yes, there *was* a bishop!"

"But that isn't why there's that chair in the hall. She only bought that at an auction."

"You know a lot, you know," granted the big other one, half-grumpily—sucking at the nail split to below the quick, making faces at the knot which had done it. "No good," she said. "No, we must give up. Another time, you'll have to have a knife."

"Men have knives. If only we had Major Wilkins."

Then it was (Emma having come humming up) that Clare boasted of knowing a knife which was like a thumb. "Though it couldn't cut knots, only cuts butter."

"Are you sure?"

"Yes. It came from my shop."

She went away, up the steps cut in the rock.

Somewhere, the orchard had Frank at large in it. Clare knew, scarcely though footfalls were to be heard on the nerveless grass, sodden with November and rotted apples. To be seen was an occasional flicker of thicker darkness in and out of the gaps between tree and tree. She stood, trying to guess his course: random and bough-hampered it seemed to be. No track ran from where she stood—she struck out blind, decided and reckless in what at least ought to be his direction. In the clearing, Dinah's and his *potager*, he had come to a stop. It was here that she brought herself face to face with him. "What, you?" he said. "I didn't know."

"Yes. Me." Stare him out though she did, in her stony way, favour and disfavour had alike evaporated from between them. She asked: "What has happened?"

"Dinah's ill. I told you that, on the telephone."

"I know. But what's the matter with her?"

Frank said: "I'm not blaming you—altogether."

"Thanks. Why?"

He thought, with difficulty. "This whole thing's been a

bit beyond you, I'm beginning to see. Not that you weren't the cause—that, I think you were. However, I dare say you were not to know: who *was* to know? Sunday, you two girls had a row, eh? And then I suppose she banged about and crashed her head. But as she is—or as she has come to be?—there was more to it than that." He looked away from her, at two or three of the *potager's* bell-glasses, misted by condensations of the autumn. "An amount more than that," he added, "you might say. That's what's been the trouble. That *is* the trouble."

Clare dug her hands into her pockets. She asked him squarely: "What do you mean, though? That's what I want to know—or don't *you* know?"

"Yes, I think I do," he said, soberly. "Or at least, can make a pretty good guess. To begin with, see the way this has taken her. She doesn't give a damn. Doesn't care a damn. Any more. Now."

"Doesn't care a damn for what?"

"Any of us, any of us round her. This life of hers here. This place. She's come unstuck."

"Unstuck's not ill," argued the other.

He again looked at her. "I say 'ill,' because what else am I to say? And there's this: in a woman who cared so much, not caring a damn *is* an illness, isn't it? Yet it's not that she ceased caring: she's switched her caring. Simply ceased to care for anything since *then*."

"Since when?"

"You ought to know," he said. "Or oughtn't you? That time you three had, God knows how long ago. *That's* what she latched on to. She switched back to you two. Don't think she meant to—didn't know it had happened to her, perhaps. But right back to you two. You more, though. You, yes. You mean more than you know. You did *not* altogether know, did you?" He frowned at Clare, for emphasis, not in anger. "That's why I don't altogether blame you."

"No, I didn't know, I suppose. Or I didn't see. I was thinking of something else."

"I took it you were."

"You were right."

One way or the other, he didn't care. "But what does matter," he drove in, "is what's happened now. Now, something has knocked the bottom out of all *that*. Late Sunday night, after Francis called me, she didn't know what she was saying. Or rather, didn't know that she *was* saying. He and I were getting her into bed, and she was in terrible distress, crying, 'It's all gone, was it ever there? No, never there. Nothing. No, no, no.' . . . And so on. Terrible to hear her. So something *had* knocked the bottom out of that, eh? So, where is she now? That is, what has she—now?"

"I wish I could tell you," Clare said.

"*I* wish you could tell me. . . . Well, there you are. At any rate, that's my guess." Frank turned away, went away —she watched him stepping over the subsided furrows of the *potager. She* then turned and went back the way she had come, into the orchard. She continued to shelter in its hiding. From where she stood, later, she watched Emma make her way round the house towards the front door. That's a game two can play, the emboldened Clare thought. After another suck at the split nail *she*, therefore, risked it —making a detour round the defoliated and swing-less beech, lest anybody be looking out of the stairs window. In front of the front door, still, remained Dinah's car. That had been Sunday, and this was Wednesday. So far, in the confusion, no one had thought of putting away the Hillman. That, might she do? No. Instead, seized suddenly by the bravado of fatigue, she tried the door by the passenger's seat: it opened. She got in, sat, and, beside an imaginary driver, fell asleep. Days had been long, nights none.

In the dark, Sheikie woke her by tapping on the window. Sheikie then wrested open the door, saying: "Well, I *must* say . . ."

"Oh, hullo. Where's *your* dog?"

"You're not drunk, are you?"

"Nn-nn. How's everything going?"

"She's all right. The sons are up there with her—why don't you slip into the house? Nobody's in the drawing-room but the children."

"They were in the garden."

"I can't help that: they're in the drawing-room. They'll be going to Mrs. Coral's at any minute, when the fathers come down."

"Fathers?" asked Clare, puzzled by the Biblical sound.

"The sons."

"Oh, all right." Clare got out of the car. "Sheikie, you won't let her know I'm here?"

"Wouldn't like me to try?"

"Not unless she asks."

The nurse, about to go back on duty, said: "One never knows, with her, from minute to minute. Just now, she was asking for curried eggs."

The nurse had her patient to herself again. She removed from the bedside the empty *bouillon* cup, made up the fire, arranged some mustard-yellow chrysanthemums, sent by a sympathizer in the village, in a crystal vase. "Turning up trumps, aren't you?" said the admiring patient, faintly, watching.

"What?"

"Turning up trumps, Sheikie, aren't you?"

Sheila (wearing the blouse into which she had changed for dinner, on her return from her stretch) looked at herself speculatively in the dressing-table glass. " 'East, West, Old Friends are Best,' they say."

"Oh, *true*! What about Trevor, though?"

"What about Trevor?"

"All by himself?"

"He was among those who considered I ought to come."

"He'll never know how much it has meant to me, Sheikie, to find him alive and safely married to you."

"Oh," said Mrs. Artworth, not seeming flattered. She asked: "Why should he be otherwise?"

"For years—years—I've been afraid that his whitened skeleton still was stuck up there in that drain-pipe. You know that dreadful Mistletoe Bough story?"

"No."

"He was *not* in the charabanc on the way home. Everybody preserved a complete silence on the subject. Mother was thinking her own thoughts. Then early next morning we went away to Cumberland—if you remember, we went away for ever. And then the war came, showing one nothing was too bad to be true. There were hundreds of reasons why I advertised for you, Sheikie, but among them certainly one was, you'd be the first person I had a hope of seeing whom I *could* ask, 'Did Trevor ever come out?' For *how* many years I needn't tell you, because you know, I thought about Trevor and his wedged-in bones. As time went on, I almost imagined I had succeeded in reasoning

myself out of that—but no. Because, when in 1940 Mr.
Churchill gave us that splendid, rousing talk about probably fighting on the beaches, do you know what my first
reaction was? 'Now they'll blast open that drain-pipe, and
there'll be Trevor.' "

"The things you think of!"

"Does he still hate matches?"

"Did he?" asked Sheila.

"He does bear me no malice? No, Trevor would never
be a malicious man; but . . . ?"

"He sent you his kind regards."

"I wish he was here," said the patient, with a beatific
sigh, staring serenely up from her pillow into the canopy.

"I can tell you who *is* here, though."

"No, don't do that—you needn't tell me. I know."

"Oh, you *do?*"

"She must go away. Please make her go. She must go."

"She *is* in a state," said Sheila, tentatively.

"And what about me? Laid low."

"It was she who got me to come here, Dinah."

"I wonder if you *are* a very good nurse?"

"You know, you go on as though she'd hit you."

"She did."

"You don't mean—you can't mean?" cried Sheila Artworth, questioningly touching her own forehead.

"No, no, no," said the patient, impatiently banishing that
small matter. "I knocked against something."

"Oh, you did? Well, meanwhile she's in a bad way. A
bad way."

"And what am I in? Tell her, I'd rather have every devil
out of every church-bell loose in this house than ever see
her again. No, she must go away. It's too late."

"Never too late to mend."

"I besought her to stay. I, I needed her. She said, 'No,
Circe.' "

"She always did swear like a trooper."

"She's been always going away. She can stay away."

"You're not being fair, Dinah."

"I never have been."

Nurse Artworth resumed her official sway. "Before I go
down to dinner, I'll take your temperature."

"I should think you'd *better!*"

Sheila popped the thermometer into Dinah's mouth. Dinah whipped it out again, to say hurriedly: "Just a minute—who was it, Sheikie, you didn't actually kill?"

"That's a long story, rather," said Sheila thoughtfully.

"Tell me tomorrow?—That's a very pretty blouse, Sheikie." (It was: being of what other than the Orient knows as shocking pink, it was of sari material, so had gold in it.) "It will cheer the boys up," their mother continued. "They're electrified by you, I know, already. They asked me about you."

Mrs. Artworth showed surprise.

The dutiful patient popped the thermometer (silencer) back into her mouth.

The long room remained empty, but for the patient. The fire burned ceremonially in the shapely grate; the dark she liked was allowed to stay pressing against the panes. Roses, roses all the way, some visible under the tilted lamplight, some not, could be known to stretch from the distant door to the distant bed. Back again into the unexpectancy which had reigned since Sunday lay the patient, not for these minutes having to arouse herself for anyone, like someone uncaringly being carried out to sea; or, still more, as though she were herself the outgoing tide.

But someone else, having once set foot on the stairs, hesitated no longer but came up warily. The step, as it neared the open door, not so much lagged as gave itself time. It seemed to be listening to itself—only waiting to be what it was counting on being, recognized. Wonderful how that hope persisted, in view of how many times the step had had to turn and go away again. This time, would there be any sign? Today was Wednesday.

Frank came to a halt where he had before, as he had before—a short way on to the carpet, across the threshold. He said tentatively: "Here I am?"

Waiting, he noted that her books were gone, since yesterday. No, there they were: stacked on top of the chest—why? He came forward by a rose or two, swaying his lowered head, looking exploratively under his eyebrows. What was the foreigner on the dressing-table? A sound, however, began to come from the pillow.—"What?" he asked, furrowing his forehead.

"I said, 'There you are.' "

"I thought I would just look in," he explained. "How are you?"

"How are you?" she wanted to know.

"What's that pot of jam doing over there, Dinah?"

"Jelly. Mrs. Coral. Where have you been?"

Crying out only inwardly "Where have *you* been?—where are you now?" he went over to verify the Coral jelly, before answering: "Oh, I've been about, you know. Round about."

"Keeping an eye on things?"

"You might say so—yes."

"Dear, don't stand right over *there*. Shouting wears us out."

"Whatever you like," he said. He came down the room and stood at the foot of the bed. He asked: "Put up your head for a minute, if you can, will you? I can hardly see you."

She raised herself on an elbow.

Awestruck, Frank more deeply furrowed his forehead. "All colours of the rainbow. . . ."

"Yes. Have *you* ever seen such a beautiful bruise?"

"You don't look too bad otherwise, Dinah. Resting and sleeping have done you good?"

"Frank, I hope I didn't give you a fright the other evening?"

"You couldn't help it," he said—turning white, looking away.

"Yes, I could have—it was stupid of me. I had no notion her masks scared you."

"Masks?" he echoed—demented, and who would blame him? He rubbed the back of his head. "Oh, what—that? It seems a long time ago. What I thought when I saw it was, you were angry with me."

"How could I—why should I be?"

"I don't know. That's what I don't know, what I haven't known. But you've been against me."

"Darling, dear Frank," she said, with a tremble of love in her voice, unavailingly reaching a hand towards him (the bed was as long as it was wide), "don't be a donkey."

"I wish to God I were one!"

"Now, now, now, now."

Without warning, he left the foot of the bed for its empty side, on to the edge of which he cast himself down, lying face buried in the pillow on which her head was not, in a sort of rigor. Between them existed the great distances. She again reached a hand out—this time sideways. But the bed was as wide as it was long.

"Frank, cheer up."

No stir, no sound.

"Frank, there's only one thing . . ."

No sound, no stir.

"Only one thing—if you would put the swing back?"

He made some sound of denial, into the pillow.

"Yes, I do know," she said. "I mean, I'm not asking—but if you *would* put it back? Straight, if you'd rather; though you'd be jolly clever. If you'd just put it back? . . . They're so disappointed."

"Cutting out?" Clare senselessly asked the children.

They did her the honour of not expecting she could expect them to answer: nonetheless they punctiliously all looked up. Three of them: three other children. Down there in the pit, that bucket of dusk, she had not counted them—on the flit, they had been innumerable. They had answered from all over the place. They had cast looks rather than shown faces. Their hands had joined hers in the battle against the knots—but that had ended. Now, all was altered. Here, lined up on the sofa, they were Three, no less excluding than had been the cave. The big old pouchy wrecked-looking outsider had the greater capacity to see herself as she now was from having been once otherwise.

Light fell on their heads from the big lamp on the table behind the sofa, photographing them clearly. They could be identified as quite unfamiliar. In the middle Emma, the robin's nestling, even her hair plump as it rebounded from under the snood. On her right Pamela, lucid Delacroix brow and brushed-upward curls; and on her left Coralie, looking respectably out through her Caliban fringe. A mistake to have seen them again—a mistake to *see* them.

However, there were flocks of magazines. Clare, barricading the children from the fire by standing on the hearthrug, bulkily stooped to pick one up.—"I'm afraid," said Pamela, scissors pausing, "you won't find very much left in *that* one."

She was right: many of the pages had been torn out,

jaggedly; others were gaping with excisions. But it was interesting to look through and see what was still there because it had not appealed to them, and to speculate as to the nature of what was gone because it had.

Emma, though she had finished work on the altar, still treasured the altar on her bare knee. She reached out, however, for the nature magazine fought shy of by Coralie, to see whether one might not yet rustle up a coloured bird. "No good starting anything else," Pamela warned her, "we're only going to have to go. We'd better clear up." Herself having done with the heart-shaped lady, she began suiting the action to the word.

"*I* don't want to go," complained Coralie, making it clear that her grandmother's machinations were no fault of hers. Also, she was a space snob: the lounge in which she was now seated, whether or not she might be in danger here from the mad lady, seemed to her the thing. "You're going to sleep where that Indian was," she informed Emma.

Clare disencumbered the hearthrug of herself. But Pamela, a minute or two later, came after her down the haunted room, holding the dinosaur between finger and thumb. "Would you like to see this? It's prehistoric."

"My goodness, yes," said Clare, looking at the dinosaur with sympathy. The other children, seeing no real reason why Francis should not finish the clearing-up (serve him right), set out to wander around the drawing-room, picking things up and putting them down again. "Those are pictures of us," said Emma, looking into the snapshot bowl.

"I tell you what *may* be here!" shouted Clare suddenly. This excited the children, who followed her to the table in the window. She slid a drawer open, slid her hand questingly into the very back of it. "Yes!" she announced. Out came the Chinese ivory puzzle. She gave herself up to it, scowled over it, was altogether obsessed by it, scarcely breathing. Intricate, interlocking ivories gave their clickety-click. She negotiated them with blundering semi-skill. *Then*, though, came the stop—the breath she'd either been holding or forgotten to draw went in and out of her loudly, exasperatedly. "To *this* point, I've always got it. Never beyond, though, never!—Now *you* try!"

She turned round, holding the puzzle out.

But the last of the courteous children had walked away. They were in the hall, giving a look over to their bits and pieces. The fathers also were to be heard, coming downstairs again from their mother's room. Clare wondered what to say to the sons if they should come in—however, they did not. Now having the drawing-room to herself, she returned the puzzle to where it lived, then stood there looking at Mrs. Piggott's clock, not to see the time.

She had no way of telling, therefore, how much later it was or was not when Sheila came into the drawing-room, pink blouse and all. "Hullo," Sheila asked, "how are *you* surviving?"

"I should imagine I'd better go?"

"All the way back?"

"I've got a room at the pub. White Hart."

"And what will you do when you get to the White Hart? What anyone does who hasn't got anything to do but be at the White Hart?"

"I'm not a drunk, yet."

"I wouldn't blame you," said Sheila, heading for the tray. "My Lord, what a Bedlam! Frank's been up there also, just now, making a scene."

"Well, to think of that."

"Yes; I soon got him out.—I'd been doing my nails," added Sheila, eyeing the results.

"Sheikie, this is how people live."

"Oh?"

" 'Enter these enchanted woods, you who dare.' "

"Will they give you anything to eat at the White Hart?"

Clare was not to be deterred:

> "Each has business of his own;
> But should you distrust a tone,
> Then beware.
> Shudder all the haunted roods,
> All the eyeballs under hoods
> Shroud you in their glare.
> Enter these enchanted woods,
> You who dare—

—I had better go," she concluded, looking about.

"And what a mess in *here*," Mrs. Artworth declared, surveying it. "Children, and everything—incidentally, you realize those berries could be poison?" She swept from the satinwood table as many as the cup of her hand would hold, and, whistling, tossed them into the fire. "How any survive," she said, "is a mystery to me."

"Children or berries, Sheikie?"

"Why, children, naturally."

"Berries are said to mean every sort of thing."

"Oh, are they?"

"I *had* better go, hadn't I?" repeated Clare.

"I can't say I see any future for you at the moment, Mumbo," said the other, with not uncompassionate frankness.

"Fine. Well then off I go, heel-and-toe."

"Where's that Mini of yours?"

"There in the village."

"I ought," said Sheila, "to offer to run you there in that Hillman she's left lying about. But the fact is, I can't stand touching anybody else's car: no. Doing that makes me nervous."

"*You?*"

"I won't touch anybody else's car, so it's no use arguing."

"I am not," said Clare, buttoning her coat. "Because I am looking forward to my walk, and that lane and all its works. I may meet the cat."

"I wrecked a car once. I wrecked somebody's car for him. 'Let her out! let her out!—let her *out*!' he kept on saying into my ear. Let her out I did: I did what he told me. I'd never handled a great big brute of a big-powered car like that new one of his before. Neither was it his, as I might have known. He was a car salesman, doing a bit of racing on the side. However, anything for excitement. He always was all shot up, at the best of times. He'd been through that war. One lung left, coughing his guts out. Still, there we were."

"That smash," Clare said, "wasn't the way you killed him?"

"No. I broke up that car, and broke up my nerve. Wasn't that enough? No, that wasn't the way I killed him."

"You now hate driving?"

"I have for years—years."

"Waste of that dashing little run-about you've got."

"Yes. I always have had a car; Trevor thinks I should."

"Stop driving!"

Sheila stared. "*That* would seem rather peculiar, would it not?"

"Do you want to tell me what happened after?"

"Why not? Well, he had worries. Some a hang-over from that smash, some not. When I say he became a sick, dying man, what I mean is, he no longer was able to keep the show on the road. No longer able to go on holding himself together. His sickness, I mean, got the upper hand. One had to know him to see how frightened he was. No doctor needed to tell him how bad he was. There he lay, in his room at the top of that house I couldn't get the dog out of the garden of the other night, saying: 'Stay with me. Stay with me,' he said, 'you never loved me, but stay with me; don't go. Stay with me, after all these years. That's all I ask,' he said, 'it's not much to ask, is it? You never loved me.'—Till the day came, Clare, when I said to him: 'That is all you know,' and went out of the room. Went out of the room, leaving him. I was not to know, but that was to happen to be the day he died. Therefore die he did."

"Oh, I see," said Clare.

"I doubt if you do. I'd loved him. I'd never ceased to. I loved him."

"Shouldn't he have known?"

"Ask me another," said Sheila Artworth. "What did he think, all those years, if he'd never known? All gone for nothing, those years—he *had* never known."

"You never show much, Sheikie."

"Love's what you feel," said Sheila, "or so I'd thought. What more *can* you do? If anybody doesn't understand, what more *can* you do? Show?—showing's another thing. I did have something to show when I had my dancing."

"I still don't see—"

"Well, there you are," sad Sheila. "Never have I told that story, and now I do it doesn't make sense—does it?"

"Never expect that.—I wish I could set eyes on her," said Clare.

"What a mess," said Sheila.

"Yes. Mistakes have histories, but no beginning—*like*, I suppose, history?"

"How long," asked Sheila, "can you hold out without anything to eat?"

"Why?"

"Because if you waited a bit longer, somewhere . . ."

"Hid for a bit longer, you mean?—Don't be refined,

Sheikie. And don't worry. *I've* found out how to hide. Well, what?"

"You could make your way up there while we're at dinner. I wouldn't wonder if by then she mightn't be asleep; she's inclined to drowse off if nobody stops her; mostly she seems to want to be left in peace. The door's open, so you could take a look at her.—If she *should* be awake, though, Clare, I wouldn't go in. . . ."

"I quite understand."

Sheila took her glass back to the tray. ("What about you?" she asked, looking at Clare. "N'thanks.") She measured herself out another drink, but then paused. She'd had a second thought. The drawing-room curtains had, at some time during the ins-and-outs since tea time, been drawn by Francis—Mrs. Artworth, going to a window, parted its curtains by inserting an arm between them (not wasting a glance by searching for the cord) and, pushing the sash up, emptied her glass out on to the grass.

"Waste of whatever *that* was?" remarked Clare.

"I don't want to get high."

"No?"

"No." Sheila's gesture, almost that of a dancer, wafted hither and thither a diaphanous sleeve. "No," she said, with that smile of hers, "not this evening."

Francis plonked a finger bowl down in front of Mrs. Artworth. She barely noticed it. Not only had he worried the dust out of the cut glass, he had seated the bowl on a circular lace mat which, bloated by much washing, concealed the delicate and probably pretty plate on which *it* sat. As dessert consisted entirely of bananas, for the first peeling then consumption of which he'd provided her with a fanciful knife and fork, the bowl might play little part as a bath: it required grapes. As a discountenancer it fell flat, under his very eye—Mrs. Artworth unfortunately regularly attended the best banquets. She removed the finger bowl and its bedding from her plate not only with *sang-froid* but absently, not ceasing to give her attention (and in a manner which during the course of dinner had settled into the motherly-ironical) to what Mr. William Delacroix was saying.

"Imagine," she then observed, "her telling you that!"

The senior Delacroix did, however, to give him his due, react. "Surely," he said, looking from one to another of the sparkling bowls, "these should have lotus blossoms floating in them, while we're about it?"

"Anybody," said William to Mrs. Artworth, "would imagine Roland had been to Simla. . . . No, but what a ceremony," he continued, "it must have been! And most exciting, of course, the moment when you each of you put in her secret thing?"

Mrs. Artworth showed, almost, surprise. "Oh, she told you *that*?"

"For ever to be secrets of the tomb?"

She smiled. "That was the idea—I think?"

"And not a word of this," William said, "not a word had one heard till this evening."

"She didn't over-tire herself, I hope?" said Mrs. Artworth, showing a glint of the nurse.

"I *don't* think so. Did you find her tired, later?"

"Well frankly, no."

"On the contrary, she seemed in wonderful spirits," said Roland, turning on Mrs. Artworth a look not rendered less amiable by its slight formality (in a way, Roland's deliberation gave his amiability more value). "Which, by all accounts, she's been anything but—lately. You have done wonders."

"Oh, I don't know," she said lightly, slighting herself. "I've done any little thing I can think of to cheer her up.— You'd heard, then, rather worrying rumours?"

Francis, professionally hovering, failed to conceal the fact that he lent ear to this. "That will be all, Francis, I think," said Roland.

"What about the port?"

"Oh, the port by all means."

Out went Francis, rigid with the intention of not being absent long. Mrs. Artworth, having waited sceptically for the door to close (or even appear to), then said: "When people are frightened they exaggerate—I suppose."

"So, in this case," William said—for the moment tense, retrospectively—"one could only hope." His brother enlarged the matter: "This whole thing began by being impossible to make head or tail of. Not only unlikely, unlike her. As a rule, as you know, she's so very placid."

That that aspect of their mother hadn't, so far, struck her former school friend was concealed by Mrs. Artworth's all-of-a-sudden interest in, well-nigh infatuation with, her finger bowl. Bunching together the tips of her pretty and manifestly unsullied right-hand fingers, she let them go in for a little dip. She looked on to her knee for her napkin —off it had slid, so, composedly, she shook the fingers dry, remarking: "That, then, was why you didn't come before?"

The brothers closed ranks. Instantly though urbanely they made it clear that they did not intend to go into *that* (with her). Without, they hoped, allowing Mrs. Artworth to feel she had gone too far (which she had) they showed themselves ready for a change of subject. Francis's coming in with the port aided them. "This, I can answer for," Roland said, as the decanter was placed before him.

Tilting a glance at the port, with genuine languor (port bored her, still more the to-do about it) she said: "You selected it for her?" Still more coolly she added: "How lucky she is."

"Except," William remarked, "that she never drinks it."

"Others do," said his brother. "She had to have some."

With a continuous swish of the pink sleeves—which, slit open downward from the shoulders, only to be gathered together again when they reached the wrists, somehow were more mellifluous than mere sleevelessness—Mrs. Artworth was peeling the banana she had, some minutes ago, broken off from the bunch on the silver dish levelled at her by Francis. Candles had failed to be found by Francis, Mrs. Delacroix and the Major having used the last; but the dining-room of which she was tonight the undoubted center-piece was not so unfavourably lit by lamps dotted over the sideboards and service tables. Mrs. Artworth, looking up from her task, beheld with awe and amazement the two wise governors brought forth by Dicey the idiot baa-lamb. "It is extraordinary to think . . ." she said.

"What?"

"Well, I don't know," she said, receding.

"Whose idea was it?" asked William. "I mean, the coffer?"

"Oh, I'm sure your mother's. She had so many."

"Who thought up those three extra-secret things?"

"That," she said, having thought, "I believe was me."

"Neither of us," said Roland—entitling himself, by a glance, to speak for his brother—"now, of course, ever can hope to rest till we know what they were."

"Oh, can't you?" said Mrs. Artworth. "That's too bad. As to what the two *others* put in, of course *I* don't know."

"To this very day?"

"To this very day.—What *she* put in, surely your mother'd tell you?"

"We asked her," William confessed, "needless to say. But no go. No—she shut like a clam."

"Adamant," Roland supplemented.

"And Miss Burkin-Jones has also stuck to her guns?"

"I should think so. Clare's always very strong-minded."

"Must *you*," asked William, "be as strong-minded as that?"

Mrs. Artworth gave one of them, then the other, the gaze of a mermaid seeing beyond horizons. "I'd feel bad if I told you when the other two haven't. And worse—in a way?—if I told you when I've never told them. Laugh at me, but tell *them* I never would! Peculiar it may appear, after all these years, but I'd go to my grave, still, rather than have *them* know."

"A-ha?"

"Really?"

"It's all very well," said she, "but *you'd* laugh if you knew what it really was."

"This is a torture of Tantalus," said William.

"Not that we'd want to tamper with your conscience," said Roland, "but—?"

"Oh, very well then. My sixth toe."

"Mrs. *Artworth*?"

"My sixth toe," she enunciated, still more distinctly. "I was born with six on one foot."

"Not on both?"

"In that case, it would have been my twelfth toe, wouldn't it?"

They bowed to her superiority in arithmetic.

"It was promptly removed, of course. But Mother, for some sentimental reason, I can only think, kept it: so there it was in a bottle—in spirits, naturally. When the day came when I thought I should have a mascot, I asked her if she would give it me back. 'What a strange idea,' she said, but didn't say no. So there I was, fitted out with a mascot."

"But Mrs. Artworth, what made you bury it? Surely a mascot's something one takes about with one?"

"Ah, but then," she said, "there's the risk of losing it!"

"Whereas, the tomb's safe-keeping?"

She congratulated them on seeing that, with a nod. " 'There it will *be*,' I thought. '*There* it will be.' Also, too, there was this—as you'll understand. I'd have had to keep keeping it hidden: this solved that problem."

"Surely, a mascot's something one goes round showing?"

"Was that an object to go round showing?"

The sons failed, for the moment, to understand. They looked at each other. They looked at her.

She outstared them. "What," she cried, "my deformity?"

A pause.

"You're a very curious person, Mrs. Artworth," Roland told her, with a deference made greater by his formality. "Am I asking too much if I ask, has it brought you luck?"

She shook a sleeve back, put a hand up: lightly the hand touched its way round her pretty hair. She looked at him sideways. "At what?" she teasingly asked.

He gravely told her: "You danced."

His brother said: "Yes, we know that you danced."

"Imagine," she said, "her telling you. Still, why not? Yes—I used to be quite a little dancer, when I was a child."

Into the cobwebby distance the bed retreated, lengthening everything: the room was an avenue at whose far end something was happening. Sleep. Deep into the curtains' shelter, the head of the sleeper was invisible. Sleep so gave this room a sensual climate that to enter was to know oneself to be in the presence of an embrace. Was it to be feared, or to be hoped, that she might not wake? Or how if she never woke at all?

Down at this end, where Clare stood, the fire was awake—sunk in the grate, fluttering vaguely like a soul. Near it burned a lamp: the triple-silk shade at an angle made a mystery of the greater part of the room. The visitant, Clare, allowed herself to imagine others—as likely as she was, with more right, more ghostly only in name. Nor need those be the dead only: for instance, twist round the lamp a little and why should light not glimmer on Trevor's spectacles as he stood in the door? The concave, bowed but not undignified man moved forward, sat down on the bed-side needle-work stool, and held out a hand, saying: "Hullo, Dicey. Nice to see you again." ("I wish I could go myself," he had said on the telephone. Are not desires acts? One is where one would be. May we not, therefore, frequent each other, without the body, *not* only in dreams?)

We were entrusted to one another, in the days which mattered, Clare thought. Entrusted to one another by chance, not choice. Chance, and its agents time and place. Chance is better than choice; it is more lordly. In its care-lessness it is more lordly. Chance is God, choice is man. You—she thought, looking at the bed—chanced not chose to want us again.

Clare turned round and, facing the chimneypiece, dared again to look into the world of china. Shepherds and shep-herdesses branched towards one another their mended arms; beautiful bowls stayed cradled within their networks of cracks; stitches held obstinately together what had been broken; handles maintained their hold on cups by grasping with tiny alloy claws. She was looking into a fragile rep-resentation of a world of honour, which was to say un-failingness.

The soldier's child also looked at the peaceful land-scapes, the some grey, some coloured scenery-motifs on cups and bowls. Within no one of those miniature planets was there anything tumultuous. Whereas Nature is *my* terri-ble nature, the exile thought. She looked with longing at the everlasting sea shores, mountain peaks, bays and lakes, even at the castles on the frail rounded sides of the cups and bowls. Never had she found them anywhere else. She had loved them because they were not for her.

You—she thought, looking back at the bed again. Me. And of course Sheikie. Entrusted to one another before we knew. Mistrustful of one another, and how rightly. You were the least mistrustful, however wrongly. To a point you were right: in our way having noble natures, we know each other's. We have our pride. Yet now, look! . . . Never should we have called each other to account: that was the catastrophe. But, see how remorseless children are—where were we to stop, and indeed how?

And now, nothing. There being nothing was what you were frightened of all the time, eh? Yes. Yes, it was terrible looking down into that empty box. I did not comfort you. Never have I comforted you. Forgive me.

Clare decided that she had better, now, get back to the White Hart. Turning to go, she thought of her last sight of the sands, from the sea wall: the wide sands and the running figure.

"Goodbye, Dicey," she said—for now and for then.

The sleeper stirred. She sighed. She raised herself on an elbow, saying: "Who's there?"

"Mumbo."

"Not Mumbo. Clare. Clare, where have you been?"

 **BARD BOOKS**

the classics, poetry, drama and
distinguished modern fiction

FICTION

ACT OF DARKNESS	John Peale Bishop	10827	1.25
ALL HALLOW'S EVE	Charles Williams	11213	1.45
ANAIS NIN READER	Ed., Philip K. Jason	33624	2.50
THE AWAKENING	Kate Chopin	38760	1.95
THE BENEFACTOR	Susan Sontag	11221	1.45
BETRAYED BY RITA HAYWORTH Manuel Puig		36020	2.25
BILLIARDS AT HALF-PAST NINE Heinrich Böll		32730	1.95
CALL IT SLEEP	Henry Roth	37549	2.25
THE CASE HISTORY OF COMRADE V. James Park Sloan		15362	1.65
CATALOGUE	George Milburn	33084	1.95
THE CLOWN	Heinrich Böll	37523	2.25
A COOL MILLION and THE DREAM LIFE OF BALSO SNELL	Nathanael West	15115	1.65
DANGLING MAN	Saul Bellow	24463	1.65
EDWIN MULLHOUSE	Steven Millhauser	37952	2.50
THE EYE OF THE HEART Barbara Howes, Ed.		20883	2.25
THE FAMILY OF PASCUAL DUARTE Camilo José Cela		11247	1.45
GABRIELA, CLOVE AND CINNAMON Jorge Amado		18275	1.95
THE GALLERY	John Horne Burns	33357	2.25
A GENEROUS MAN	Reynolds Price	15123	1.65
GOING NOWHERE	Alvin Greenberg	15081	1.65
THE GREEN HOUSE	Mario Vargas Liosa	15099	1.65
HERMAPHRODEITY	Alan Friedman	16865	2.45
HOPSCOTCH	Julio Cortázar	36731	2.95
HUNGER	Knut Hamsun	42028	2.25
HOUSE OF ALL NATIONS	Christina Stead	18895	2.45

BD (1) 10-78

SUN CITY Tove Jansson	32318	1.95
THE LANGUAGE OF CATS AND OTHER STORIES Spencer Hoist	14381	1.65
THE LAST DAYS OF LOUISIANA RED Ishmael Reed	35451	2.25
LEAF STORM AND OTHER STORIES Gabriel García Márquez	36816	1.95
LESBIAN BODY Monique Wittig	31062	1.75
LES GUERILLERES Monique Wittig	14373	1.65
A LONG AND HAPPY LIFE Reynolds Price	17053	1.65
LUCIFER WITH A BOOK John Horne Burns	33340	2.25
THE MAGNIFICENT AMBERSONS Booth Tarkington	17236	1.50
THE MAN WHO LOVED CHILDREN Christina Stead	40618	2.50
THE MAN WHO WAS NOT WITH IT Herbert Gold	19356	1.65
THE MAZE MAKER Michael Ayrton	23648	1.65
A MEETING BY THE RIVER Christopher Isherwood	37945	1.95
MYSTERIES Knut Hamsun	25221	1.95
NABOKOV'S DOZEN Vladimir Nabokov	15354	1.65
NO ONE WRITES TO THE COLONEL AND OTHER STORIES Gabriel García Márquez	32748	1.75
ONE HUNDRED YEARS OF SOLITUDE Gabriel García Márquez	34033	2.25
PARTIES Carl Van Vechten	32631	1.95
PNIN Vladimir Nabokov	40600	1.95
PRATER VIOLET Christopher Isherwood	36269	1.95
REAL PEOPLE Alison Lurie	23747	1.65
THE RECOGNITIONS William Gaddis	18572	2.65
SLAVE Isaac Singer	26377	1.95
A SMUGGLER'S BIBLE Joseph McElroy	33589	2.50
STUDS LONIGAN TRILOGY James T. Farrell	31955	2.75
SUMMERING Joanne Greenberg	17798	1.65
SWEET ADVERSITY Donald Newlove	38364	2.95
62: A MODEL KIT Julio Cortázar	17558	1.65
THREE BY HANDKE Peter Handke	32458	2.25
THE VICTIM Saul Bellow	24273	1.75
WHAT HAPPENS NEXT? Gilbert Rogin	17806	1.65

Where better paperbacks are sold, or directly from the publisher. Include 25¢ per copy for postage and handling, allow 4-6 weeks for delivery.

Avon Books, Mail Order Dept.
250 West 55th Street, New York, N.Y. 10019

BD (2) 10-78